DAY BREAK

DAY BREAK

SORROWSONG UNIVERSITY SERIES

AUTUMN WOODS

SLOWBURN
A zando IMPRINT
NEW YORK

zando

Slowburn is an imprint of Zando.
zandoprojects.com

First Edition: July 2026

Text design by Neuwirth & Associates, Inc. and Kevin Ullrich
Cover design by Emily Wittig
Cover art: (window) bruno135_406 / Adobe Stock; (silhouettes) vladmarko / iStock; (florals) Eclectic Anthology / Creative Market
Interior illustration by Summer Grove

Library of Congress Control Number: 2026936114

978-1-63893-375-5 (trade paperback)
978-1-63893-376-2 (ebook)

10 9 8 7 6 5 4 3 2 1
Manufactured in the United States of America
LSCC

Do you ever feel like you're being seen?

DAY BREAK

AUTHOR'S NOTE

THANK YOU SO much for picking up *Daybreak.*

You should be aware that this book forms the second half of a duet, and that in order to follow the events of this book, you should read the first part, *Nightshade.*

This book is intended for an audience aged eighteen+ and contains themes of murder, depression, bereavement, drowning, suicidal thoughts, declining health of a parent, violence, as well as sexual content.

Prologue

ANONYMOUS

Do you know how frustrating it is to trust someone, to let someone be your final hope, to believe you might be *friends* with them, only for them to turn out to be a fake?

I don't know why I'm surprised. Everyone, *everyone*, has let me down.

When I die, there will be no headstone. No funeral. Forgotten.

I used to think kindness was genetic. That bad people were born bad, and good people were destined to be that way from birth. But now I see that I was so wrong, because I have watched myself decay from a bright-eyed, hopeful child to a hollow, bitter adult who wants nothing but bad things for others.

At the kitchen table, rotting with damp like the rest of the motel, I stare at my phone. At the blurry photo of two figures standing over a dying man, a man who deserved to die.

They all deserve to die. The girl, the lecturer, the businessmen. Every single one of them deserves to die.

I swipe from my photos to my messages. Finding out Ophelia Winters had a stalker was not surprising. She seems to gather enemies so effortlessly that it's almost admirable.

Two days, and my message to her is still unanswered. I stare out the window, but the view is obscured by the rain, deafeningly loud.

My laptop chimes with a notification from an encrypted messaging site.

Anon
I have confirmation she's back at the university.

Her silence is my answer. If she doesn't want to come to me, we'll have to do it the hard way.

Anon
I'm finished here. Any other jobs require further payment.

I bark out a cold laugh, my breath white in front of me. I couldn't pay another hacker even if I wanted to. Everything is gone. House, jewelry, cash. Family, hopes, dreams. All gone.

I'm done with this life. Ready to leave.

But leaving without watching that Winters girl begging for her life, begging for forgiveness? Absolutely not.

Chapter 1

ALEX

[DRAFT]

From: Alex Corbeau-Green
Subject: Consumerism (noun) *the selfish and frivolous collecting of products*
To: Ophelia Winters

An interactive billboard has appeared outside my office building. You'd hate that. Advertisements and forced interaction - your two least favorite things. I can already picture the expression on your face.
Fuck, I miss you.

"ARE YOU AIDING the cops in their search for your father, Alex?"

"Are you polishing your head to make it that shiny, Andre, or is it natural?" I bite back, as the reporter desperately follows me toward the ground floor entrance of Green Aviation's office building for what must be the tenth time in two weeks.

My cigarette hisses against the trash can outside. The flash of a camera somewhere behind me has me gritting my teeth.

"How's your mom coping? Any comment on her health?"

I swallow the vitriol sitting in my throat and let Green's doormen shove the prying media away.

The automatic doors close behind me, and despite all the garish grandeur of Green's lobby, I'm instantly claustrophobic.

If Green is a pandemic of greed and corruption across the globe, then this shiny office is the rotting epicenter of it all, the sparkling jewel in my father's empire.

My empire now.

Though, hopefully not for long.

I nod in response to a few overly cheerful *good morning*s, drumming my fingers on my thigh and willing the elevator to hurry up.

Sonya, my publicist, appears beside me, the cloying scent of her perfume scratching the back of my throat. "Ah, Alex. I was hoping I'd catch you."

I search the immediate vicinity for an outlet to ram a fork into but come up short. "About?"

"Your press conference for tomorrow. I thought you might want to speak a little on your family at the end."

Apparently all six elevators are stopping at every floor this morning. "It's a business conference."

"I know, but it'd be great for your image. Family man, a united front, even with what's going on with your father."

I press the call button three more times, like that'll do anything. That goddamn reporter has me well and truly rattled. "Would using Andre Jackson from Insider Weekly's head as a bowling ball be good or bad for my image?"

"Alex, it's a great opportunity to reassure the shareholders that whatever is going on at home isn't going to affect—"

The elevator finally arrives, and I hit the button for the penthouse floor and wait until just a sliver of her face is visible between two silver doors to say, "I'll have Jacqueline put a call in your diary later."

I slump against the mirror, exhausted before the day has really begun. The claustrophobic metal box fires me unnaturally high in this glass monstrosity of a building, but my mood remains somewhere in the basement garage.

Still, I straighten my collar, smooth the cracks in my mask, steady the shake in my hands, and think of the seven women I do it all for.

The doors slide open after what feels like an age, spitting me out in front of Jacqueline's desk. It's quiet on the top floor, thankfully, just the sound of my hammering heart working overtime in my chest.

I rap my knuckles against the desk, an annoying habit of my father's that I've somehow absorbed. "If Sonya emails you about a publicity call—"

"She already has. She's coming up at three thirty."

Damn it, these people work fast. "I'm busy at three thirty."

Her eyes drop to my calendar, open on her laptop screen. "With?"

"I have to . . ." I rub the back of my neck. "Pick the lint from between the keys on my keyboard?"

"A noble attempt," she says, handing me a coffee. "Enjoy your meeting."

Great.

Jacqueline is a short, chaotically dressed woman in her late thirties, and though I like her very much, she genuinely *sucks* at her job.

I interviewed twelve people for this position, and eleven of them were ruthlessly organized assistants with a résumé an inch thick. It felt more like they were interviewing *me*. With their sharp stilettos, predatory glances, and scarlet fingernails that lingered a little too long on my forearms, they reminded me too much of the women I'd find my father taking out for wholly inappropriate dinners.

Then Jacqueline rocked up, perfectly on time but covered in kids' stickers. My background check told me she has three young children, living in an apartment in Queens. She looked like a deer in headlights—how I felt inside. She was as lost as I was, but when I asked her the final question, she squared her shoulders beneath her ill-fitting blazer and said, *I'm not sure, but I just know we'll figure it out.*

She put so much faith in those words, my daddy issues and I just couldn't say no.

And she makes a great double espresso.

And like she said we would, we're figuring it all out. The Green share price is recovering, the media storm is still intense, but we're not on the front cover of *every* newspaper anymore.

On the surface, everything is working out. Beneath? I'm fighting for air.

My father is missing. The FBI showed up here to arrest him, and he was nowhere to be found, nor has anyone seen a trace of him since. A team of private detectives and the FBI's best can't even catch his scent.

It's driving me crazy, plaguing my sleep, squashing my appetite.

Oh, and I'm the CEO of an almost-billion-dollar company. The *Financial Times* called me Manhattan's wunderkind, when my most tangible experience managing any kind of business was starting a restaurant chain on *The Sims* with Charlotte and Mia.

I don't think our "experimental" food restaurant even had walls or a roof.

I had a vague idea of how my life would look at twenty-three. I thought I'd be a fresh-faced architect, or running a smaller company I'd founded myself. Maybe I'd be traveling the world with no responsibilities.

I didn't think I'd be a CEO with parental custody of my six sisters. Didn't think I'd be trying to sneakily arrange my mom's hospital visits or pay the nanny overtime while I'm stuck in a glass boardroom. Didn't think I'd spend my evenings arguing with them over how much they hate having security following them around all day.

And despite *all* this, it's a brown-eyed redhead that occupies the majority of my headspace. In the month since I last saw her, I've thought of little else.

In my father's—*my*—office, a low sun bleeds out over the New York skyline, staining the wall in front of the desk a macabre shade of red.

The glass of the window is cool against my forehead, each heavy breath obscuring the busy comings and goings of a morning in the city. The light on the river is the same color as Ophelia's hair.

I left her without a word.

To make looking in the mirror a more bearable process, I convince myself that my lawyers asking me not to contact Ophelia is the only reason the draft emails piling up on my laptop never get sent, but I know it isn't true. There's a part of me that thinks I don't deserve her, and another part of me that's hurt. One likes to remind me that I've turned her life into a mess of public attention and online hate, and the other plagues my nights with a question I wouldn't dare to ask myself during the day.

Was any of it real?

I think I've accepted by now that Ophelia's motivation for appearing in my life was so she could gather information, but it's trying to imagine exactly when her feelings changed that's keeping me awake into the early hours of the morning. Was it real when she lay beneath the sofa at Carmichael's office? Was it real when I found her drowned at the tarn? Surely, it was real in the car on Boxing Day, when she held my gaze and gasped my name and made me feel like I was more than enough.

I really, *really*, need that to be real.

And beneath all of this is one tiny question, one I'm not even sure I have the right to ask.

How could she? I don't know how that article got leaked to the media. Deep down, I struggle to believe it was her, but she wrote it, nonetheless. She must've known what it would do to my family when she typed it all up. It sent my father into a frenzy, throwing guns and clothes into a bag and threatening Fleur and the housekeeper when they tried to stop him from escaping. It's put my sisters on the front page of every newspaper, every gossip forum.

What a mess.

Every time I shower and shave in the morning, I see a little more of my father looking back at me in the mirror.

I'm turning into him, like he always said I would. I can try to pretend I'm all my mother, soft and kind and *good*, but the illusion is cracking. I'm fifty percent my father, and that's a fact I'll never be able to escape. Every positive thought has a shadow that trails behind it, biting at my heels no matter how fast I run.

I hate how naturally this role comes to me. How I can hear his voice guiding me through meetings, through finance reports, through tough negotiations.

He trained me to be a CEO, but I wish he'd taught me how to be a man.

There's this sort of sickness that comes with money: The more you have, the more you crave it. We've always been rich, but when the zeroes started piling up on my father's net worth, he became a different man. It's an addiction. A total loss of sight of the important things.

Vacations stopped. Family dinners stopped. Christmas presents stopped. All the things he *should've* been doing with his money stopped. Everything went back into Green.

He traded his soul for the promise of more wealth. And for my sisters, I cannot let myself fall down the same hole.

Somewhere in the periphery, Jacqueline hovers in my doorway and clears her throat to read from her tablet. I'm only half listening, lazily sketching a female form on my notepad. Like all my sketches these days, it comes out looking like Ophelia. The gentle swell of her hips when she walks, the soft lines across her stomach when she sits, the muscles of her arms, they sit on my brain like a tattoo I can't erase.

I'm incapable of producing a drawing that doesn't curve, bend, flow in the same way that her body does. I love her. God, I *love* her, but maybe she was right. She and I are the right people in the wrong universe. It's too messy, too *complicated*, like she always said it would be.

When I get home, when my sisters are in bed and my work laptop is off, there's nothing to dilute her in my head. She becomes every thought I have and every shaky exhale I make. She's the subject of my most rattling nightmares and my most carnal dreams.

Without her soft thighs, miserable cynicism, and runny nose, my life has faded back to gray. It would sting less if I hadn't had a taste of how sweet the other colors could be.

I'm as bad as Harwood says I am: fixated on her in an unhealthy and immature way.

Harwood. That's what I need. Maybe my therapist can fix me. *Low* isn't a strong enough word to describe my mood the past few days. I'm itching to speak with him, but he's with family in Nigeria for the rest of the week.

Snapping myself out of my thoughts, I dismiss Jacqueline and buzz in Mike and Luis, two other execs who help me run the company. The media can give me as much praise as they like, but half of the decisions I've claimed credit for in the past weeks were based on their advice.

Once I've finished phase one of my Green plan—steady the ship—I'll move on to phase two—find a replacement CEO. I'm not stupid. I know a twenty-three-year-old with no passion or drive for the company is not the best fit. These two are the best options I have at the moment. I just can't trust them fully. I need to make sure I'm not putting Green into the hands of someone like my father.

In the meantime, the pay isn't so bad. I've hired a chef for weekdays, a security team, and another nanny, as well as secured the best care for my mother. I paid a ludicrous amount of money to buy the Land Rover I rented over the holidays to visit Ophelia and have it shipped here—letting it stay at the rental office felt like a crime. Now it sits in the underground garage like a priceless artifact, a museum of my time with her. Sometimes I sit in it just to try to catch her cinnamon scent.

It's probably fair to say I'm not taking the breakup well.

IT'S GETTING DARK by the time I pull into the garage of our brownstone, flanked by a black security vehicle. I swing into the empty space between the Official Land Rover Ophelia Winters Museum (trademark pending) and the white Audi I bought Fleur for her seventeenth birthday last week.

I step out of the car, giving it a once-over for any trackers. I'm not sure where my father is, and I'm not sure whether he's feeling immense pride that I've protected his precious company from complete collapse, or murderous rage that I've taken his job because my girlfriend gave him the biggest metaphorical middle finger in history. Somehow I strongly doubt it's the former.

I take the elevator into the house, unlocking the door to the main foyer. My little sister, Josie, barrels toward me in a Batman costume, cape flying behind her. "Alex is home!" she shrieks, at a pitch only a sugar-fueled seven-year-old can.

Slamming into me, her arms wrap around my waist. She lets out a dramatic *ugh*, mumbling something about how much she missed me, how the twelve hours since we last spoke has been the longest amount of time in history, *ever*. I'd be lying if I said it didn't warm my chest *just* a little. "Taking the night off from fighting crime?"

She swishes her cape. "Yep. I'm on vacation. Did you have a nice day?"

"*Nice* is certainly one word for it." I place a gentle hand on her upper back and guide her into the kitchen, where my other sisters, Mia, Evie, Éléanor, and Charlotte, are arguing over how big to roll out the dough for their cookies. My eldest sister's absence is not surprising; Fleur hasn't handled any of this well, nor should she have to.

I hate how much they've all been through. Hate that the article going live was a grenade in their lives and that the pieces will never return to the way they were before.

I swipe the bowl of cookie dough from the marble counter. They've managed to use every pot, pan, and utensil in the kitchen, which is impressive. "Oh, nice of you guys to make me cookies."

"They're for my class tomorrow!" Charlotte protests, trying to grab it back.

I steal a bit of the dough. *Man*, it's good. It tastes like vanilla. It tastes like my childhood, when my dad still loved my mom and my mom still loved herself.

"How was school?" I ask, setting the bowl back down and opening the fridge for an alcohol-free beer. Five different answers fire back at me as the chef pops his head around the door of the back kitchen.

"Good evening, sir. Chicken pie okay?"

I pop the lid off the bottle. "More than okay. Thank you."

Having someone cook is a godsend. Without the staff, we'd be a box-mac-and-cheese-fueled mess.

I pick at the label on the bottle, a sinking sensation somewhere in my chest.

Who'll cook for Ophelia when she has to go back to her parents' house over the Easter break? The woman won't even chop an onion.

Staring at six overflowing shelves of fresh produce and home-cooked meals with my sisters' arguments a familiar soundtrack behind me, I'm struck again by the privilege of it all. I push the fridge door shut, but the rush of cold air that follows has nothing on the chill that hit me when I stepped inside Ophelia's house at Christmas.

I can't rid that day from my mind: the silence in her house, the emptiness, the ocean of resentment she crossed just to let me into her life and *oh God, I've messed up so badly.*

I think I've broken us beyond repair.

I sit down at the kitchen island, watching the five of them cut the dough into erratically sized circles. I've lived in an all-female household for long enough to know that when they're quiet, it means I've interrupted something.

"All right," I drawl, taking a swig from the bottle, "who has a homecoming date?"

Silence.

"Fleur has a new boyfriend," blurts Mia, eventually. The others glare at her.

Remain calm, Alex. Act rationally.

I tighten my grip on my phone as I flip through the security feeds in the house, paranoid. "Who is he?"

"He's a fashion model."

I shut my phone off, trying to control my protective tendencies. Models are the *worst*, especially the ones in Fleur's circle. There's something ironic about men who paint their fingernails and still manage to be the biggest misogynists on the planet. He's probably using her as a publicity stunt. "Is he here? Upstairs?"

They all fall silent, obviously sworn to secrecy. Even Mia stares at her feet, the tips of her ears reddening. My mood sours. I head back into the foyer and up the left-hand staircase, stomping as loud as I can so they have time to stop . . . whatever it is they're doing. "Fleur?"

"What?"

"Can I come in?"

"Nope."

I put my forehead against the door. "Are you coming down for dinner?"

"Nope."

"What's your friend's name?"

"Freddie," comes a male voice. He sounds like a wanker, as Ophelia would say. "Hey, bro."

"How old are you?" I ask, and I hear Fleur mutter an insult under her breath.

"Eighteen."

I can hear Harwood's voice in my ear, reminding me for the four millionth time that my sisters are their *own* people with their *own* lives, allowed to make their *own* mistakes. Through gritted teeth, I try to make the bastard feel welcome. "Be good to see you both down at dinner, man."

And get your slimy hands off my sister.

"Let her live, Alex," comes a soft voice. My mother steps out of her bedroom at the end of the hall, dressed in cream cashmere loungewear. Her dark hair is loose around her shoulders, glossy, but thinner than it used to be. She looks okay, though, tightrope walking the equilibrium between a manic high and the impending low.

The events of the past month have not been kind to her. If I thought she couldn't get thinner, she's managed to. Every hospital visit, they tell me her heart is weak, atrophying like the life behind her eyes. The paranoia seems worse, the anxiety that everyone is plotting against her. Her bipolar diagnosis went untreated for so long with my father it's hard to catch up with the effects on her health. These days, these level days where it's easy to recognize the woman beneath the exhaustion, are becoming more and more uncommon.

It sounds morbid, but it's always a relief to see her alive when I get home. She probably says the same about me.

"I'm trying. But fuck knows what he could do to her in there. We don't know him at all."

She hooks her arm around mine as I walk her bony frame down the stairs. "Your first girlfriend was a nasty piece of work. Do you think I couldn't see that the second she walked through the door? She used you for your fame and your wealth. But I let you figure it out for yourself."

I smile. "And now I know to avoid the ones who livestream our first date."

Her laugh is quiet, but it's there. "Exactly. How is Ophelia?"

A twinge of pain spears my chest. "She's okay."

She gives me a knowing look. "You're still having someone watch her, aren't you?"

"Ophelia was as much involved in this whole mess as we were. It'd be foolish of me not to ask Vincenzo's men to keep half an eye on her. It's smart business." And the thought of someone hurting her keeps me up at night, but yeah, *smart business.*

"Have you spoken with her?" she asks, as I tug her into my father's—*my*—enormous home office and sit her down on the desk chair.

"No."

"*Alex.*"

"She used our homelife, your illness, Dad's . . . whatever the fuck is wrong with Dad, against us."

"Against your *father*," she corrects. "Not us. I don't believe she wanted to hurt us."

I pull the spare chair beside her and sit down, logging on to my laptop. "She mentioned your name in it."

"Before she knew me, darling. Imagine I died tomorrow. Imagine Fleur and I were killed in a targeted hit-and-run on the highway tomorrow."

I shudder as I bring up my emails. "Don't say things like that."

Her nails scratch in my hair. It makes me want to cry. To curl into the lap of a woman who doesn't really exist anymore, not the way I want her to. "But *imagine*, love. What would you do if you knew who was driving the car?"

"*Maman*," I sigh, scrubbing my hands down my face. "I've overanalyzed it enough already. I don't care what she did to Cain, I care what she did to you, to the girls. And it's not like she would forgive me for leaving the way I did, anyway. *And* the distance. I could go on forever."

"Tell her your lawyer asked you not to contact her."

"It's a cheap excuse. I haven't contacted her because I can't bring myself to. Helen's advice has nothing to do with it."

"She might've written it, but I think we both know she wouldn't have leaked that article," she continues, like she's bringing up a point I haven't already thought of during the countless sleepless nights of the past month. Like this isn't the hundredth time we've had the exact same conversation.

Ophelia and I are separated by thousands of miles and a *vast* ocean of mistrust, all the progress I'd made with her shipwrecked at the bottom of it.

"It doesn't matter, Mom. I'm desperately trying to move on. Even if we did work it out, I'm here and she's over there. She can't get on a plane to visit."

"But once you quit—"

"*Mom*," I say, gently. "Please drop it."

Gentle fingers swipe a lock of too-long dark hair away from my forehead, eyes full of some unidentifiable emotion. Tears pool on her thick, black lashes.

"Don't say it." I can't hear it again.

"Say what?"

"That I look like him. It's the first thing anyone says when they walk into my office."

Her bottom lip wobbles. "I was going to say how sorry I am that you've ended up in this position, that you've ended up in the one job you always made it clear you didn't want. That you're the only father figure in their life. I was going to say how sorry I am that you've . . ."

"Maman, don't."

A lone tear trickles over her cheek. "Ended up with me as a mother and him as a father."

"You're the best mother I know," I whisper, snaking an arm around her bony shoulders. "And I mean that."

"I'm just *so* sorry."

I swivel her chair back to face the laptop. "Enough of that talk. Look at this."

I bring up an email that I read earlier from Jack, my rugby teammate from Sorrowsong. It's a forwarded chain of emails between his parents: a top-ranked neurosurgeon and a psychiatrist.

She peers in at the screen, the blue light spilling over her delicate cheekbones. "*Another* medication. Alex, I . . ."

"It's been really promising in trials. They're still rolling it out."

"Do you know them?"

"Their son is on my rugby team—my old rugby team."

"You can go back to Sorrowsong. Don't rule it out."

"I'm twenty-three, Mom. Too old to start again."

She laughs, brushing her hair out of her face with a shaky hand. "I was like that at your age. Thinking I was running out of time even though I was just a baby."

"I was going to schedule a call with his parents so we can learn a bit more. They're willing to fly here from California to talk to you. Are you interested, hypothetically?"

"I am, but . . . I've had a lot of treatments, Alex, and they've all seemed promising in the beginning. My mind is tired and my body is beaten. I don't want to die on a table on the small hope of a longer life. I just want to live to see you get married."

My fingers freeze over the keyboard.

Ophelia at the altar. Flowers in her hand, raindrops in her hair. Some ridiculous, thrifted, too-big, probably brown dress. Stuttered vows from nervous lips, and a lifetime of peace.

Even in my imagination, it's hazy. Some distant future I'll never deserve. I could dream of it until the last threads of sanity have slipped through my fingers.

But it'll stay a dream. I haven't the heart to tell my mother that, though. Or maybe I just can't quite admit to myself that I've given up on it yet.

I start typing out an email in reply, ignoring the sixty new emails I've received since leaving the office. "I'll put a call in their calendar."

INGRID AND EMILY—THE housekeeper and the nanny—join Charlotte, Evie, Mia, Josie, Éléanor, and me at the table in the all-white dining room, the conversation surprisingly cheery. Ingrid is animatedly complaining about her husband, Russell, which is a terrible idea because Russell is our driver and Josie repeats everything she hears verbatim. But there's no stopping her reenactment of Russell's loud chewing, and it's worth it to hear the girls laughing.

Ingrid is one of those people: like if home-cooked sauce with way too much oil, hugs that smell like old perfume, and coffee breath managed to manifest themselves into a human. And I mean that as a compliment. She's worked here for years under the guise of being a housekeeper but doing so much more.

When my father would come home and take his frustrations about the supply chain out on me, she'd clumsily bumble into the kitchen long past her bedtime, taking half an hour to make herself a cup of tea just so he'd get bored enough to leave me alone.

And Josie won't eat a sandwich that Ingrid didn't make, so there isn't much I wouldn't do to keep her around.

Fleur and Freddie come down when we're all halfway through our dinner. Freddie is still pulling his Ralph Lauren quarter zip on when they come in, which makes me want to put my knife in his retina. His blond hair is slicked back, his chinos perfectly pressed. Just another Shawn Miller lookalike. *Idiot.* I give him a brief nod, for Fleur's sake.

"Hey, bro. Loved your shareholder statement yesterday."

"Cheers," I mutter, even though I want to tell him to find a more impressive hobby than watching press conferences at eighteen years old. "Take a seat. There's enough food."

He does, flicking his stupid hair out of his eyes.

"So, are you thinking of college, Freddie?"

"Nah, probably not. I'll probably start a business, or a podcast, or something."

Fucking hell. Code red. He's a wannabe podcaster.

"I think you should both at least consider it," I suggest.

Fleur rolls her eyes, as tired of this conversation as I am. "Shut up, Alex."

"Fleur!" scolds Mia, pushing back her curtain of thick, dark hair to glare at her. I shake my head at her, trying to defuse the situation. Mia, more than any of us, has inherited Dad's stubbornness, never one to turn down a confrontation.

"You're not my parent, Mia." Her gaze lands on me. Fleur's interest in any form of relationship with me died the day I, in her mind, chose Green over her and my sisters when the article went live. "And neither are you."

"Legally, I am." For now. Until Mom is better.

Mom's not getting better.

"I bet you love that, don't you? A chance to turn into *him*."

"Fleur," I warn, tone sharp.

"But you are, aren't you?" She checks her watch. It's well past 9 p.m. Way too late for a seven-year-old to be eating. "Late dinner, again? Another shareholder to appease? Another meeting running over?"

"Fleur," snaps Mia, slamming down her cutlery. "You should be grateful he's trying to hold this family together."

"He's coming home late, putting Green first. He chose the share price over us when we needed him most. When we could've *died* because of our own father, he chose to run to the New York office. Sound familiar?"

The food turns to ash in my mouth. Little pieces of the monster inside me slip into my bloodstream, but just like they always have, they stay just there. I couldn't lash out at them even if I wanted to, can't let that black cloud fill this dining room and suffocate my sisters. So, it eats me from the inside out instead.

I need to fix this before there's nothing left of me at all.

I'm desperate to leave the table. Desperate to storm away and lock myself in the office and prove Fleur right. But I don't. I stay and listen as she fires her bitter hatred at me, because leaving would make me my father, and I can't do that to them.

"I'm very sorry you feel that way about me, Fleur," I manage, as she pauses for air.

I don't blame her. I went to New York and my father gave her a black eye. I went to New York, and Fleur used her debit card to hide all of my sisters in a hotel in Paris when an army of cameras and reporters gathered on the street outside. I *chose* New York, and Fleur stood between my father's fury and our housekeeper.

I can analyze whether I made the right or wrong decision as much as I like, but it won't change the fact that they needed me and I wasn't there.

Mia credits me with holding the family together, but it was Fleur who controlled the explosion. I'm just tightening the knots she tied under astronomical pressure. It's me who's booking physicians appointments, ensuring the fridge is full, keeping security tight, catching up with schoolteachers, and interviewing nannies, but it's Fleur who's doing the work that the staff cannot.

She's the one dealing with my sisters' friendship dramas, the confidence issues, and all the difficulties that accompany being a teenage girl. She's the one that does the things my mother did before her sharp decline in the last two years. It shouldn't have to be her, but it is.

Fleur and I are on the same team, but we're both drowning.

"Maybe Ophelia wants to kiss you again, Ally," interjects Josie, helpfully. I lean over and wipe the sauce from her chin.

"What makes you say that?"

"Someone made an edit of your shareholder press conference," says Evie, seemingly as desperate for a conversation change as I am.

"An edit?"

"Yeah, like edited clips of you with music."

That doesn't sound sexy, but I'll take it as a much-needed win.

"*It's a new age for Green Aviation, and I'm privileged to be a part of it*," says Éléanor, mimicking my voice. Even Fleur laughs a little.

"Fuck you all," I say, the mood lighter.

"*It's a new age for Green Aviation*," repeats Charlotte, undoing the top button of her blouse and flexing her shoulders.

"Oh my god," I mumble around my dinner, but it's drowned out by laughter. Every time I almost summon an ego, these idiots humble it back down again.

We manage dinner without another fight. Fleur doesn't touch her pie, so I put it in a box in the fridge in the hope she'll eat it later.

I get Josie and Charlotte to bed by ten thirty, catch up on a few emails, and miraculously still find the time to work out in the basement gym.

"It's a school night," I say, racking the weights as Mia bumbles in with her giant water flask and a bag of chips at almost midnight. My frustration is unconvincing. Mia *always* joins me for a workout. I lift dumbbells and she usually lifts cookies into her mouth.

"I'm sorry about Fleur," she says, sitting on the treadmill with her snacks.

I nudge her with the toe of my sneaker. "Move, squirt. I'm about to run." She shuffles onto the mat beside us, spilling chips over the belt. They crunch under my feet as I step onto it. "Have fun sweeping that up."

She crunches another chip, preoccupied with her thoughts. "Ignore Fleur."

"I don't want to ignore her. Ignoring her got me into this mess. I want to help her."

"Why *didn't* you come, Alex?" she whispers, so quiet I barely catch it over the whir of the treadmill. I decrease the speed slightly so I can hear her better.

"I wanted to come, Mia. More than anything. But I was—*am*—so tired of him, desperate to clear him from our lives. If Green fell into the wrong hands, if one of his equally corrupt buddies became CEO, then Dad may as well have not been fired. He'd still have endless power, he'd have buried the articles, spun the story, bought more people's silence. He'd still be fucking us all over—fucking *Mom* over, choosing her doctors, choosing her meds. I didn't choose Green over any of you. I was choosing long-term safety."

"What if Fleur got badly hurt?"

Lord, give me the strength to cope with my sisters. "God, Mia. I had to make a decision, and I can't change it. If I hadn't taken Green . . . Dad would've taken his anger out on all of us."

"Did he ever hit you?"

My eyes snap to hers, wide with alarm. Everything I thought I knew about their relationship tilts on its axis. "He hit you?"

"Never," she whispers. "But your football bruises always coincided with the dips in the share price."

I wince at the memories that flit through my mind. At cruel hands that should've been loving. "You're sixteen, M. You shouldn't even care what a share price is."

"Oh, I don't care. Like, at all."

I grin through the burn in my legs. "Good."

I crank up the speed again, hoping the fire in my legs will burn the confusing mixture of emotions in my chest.

Another day down. God knows how many to go.

I run until I can barely breathe out a goodnight to Mia when she leaves, until I've carved myself a shred of hope that I might be tired enough to fall asleep quickly tonight.

I got used to anchoring my own breathing to Ophelia's, got used to wanting to fall asleep just to wake up beside her. The fierce copper of her hair was my sunrise, and those two torturous dimples at the base of her spine were my grip on reality.

Now just the weight of my confusion and regret sit on the pillow beside mine.

Ophelia's betrayal isn't enough to make me hate her. Article or not, I love her. I don't know how to make that go away.

Chapter 2

ALEX

[DRAFT]

From: Alex Corbeau-Green

Subject: Torture (noun) *the act of inflicting severe pain as punishment*

To: Ophelia Winters

Dreamed about the freckles on your thighs last night.

MY COFFEE SCALDS my lips as I take a sip, unlocking my laptop. Just how I like it.

Rain patters against the glass wall behind me, staining the city a drab shade of gray.

It's dark out, thanks to a thick blanket of black cloud and a heavy fog that snakes its way through the skyscrapers of lower Manhattan.

I hang up on my morning call with Luis and scroll to the website of a nearby culinary school campus. I book myself and Mia a tour in a couple weeks' time. Fleur has wanted to be a model for as long as I can remember, Evie has dreamed of being on Broadway since she could walk, Josie's pretty dead set on a career as Spider-Man, but Mia has never been sure. After making pro and con lists beneath nurse, personal trainer, sports coach, engineer, and athlete, she sighed at the kitchen island and said, "I wish I could just cook food all day."

Chef, Mia. You want to be a chef.

Idiot.

I love all my sisters equally, but Mia is the one who most often feels like a friend. The idea of her moving out and chasing her dreams of becoming a chef is terrifying; I'd miss her. In my head she's still six years old.

Jacqueline buzzes me from her desk outside my office. "Mr. Corbeau? Mr. Morello is here."

"Send him in."

Rocco Morello is a mountain of a man. I remember meeting Vincenzo, double the size of the other kids his age, and then seeing his father across the room and thinking, *Ah, that makes sense.* Buzzed hair, watchful eyes, tattoos all the way up his neck, a nasty scar across his forehead. Six foot six with shoulders broader than your average doorway, he used to terrify me as a boy.

Now we've ended up here, feeling more like equals.

"None of that instant crap. I don't want no pods, either. Or coffee bags. *Fuck* coffee bags. And *fuck* decaf. You got that?" he barks, on his way in.

"Yes, Mr. Morello," replies Jacqueline, sounding a little faint.

Rocco shuts the door behind him, isolating us in my oversized office. He bypasses the sofa, sprawling out in the armchair opposite my desk. "You get her from the unemployment office, or what? Woman doesn't know how to work a computer."

"She's fine."

"She sucks at her job."

"Like me."

Despite the early hour, he lights a cigar, smoke obscuring his frosty blue gaze. The tattoos all over his hands have spread with age, but his wife's name is still legible just above his knuckles. "Not according to the *Wall Street Journal*."

I pull a cigarette from my desk drawer, joining him. "I appreciate you watching over my sisters the week it all happened."

His smile doesn't touch his eyes. He sits forward, the faint wrinkles in the tanned skin on his forehead deepening. "I've got a bone to pick with you, Corbeau." The steroid-enhanced muscles in his shoulders tense, fingers drumming together. "You endangered my children at Sorrowsong."

I shake my head, taking a drag. "Not how it played out."

"No?"

"I didn't ask anything of them."

"You sent my daughter on a hunt for a killer in that forest outside the castle. If you hadn't have left her with a weapon, I'd have pulled your intestines out your mouth by now."

"Consider us even, then, for the cleanup I did with the Ivanovs."

When Ophelia's roommate—the daughter of Rocco's bitter rival—was found dead at Sorrowsong last year, Vincenzo looked like the obvious culprit.

The rift between the Morellos and the Ivanovs is decades long and is often only worsened by each family refusing to send their kids anywhere other than Sorrowsong. There are too many influential people there to let the other family have free rein over the secrets and societies that hide between those crumbling walls.

Thankfully, by the time I got to Ophelia's stalker—some sad, sniveling psychology lecturer—he was alive enough to confess to the murder. Three days of pleading with the Russians to see sense and they eased off on the attempts to kill Vincenzo.

It's never boring in their world; I'll give them that.

He scoffs. "I could've handled the Ivanovs on my own."

"With bloodshed," I argue.

The skull tattooed on his hand stretches into a nasty grin when he clenches his fist. "Yeah, and explosions, probably. Risk my daughter's safety again and I'll kill you."

"Have you ever tried to stop Belladonna doing anything, ever?"

That earns me a genuine smile. Rocco Morello and Cain Green may share many characteristics, but there's one where they differ: Rocco loves his children with every piece of his soul. He wears the capo hat well, but when you pull it off, the father hat sits closer to his skin. His life revolves around Belladonna and Vincenzo. He cried like a baby at her sixteenth birthday party.

For all the wealth and power he sits on, I know he'd trade it all for them if it came to it.

Rocco gave me my first condom. Bought me my first bottle of whiskey. Told me which women to avoid and which ones to trust. After my first breakup, he called me to talk about it. In many ways, he was more of a father than Cain ever was.

He's like Vincenzo: His morals are marbled in the shiniest gold and darkest shade of black.

He claps both hands onto his knees. "What gives me the pleasure of being here today?"

I exhale a breath of smoke over my desk. "A new deal."

"I'm listening."

"No more hits."

His gaze ices over. "I'm no longer listening."

"No more hits. Not for you, not for anyone. You want someone dead, do it yourself."

My father was malleable, easily used by whichever criminal was willing to pay him most. He built himself a monopoly on the private aviation market. If anyone rich, anyone important was flying anywhere, my father knew about it.

If Rocco Morello wanted someone off the face of the earth, my father would make it happen, tidy it up with a fake story and an NDA. *He had a heart attack just before takeoff; he tried to hijack the aircraft—we had to shoot him; he never showed up for the flight.*

For the right price, Cain Green would do anything anyone wanted.

It's a legacy I do not intend to continue.

"No deal. It's not about doing it myself. It's about getting multiple important people in the same place at the same time. A helicopter is a sitting duck."

"No. More. Hits."

"You don't want to make an enemy of me, Alex."

It's true, but for the first time, he doesn't want to make an enemy of me, either. Temporary or not, I'm as rich as he is. Better connected than he is. More reputable, believable, *trustworthy* than he is. He has power, but so do I.

"I can't think of another airline that'd be willing to ferry you and your men around all day, willing to splash as much cash as Green does on covering your tracks from the Russians."

He narrows his eyes. "Why are you doing this? For the woman?"

"For the woman."

"I warned you about women," he growls, temper fraying. "They make a mess of it all."

"I'm scrubbing Green clean. I shouldn't even be partnering with you, Rocco, but I'm willing to continue. But no more hits."

"I'm saying no."

"I'm saying you have no choice."

He huffs out a laugh. "You have nothing over me."

I bite down my smile, glancing down at the watch that hugs my wrist: 9:01 a.m. The news will be live. I type a quick search into my phone, standing to put the device on the coffee table.

Green Aviation Acquires New York Based Cybersecurity Firm Synx in $540 Million Deal.

Synx covers every digital trace Rocco leaves. It encrypts his messages, buries his finances, and hides his illegal business behind his legitimate one. It's also a *very* profitable company.

"Would be a shame if your security company turned evidence in to the Feds."

Rocco looks the same color as the ugly chartreuse curtains he let his wife put up in the Morello mansion last Christmas. His fists clench and unclench over the expensive wool of his slacks. "You're losing your mind over a piece of ass, Corbeau."

"Call her that again and see where it gets you." And that ass is *such* an ass. Couldn't have picked a better one to lose my mind over.

"You hold far too much loyalty for a girl who plotted against you."

"Didn't Francesca blow up your car two weeks before you got married?"

A fond affection joins the venom in his eyes. Rocco and Francesca Morello might be the only reason I still believe in true love. "She's a firecracker, that one. She did me a favor, really. Car needed replacing."

"As did my father."

His snort of amusement tells me we're back on safer ground. He had a profitable arrangement with my father, but he never really liked him, didn't really like the way he treated my mother the last few years.

Abruptly, he slams a giant fist down on the coffee table and curses. It's easy to step on a land mine with Rocco. If Jacqueline comes in with an instant coffee, God himself wouldn't be able to save her. "You're not scrubbing shit clean, *coglione*, you're blackmailing just like he did."

"For the right reasons. For my sisters, for my mother. No more hits, Rocco."

An inch of gray ash tumbles into the porcelain tray on the coffee table, his eyes wide with manic exasperation. I'm still half expecting him to reach out and snap my neck. He's unpredictable, possibly a little unstable. I think you have to be, in his job. "You kids will be the death of me." He leans back in the seat again. "Fine. Deal. Only because Francesca likes your mother, and Vincenzo likes you."

I didn't need his acceptance, but I take it anyway.

"How is she?" he asks.

"Ophelia?"

He snorts. "No, dipshit. Your mother. I don't give a fuck about the sad ginger girl."

"She's the same."

He draws a graph with his hand, up and down and up and down. I nod. That's about it. Highs and lows, over and over, with increasing volatility.

"When Francesca got shot in the back, I thought my kids would have no mother. It's fucking terrifying, the idea of losing her."

"And?" I say, waiting for the inspirational speech. The *it'll get easier*, or the *she'll always be in your heart*.

He shakes his head, tossing the remainder of his cigar in the tray. "That's it. It's bullshit, it's terrifying, and it'll hurt like hell. Nothing anyone tells you, no shitty quote regurgitated from a sign on a bathroom wall is gonna fix it. Your mom will be gone, and that's shit."

"A cheerful conversation for my Tuesday morning," I chime, but really, I do appreciate his honesty. Everyone is obsessed with telling me that everything will get easier.

I can't imagine that ever being the case.

IT'S INCREDIBLE HOW fast things decay. My relationship with my father, whatever it was I had with Ophelia, my mother's health. My mood today is no exception.

As I saw Rocco into the elevator just before lunch, I felt buoyant, another job off my list, another weight off my shoulders. And here I am at quarter to three, struggling to imagine how I'll make it to five.

I can't identify a trigger. No disastrous event occurred between Rocco's polished oxfords shuffling out of my office and now. But there's a gray cloud looming over my head again, casting all my thoughts in shadow.

Fat droplets of rain slide down the glass windows behind me, staining the sidewalks an inky charcoal.

On cue, my phone buzzes where it sits on my laptop keyboard. *Robert Harwood.* I pick it up on the first ring.

"Robert."

"Alex. How are you?"

I don't even bother answering that. He knows the answer. "You're not very good at being on vacation."

I hear his smile. "I can find time to check in on my favorite clients."

Yeah, *right*. He just wants to make sure his paycheck is still breathing. "Your most unstable clients."

He laughs. "I think you take both crowns."

"How is Lagos?"

"Busy. Humid. How is New York?"

I drum my pen on my thigh. Suffocating. Depressing. Freezing. Gray. So fucking lonely. "It's fine."

"Tell me more."

"Enjoy your vacation, Robert."

"I have time. It's this or drinks with my great aunt, so if you could keep talking, that'd be fantastic."

I shrug, even though he can't see me. I stare down at the traffic on the street far below. It's all so pointless. "I'm just tired."

"Bad day?"

A headache thuds at the base of my skull. The number of unread emails on my screen ticks up. A taxi rear-ends a bus at the intersection. The pedestrian light turns green. A crowd of people burst into action, and I find myself skimming each one for my father's graying blond hair. I wonder for the millionth time where he is. "Just tired."

"Let's break it down, then. Are you stressed at work?"

"Not really." I don't care about Green that much. "I met with Rocco Morello this morning."

"And your head is still on your shoulders. A miracle."

That drags a small smile out of me. "Yeah. I'm just . . ." *I'm lonely.* It feels so ridiculous to say out loud. I'm an adult man, with a big family at home. Vincenzo is just a text away. I have friends in the city. But I am. Loneliness gnaws at my bones the second I swing my eyes open in the morning. It sits on my shoulder while I'm at my desk, fills the car when I drive home.

And when I get into bed at night, it's so heavy on my chest that I can't take a full breath in.

"I miss *her.*" I miss Vincenzo. I miss my free time. I miss my mom, I miss my hopes and dreams. The words are out without my permission, but they aren't news to Harwood. "And I feel trapped by my sisters."

"Trapped into staying alive?"

"Yeah," I whisper, even though I know how awful it sounds. But Harwood doesn't scold me. Doesn't tell me how grateful some people would be to have a family. Doesn't tell me how lucky I am to have reasons to stay alive.

An accepting sort of silence unravels between us for a moment. "I think that's a very valid way to feel, Alex. It's not ungrateful, if that's what you're telling yourself. Let's talk about it when I'm in your office next week. I was mostly calling to see if there was any news on your father."

The gray cloud clogs my throat. Forcing the words out feels like wading through syrup. "No news. He's vanished."

"Could he be dead?"

"Unlikely." He's not one to go down quietly, nor one not to be ruthlessly efficient. I doubt he'd shoot himself unless he knew the shot would pass through someone else on the way. Double the return on investment. "I worry about him getting to my sisters and me being too far away to help."

"You've hired very capable security for them, and should he surface for air, he'll be caught. You've done all you can. You've done enough."

Maybe. Maybe not. Even with his credit card blocked, my father is rich enough to slip through the nets of the law. Rich enough to silence people, rich enough to buy his freedom. He has blackmail on police departments, hospitals, insurance firms, airlines, billionaires, crime gangs, *everyone*.

His absence looms over me, unsettling and threatening. A knife above my head tied to a fraying string. I get the sensation we're all just treading water, and somewhere beneath us, my father is a shark just waiting to bite.

I wrap up my call with Robert and text Mack, my private investigator, and Jordan, my contact at the FBI, asking if either of them has any updates. Mack replies immediately. *Nothing.* On the app on my phone, I check the security feeds at home. The lounge is empty, the basement, the hallway, the foyer, the games room, all unoccupied. In the kitchen, my mother is sitting at the island having coffee with the housekeeper.

All is well. I close the security app and get back to work.

A twisted part of me wishes I had a camera on Ophelia. Day and night. Every room. I'd watch it like it was my favorite TV show, watch it when I couldn't sleep.

But she isn't mine anymore. She hid the truth from me, and I left her. I lost all right to watch her, and she lost my trust.

I have a feeling I'll be watching her for the rest of my life, though.

I slap a hand onto my keyboard just to get rid of the reflection of my face in my laptop and try to focus on something, *anything*, that isn't her.

Chapter 3

OPHELIA

Stalk me once, shame on you. Stalk me *twice*, and clearly, I must be a fucking idiot or something.

Or however the saying goes.

I don't understand how I've managed to be stalked twice in one year. I'm the kind of person who has to hype myself up in a mirror to tell the barista I got the wrong drink. I cry at kids' movies. How is it *me* who ends up with the stalkers? Belladonna punched someone who looked at her funny at a party last week, and to my knowledge, she's not being stalked.

Another crack of thunder reverberates through the castle, dragging me back to the present. Divya lets out a stomach-churning yodel, and the cocktail glasses on the gold bar cart chatter in time with the flickering lights. Colette shoves a sofa cushion over my head like she's trying to finish me off. Her friend Magda lets out a tuneful hum.

Their attempts to distract me from the thunder are working, but probably not for the reasons they think they are; I'm genuinely fearing for my life, too scared to even *think* about helicopters as Colette mashes the velvet tighter against my ears.

"Are you feeling better yet?" she demands, her voice muffled.

"I can't fucking breathe!" I screech.

"Oh, sorry." She eases the pressure on the cushion, and I heave in a grateful breath. My laugh is buried in the stiff fabric.

The article about Alex's family going live may have sent so much of my life into chaos, but it's tied what few friendships I do have closer. Divya and I whittle away our evenings studying in the library in companionable silence, and Colette's best friend, Magda, has become one of my best friends, too.

After the bomb exploded between me and Alex and fractured the delicate thing we were building, I did what I've only ever been able to do. Withdraw. Isolate myself. Deprive myself of human connection because how could loneliness ever be worse than the pain of losing someone you thought was here to stay?

I'm never one to miss a good opportunity to wallow, and man, did I wallow. Like, crying into my dry bowl of cereal and listening to sad music just to make myself cry harder. Scurrying across the floor like a greasy orange sewer rat to collect the snacks that Divya left outside my door but refusing to let her in. *That* sort of wallowing.

But my new friends are not so easily dissuaded, and when Colette's thousand-dollar ankle boot snuck in the door before I could close it on the fourth day, I knew I was done for.

A nutritionally balanced meal and a tipsy pep talk later, I told my new friends everything. I told them about my parents, about

Bancroft, about Cain Green. I told them why I could never get on a plane, why the sound of the helicopter terrifies me, and why thunder crashing in the valley makes me think of my parents' death.

I told them I felt like Alex leaving was one thing too many, that it hurt me so much I didn't think I could survive it.

By the end, all three of them were sobbing with me. And since then, by the time the first flash of lighting illuminates Sorrowsong's crumbling walls and well-buried secrets, they're already at my bedroom door, armed with snacks and blankets. Which, when you're as well-acquainted with the Highlands' storm warnings and howling winds as we are, is serious dedication. Every frantic run from the castle's walls to the mansion feels like a deadly trial.

And yet, they think I'm worth it.

For the first time, I find myself with fledgling friendships, delicate roots finding their place in my broken heart and filling up the smallest cracks.

I'm *desperate* not to damage them.

Alex's absence gnaws a gaping hole in my chest every day, but there are people looking out for me. I'm getting to know the reflection in the mirror. I'm learning what she likes, what she's passionate about. I'm learning her insecurities and her dreams and all the other things she put on pause for five years.

I see the next flash of lightning through the pillow, and when Colette finally removes it from my face, the power is out. The lush amber curtains and art deco wallpaper of the Cortinar halls are cloaked in dim candlelight.

"Fuck this weather," I mumble, letting out a heavy exhale that has me sinking farther into the soft velvet of the sofa.

"Fuck this weather," the three of them echo, in perfect unison.

"And fuck this group chat," I add, phone open on one of the many group chats I was advised to join "because they're a great way to network," like having an oil tycoon's son on speed dial is something that'll come in handy for me.

With his good looks, online speculation of how badly his father treated him, various paparazzi images of him dropping his sisters off at school in his rugby shorts, and Green's rallying economic performance, Alex has become somewhat of a national treasure. And people love to talk about it, which unfortunately means everyone *hates* me. More messages ping through in the Sorrowsong first years group.

Annabelle Young
Apparently a guy in second year is missing

Lawrence Carlisle
Someone check Ophelia Winters's
hard drive.

Rose Hanover
Lol. Or under her bed.

Lawrence Carlisle
He's probably in the trunk of her car
with Sofia Ivanov.

The inside of my cheek bleeds from how hard I have it clamped between my teeth. I want to march into lecture halls and scream at them, but that won't help my case.

Tabby Jones
You think she can afford a car?

Gabriel Bristol
Careful, Lawrence, she'll dig up your private affairs and sell them to the press.

Lawrence Carlisle
Anything for a few dollars, right, @Ophelia Winters?

"Ophelia," Colette scolds, snatching my phone away to close the app. "You're going to have to learn to ignore what they say to you."

But I can't. It feels like the rest of the students are creating a movie about how awful I am. How *I* was the one who killed my parents, how I ruined six girls' lives, how I led Alex on for months. And I, servant to my own morbid curiosity and apparent need to see myself suffer, haven't left any of the group chats, haven't asked any of them to leave me alone.

"One of them said I was bland, Colette. *Bland and meek.*"

It's not remotely the worst thing they've said, but it has stuck with me.

Meek.

"Well . . ." says Magda, tilting her head from side to side like that might be a fair assessment. "You haven't exactly got a zest for life."

Colette throws the pillow at her head. "Magda!"

"She's right," says Divya, through a mouthful of popcorn.

"There's never any whimsy with you. You stomp around."

"So does Magda!" I protest, sweeping a hand in the direction of the heavy platform boots that sit over her fishnet tights. Magda's fashion sense lies somewhere between a ghost bride and Wednesday Addams, and she's always matching her eyeliner to her braids.

See: Magda has it together. I really don't.

"It's part of her charm."

I don't even attempt to argue that I have charm. Whatever the opposite of charm is, I've got it.

Alex thought I had charm. Alex made me *feel* like I had charm.

Until he left me without giving me a chance to explain myself, that is.

I shrug the thought away, rising to my feet in the dull gloom of the Cortinar common room. It's Saturday, so students are strewn about the large space, slouched on sofas or studying at vintage desks. The gold coffee machine at the far end of the lounge coughs and splutters, kicking out the rich smell of warm espresso.

I'm still upset that I wasn't put into Cortinar.

I stretch my arms above my head and grab my swimming bag, ignoring the spiteful looks I get around the room from students who want me dead for betraying their rugby-thighed, messy-haired prince.

"Nice sweater," sneers the guy studying by the exit, eyes sweeping up and down my father's jumper with a poorly concealed look of revulsion on his face. He's said far worse about me this week, but my anger bubbles up in my throat all the same.

I plaster a sweet smile across my lips. "You're nineteen, Hugo. Worry about your receding hairline first."

An orchestra could play on that forehead.

I turn back to Colette, cocking my head toward the door. "Let's go."

She clambers to her feet, all long Bambi limbs and honey-blond hair that falls in big, loose waves around her pretty face. Her glossy bottom lip juts out, telling me she's no keener to go to swimming practice than I am. But with my first term's performance in the pool—or lack thereof—it's a miracle I've not been kicked off the team yet.

My relationship with swimming, like my relationship with most things since the events of the past few months, has grown more complicated. Swimming was my mother's hobby. Something we did together, from when I was floating in orange armbands to when fuzzy photos of me with cheap plastic medals made the local newspaper.

Then she died. Competitive swimming lost its charm. The two faces I'd always looked for at the side of the pool, warm and reassuring, just weren't there anymore. Burger and movie night to celebrate a new personal best became a memory so distant that it was hard to imagine it was ever real. The chopping boards grew dusty, the fridge shelves stayed empty, and my school swimming gear never made it out of the bag again.

But I never stopped swimming. I may have traded the pool for lakes and rivers, lost the stopwatch, lost the passion, but I never stopped. It was the only thing that made me feel close to them. The only thing that numbed the jagged wound their absence left.

Now I'm not sure if I want to feel close to my mother at all. Her affair with Bancroft feels like a ruthless betrayal of my father, which feels like a betrayal of me, of every Christmas and birthday and movie night we all shared together.

My life at the moment is an endless string of *not sure*s. I'm not sure who my mother was, not sure if my father knew about her cheating, either. I'm not sure why Alex left without a word, not sure if he'll come back. I'm not even sure if I'm angry with him, or if I'm just heartbroken for a boy who has let his life become the bridge that others walk on.

And I'm really, *really* not sure why I didn't tell him about my plan to out his father, or that my intentions at the beginning of our relationship were not genuine. I replay them now, all the opportunities I had to come clean, all the opportunities I had to delete the document.

I guess I just didn't want to let my parents down, to give up on getting some sort of justice for them, to feel like I was trading them in for Alex.

Now I have none of them.

Colette snorts beside me, taupe fingernails tapping at her phone screen. "Vincenzo is *so* funny," she sighs, grinning at the string of blue and gray texts. I smile back but don't reply. Vincenzo doesn't speak to me anymore. I'm embarrassed to admit I miss him, too.

We wind our way out of the labyrinth of tunnels in the eastern wing of the castle, a poorly lit archway spitting us out into the valley outside. It's not long past midday, but Sorrowsong is laden with thick, heavy clouds that make it look like it's early evening. The damp air is rich with the smell of rain, but the storm looks like it might finally be easing off. A few white wisps of sunlight trickle through the patches where the cloud cover thins.

Colette slides her phone into the pocket of her fluffy white coat, giving me a serious look. "My love, if I read and believed everything that's said about me by people who hardly know me, I'd never get out of bed. I get it: It's new and novel to you. It's unthinkable. Abhorrent. But it's just the way it works. We ignore it."

"Do you think I'm bland?"

"I think you're wonderful."

"But am I wonderful in a bland way? Like salted crisps, or white bread?"

Her grin widens as we trudge up the path to the large, ornate Victorian glasshouse that encloses the pool. "I think you're wonderful like roses. Beautiful and prickly."

Christ. "Is this about my unshaven legs?"

Her laugh is bright, too cheery for a place like this. "Mine are prickly, too. I miss my wax lady."

Even if you melted down the entire contents of Madame Tussauds, it wouldn't be enough wax to fix the state of my legs.

"Hey," she says, changing the subject. "Still no more anonymous texts?"

That sours my mood further. I still don't know who sent that message to me in the airport. The person with the most motive is Cain, but would he really waste his time with me? I have zero power and influence. Vin and Belladonna? They aren't my biggest fans these days, *especially* Belladonna. But somehow, I can't believe it of them. Shawn's friends? I'm sure they don't love me, either. I run away from Carmichael at every opportunity, but he probably has my face on a dartboard. And there are always a few students up to something in the woods at night. Anyone could've stumbled upon us.

My friends and I have been trying to figure out my anonymous texter for weeks. Last Monday, they all sat in the high turret windows while I walked round the courtyard for an hour like a fly that can't find the door. We were hoping they'd catch someone taking a photo of me, but no luck.

And when we caught Lettice Hartwick following me down to the tarn a few days ago, we thought we had it figured out, but no, it wasn't her. Which I was quite pleased about, because being stalked is bad enough, but being stalked by someone called Lettice would be a new low, even for me.

I'd have gone straight to the police, if the image attached wasn't a picture of Alex and me burying a body.

We killed a man together. *Buried* him together. And now I'm trying to deal with the consequences of that alone. Maybe killing someone doesn't seem so significant in Alex's world of wealth and power, but in my world of multipack crisps and laddered tights, it's enough to keep me up at night.

I hug my knees to my chest on the bathroom floor in the early hours of each morning and try as hard as I can to justify a man's death, scrub my fingers raw like they're still caked in damp earth from the forest, and beg the universe to erase the things I saw that night from my memories.

He killed my parents because of his unhealthy obsession with my mother, because she wouldn't run away with him. He had Cain make them disappear as payment for upholding his family man image.

A video of Cain sleeping with Carmichael's secretary. That was the price of my parents' existence. And so, the helicopter crash became the price for Bancroft's existence.

It's *that* way of thinking, like all of this is just a set of equations to be balanced, that scares me. It feels like Sorrowsong is rubbing off on me, lacing those first few threads of corruption through my conscience.

Everyone has a limit at which they abandon their own morality, Ophelia Winters, even you.

It was one of the first things Carmichael ever said to me, the two of us beneath Achlys's haunting stare on my first day here. I guess I reached that limit sooner than I thought.

"No, no more texts," I finally breathe out, realizing Colette has stopped walking in favor of watching me with great concern.

My new stalker had asked me to hand myself over, but if it's Cain, I have no idea where he is, and if it's not, I have no idea *who* this person is. So, I decided to remain silent, surrounded by friends. Weeks later, it seems to be paying off. I haven't heard from that number again. If Cain wants to find me, he'll have to walk onto a busy university campus.

With Belladonna in it.

At the rusting entrance, I swap my fading leather boots for sliders and head to the pool, where the aforementioned Mafia heiress is gliding through the water at a pace that makes it clear why she's the captain. One toned, tattooed arm hits the tiled edge and she surfaces, pulling off her cap and goggles and glaring at us. Even if I did manage to grow a backbone—even if I managed to grow *nineteen* backbones—I'd still be scared of her.

"Go and warm up," she barks, more at Colette than me. She's made it clear that she believes that what happened to Alex was my doing and wants nothing to do with me, either. For the most part, I can handle the online abuse, the stares and the venomous looks, and the snickers whenever I ask a question in a lecture, but when they come from someone I'd hoped might be my friend one day, it feels a whole lot worse.

* * *

SWIM PRACTICE IS grueling. I stay long after the others leave. Length after length with Belladonna shouting at me. Too slow, too sloppy, too tense, too *relaxed.* Steve, the *actual* swim coach, can't get a word in edgewise. He's a short, wiry man who wears a navy tracksuit that tells me he's clinging onto his youth as hard as he is to the remaining strands of hair dotting the back of his head.

He might be the only person more scared of Belladonna than I am.

My final one hundred is fueled only by frustration and spite. A determined chant of *don't cry don't cry don't cry* rattles around my brain.

Miraculously, it's my fastest time of the day.

I haul myself out of the pool, thighs landing on the edge with a wet slap as my mantra of *don't cry* turns to *don't vomit.*

"Good job, Ophelia," Steve says, like it has *just* occurred to him that he is a coach.

Belladonna crosses her arms. "Keep swimming like that, and there's a slim chance you might not lose *everything* this season."

From her, it's high praise, and I take it as a win.

She's the only one in the poorly lit changing room when I emerge from the showers, tugging a hoodie over my head. Industrial iron lockers line one wall, oak benches along the other. The stained plaster is peeling to reveal gray brick beneath. It looks postapocalyptic in here, like a war bunker.

Belladonna doesn't glance in my direction, focusing instead on stuffing a folded towel into her bag. The atmosphere is awkward as I pull my duffel from my rusty locker, half expecting a knife to land in my back.

"How is he?"

It takes me a minute to realize it's *my* mouth those words have slipped out of. Those words I've held on to so tightly, swallowed down at every opportunity, creeping out without my permission.

She looks like she can't believe I've just said that. *I* can't believe I've just said that.

"How do you think he is?" she snaps, picking up her bag with far more force than is required.

I don't know why it makes my stomach sink; it's not like it's a surprise that Alex is suffering. I know how sick his mom is, how lost his sisters are, how heavy his father's disappearance must weigh on him, how busy Green must keep him. I've seen videos on social media of Fleur lashing out in clothing stores, smoking outside bars she's far too young to be at, arguing on the street with her new boyfriend.

Deliberately or not, I did that to them.

"*He* left, Belladonna," I say, not convincing enough for either of us. "He left without a word."

What happened between Alex and me was a mess, a complete injustice to what I felt for him, to what I'd dreamed of for our future. I let my desperation for revenge take the reins on my life for four years. I let the grief I felt over my parents prevent me from doing the one thing they always wanted me to do: live.

But he believed them. The papers, the media. The lies and the deceit. I made a space for him in my heart, and he walked away.

Belladonna is facing me now, stalking over until she's almost nose to nose with me. She's taller, wider, *stronger*. The delicate vine tattoos that peek out from the neckline of her hoodie stretch as her jaw ticks. "He left because you put six girls into a relentless wheel of media attention. Didn't you think his mom was sick enough already?"

"It. Wasn't. Me." I've said it so many times, I'm convinced the words are etched onto my tongue, bleached onto my soul.

Her nostrils flare, pale blue gaze icy. I'm sure she can smell my fear. I don't doubt that Belladonna would kill—maybe even *has* killed—for those she loves. "Do us all a favor and stay out of his life, Winters. He doesn't need any more mess."

The final word comes out laden with so much malice, so much intention, that despite my desperate efforts to thicken my skin over the past few weeks, it slips inside like a hot knife through butter.

Mess. That's what she thinks I am to Alex.

She stalks away before I can think of a clever reply, shouting over her shoulder as she leaves. "You're kicking too wide on your breaststroke. That's why you suck."

The door slamming rattles my bones, teeth chattering as wind slips through the cracked windows. I sink down to the bench, letting my head hang in despair.

A heavy silence settles in the locker room.

My fingers fumble with the laces on my boots, hurrying to zip up my bag. Like every time I'm alone here, my heart rate spikes where it thuds in my throat. Bancroft may be dead, but it doesn't stop me feeling watched everywhere I go, hearing twigs snap behind me in the forest, sensing someone standing on the other side of every door.

I glance over my shoulder whenever I walk along the path to the Nightshade mansion. I double lock my room each night, slide the chair beneath the handle.

Someone took that photo of us in the forest. I'm 99 percent sure it must've been Shawn. Who else would be following me? No one on campus other than him has shown an interest in me at all.

And that 99 percent is enough for me, until the early hours of the morning, where sleep deprivation has made me paranoid, and that extra one percent shouts louder than the rest. I've buried one stalker. I just hope my silence is enough to stall the anger of whoever sent that photo.

I don't feel safe here, and I don't feel safe back at my parents' house. It feels so ridiculous that despite the magnitude of the last few months—falling in love, learning to trust, almost being killed, taking down Cain Green—I don't feel any safer than I did when I first arrived at Sorrowsong last autumn.

My phone buzzes in my bag as I head out of the changing rooms and leave the glass pool house. A dangerous bulb of hope illuminates at the back of my mind.

Could it be him? Do I even want it to be him? I hold my breath as I rifle around in my bag, thinking of what it is I'd say. I'm sorry? Why did you leave? I'm angry with you. How is your mom? I passed the exams I thought I'd fail, beat the freestyle personal best I never thought I would.

I think about you all the time.

A hundred and one things flit through my brain as my hand finally finds the device amongst the empty cereal bar wrappers and lip balms.

It isn't him. It's an unknown number.

A shadow moves in the corner of my vision, making me jump. But nothing is there, just a bush rustling in the wind.

I pick up the call but don't speak, waiting anxiously as I scan every single gap in the trees.

A gruff American accent breaks the silence. "Ms. Ophelia Winters?"

"Speaking."

"My name is Mack; I lead a firm working for Mr. Corbeau-Green to investigate his father's disappearance."

"Oh." Even his name hurts. "I see."

"I wondered if you had time to answer a couple of questions?"

I glance over my shoulder at the sound of footsteps in the trees but see nothing. "Uhh . . . okay. How do I know you're . . . real?"

"I can fly to Scotland tomorrow, if you'd prefer. Or have you flown to New York."

"No!" I drag in a ragged inhale, trying to calm my tone. Even the idea of getting on a plane has my hands clammy. "No, thank you. I'm afraid of flying, and you don't need to come here."

"I can put you on the phone to Mr. Corbeau, to ease your worries?"

A long silence stretches out over the line. I imagine a brief phone call, sandwiched between meetings, curt and businesslike. I'm not ready for that. "No, no. Bear with me."

If I texted Belladonna now, she'd probably use her influence to make my phone explode in my hand, or something. I don't know where I stand with Vincenzo these days, but I know he wouldn't lie to me.

Ophelia Winters

Do you know a guy called Mack?

Vincenzo Morello

Alex's investigator?

Ophelia Winters

So he's legit, then.

Vincenzo Morello

One of the best.

"Okay, fine," I breathe, suitably appeased. "What do you want to know?"

His voice is crackly from lack of signal. "Have you seen, heard, or received anything suspicious since Cain Green went missing?"

I open my mouth to tell him about the text I received at the airport but shut it just as quickly when I remember what was *in* that text message. A photo of Alex and me, both dirty and bloodied, standing over a dying man in the forest. If this guy is working with the police, that's probably not the best idea.

I'd die burying that photo if it meant those girls didn't lose another parental figure in their lives.

But hiding the truth from Alex is something I'm trying to leave behind.

"I . . . I think I need to speak to Alex first."

"You're free to say as you wish without judgement."

Yeah, but is that *I stole a cookie from a bakery when I was nine* sort of no judgement, or *I stabbed my lecturer and spat on his dead body* sort of no judgement. "I got a text from someone."

I snap my mouth shut before I say any more.

"And this was before or after Alex buried your stalker?"

Oh. Well, that clears that up. "I . . . you . . ."

"I'm not interested in putting you behind bars, Ms. Winters. I'm more interested in keeping Alex and his sisters safe."

"It was after. It was the day the article went live. It had a . . . it had a photo in it."

"To your personal phone?"

"Yes, it's my only phone."

"Are you busy tomorrow? I'd like to have a look at your phone to see what I can gather from the text."

I toe my boot in the wet mud beneath my feet, desperate to leave all of this behind. To leave Bancroft behind, Cain behind, Sorrowsong behind. "I'm not busy."

His tone is sharp and efficient, like I'm helping him get through his boring to-do list. "Great. I'll fly in later tonight."

The line drops before I can ask him anything else, leaving me stranded and shivering on the forested path back to the castle. A shudder up my spine sends a puff of white breath into the frigid air, and when I walk toward my lecture in the tallest spire, eyes weigh heavy on my back the whole time.

A STRONG GUST of wind sweeps through the valley, rattling the ancient window in its frame.

A thin strip of moonlight illuminates the dust on the cold tile of my bedroom. I can hear a few students laughing outside the mansion, despite it being past three in the morning.

I'm fighting sleep. This is how it goes every night: deluding myself into thinking I'm some new breed of human who just doesn't need rest.

My friendships may be growing, my fitness improving, my

grades recovering, but my nightmares couldn't be any worse. It's so bad, the guy across the hall has filed a noise complaint.

I was sleeping better when Alex . . . never mind.

Why did he leave without a word?

I should let this go, move on, think about something else, but I can't. I understand why he left that day, I understand why he took the CEO position, I understand why he dropped out of university, I understand everything except one thing.

Why didn't he wake me up and fight for us?

I can only imagine his mental state that morning. Alex was doing better in the months before he left, but I'd still seen him at his lowest. Those sporadic evenings when he'd ask me to leave, tell me he felt so low that he might never get out of bed again.

Depression can be a cruel illness. When I checked the news every ten seconds for the rest of that day, it wasn't for news of his father's demise, it was for his.

So like I always do at this hour, when the Nightshade mansion howls and groans under the biting wind, I allow myself to hunt for any scraps of Alex I can find.

He makes it all look easy. I've watched each press conference, each blurry paparazzi video. Christ, I even got a one-month subscription to the *Financial Times* to see an article about him.

When you find yourself reading your third hedge fund managers' take on the upcoming quarter to get full value out of your news subscription, you know you've fallen a bit too hard for a man.

It can't get lower than this.

Fleur's Instagram story is a mirror selfie with her new boyfriend. If I wasn't trying to be less skeptical and judgmental about the world, I'd say he looks like an absolute wanker.

But I am, so I won't.

Mia still lets me follow her private account with a hundred followers, but she, like the other five of her siblings, has been radio silent for the last month.

I'm worried about him. I hope he started those antidepressants, is keeping up his sessions with Harwood. I hope he's not spreading himself too thin, but I know he is.

In the eerie darkness, I furiously brush away my tears before they have the chance to fall. I'm angry with myself, frustrated that no matter how many times I try to toughen up, feel less, *move on*, it doesn't work.

I want to be more like Belladonna, but it sure is harder than she makes it look.

I shut off my phone, plunging the room into darkness. I squeeze my eyes shut before they can adjust, before I can see Sofia's untouched bed, the cobwebs on the walls, the knife on the bedside table. With the bitter chill of an overnight snow seeping through the walls, I bury my head beneath the blankets and try, try, *try* to relax.

Ping.

A text notification rings through, loud and clear in the silent room.

I can't explain the bad feeling that washes over me, the way that ping sounds so much more menacing than the other identical ones today. The note is too high, too shrill, too out of tune. It echoes between the decaying beams above me and lands right in my stomach with a nauseating thud.

Through one squinted eye, as if that might make it any better, I risk a glance at the text.

I let my phone clatter back down to the side table, let my head fall back to the bed. It's not dread, or horror, or fear that runs through me. It's exasperation. A complete exhaustion, sapping the fight out of me.

I can't do this again. I can't take this anymore.

I turn over, burying my face in the blanket so I don't have to see the blurry photo, sent from the anonymous number, of me walking out of the swimming pool greenhouse earlier today.

Chapter 4

ALEX

[DRAFT]

Subject: Sudoku (noun) *Please teach me*

To: Ophelia Winters

I don't understand how you could possibly enjoy Sudoku. They're making me angry.

I KNEW MY day was off to a rocky start when Josie, unsupervised, ate six bowls of marshmallow cereal for breakfast and then proceeded to vomit it all up on the way out the door. Crisis managed—I owe Emily, the nanny, a day off for that one—I made it into the office by nine, despite the traffic that a Monday morning in the city brings.

Jacqueline has my weekly schedule in my inbox by the time I slide into the chair behind my desk. A double espresso steams on the coaster beside my laptop. I text her a quick thank you and open the shitstorm that is my emails after a busy weekend at home.

Two notifications ping through at exactly nine. My daily reminder, *Don't call Ophelia*, sits beneath a text from Harwood, punctual as ever.

Robert Harwood

Morning. I'm back in the city today.

Lunchtime?

Alex

Lunch sounds good.

I stare at the reminder, glaring at it like that might make it go away. *Don't call Ophelia.* It sits on my lock screen all day, obscuring her warm brown eyes in the photo I took in the back of the Land Rover on Christmas Eve.

It was the first text I got from my lawyer and investigator the day it all went south. Don't call Ophelia. Cease all contact. Don't incriminate your family further. Don't give Green a reason to sue you for defamation, to suspect that it was you who helped her put that article together. Don't be seen together, not until all threads of Bancroft's life have been buried.

Fifteen infuriating letters that have made all of this so fucking lonely.

My first call of the day is with Mack and Brendan: the two private detectives I hired to assist the FBI in their search for my father. My dad has a lot of connections there, so I need two people who are definitely on my side. They've worked with me before to find the leak of various medical records belonging to my mother over the years.

Brendan appears on my laptop screen, a hoodie covering his messy hair. Through his half-an-inch-thick glasses, he's frowning at his screen, telling me I only have half his attention. With a background in cybersecurity and an IQ the rest of us mortals can only dream of, he handles anything that can be done behind a desk.

I don't think Mack could sit behind a desk even with a gun to his head.

"Morning, Brendan."

He pushes his glasses up his nose. "Morning. We have an update for you. I'll wait for Mack to get online."

No problem, I'll just have an internal meltdown until then. "Great."

Mack takes forever to arrive, finally joining on his phone with his AirPods in. "Guess where I am."

"Do you actually want me to guess? Because I have another call at nine thirty."

He rolls his eyes at my mood, panning the camera round an empty airport.

My breath hitches, fingers freezing as they type an email on the other half of my screen. The last time I was at Inverness Airport, the walls of my universe were crumbling around me.

The last time I was there, I told Harwood I genuinely couldn't survive the day, that I couldn't do it anymore.

The last time I was there, Ophelia was there, and I turned away.

I thought distance from her would make it easier. Easier on me if I chose to live, easier on her if I chose to die. Easier managing my time between my sisters and work. It hasn't made anything easier.

Mack's voice drags me back to the here and now. "You're not our chattiest of clients."

"What are you doing there?" I sit up straighter in my chair, realization suddenly dawning on me. The idea that my father might be in Scotland, anywhere near Ophelia, makes my hands curl into tight fists atop my desk. "Is he there?"

"Well," begins Mack, like he has all the time in the world, and not twenty minutes, to deliver this story. "I just left Sorrowsong this morning."

My stomach drops, landing with a splat on the ground floor sixty-two stories down. "Is she okay?"

"She got a text in the airport the day you left."

I flinch at the last two words. I don't need a reminder. "You asked me to stay away from her," I spit out, teeth gritted.

"And I stand by that, given you don't want a murder on your record. Or hers, for that matter."

"No one will give a shit that Bancroft's gone."

"Please don't text Ophelia, Alex. Don't risk incriminating yourself."

"Rocco's men have scrubbed the site clean. All pieces of Bancroft—digital *or* physical—have been wiped."

"Ah. About that." My phone pings. It's an email from Brendan. ***Delete it once you've opened it. I'll erase all trace from my end.***

I unlock my phone and open the photo attached. It's blurry, taken with some kind of cheap night vision camera. When I realize what it is, the rest of my internal organs join my stomach seven hundred feet below me. "Fuck." I rake my hands through my hair, imagining what this could mean for the eight women that own every cell of my heart.

For Ophelia, it's jail time. It's the end of all the dreams she deserves so much to achieve, the dreams I crave for her. This would be the end of my mother, the final straw. "Fuck," I repeat, zooming in on Bancroft's dying form in front of Ophelia and me.

I drop the phone back on the desk. "Fuck."

Mack purses his lips like he's actively enjoying himself. "Triple fuck. Haven't had one of those before."

"This isn't funny, Mack. I have the girls to look after. And Ophelia . . . this can't come out."

"I can't match the text to either of your father's phones," says Brendan, more serious than his colleague.

"A burner phone?"

"Maybe, but I'm not sure. I don't know how he'd have a burner phone ready so soon after that article went live."

"He could've." He had a hundred phones for a hundred crimes. "But he couldn't have taken the photo. He was in New York that week."

My mind whirs like a flip-book, a hundred different faces flashing up in quick succession. Shawn feels like an obvious possibility. Carmichael, maybe. I can name more than a handful of business and finance students who think of my father like some sort of hero, who'd do anything for him.

My question from earlier lingers, unanswered. The knowledge of what this truly means seeps beneath the fragile barrier of my skin, joining the grief and the exhaustion and the anxiety that already sit there. Ophelia is dealing with another anonymous threat. "Is she okay?"

"She's in one piece, if that's what you're asking. She looked exhausted."

Fuck. I look at the email again, trying to imagine the mental toll that sitting with this photo has taken on her. My presence—my family's presence—in her life is an abscess, infecting all the healthy tissue around it. "I need to call her."

"Not a good idea, not with this picture in the equation."

My frustration is dangerously close to bubbling over. "Like me calling Ophelia is going to incriminate us any more than a photograph of us next to a body?"

"It's not a great photo of you. Obviously, we're aiming to track this photo down and bury it, but if it did get leaked, we have a solution. If we can claim you and Ophelia split before that night, you'd probably pass for someone else. That photo isn't clear enough to identify you in a criminal case, in my opinion."

Something clicks into place, and with it, a hot wave of fury boils my blood. I've been too busy to fully understand Mack and my lawyers' decision to distance me so far from Ophelia.

They want her far enough from me that she can be thrown under the bus if required.

Mack mistakes my silence for confusion, or a lack of confidence in his plan. "It's not like you had a motive for what happened to Bancroft."

But Ophelia had the perfect reason. He doesn't say it, but it echoes around my office, deafeningly loud. Ophelia was looking for revenge for her parents' death, and that makes her a perfect scapegoat for all our problems. "That is *not* our angle. I am not taking that angle if it comes to it."

"Alex, you have an airline, six minors, and your mother's healthcare depending on you. Ophelia . . . to put it respectfully, if she went to jail—"

My knuckles turn white. *I* would care. It would matter to *me.* "I wouldn't finish that sentence, if I were you."

The ice in my tone must make them realize their jobs are on the line, because they both drop the idea completely and don't mention it for the rest of the call. The rest of their updates are just filler, delicately placed to keep me sweet. We *almost* found this, we're *nearly* there with this, we're *hoping* to do this.

Why is it that the best of the best can't even catch my father's scent?

"He will have to surface, Alex. Visit an ATM, rent a car, get gas, eat food. He will surface, and we'll get him the second he does. Talk to your lawyers about whether calling Ophelia is a bad idea."

I hang up and scrub my face in my hands. I swivel in the chair to face the bustling city below, trying to get a hold on my quickening breaths. Everything is piling up. Everything is too much and not enough. I can't shake the feeling that Ophelia is in danger, that someone else is after her.

The chime of my laptop tells me my next meeting has begun, but my chest feels like it's wrapped in chains.

I stare down at my shaking hands, trying to count my fingers through the panic that sinks its claws deep into my throat. I can't catch my breath, can't get a full inhale. I almost drop my phone, fingers trembling as I dial Harwood. He picks up on the third ring.

"I can't breathe. I'm not going to make it to lunchtime."

"You will. You can and you will."

"I can't breathe."

"It's a panic attack, Alex."

A cold wave of dread washes over me. "Not this time. It's worse. I can't breathe. I can't do it."

"What's happened?"

I can't do it. Can't survive the next thirty seconds. My heart is hot and sticky in my throat, clogging my airway. "He's nowhere. He's fucking nowhere. But he's going to surface and he's going to hurt one of them when he does. And Mack . . . Mack saw Ophelia and . . ."

And I'm not there to hold her, to walk her to her lectures. I can't keep her safe.

"Alex, stop. Good, okay. Now breathe. *Breathe.*"

I manage a sorry excuse for a deep breath. "Mack visited Ophelia, and she got an anonymous text, and it . . . it's a photo of us. A *bad* photo. And this could be the end of her."

"Ophelia is stronger than you're giving her credit for. She can hold her own. Tell me about the photo at lunchtime. I have another appointment in two minutes."

The small crack in my voice fills me with disgust. "I can't make it to lunchtime."

There's a smile in his voice when he next speaks. "Tell me about that at lunchtime."

A small, disbelieving snort slips between two ragged breaths. "I struggle to like you sometimes."

His laugh is genuine. "Survive until lunch, Alex. Then we'll talk more. And ask Jacqueline for decaf for the rest of the day."

I hang up, puffing a slow exhale from my cheeks, drawing random lines in my notebook. My heart rate slows gradually. This whole situation is laughable—me, twenty-three, sitting behind a CEO desk with no idea what I'm doing and a crushing sense of existential dread.

I breathe for another moment, sketching a robin in the corner of my page until I'm calm enough to join my call. I switch my camera on and attempt to tame my unruly hair. "Sorry I'm late."

I'M ON THE treadmill at 11 p.m. with Mia crunching through a bag of chips beside me when she mumbles something. I slow the treadmill to a jog. "Huh?"

"Who's Brendan?"

I hit the Stop button. "Why?"

"You've got two missed calls from Brendan. You got a boyfriend?"

An uneasy sense of alarm prickles my nape. I already know from the late hour and the fact that it's Brendan calling and not Mack that it's probably something serious. I pray to a god I've never believed in that Ophelia is unharmed. I grab my water and my phone from where they sit beside my sister. "I need to call him back."

"Is it work stuff?" she asks, holding the bag of chips toward me.

I shake my head at the bag, trying to catch my breath. "Get yourself to bed, M."

I head out the kitchen doors and into the garden outside, pacing the length of the small space while the phone rings and rings. It's unbearable. I call him for a fifth time, raking a hand through my hair. I fire Belladonna a text asking her if she knows if Ophelia is okay.

Belladonna

Let her go, Alex. She's the human equivalent of wet cardboard.

Great.

When Brendan picks up, I half expect him to have been shot, or for someone to be holding him hostage, or something. He *never* fails to pick up immediately. His voice is muffled when it comes. "Sorry, was refilling my cereal bowl. Do you think they're putting less marshmallows in Lucky Charms?"

We've put people on the moon, yet we can't punch people through the phone line yet. Science is letting us down. "You're thirty-five, Brendan. This better be fucking good," I grit out. "Is she okay?"

"Ophelia? I think so, yeah. Can you see my screen?"

I look down at my phone, where Brendan has started sharing a photo. It's blurry, like the camera it was taken on was greasy, but I'd recognize Sorrowsong's distinct glasshouse swimming pool anywhere. "Yeah, I see it."

"Ophelia got sent this. Only just told Mack about it."

I zoom in on the small screen, realizing why he's showing me it. Ophelia is in front of the door to the pool, glancing over her shoulder like she knows she's being watched. Even with the low quality, I can make out the worry on her expression. "When was this taken?"

"Yesterday."

My eyes flick to the soft glow emanating from Fleur's bedroom window to the silhouette of Mia brushing her hair in hers. I feel like I'm stretched too thin to protect everyone who's important to me, despite my best efforts.

I chose the girls over Ophelia, I chose my family over her. It's the decision I always knew I'd have to make; it's the right decision. But I can't help but imagine how it feels for Ophelia. Left behind, like she always has been.

Fuck.

I drag a cigarette out of the box and light it. "And you of *all* people can't trace it?"

"I can trace it, but it's no help. It was taken at Sorrowsong, obviously," he says, like I'm three years old.

"But sent from New York?"

"Sent from Sorrowsong, too."

"So either Ophelia has herself a new enemy, or . . . ?"

"Or your father has made his way to Scotland to punish Ophelia for the article. Would he do that?"

I open my mouth to ask how my father would cross continents with an international arrest warrant but don't bother. He has endless connections in the aviation industry and bottomless wealth, both in cash and in private banks.

Would he do that? It's a good question. I try to put myself in my father's shoes, imagine I'm on the run with nothing left to lose. "I'm not sure that he would. She's a nobody in his eyes."

Ophelia lost a lot when that article went live, but from an outsider's perspective, I won. Inherited a company I had no right to inherit, gained the favor of the media, got rid of the father I never liked. I imagine my father hates me more than anyone else right now. "I think if Cain were to want to punish anyone, it'd be me."

"That's what Mack thinks, too. He thinks your father is waiting for a good time to corner you. He might still believe he can get his life back."

Dread trickles down my spine, too hot, too sticky. I'm not afraid of whatever he has planned for me, but if one of the girls were to get caught in the cross fire . . .

I shudder, my next drag on the cigarette a burning fire beneath my freezing skin. "I have to go to her."

"I think your team is really against that idea."

The unspoken reasoning behind his statement drums up a visceral rage, boiling and volatile in my chest. "We are not throwing Ophelia under the bus for what happened to Bancroft."

"If Rocco has done a good enough job of burying him, we won't need to, as long as we silence whoever's texting her before they leak the photo."

"Leak or not, it's not happening," I bite out. "If she's getting a manslaughter charge, I am, too."

"Do you hear how you sound? You have a family."

Maybe I sound ridiculous to him, but for me, there is no debate. I will not be one more person using Ophelia like that. My father used her parents' death to mop up the evidence of an affair. I won't use her life to mop up the evidence of a murder. "Drop it."

"Okay, okay," he says, defensively.

"I'm going to visit her," I declare into the cloudless night, more to myself than Brendan. Like I'm giving myself a little pep talk. *This'll all work out marvelously, Alex. Ophelia will be delighted that you came and definitely* won't *tear you a new one as soon as she sees you.*

A sigh is all I get in return.

"There's an aviation conference in London this weekend anyway."

"Oh, is there?" he says, and I think he's convinced I've lost it. "Amazing. I, too, love to take eleven-hour detours when I'm on business trips. Do me a favor and keep your trip to Scotland off any electronic records. Don't fly to Inverness. I'll book you a rental car from London under an alias."

"Will do," I say. "And my seven-year-old sister thinks they're putting less marshmallows in."

"Fucking knew it," he mumbles before hanging up, like he's just solved the biggest case of his career.

With the New York February chill biting its way through the thin fabric of my gym top, I open up my texts and ask Jacqueline to book my flights.

I'm going to see Ophelia again.

I should text her first. Give her some kind of warning.

My fingers hover over the keyboard, cigarette dangling from my lips. *Hi.* Absolutely not. *Hey.* Even worse. *We should talk.* Jesus, no. I sound like I'm about to suggest a divorce. *I'm coming over.* I spam the backspace button, reminding myself that I'm actively trying *not* to get a restraining order from her.

Above the dread that sinks itself right into the marrow of my bones, an unfamiliar buzz of excitement skates along my skin, and as I let sleep drag me under later that night, for the first time in a while, I actually want to wake up.

Chapter 5

OPHELIA

I paid sixty pounds for a private remote GP appointment—it was cheaper than making the forty-minute journey to the nearest doctor's surgery—about my lack of sleep, only for her to tell me I'm sleep-deprived and need to sleep a bit more.

So, with that invaluable wisdom tucked neatly under my arm, I skipped my final lecture of the day to go back to my room and go to bed early

And naturally, I've been lying awake for six hours.

My windows aren't good enough to stop the breeze slipping through the frame, the crunch of snow and gravel under feet outside too loud for me to fall asleep. My mind is whirring so fast that it might take off, like the staff helicopter that hasn't flown once since Alex was appointed CEO of Green Aviation. Instead, I pull my phone from where it lies beside the knife beneath my pillow and open a text thread with the newest contact in my address book.

Mack

Thanks for your time.

Mack

I'm going to try to track down the texts to see if they match anything I have on Cain Green.

Mack

In the meantime, Brendan is looking into the article leak. If it was you, now would be a great time to tell us. You'd save him a whole lot of time.

I send a reply, typing my new favorite phrase.

Ophelia

It wasn't me.

He asked me that when he was here, too, the two of us talking over steaming coffee in the darkest corner of the Nightshade library, where the lamps and the candles don't quite reach. And like usual, I could see disbelief reflecting back at me when I looked into his eyes and told him it wasn't me.

But who was it? That's the question that truly stumps me.

I feel like I did last term: second-guessing every friend, stranger, and act of kindness that I stumble across. This is probably exactly what they want, for my new connections to be eaten away by suspicion, for me to become isolated. Easy to reach.

I'm missing something. *Again.*

As I stare at Mack's texts, another one pings through. It's a phone number.

Mack

Alex's new phone number, in case you need it. He said I could pass it on.

What?

I sit upright in bed, the duvet sliding down to my midriff.

What?

I've spent the first part of this year desperately trying to get over him, trying to get my life back, and now this?

Is he asking me to text him?

Complete radio silence for a month and a half, and then . . . *here's my phone number, Ophelia*, like some customer service representative. *Please don't hesitate to reach out if you have any issues.*

"Hi, yes, my boyfriend left without a word. I'd like a refund," I mutter, as I shut off my phone without saving the number.

My lungs ache, and whatever protection I thought I'd built against the harsh slap of Alex's silence crumbles away. Anger rejuvenates my tired mind, the blood rushing through my veins almost an audible thrum beneath the duvet.

Why has he given me his number?

I throw my phone to the end of the bed before I do something stupid like text him.

Silence descends around the valley, a break in the wind offering a brief reprieve from the whistling and the whispering that snake through the trees. Somehow, it's worse than the noise.

Loneliness is like a physical presence in my life. A person more than it is a feeling. Faceless, nameless, back turned to me. Teasing and taunting, laughing at me whenever I have to eat dinner alone.

Like I always have been, I think I was a bit naive about how my life would change once I had friends. Friends were a panacea, a big, shiny, glowing orb that if I could only reach, would turn all the shit in my life into gold. The yawning chasm left by my parents' deaths would shrink, and silence wouldn't feel like an ache.

Now I have some, it hasn't quite worked out that way. The introduction of friends to my life has filled a *different* void, numbed a *different* pain. My friends make the mornings pass quicker, fill the afternoons with noise and laughter, but when the night has stripped the day of its color and the day has stripped the resolve from my bones, my past still eats away at me.

I trace my finger round the lucky key ring my dad gave me on my twelfth birthday. It's actually a shopping cart token, but I don't think he knew that. He just liked the fact that it was orange.

He loved my mother's hair, always said it was the reason he loved her at first sight. I think that's the reason I don't hate mine. I struggle to pick holes in my reflection when it's the combination of the two people I loved more than anything else.

I startle, the key ring falling from my hand when footsteps sound outside my door. I wait for them to fade, wait for the guy down the hall to close his bedroom door, but everything is silent.

My breath is suspended, whole body frozen as I watch two black shapes come to a stop in the dull strip of light beneath my bedroom door.

No knock comes.

Did I lock the door? God, I hope I locked the door.

My fingers tighten around my knife, my own voice making me jump. "Hello?"

I cringe at the rustling of sheets as I slowly rise from the bed, bare feet silent against tile. I don't dare breathe, mouth clamped shut as I wrap my hand around the door handle.

With my heart beating a rapid, sickening rhythm in my throat, I count to three and yank open the door, holding my knife out, just in case.

It meets . . . nothing, no one.

The hallway is deserted, the shadows between the doorways eerily still.

The only sign I'm not going completely mad is the remainder of two rapidly fading wet footprints at my feet.

A KNOCK AT my bedroom door has me jumping out of my skin.

This is it. I'm about to get murdered. Probably.

I've hardly slept for two days. I spend my nights covering and uncovering the thin gap beneath the door, unable to decide between *yes, I'd really love to know that someone is standing outside my door*, and *no, thanks, I'd rather just die a quick, ignorant death.*

"Ophelia," sings Colette on the other side of the gnarled wood. "We have snacks and plans."

"I'm busy."

Divya's voice comes next. "Sitting on the bed in a towel while plucking hairs from your stomach doesn't constitute *busy.*"

God, I'm getting predictable.

"Rude!" I shout, throwing the tweezers to the back of my drawer. I drag on a hoodie and pull the door open.

Project Pheelz.

The letters are written in Colette's loopy handwriting on a chalkboard that Divya is holding.

Colette finishes putting a little love heart above the *J* while Magda draws sparkles all around it in yellow chalk, the three of them making quite the spectacle in the dark, dusty hallway.

Magda pops her chewing gum as the three of them file in. "This is a home invasion," I declare, watching Colette slip out of her fluffy boots and dive onto my bed.

"Would a home invader bring cookies?"

"Probably, if they were trying to convince me it wasn't a home invasion."

"It's too snowy to do anything outside, rugby and hockey games are canceled, the roads are pretty much undrivable, the power is shaky, and we're bored out of our minds."

Colette hangs the board from a rusting nail between two crumbling stones. "Hence, Project Pheelz."

Magda shudders, shuffling away from the thick cobwebs over the broken sconce on my wall. "Can't we do this somewhere else? I fucking hate this place."

I don't blame her. The Nightshade mansion is terrifying, especially this time of year. The lights haven't worked all day.

"Project Pheelz," declares Divya, giving us a look like a teacher who has just caught two students talking. She whips a laser pointer out of her pocket. I stifle a laugh, but my heart is warm.

They love me.

"We have three main aims," explains Colette, drawing heart-shaped bullet points as Magda throws a pillow at Divya for shining a laser in her eye. "Mini makeover in time for the Winter Ball."

"I'm not going."

"We're all going. Wardrobe refresh—on a budget. Murder Cain Green."

My laughter bubbles out of me as Magda draws a wiggly line and a sparkle beneath the final bullet point.

Magda snatches the pink chalk from Colette, messily scrawling a fourth sentence: *Find a rebound.*

"Absolutely not." For a multitude of reasons: My heart hurts too much. No one would compare to Alex. I've sworn off men forever.

A nasty thought pops into my brain, unwelcome. Has *he* found a rebound? The thought of Alex with someone the way he was with me . . . the whispered French, the eye contact, the swipe of his tongue along his lower lip, the way my name on his lips as he comes sounds like a desperate plea.

I feel nauseous.

The others must catch the shift in my expression, because Colette's gentle hands push me down to a sitting position on my bed. "All right, let's forget the rebound idea. You don't have to do that one."

"Okay," I whisper, voice distant. I take a steady breath, thinking rationally. I know in my heart that Alex hasn't found a rebound, that it'd be as abhorrent to him as it is to me.

"Let's skip to step three. Let's just skip straight to murder. Way more fun than makeovers, anyway."

Colette sticks her bottom lip out. I think she's been desperately waiting for me to ask her if I need a spring or autumn palette for months. But I need to master a routine of eating, showering, and brushing my teeth before figuring out if wearing yellow makes me look even more like a corpse than I already do.

"Okay," I say, sounding more assertive than I really am. "I don't think we are the people to catch Cain Green. The FBI and the best private detectives are already on it."

The three faces opposite me are wrought in disappointment. I see them lower their metaphorical pitchforks. Magda looks like I've canceled Christmas.

"We tried to change Divya's tire last week and three of us were in tears by the end," I argue. That gets me a few reluctant nods of agreement. "But we *can* figure out who leaked the article."

"And figure out if it's Cain texting you."

Divya pulls out a fucking clipboard. Colette hands her a highlighter in every pastel shade you could imagine. My spirits lift.

"Okay, let's start at the beginning again. Who would have a motive to hack your laptop and spread all that information?"

I trace my fingers over my chapped bottom lip. This is what I don't understand. Cain, Shawn, Carmichael . . . they all had a reason to hate me, to want me to be unhappy, but they also had no reason to want the downfall of Green, *especially* not Cain. "I have no idea."

"And once again we're off to a flying start."

Now we're all laughing, driven hysterical by the shambles that is my life. "Shall we just leave this to the detectives and get drunk?" I ask.

"No!" They all yell, revenge hungry and fueled up on too much caffeine.

I hold my hands up in surrender. "Okay, okay. Umm . . ."

"Does Alex have any angry exes?"

"Not that I know of. And how would they have known about the article I wrote, anyway?"

Divya hums. "Good point."

I drag my hands down my face. "I am definitely missing something. It could've been Carmichael?"

Colette sprawls back on my bed. No one is brave enough to lie on the other one, where Sofia's side of the room remains untouched. I'm scared that if I do so much as move the bed closer to the wall, the Ivanovs will know, somehow. "But *why*? This whole ordeal hasn't done wonders for his reputation, either."

"Ophelia, don't give up on this," says Magda, snatching my phone out of my hand after I bring up a Sudoku app. "You deserve to have your name cleared."

"I don't care about my name," I grumble, because it's true. People can think what they want about me. I know the truth; my friends know the truth.

"If your name gets cleared, you and Alex can . . ." Divya trails off, an awkward silence hanging in the stale air.

"Can what? Reconvene? Pick up like nothing happened? Like his father didn't kill my parents, like he didn't walk out on me, like I didn't hide that article for months? Work through the fact that we're three thousand miles apart, and that I'd never move to the US?" My laugh is bitter on my tongue, words I've kept buried for weeks finally spilling over. "He left me. He blocked my number."

"He went through a lot," says Colette, quietly. "He's shut everyone out, even Vincenzo."

It's petulant, but a flash of hurt spikes my chest. The words *Team Alex* might as well be flashing above her head. "Whose side are you on here?"

"I'm on Team Alex and Ophelia. The two of you. Together. He made you happy."

The sting of tears in the corners of my eyes makes me turn away. Rummaging in my bag for anything to distract me, I pull out a crumpled paper bag, haphazardly covered in brown tape. "You guys keep brainstorming. I need to drop this off at the post office. Back in ten."

Colette's delicate fingers close around my biceps as I leave. She must notice the glassy sheen over my eyes, because one appears over her eyes, too. "Ophelia—"

"It's fine. I just need some air."

"I'm on your side. I'm always on your side."

I nod, eyes on my boots. "I know. I just need to post this."

Her grip on my arm vanishes. "Okay, honey."

It's raining when I step outside. Heavy gray rain that melts the snow into sludge. I'm too petty to go back and grab my waterproof jacket. Laura's father's confession tape, the final nail in Cain Green's coffin, feels hot and heavy tucked under my arm. Though none of this played out the way I wanted, I hope it's brought Laura some peace.

I've been meaning to post it back to her for weeks—I know how important it is to her. I've been meaning to text her, too.

I've been meaning to do a lot of things and failing.

Trying to move on from Alex is taking up all of my emotional strength.

As I trudge through wet snow and freezing mud, I vow to myself not to let this continue. I've lost my last four years to grief. I won't find something else to grieve over now.

I need to find a hobby that isn't being miserable.

My breath is a white cloud filtering through my chattering teeth as I hand the parcel to the woman at the small post office in the castle's main structure. The brown paper is a little bit soggy, but it'll do.

The rain has slowed to an icy drizzle when I leave the castle and slide my hands back into my mittens. March may be on the horizon, but winter still rules in the valley. I thought February here would be picturesque: snow-capped turrets and deer running through the frozen forest. Instead, it's beige-gray and depressing. Leaky ceilings and single-glazed windows. Thick fog that veils the beautiful views of the Scottish Highlands.

If soup didn't exist, I'd have given up by now.

A text from Colette pings through on my cracked phone screen.

Colette

Power is back on in the Cortinar halls!

Meet us there.

Colette

I'll microwave popcorn!!

Popcorn sounds good right now. I tuck my phone back into my pocket and duck under the branches that sag over the overgrown trail back to the mansion. A twig crunches somewhere ahead of me, and I freeze in place. The pea-sized rational part of my brain reminds me that this is a university. That there are students all over the campus. That not everyone here is a stalker.

A figure steps onto the main path, and I stagger backward. My rib cage feels too small, a constrictive cage preventing my lungs from inflating.

It's not a stalker.

It's not an angry student.

It's worse.

It's Alex.

My brain asks my feet to turn and run, but they kindly decline. I stand there, mouth opening and closing like if I keep going, something good might come out of it. The hundred things I want to say to him have all rushed up at once, forming a gelatinous ball that clogs my throat.

His black boots are covered in snow, but he's perfectly dressed. Shirt ironed, slacks pressed, damp hair falling in that messy middle part. The cherry of the cigarette in his mouth glows, the look in his eye agonized. He doesn't move, doesn't speak, like a hunter desperate not to scare off his prey.

I don't know why, but I thought he'd look different. More menacing, taller, bigger, *older*. The CEO I read about in the news feels like a different beast than the boy who spent his boxing day stringing up fairy lights in a rental car so I could experience my first Christmas in years.

But he just looks like . . . Alex.

He opens his mouth to speak, but I can't bear to hear it. There's nothing he could say that would ease the sting of the past couple of months. I shake my head at him, desperate for silence for once in my life. I'm not ready for how much hearing his voice will hurt.

Whatever it is he wants to say, I'm not ready for it. I just hope it isn't something idiotic like *hi*.

Chapter 6

ALEX

"Hi."

Five days of rehearsing my speech for Ophelia, and those are the two letters that come out of my mouth.

I'd like to reach out and snatch them back from the space between us, but I can't.

She's frozen in place, staring at me like she's half a second away from running. "Ophelia, I—"

"Hi?" she whispers, voice hoarse. Just the *sound* of her aches. "*Hi!?*"

A lump forms in my throat, sliding down my esophagus until it's a heavy stone in my stomach.

I'm so fucking sorry.

I run a hand through my hair. "Not my finest work. Fuck, Ophelia. Please hear me out."

"No," she croaks, shaking her head. "Please, no."

I take a step forward. She takes one back. We've been here before, on this same path, right after she hid under Carmichael's couch. Only then, I felt like I was *finally* on the edge of having her. Now I'm inches from losing her forever.

"Please let me talk."

"You *left* me," she bites out. The very tip of her nose reddens with anger, and I want to ask her how she could dare to do something so endearing while not allowing me to touch her. "You and I are doomed, Alex."

Right people, wrong universe. That's what she thinks about us.

It's bullshit. I need it to be bullshit.

"Come on a drive with me."

Her spine straightens, shoulders squaring. A determined look solidifies in her gaze, and *there's* the woman I fell in love with. She's so beautiful.

"I'd rather put myself into a blender."

"I can put some rotating blades in the car, if that'd help."

"Only if you put your head through them."

"Oh, you know very well that I'd put my head wherever you ask me to, Ophelia," I reply, much too quickly.

That has the pink tinge of her nose spreading over her freckled cheeks, and suddenly the low fog that hugs Sorrowsong castle doesn't feel so cold. "I . . . that is not . . . I didn't mean it like that."

She's flustered. The thrill it gives me is dizzying.

I take two cautious steps toward her. She doesn't bolt, but she does look like she might snap my neck. At least her hands would be the last ones to touch me. "Just let me talk."

"The time for talking has long passed, don't you think?"

"No, not really."

"You're impossible."

I chance another step toward her. "Determined."

"Desperate."

Another step, and she's so close I could almost touch her. "Lovesick."

She flinches at that one, and I'm finally close enough to her to see the hairline cracks in this steely facade she's put up. She's pale. The circles beneath her eyes are vicious, every shade of purple a knife to the heart. The hard shell of anger is chipping, and I can see the hurt beneath it.

I've been so wrapped up in work, in my sisters, in my mom, in my dad's disappearance that I hadn't really appreciated until now what I've done to her. Lured her in, spent months convincing her to open up to me, threw it all back in her face.

Jesus fucking Christ, I'm so sorry.

I can see it now, her rebuilding that wall I spent so long dismantling. But I can't let that happen. And maybe she's right, maybe I am desperate, suffocated by the black cloud that just won't shrink, no matter what I do. I thought I was doing the right thing by staying away, but it might actually be *worse* this way around.

The idea of losing her is one thing too many.

"I shouldn't have left."

Her laugh is cold and disbelieving. "And it's taken you this many weeks to realize that?"

I tilt my head back and blow a long breath of smoke away from her, silently asking the universe for help. "That's not true."

She's on a roll now, her tone utterly incredulous. "And the phone number thing?"

"I know, I'm sorry. I had to deactivate my old number. Someone leaked it. I was going to text you. I *tried* to text you, I just . . ."

"Didn't."

"Get in the car with me."

I just need her to get in the car. She can't run if we're in the car. The lines between kidnapping and romance seem to be getting increasingly blurred, but oh well. One to tell at our wedding: *I held her hostage in my car and forced her to fall back in love with me.*

Ophelia shakes her head, so I give up on being fair. "I'll tell you Mack's updates if you get in the car."

That gets her attention. Whisky-colored eyes turn wide and curious. "Why? What happened?"

"I'll tell you in the car."

"Tell me here."

"No, because you'll run."

"This is blackmail."

"It's negotiation."

"Fucking hell," she grumbles, storming over to me.

It's the greatest victory I've had over the past month. My hand lands on her lower back, but she slaps it off as soon as my fingertips make contact with the damp fabric of her jacket.

She's furious. "Touch me again and I really will shit on your dashboard this time."

I stuff my hand into my pocket, trying to distract myself from the desperate need to feel the warmth of her skin. "Duly noted."

She stops in the parking lot, where I unlock a black Land Rover, parked beside Belladonna's Bronco. "Where's the dark green one?"

"Uhm . . ." I scratch the back of my neck, remembering I really am trying *not* to get a restraining order. Better not tell her I sit in it most nights. "It was a rental, remember?"

"Oh, yeah," she mumbles, looking a little disappointed. Hope inflates between my ribs. Maybe she thinks about *that* night as often as I do.

She shoves my hand aside when I go to open the passenger door for her, yanking it open herself. Her expression is thunderous. "*No*, Alex. I'm not . . ." Her tone switches from angry to the kind of patience you'd give a toddler who's struggling to understand something, which feels even worse. "I'm not yours anymore."

I hold two hands up and step back, trying to act like that statement wasn't a serrated blade to the neck. She goes to get into the car but stops, turning to face me. "Don't touch me. Don't talk about *us*. Don't take this as a reunion. Tell me about Mack and then let me out of the car."

"Okay," I whisper. I don't allow myself to feel disappointed. It's more time with her than I deserve, and I know she's just protecting her heart.

If anything, I respect her for it.

She climbs into the car, and I walk around and do the same. She's as far to the left of the seat as she could possibly be, shoulder pressed against the window.

Still, with her in the car, safe and unharmed and within arm's reach, I take my first full inhale since the second week of January.

"That morning, when I woke up and saw what had happened—"

"You're already in violation of rule two."

A ragged growl of frustration leaves me as I start the engine. "Seriously?"

"I'm not here to talk about us. And there's no need to drive anywhere."

I reverse out of the parking spot, ignoring her protests. If I drive away from the castle for the whole Mack story, we'll have to fill the silence for the journey home.

"This is kidnapping!" she shouts, reaching down to fiddle with the gear stick. I hit the brakes. I told her months ago that I wanted to kidnap her, so she can't *really* claim ignorance.

"Ophelia, what the fuck are you doing?" I ask, as she probably mangles the transmission of the rental car.

"Putting the car in reverse."

"When we're doing twenty miles per hour?"

She lets out a cry of frustration, flustered and angry. A red tinge sweeps over her pale face, and I fall in love all over again, painfully and violently. "Why is this thing so hard to move?"

"Because my foot isn't on the clutch."

"Put your foot on the clutch, then."

"I'm all right, thanks."

She tries the passenger door—locked, *obviously*, that's rule number one of kidnapping—and presses the heels of her hands to her eyes. "Alex!"

My tone is butter soft. "Ophelia, my darling."

She goes quiet as I drive out of the university gates and onto the bumpy country lanes beyond. The roads are icy, but the car has four-wheel drive. I revel in the feel of her, the heat of her body, the cinnamon smell of her hair, the sound of her breathing. "I'm *so* angry with you," she says, eventually.

"Yeah, well I'm not delighted with that article you put together and failed to tell me about," I say, now that I have her trapped. "But I thought we could discuss this like adults."

She laughs bitterly. "Where was this logic when the article went live? Tell me about Mack."

I rub my palm over my jaw, the stress I'd momentarily forgotten coming back tenfold. "Brendan traced the texts you're getting back to Sorrowsong."

"I know. The pictures of me are taken here."

"They're sent from here, too."

If I thought she couldn't get any paler, I was wrong. "But . . . that would mean . . . your father is here? In Sorrowsong?"

God, I hope not. The thought has kept me up at night, but it feels so remote, so unlikely. "What makes you so sure it's my father sending these?"

"I've barely spoken to another human for four years. Surely, I can't have many more enemies. It *has* to be him. I mean there are other options but . . . he's the only person who'd want me ruined."

My expression must betray the fact that I disagree, because a long, tired sigh mists the window on her side, her solemn gaze fixed on the naked branches outside. "You don't think it is."

"I think it's beneath him, tormenting you like this."

A small smile cracks her frosty expression, and *there's* that little glimmer in her eye. "Wow. Thanks. Gonna add *not hot enough to be cyberstalked* to my list of attributes."

"You're definitely hot enough to be cyberstalked. *Too* hot, even."

"Aww," she says, swishing her hair. "Maybe if you got a haircut, you could be cyberstalked, too."

My laugh bubbles out of me, surprising us both. I don't need to look in the rearview mirror to know I look a mess. I run both hands through my hair, trying to rescue it. "Better?"

Her smile is soft when she reaches out to pull a lock of hair out of place, letting it hang over my eye just how she likes. When her finger grazes my skin as she withdraws her hand, I swear I feel a crackle of electricity. My heart stumbles around a heavy, thick beat. I hear her breath catch in her throat. Somehow, we're close. So close I can see each and every one of the freckles that are scattered across her nose, cheeks, forehead, chin.

So close, I can hear how her breathing has changed, dragging air into her lungs through the hot, heavy tension in the car.

Her tongue darts out to wet her lower lip, and maybe the world isn't such a terrible place, after all. Maybe everything will work out.

She catches herself, shaking her head as if trying to dispel this intoxicating atmosphere. "There," she rasps, her throat hoarse when her eyes flick back up to my hair. "You'll get a threatening text in no time."

And just like that, the bubble bursts. The love and the lust and the desperate hope, they all seep out of the car and into the crisp air beyond when she turns away from me.

I swear I almost see the world outside turn grayer, more muted in color.

I'm not naive enough to think that being with Ophelia will simply cure me, but she's a million and one little reasons to keep going, neatly wrapped up in a holey jacket and moth-eaten scarf.

"Colette says you've shut Vincenzo out."

My hand pauses where it turns on the heater beneath her seat, the question taking me by surprise. Guilt swirls somewhere between my ribs. Vincenzo deserves better. I've shut *everyone* out. "I haven't had time for friendships, lately. I haven't had time for much except . . ."

"Treading water," she finishes for me, when I cannot find the words.

I breathe out a soft laugh, but it's devoid of humor. It's the perfect analogy. I'm not making any forward progress, not getting anywhere. I've forgotten what it's like to start the day with an aim that isn't just getting through it.

Making no progress has never felt so exhausting.

I undo my top button, suddenly too hot, the conversation uncomfortable for me. "Back to your stalker," I say.

She either doesn't hear me or doesn't listen. "Promise me you'll keep treading water."

"You said we can only talk about the investigation."

She stares at her lap, fiddling with the friendship bracelet my sisters made for her. I trace my fingers over my matching one, the braided rope smooth and worn. "Shutting me out, shutting your friends out, I know you think it'll make things easier. I know your depression convinces you that shutting people you love out is the right thing to do, because it'd be easier to disappear if no one would come looking—"

My voice comes out soft, pleading for her to be gentle with my fragile mind. "Ophelia."

"It's lying to you, Alex. Shutting people out will fix nothing. Believe me, I tried it for four years."

"You and Harwood would be friends."

She gives me a look I've missed so much. Amused exasperation, I think. But she drops the topic, which I'm grateful for. "I'm not afraid of your father, Alex. If he really is here, I wouldn't run."

God. Even the thought has me white-knuckled around the steering wheel. "Well, you should."

"He doesn't scare me."

Too stubborn for her own good. But then again, that might be why I fell in love with her.

"I need you to cooperate with Mack, Ophelia. Anything he asks, tell him. If anything happens to you, anything suspicious, any strange mail or emails, anyone says anything unkind, you tell him straight away."

She snorts. "Plenty of people have unkind things to say about me."

This is true. The reaction to the article has been broken and backward. The only person who has received more hatred at Sorrowsong and on social media than my father—the man with a rotting mess for a heart—is Ophelia.

It's the story of my mother's life, and I hate how much it's become Ophelia's. The media will hold anyone accountable except those who are truly responsible.

Men like my father play chess with real people's lives, and it's always them who come out holding the medal.

The family divider, the torturer of an already sick woman, the disrupter of six little girls' homelives, the betrayer of Alex Corbeau-Green. An elaborate painting has been constructed of Ophelia this past month, and it isn't flattering. Each brushstroke is a new way to pick her apart. I'd throw every penny I can into having it taken down, but like with what people say about my mother, there isn't a net big enough to catch it all.

Ophelia is the strongest person I know, but I see the heavy weight of it, the abuse, the texts, the attention. I want to pull over and wrap her so tightly in my arms that we both forget what it feels like to be splintered into so many pieces.

I can't keep the pain out of my plea. "Please don't believe what they say, Ophelia."

"I try not to." She shrugs, and though the tears that she blinks away gut me, it's the fact I can't pull her into my lap that delivers the killing blow. She should still be mine. None of this is the way it should be.

"Ophelia." Her name is a desperate prayer. I slow the car to a stop in the middle of the deserted road, trying to recall the worst things I've read about her in the past few weeks. *It's no wonder her parents couldn't put up with her any longer. I'd get in a broken helicopter, too.* If that's what people say online, I can only imagine it's worse in the private confines of Sorrowsong's dark hallways. "Shit, Ophelia."

"I don't need you to defend me."

"I know."

"Can you just drive?" she begs. "And talk about your father and Mack?"

She needs a distraction, and I'd do anything for her, so I talk. I tell her about Brendan, how even *he* is struggling to get anything about the article leak. I tell her about Mack, about his time in the military, about how he's tracking down my father, how Brendan hacks into CCTV feeds all over New York City in his search.

I don't turn around to go back, not until she's completely out of questions.

I slow to a stop in a passing place on a narrow lane sheltered by trees. Fat droplets of rain and the occasional twig hit the windshield. The radio crackles quietly over the soft sound of Ophelia's breathing.

"I'll be careful if you will," she says, looking up at me.

This is horrendous. To be this close to her and not allowed to touch her, not allowed to trace my finger over each freckle to see if she's gained any more since I last lay my head on a pillow beside her.

I deserve punishment for my actions, but this is torture. "I'll be careful, Twist."

She smiles at the nickname, but it's soft and sad. "How is she?"

"My mom?"

"Yeah."

"She's okay. She's actually starting a trial for a new treatment soon."

Her expression brightens, warm and genuine. "Oh, that's good, right?"

"Yeah." I rub my forehead. "I mean, I think so. It's not without its risks, but leaving her on the trajectory she's on isn't going to do anything."

"I'll be crossing my fingers for her every night."

I force a smile. It's hard to talk about my mother. She's going to die too young, and I'm *so* deep in denial about it. In my visions of a future with Ophelia—wedding or no wedding, kids or no kids—I picture my mom there throughout it all. But she won't be.

I'm just trying to snatch years back from the cold grip of her weakening body, battered by too many drugs taken too young, too many years with her declining mental health ignored, too many letdowns by my father. "I'll tell her."

"Alex, she'll—"

"Don't," I manage, tone harsher than I mean. I'm tired of that stupid promise. *She'll be okay.* People say it on autopilot with zero thought behind what they're actually saying. "Don't tell me she'll be fine. Please don't tell me she'll be fine. Can we talk about something else?"

"Yeah," she says, but the car descends into silence. Between us, our meager bingo card of acceptable conversation topics is exhausted. Everything else is covered in red tape.

I stare out the window, at the rolling hills and distant Munros that peek between the trees. Ophelia turns down a call from Colette, typing out a text. She puts her phone back in her pocket, but neither of us speaks.

It's awkward, this silence. And it's awkward that it's awkward—that we've gone from being two people who couldn't make a silence awkward if our lives depended on it, to being two people with nothing left to say.

I start to speak, and so does she. We both stop. I watch her cheeks turn pink, her freckles lost in her blush.

"Sorry, what were you going to say?"

That I love you more than life itself. "You go first."

"They started putting crispy onions on the mac and cheese in the dining hall."

I huff out a breath, unsure whether to laugh or cry. "And your review?"

She picks at her fingernails, forehead creased in a frown. I wish she'd look at me. "Not good. Why must we over complicate everything? First it was chives, and now this. They keep trying to be clever with things. What were you going to say?"

"I was actually just wondering how the mac and cheese from the dining hall is at the moment."

Her laugh heals something inside me. "Oh, you were?"

I lean my head back against the seat, heavy gaze on her. Her T-shirt is tight beneath her jacket, molded to her chest in a way I'm struggling to look away from. "Mmhmm."

"Can you drive me back now, please?"

"My lawyer asked me to cut ties with you."

Her whole body goes rigid, her lungs stall around her next inhale. "Not before you left, surely?"

"I left because I felt like dying. But it's the reason I didn't call you after I landed in New York."

"You blocked my number."

"Mack deactivated the number."

"That's not an excuse. You could've texted me."

"I know."

She's holding her breath, staring out of her window. She can't even face me. "If you'd have just woken me up, Alex . . ."

"I know."

"I didn't publish that article."

"You wrote it," I counter, regretting the low blow immediately. She doesn't need any more guilt over what happened. She's already taken a share of the blame. I can see it in the slope of her shoulders, in the shadows beneath her eyes, in the reddened, raw skin around her fingernails.

I know she didn't release it. Seeing her now, I don't know how I could have ever doubted it, too untrusting of the world to let myself believe that good things are genuine, that good people won't let me down.

"Yeah, I wrote it," she whispers, like a dying confession. I can hear the pain in her voice, and despite my effort, I can't drum up any anger over it. Not anymore. I don't know what it is—maybe it's watching my mother's health slipping down the drain, maybe it's the defeat in her eye, but I just can't waste another hour resenting Ophelia when I could be loving her instead. "I wanted to break your father. I wanted him to lose everything. I wanted his family shattered, his business bankrupt. I *wanted* this. All of this. I wanted your mom to suffer because I wanted *him* to suffer."

"You didn't."

She whirls around to face me, eyes alight with anger. "I did. Don't you see? This is exactly what I prayed for, night after night. I wanted your family to break."

"Not like this. You didn't want it like this."

"It's no different, Alex. You and I are doomed."

Her pessimism is usually charming, but not now. "Stop saying that."

Her teeth sink into her bottom lip to stop it trembling. "And I was wrong. But you left me. You didn't give me a chance to speak, to explain. And now you're asking me for the exact same thing."

The second sentence is so full of anguish, I almost hear her heart crack when she says it. "I had to do what was right for the girls."

"But you could've just woken me," she says, raising her voice. Her eyes are glassy, shrink-wrapped by unshed tears. She's fighting so hard not to cry in front of me, to save it for someplace else, someone else, and that might be the only thing worse than watching her fall apart. "We buried a *body* together, Alex. We killed someone, and then you left me to cope with that alone."

Fuck. If she notices me wince at her words, she doesn't let on. The list of ways in which I failed her grows longer, the regret that's eaten away at me for weeks gets heavier.

Maybe the monster my father nurtured inside me is bigger than I'd hoped, because I hadn't considered that at all, hadn't really considered Bancroft as anything more than a photo that needs burying.

I hadn't thought about how she'd cope with what happened to Bancroft, how it'd affect someone who isn't used to all of this . . . mess.

"Just tell me how I can fix this."

"You can't fix this. I'm trying to just . . . I'm trying to move on with my life and now you've shown up here and ruined what little progress I've made."

I shut my eyes and lean my head back against the headrest. "I can't move on."

She wraps her jacket tighter around herself. "That's not my problem. You're living thousands of miles away. It's hardly been any time." She wipes her nose on her sleeve, and it pulls my chest tight. "We just need to give it more time."

I don't want to give it more time.

I just want *her*.

I think back to that dreadful morning, waking up beside her with the first few streaks of sunlight washing their way across the valley. It was so serene. So quiet. With Bancroft buried, I'd woken up with an unfamiliar lightness.

And then I'd checked my phone, seen the chaos. It's *that* moment, those horrible next couple of hours that cost me this. Cost me *her*.

I did what I knew to be best for my family, but it feels *so* wrong.

I ball my fists to stop myself from touching her.

"Ophelia, I don't think I ever really believed you published the article. Maybe for five minutes, before I'd given it any thought—"

"That's not what this is about." She rubs her forehead, smoothing out the lines of her frown. It's something more and more people seem to do in my presence, lately. Her bitter laugh fogs the window beside her. "*God*, Alex . . . how can we ever trust each other again? How could you survive being asked to choose between your family and me again?"

"I won't choose."

She turns to face me. Her feet have slipped from her boots, white knitted socks perched on the edge of the seat, and my traitorous heart decides now is the time to fall in love with her for the hundredth time.

With her chin resting on her knees and my pulse a stuttered, desperate beat, I think she might be about to agree. To give me the second chance I don't really deserve. But she opens her mouth and says, "Please can you drive me back now?"

I let out a defeated sigh and turn the car around in silence.

"How's . . . how's work?" she asks.

"As shit as I always knew it'd be. How's Sorrowsong?"

"It's okay," she says, quietly. She hates it there, I know. "It'll do."

"Did you pass your exams?"

"Yeah."

I can't help my smile. I glance down at her while I drive. "You did?"

The little bit of pride in her expression makes my grin widen. That's *my* girl. "Yeah."

"That's amazing, Twist. You're amazing."

She's stronger than she gets credit for, just like Harwood reassures me.

"I need you not to come back again, Alex," she says calmly. I pinch the bridge of my nose. "I lost my parents, and I said I'd never open myself up to that sort of loss again, and I understand why you felt like you had to leave that day. And I'm not angry at you. I *forgive* you, even. But my heart can't take it happening again. And you deserve not to have to choose between us ever again."

"I won't leave."

She shakes her head. "In what alternate universe do you and I get a happy ending, Alex? One where you don't have a family tying you to New York? And I don't have a whole load of baggage and a complete inability to open up to you? One where I'd be comfortable dating someone in the spotlight? One where I'd be happy to just hop on a plane and move to New York? Or Paris? One where you wouldn't resent me for what happened over the past few weeks? Where we *really* trust each other?"

"You're giving up on us before we've even tried."

She looks like I've slapped her when I glance to my left. "We've tried. This year won't be the only time in our lives that things get hard. Other terrible things will happen, and I don't trust that you won't leave me again. That's it. That's all there is to it."

I keep my gaze fixed on the road ahead, letting her words sink in.

She wants someone more stable. She *needs* someone more stable. She needs to look after her mental health, and I, of all people, can understand that.

"Okay," I whisper. We're plunged into silence. Not awkward this time, but final. Neither of us is scrambling for things to say.

I pull into the Sorrowsong parking lot a short while later. It's raining again, harder this time. I kill the engine, pull an umbrella from the back seat, then round the front of the car to open the door for her.

She steps out of the car and under the umbrella I'm holding. I hate how sad she looks. "We're just in the wrong universe, Alex."

"Yeah," I say, flatly. I force a small smile, hoping it makes her feel better. She doesn't bat me away when I brush the tear from her lower lashes before it has a chance to fall.

"I love you," she whispers, like a goodbye.

I smile, letting my thumb trace her jaw. I swallow my own tears down. We didn't get a goodbye in January, but this feels like it. It's *agony*. "I love you more, Twist."

She shakes her head, lip trembling beneath my fingers. All I can think about is kissing it. "You don't."

"I do."

"It's *because* I love you that I can't do this."

"I get it," I say, because I do. She's protecting her heart and mine the only way she knows how. "And it's because I love you that I'm letting you."

I let myself touch her. A featherlight touch over her cheeks, her neck, her nose, her lips. I let myself brush the damp hair from her forehead. I can't live without her. The thought is insurmountable.

Her eyelids drift shut, face leaning into my touch so lightly that I wonder if it's a product of my hopeful imagination. Her lips part on an exhale that seems to leave her lungs in slow motion.

It would be so easy to press my mouth to hers, to glide my hands beneath her wet jacket and press her against me. Her hands tighten where they grip my shirt, her tongue darting out to catch a raindrop from her bottom lip. I swallow my groan down, completely drunk on desire without so much as a kiss.

Her pulse drums beneath my thumb, hard and fast and in perfect time with mine. She looks back up at me, and the look in her eyes lets the penultimate thread of my self-control slip. The cold, stiff air has turned hot and humid, thick with tension. *Fuck.* I glance to the back of the car. The windows are tinted, back seat more than big enough. She must feel my arousal, because her thighs press together beneath her skirt.

We're teetering on the edge, toeing the border between goodbye and hello, tame and feral, respectful and something so much more tempting.

My lips hover over hers, separated by half an inch.

Time seems to grind to a stop.

But that half an inch between her and me holds *so* much. So much trauma, so much reverence, so many reasons that closing the gap would hurt her heart. Desire is like a drug in my veins, dizzying my thoughts, shortening my breaths, but my respect for Ophelia overpowers it all, so I step back.

The tension bursts like an over-inflated balloon, running into the waterlogged earth at our feet.

The air goes back to frigid and bitter. My mood fades back to gray.

She catches herself, eyes wide like she can't believe we almost kissed. The look she gives me is grateful.

I straighten her jacket with a sad smile, opening her curled fist to slip my umbrella into her warm hand. "Stay out of trouble, Twist."

She smiles, taking a few steps back. Away from me. Away from us. I can't bear it, but I have to. "Promise."

And then she's gone again, hurrying away from my car and into the castle just like that first day we met, leaving me and my punctured heart in the torrential rain.

[DRAFT]

From: Alex Corbeau-Green

Subject: Ophelia (gone) *Alex, you fool*

To: Ophelia Winters

A future without you in it doesn't feel like much of a future at all.

AN HOUR PASSES, maybe two.

I sit in the driver's seat in the Sorrowsong parking lot, smoking my way through a pack of cigarettes until only two remain. My head is tipped back against the seat when the rain that splatters my cheek from the open window suddenly stops.

I peek open an eye to see Vincenzo's stupid, giant head filling the space. The scar over his eye crinkles, a crooked smile brightening his face. He leans even farther into the car, like those overly friendly ostriches at safari parks that just want to eat all your food. "Hey, man. Why'd I have to hear it from Colette, who heard it from Ophelia, that you were here?"

He's gone before I can reply, rounding the hood of the car and folding his ridiculous frame into the passenger seat. He leans over me to steal the penultimate cigarette, raindrops running over the dagger tattooed on his index finger when he cups a hand around the flame. His blue gaze turns to mine, never one to let his questions go unanswered.

Man, I've missed him.

"I'm not in the best of moods, lately."

"Doesn't bother me."

"You and Colette, huh?"

His grin is face splitting. "She's so hot. I . . . we . . . do you know what a spreader bar is?"

I wave my hand in a *cut it off* motion. "No details, please."

"Your loss."

"I sincerely doubt that. She your girlfriend?"

His face falls. "Nah. She doesn't want that. We're just . . ."

"Friends?"

"She texts me when she wants to fuck."

"And?"

"Then we do."

"And?"

"And then I go back to the mansion."

This is a familiar pattern with Vincenzo. "And you're fine with that?"

"Well . . . I'm hoping she'll want to hang out more as time goes on. You know . . . go on hikes and stuff, meet my mom."

"And have you spoken about it? Does she know you want a girlfriend?"

"Kind of. Probably. Yeah. She doesn't want commitment."

Christ. I've been so caught up in my own world, I forgot other people have relationship issues, too. "Then she probably won't want to go on hikes and stuff, Vin."

"We'll see."

Vincenzo is a mass of contradictions. Trained by his father to be a ruthless killer, he also has this soft, gentle faith in the world that only people with a stable homelife and two loving parents can have. He has an unfair reputation as someone who sleeps around, but he's desperate for a girlfriend. Something steady and reliable in his world of crime and chaos.

A hand squeezes my biceps. "You look good, bro."

He might be the single most punchable human in my life, but I have to admit that it's good to see him. "Thanks."

"So . . . how did it go with Ophelia?"

I take a *long* drag. "We've split. Officially, now, rather than unofficially."

"Fuck. Like . . . forever?"

"Yeah."

"She might not want to lose you completely. She might want to be—"

"Don't say friends," I bite out. He shuts up.

We smoke in silence, lost in thought. He opens and closes his mouth every now and then, like he wants to say something.

"How's Elise?" Is what eventually comes out, but I can tell it's not whatever is sitting on his tongue.

I'm grateful for Vincenzo. Grateful I never need to sugarcoat anything. Grateful for his unwavering friendship. I hope I never lose it. "I think she's dying, and I don't think I can do anything to stop it."

He doesn't deny it. Doesn't tell me it'll all work out fine. He just sighs, passing me the final cigarette. "I'm sorry. That fucking sucks."

"It does."

"The girls?"

"They're good. They're all stronger than I am. I don't know how they stay so positive all the time."

"Kids are crazy. Shit just bounces off them." He reaches behind him for his seat belt. "There's a kebab van near Ullapool that does the *greasiest* burgers. You wanna go?"

A greasy burger does sound good, and I haven't eaten anything all day. I hand him my phone to plug it into the GPS. "Sure."

I pull out of Sorrowsong's black iron gates for the second time this afternoon, marveling at how my mood plummeted from hopeful to completely lost in the space of two hours. I have no one to blame but myself.

A low fog is seeping across the landscape, clouding my already addled mind. After fifteen minutes of silence, I'm sick of Vincenzo's loaded inhales. "Just say it."

"Really?"

"Yeah."

"I think you're being a complete fucking fool, and I want to bash your face in."

The engine purrs as we climb a hill against a sheet of rain. "Great."

"You *love* her."

"And she has asked me, respectfully, to remove myself from her life so that she can move on."

"She doesn't mean it."

I spare a glance at him while I drive us through a flooded road. I don't like his tone when talking about her, like she's a fool. "Are you suggesting she doesn't know what's best for herself?"

He throws up a tattooed hand in frustration. "That's *exactly* what I'm suggesting. Neither of you knows what's good for you. You're both drowning in emotions and shit. But I'm an outsider with a better view, and I'm telling you, *categorically*, that walking away is the incorrect choice, and probably an irreversible one."

"And I'm telling you that not walking away would be me completely disrespecting her wishes."

He growls into his hands like I'm driving him up the wall. "You don't give up anywhere else. You practically stalked your mom's doctors until they agreed not to give up on helping her last year. You moved across the Atlantic when you thought it might help you take Green from your dad. When I thought I was gonna die when we hiked Mount Suilven before Christmas, you dragged me up it. And now you're turning away from Ophelia at the first obstacle."

My laugh is hollow, devoid of humor. "That's what you'd call this? An obstacle?"

"Yeah. In ten years, you'll look back and see it that way."

"My father letting her parents die is not an obstacle, Vincenzo. It's a concrete wall."

"*You* letting her parents die would be an obstacle. You are not your father."

It doesn't feel that way lately.

"Look . . . it's the Sorrowsong Winter Ball the day after tomorrow."

Panic slices through me, the gash it leaves behind stained green with envy. "Is she bringing someone?"

"Yeah, you dick. Me."

"What the fuck?"

"I'm gonna ask her so some other guy doesn't! She attracts attention, you know?"

I grip the steering wheel until my knuckles are the same shade as the snow-topped mountains that come into view. "I know."

"So go to the ball with her."

I am at the center of a media frenzy, and the talk of Sorrowsong's dusty hallways. God knows how much more insufferable they'd all be if they knew I was here. "I can't put her in the spotlight like that."

Vincenzo looks like he might actually poke his eyes out with his thumbs. "More than she already is?"

Fair point.

He flings his hand into my peripheral vision, curling his fingers in a beckoning motion. "Go on. Next excuse. Let's work our way through them."

"I have a dinner hosted by the Minister of Aviation tomorrow."

Vincenzo sucks a breath in through his teeth. "*Alex.* Listen to yourself."

"What?"

"Green over personal life? Green over one of your eight people?"

I'm not sure if he means it as a harsh slap, but it lands like one. A cold bucket of reality over my head.

When I flick my gaze up to the rearview mirror, it's my father's eyes that glare back at me. I glance away and run my hand over my jaw, over the day-old stubble there. "If she rejects me again . . . that'll be it." And I'll be a fucking mess.

"And if you walk away, that'll be it. *Oh my god.* It's like your brain has turned to mush in there. Should you even be driving if you can't even form a rational thought?"

Finally, I turn us onto a road that at least *looks* like a road. "Fuck you, man."

"She's borrowing a dress from Colette."

Fuck.

"Pretty sure she said it's backless."

Fuck!

"Ask her to be your date, Vinnie, and it'll be the last thing you ever do."

Chapter 7

OPHELIA

The list of stupid things I've done in my life is probably long enough to wrap around the perimeter of the castle twice, but telling Alex to walk away felt like it should go somewhere near the top.

But if feeling stupid is the price to pay for shielding my heart from a final, damaging blow, then I'll do it.

The pain in his eyes when I was turning away is burned into my soul. I felt like I was watching him give up. Not just on us, but on everything.

I asked Colette to send Vincenzo to find him, hoping he'd be able to convince him everything will be okay. I don't want him to feel like he can't call anyone when he's at his lowest.

It's so cliché, plucked from the top comment of any relationship advice thread on the internet, but Alex and I have a long way to go in terms of self-acceptance before we can try again. I think we're too damaged to fully trust, fully open up to anyone.

I draw my knees up to my chest where I sit at the back of the minibus, the AirPods he got me in my ears. We're most of the way through the drive back from a meet in Manchester, and while the silver medal in my bag was enough to make Belladonna want to drown me, I think it's my proudest achievement here.

Belladonna took gold for backstroke; I took silver for the four hundred medley. Colette came in sixth, but she seems pretty happy.

The bus is quiet now. Illuminated only by blue striplights along the floor and the dim streetlamps on the dark road outside.

My parents would lose their minds if they knew I'd gotten a medal at such a big tournament. *Who knew it, Dad, exercising actually works.*

My phone pings, and I wonder how long it'll take before that sound doesn't fill me with dread.

It's Alex. The first text from his new number.

My stomach sinks. I open up the message. It's a picture of his laptop, this weekend's swim results on the screen.

Alex

Nice silver, Twist.

I shut my eyes, let my forehead drop to my knees. One day. He stayed away from me for one day. I don't reply.

That nonexistent kiss was . . . that was everything I've needed and everything I need to avoid. My fingers trace my bottom lip, the sound of his swallowed moan echoing in my ear.

Colette taps me on the shoulder, a worried crease between her perfect brows. "What's up?"

I tilt my phone toward her, to the only text between myself

and Alex's new number. She frowns, probably thinking something along the lines of: *Why did I let you cry into your cereal in my bed all night if he was just going to text you the next day?*

"Do I reply?"

"Obviously."

"You're only saying that because you want us to get back together."

"Quite right."

"I don't want to lead him on."

"Just say thank you. Nothing flirty. That way, he knows he still has you if he's really low, but you're not giving him hope."

I squint at Colette suspiciously. I'm not sure if I trust her, given that she is, in my opinion, giving Vincenzo hope even though there is zero chance of her ever dating someone linked to a crime family.

I type out a stiff reply, keeping it firmly out of flirtatious territory.

Ophelia

Thank you.

Alex

You gonna celebrate?

Ophelia

Hopefully with sleep.

Alex

You've earned it.

I run my thumb over his name. If I could swap his sick brain with mine, I would. He deserves peace. He deserves *life*.

All I've thought about since he left is his mom. How he's watching her slip away. I can't imagine it—this long, slow acceptance that she probably won't grow to be very old. I lost my mom, too, but quickly. She was here and then she wasn't.

I don't reply to him, even though I feel bad. But the texts give *me* hope. Maybe one day, when all of this is over and his dad is withering away behind bars, we could be friends.

I almost laugh out loud at my own stupidity. Having to force my feelings for Alex into a friendship-sized mold, to take the love and the anger and the desperation and try to make them something beige and neutral, might be the final straw for my miserable existence.

Luckily, he ends the conversation for me, and I vow to myself that unless I think he's in real danger, that is the end of it.

The end of *us*.

Alex

Goodnight. Sleep well.

I shut off my phone, hearing my name uttered a few rows in front. Most of the swimmers are sleeping, except a guy in third year and his girlfriend who are just one inappropriate pair of shorts away from fucking in their seats. Colette yawns, lashes fluttering sleepily. "Are we nearly there?"

"Yeah."

Her phone dings. Someone has sent a link into the swimming group chat that I refuse to join. She opens it and angles her phone away from me.

This is never good.

"Show me."

"It's stupid."

I snatch it from her grip. It's on some social media platform I don't have. A not particularly flattering—though my triceps look *fantastic*—picture of me getting out of the pool earlier today sits beneath the caption *TFW Alex Corbeau-Green's crazy ex is at your swim meet.*

"What's TFW?"

"Just like . . . *that feeling when* . . ."

"*That feeling when* Alex's ex is at your swim meet?"

"Yeah."

"What's the feeling?"

"What?"

"What does that even mean? What's the feeling? She didn't even say what her feeling about it is."

Colette frowns, texting Belladonna and asking her to use her admin privileges to delete the link. "It's just an internet expression."

"Well, it's a shit one." I take her phone back and open up the replies. They're pretty terrible. I hand the phone back after my eyes coast over the words *helicopter whore.*

It's not the nickname I would've chosen for myself. Biscuit whore might be more fitting.

"Don't they have something better to do?" I ask, refusing to let their words sink in. This is just one of many reasons I can't be with Alex. Me and the spotlight don't mix well. I'm a ginger, for heaven's sake; I'm *made* to hide in dark corners. All this media attention is the sun, and I'm thoroughly sunburned, tired of it all. "Why do I get more hate than Cain?"

"Because the world will turn a blind eye to the actions of a rich man if there's a defenseless woman around to take the hit instead." Her expression brightens at a text on her lockscreen. "My dresses for the Winter Ball have been delivered!"

"Fun," I say, failing to hide my lack of enthusiasm.

"Ophelia, you have to come."

"I'm ill tomorrow."

She scowls at me. "You're ill all the time."

"Then I'm busy tomorrow."

"With what?"

"I have to hang up my used tea bags."

"You're going," she declares. "And you're going to wear green."

"Great. That'll look good with the wine that inevitably gets thrown on me."

I burrow deeper into the seat, tugging the sleeves of my hoodie over my cold hands while the others laugh at whatever jokes they're reading about me.

My phone lights up again on the foldout table in front of me.

Unknown

I'd hate for something to happen to your
Prince Charming because of you.

Unknown

This could all be over so easily.

Anxiety prickles the back of my neck. Colette swallows, eyes wide. "Don't agree to meet them, Ophelia. Don't let them use Alex to lure you into a trap. Let the investigators work on it."

I attempt to run my hands though my hair, though they're thwarted by the endless tangles that never seem to go away. "But they're not getting anywhere."

"It could just be a student playing a truly stupid prank. You are in the spotlight right now. Keep ignoring it and it'll go away," she reassures me, snaking an arm around my shoulders.

Everyone seems to think that, but I'm not so sure. If it was a student, surely I'd have found something out by now.

I slide my phone into my pocket and let her maneuver the conversation to an art gallery opening she's attending next month, but unease prickles my gut. *Prince Charming.* Did they see me with Alex in his car?

Threats to my safety have become this constant, dull toothache during my time here, irritating and persistent but feeling increasingly . . . manageable. Which is a ridiculous thing to say, but it's true. They're a part of my daily routine now. *Wake up, eat slice of toast, receive death threat, eat second slice of toast, go to a lecture.*

But it's not just about me now. A threat to Alex's safety?

That, I cannot ignore.

DIVYA STEPS OUT of the bathroom, her mouth dropping open when she sees me. "Oh my god. You look hot."

I feel embarrassment heat my cheeks. "Don't sound surprised."

"I'm not. It's just been a while since you've not worn pajamas."

"Rude!" scolds Colette, laughing as she dusts something over my cheeks and nose with her brush. "Shut your eyes."

I do, and a smaller brush tickles across my eyelids. Colette sighs contently. I think she might be in her happy place. She's given me a dress that she supposedly didn't want. Except it's a deep shade of green—my favorite color—and at least a size too big for her, tags still attached.

But she rejects any claims that it's anything but an old dress she doesn't want anymore.

Something settles beneath my lash line. Hopefully a mascara brush. "Okay, blink. And again. And again. And again. And again. And again. And again."

"Oh my god."

She makes me do it all again on the other side and then puts loose waves in my unruly hair.

It feels foolish, getting all dressed up for an event I wasn't even planning to go to until Colette convinced me yesterday. I'm already anticipating the lingering glances, the looks that sit anywhere from pity to hatred. But I've longed for a night out with friends for so long that not attending feels like a disservice to all the progress I've made since getting here.

Dressed in a spectacular gothic gown with black lace sleeves like vines that creep over her dark brown skin, Magda tops all of our cocktails up with champagne.

"Finished!" Colette steps back, impressively steady on the pinpoint heels of her navy Louboutins.

I dare a glance in the mirror, unable to hide the smile that sneaks across my glossy lips. There's a little eyeshadow wing on my lash line, and all the blinking was worth it, because my lashes look *great*. The purple circles that hang beneath my eyes are gone. The dress is backless, save for a few thin straps that pull my waist in.

Divya grins. "You look so good, right?"

Colette claps. "Well, with such a pretty canvas . . ."

"I like that you didn't cover my freckles."

"Of course! I would die for freckles like yours."

Magda and Divya are arguing over some TV show they're both watching. Colette is humming quietly as she swipes a final coat of gloss over her lips. For a tiny, begrudging second, I'm glad she convinced me to come, because this easy, comfortable friendship is everything I've been missing the past few years. I can feel it slipping beneath my skin, making me stronger, nurturing that lonely teenage girl who wanted nothing more than to be included.

When I catch Divya's eye in the mirror, I realize with great horror that I'm *smiling*.

I slip my feet into my Converse just as a quiet rumble of thunder cracks across the valley. Perfect weather for a Sorrowsong party, I suppose.

We run across the cobbled courtyard and into Achlys's Hall, the four of us trying to hide under one jacket. The ball is already in full swing when we arrive, the room bustling beneath the watchful gaze of the painting that has set me on edge since the day I arrived.

Candles line each wall, hanging from chandeliers above us like a twinkling night sky, heels clicking against the tiled mosaic beneath our feet. The last shards of daylight slip through the high arched windows on the two longest walls, failing to brighten up the place. A small orchestra play in almost complete darkness at the far end. The paintings and vases that decorate the near side of the room are all winter themed: frozen landscapes and icy lakes behind white roses and pale blue delphinium that rise from the vases like icicles. But at the far end of the hall, the lakes in the paintings have thawed, the flowers turning to pastel shades of pink and orange.

A reminder that we are teetering on the edge of spring.

I try to twist it into something clever about fresh starts and new beginnings, but I can't.

I can't spin anything positive out of losing Alex.

If I thought Magda's dress was something special, Belladonna's is on another level. In a black gown that looks like it could've been plucked from Sorrowsong's dusty crypts this morning, she's somewhere between a gothic witch and a regency bride, accessorized with a black spider necklace and the captain of the women's rugby squad.

"Winters," she mutters, gazing down at me. Her eyes are unreadable beneath the wing of eyeliner that looks sharp enough to cut someone.

"Belladonna."

"Glad you came," she says, like she knows something I don't.

I open my mouth to ask her why, but she turns and stalks away.

"*What* is her problem?" Divya says, rolling her eyes. "She'll regret it when she dies alone."

I shrug as we head toward the bar, grabbing four cocktails from the tiered silver tray that's almost as tall as I am. "I find her really hard to dislike. I don't know why."

"Me too! I feel like . . . growing up in that family, she has to have seen some things, right?" says Colette, who may well be tipsy already. "Like Vincenzo—he can hardly fall asleep at night."

I frown. "Really?"

"Yeah. He definitely has something going on."

Magda clinks her glass against each of ours. I bring mine to my lips, the welcome burn of whisky sliding down my throat, leaving the honey aftertaste of Drambuie behind. "Well, the Ivanovs keep trying to kill him, so that can't exactly help."

Colette scans the crowd, looking for him. The Nightshade students seem to lurk in the shadows, stolen kisses lingering between hushed conversations and whispered threats. Hemlock have flooded the dance floor, Snakeroot mingling around the edges in deep and thoughtful conversation. For those I know in Cortinar, this is just another opportunity to show off their extensive wardrobes and family millions. Colette is no exception, dripping in jewels and a powder blue, off-the-shoulder tulle dress that has her looking like she might lose a slipper and find a prince this evening.

Knowing her, she probably will.

Or maybe not, I think, as I spot Eike, her driver-turned-bodyguard-turned-killjoy keeping a watchful eye on her from his position leaning over the ornate banister of the two curved staircases behind us, smartly dressed in a black tuxedo.

I doubt he'd let her breathe if her stepfather didn't allow it.

"Can you ballroom dance?" she asks, face lighting up as the song changes.

"Colette, do I look like a woman who can ballroom dance?"

She pouts, but Magda gladly takes her hand. Of course Magda can ballroom dance. I'm content to stand and watch them, unable not to let Colette's infectious joy tease a small smile out of me when she swaps partners to dance with her friend Hattie, the daughter of a princess and a famous dressage rider.

Divya gets tugged away by some medical student friends, and immediately, I become hyperaware of another presence beside me, a Scottish accent softened at the edges.

"It feels like no time at all since we met in this very spot."

I glance up at Achlys, at the way she sneers at me in the darkness of the hall, painted in such great detail that it looks like she might reach out from her frame and stroke her dirty fingernails down my cheek. "It feels like a lifetime ago."

"Isn't it quite peculiar how time passes so differently for each of us?"

Carmichael is looking right at me when I glance his way, eyes burning into my soul.

He's always creeped me out. He feels like an extension of Sorrowsong Castle, rather than an employee of it. If I look hard enough, I find him at every event, every rugby game, every exam, watching me with that lifeless stare.

"Time would pass faster for me if you hadn't let my parents' murder slip through your net."

His smile is cold, eyes colorless. The flowers that peek out of the breast pocket of his merlot-colored waistcoat are dead and dried up. "I would be careful not to wish for your life to pass too quickly, Miss Winters."

I wish he'd just *leave*. "What do you want from me?"

"I want you to convince Alex to come back to Sorrowsong."

That takes me by surprise. "Why?"

He runs his thumb and forefinger over his mustache, deep in thought as he watches a couple waltz across the polished tile. "For a friend."

I narrow my eyes at him, trying to piece a jigsaw together with a feeling that I don't have all the pieces. "His mom? Elise?"

"I told her I'd watch over him."

"Why?" I ask, following his gaze back to the couple that twirl under the candlelight. "Oh my god. You're in love with Elise."

"I was, once. But she was young, and I was old. She is all the good in the world, and I am the bad. Cain Green covered her wings in oil, caught her in a trap. When her health started to spiral and Cain's intentions for Alex's future became clear, she asked me to keep an eye on him."

I chew on my lip, unsure why this man sets me so on edge. "You cannot convince me you're a good man, that you're doing this because you care about what happens to us."

He chuckles, fiddling with his pocket watch. "I'm not a good man at all, Ophelia. But I *am* a man of my word."

"Is that what you think? That you're protecting Alex?"

"I told the police that Clint Bancroft had suggested to me multiple times last year that he intended to kill himself. They lost all interest in his death after that."

My breath catches in my throat, lungs stalling under his lifeless stare.

He knows we killed Bancroft.

My phone burns a hole in my hand. Carmichael could've taken the photo and sent it to me. Carmichael could've posted the article to remove Cain from Alex's life.

I make a note to suggest it to Mack when we speak next.

The cocktail slips down my throat so easily, stoking the dwindling fire in my soul. "Alex and I aren't together. Convince him yourself."

"He only listens to you and the psychiatrist."

I drop my empty tumbler onto the silver tray of a passing waiter, meeting Carmichael's eyes with my shoulders back and my head high. "Alex's decisions are his own to make, and I owe you nothing."

I shove through the crowd of students toward the double doors that lead to the hallway, desperate for some air.

The atmosphere shifts as I near the staircases, the loud buzz of chatter quieting to a hum. The sea of people seems to part, a few murmured sentences filtering through the crowd. I turn around and strain my neck, trying to see what the fuss is about. People glance at me, then back at whoever it is who's just entered the hall.

And I just *know*.

I know it's him before he comes into view. I know it's him from the way people look at him. I know it's him from the way the oxygen in the air seems to fizzle up and burn.

But I'm still not prepared when he stops in the middle of the dance floor, looking at me like I'm his only hope at a happy ending.

Alex in a suit is a sight for sore eyes. Droplets of rain glisten on the black fabric of the jacket, drip from the lock of hair that curls over his forehead, trickle over the curve of his bottom lip, glue his white shirt to his skin.

I stumble backward, the whole room waiting on my reaction. He gives me an infinitesimal shake of his head. *Don't run from me.*

He clears the space between us in a second, a hand running through his hair as he takes in the green gown that clings to my upper body like a second skin. He looks like he's forgotten whatever it was he was here for. "Fuck, Ophelia. I had a whole speech planned."

I open my mouth to argue, but the weight of hundreds of eyes stops the words from coming out. Colette is stood beside Belladonna on the edge of the crowd, not a lick of surprise in their expressions.

Traitors.

Go. The word is sitting on the top of my tongue, heavy and uncomfortable.

The song changes to something softer, slower. Even the staff that hurry around with trays of drinks seem to have frozen, suspended in time until Colette drags Vincenzo onto the dance floor. "I'm sure Alex and Ophelia would love to have a dance?" she says, loud enough for half the student body to hear.

I catch her gaze. *I'll murder you in your sleep*, my glare says.

Not if you're busy banging Alex, hers says back.

Alex's hands settle on my waist, wide and scorching through the thin material of my dress. Panic flares up in my chest, frantic flames that lick the wall around my heart. "I don't dance."

I try to step back, but he has me ensnared in his grip, bright green eyes glittering with something that's so comfortingly familiar that a shard of pain slices through my chest. "*Alex.*"

His fingers flex and unflex around my waist, as if testing that I'm real. The weight of so many eyes has my shoulders drooping, fighting that lifelong urge to fold in on myself and disappear. "Ophelia."

"You agreed to leave."

A small smile lifts his lips. "I was young and foolish back then."

"*Two days ago?*" I breathe out, in disbelief.

He pulls me to his chest as more drunken couples surround us. His voice is a deep rumble beside my ear. "Yeah. Old news. Forget that ever happened."

I fight to stay focused, fight to keep my brain still and steady when it feels like the rest of my body is being dragged into his orbit. *He doesn't look good. His hand sliding down my back doesn't set my blood on fire.* "It wasn't foolish, Alex. It was the only sensible thing we've done in the last two months."

He lifts my hand in his, twirling me once. When he drags me back to him, my back is pressed to his front, his arms snaking over the soft flesh of my stomach. His lips press just beneath my ear, his next exhale bordering a moan. My knees feel like they can't be bothered to hold me up anymore. "It was foolish," he rasps, "because I'd have to be unthinkably stupid to give up on a chance with you."

My lashes drift shut as I revel for a split second in the feel of his warm, hard body around mine. His scent soothes my senses, the rapid thrum of his heart against my back in perfect time with my own. "And do you think you have a chance?" I ask, letting my hands slide behind me, clumsily finding their way beneath his jacket. "This isn't Monopoly."

His laugh is a husky, treacherous thing. The music seems to slow, suspended in treacle like the rest of the world around us. The hall is full of laughter and conversation, but I can hear our breath louder than anything else. "If it was, you'd be Mayfair."

My head is swimming, a heady combination of alcohol and Alex Corbeau-Green's hands that run up and down my body like he can't get enough. "And you'd be in jail."

"But I get three tries to get out, right?"

Fuck. "Not in this game."

"I've used one," he breathes, lips tracing the shell of my ear. Desire is a punishing drumbeat somewhere low in my belly. "And I won't need a third."

"You used your first when you almost hit me with your car."

He spins me back to face him so fast that I'm pressed flush against him before I can blink. "That's not fair. You were standing in the middle of the road."

"When you ate the last Jelly Baby our first night together, then."

The blush that accompanies his small, hopeful smile chips away at me. "One last chance to get out of jail, Twist. *Please.*"

I press my cheek to his chest, let out a ragged, tortured sigh.

Even with my eyes closed, I see it. The flash of a camera, jarring me out of whatever trance I was in. Another comes, and it's too bright, too harsh, like that blinding light that hovers too close to your face at the dentist.

And here it is. Another reminder of why he and I are oil and water. Our worlds don't mix. I pull my hands off the hard, warm muscles of his back like he's on fire.

When I swing my eyes open, Vincenzo is punching the phone out of someone's hand and Alex is hiding my face with his body. A few other students take pictures like this is the most interesting thing to happen all year, and I know they'll be somewhere online before the evening is up.

"Fucking idiots," Alex mutters, dragging me toward the bar.

But I don't need a drink. I don't need more eyes on me, more pictures of me traveling around the university's depressing hallways. I need to get *out*. I yank myself from his grip, instead making a jog for the small wooden door to our right.

The rain is hammering down outside the castle, running down Sorrowsong's rusty pipes and pattering through the dense tree line in front of me. I tip my head back, letting the icy droplets snatch my breath away in a desperate attempt to wash the sticky, hot desire from my body.

I hear the door clatter shut. My stomach sinks into the wet earth at my feet. "Just go."

"No."

"I—" My reply fizzles out on my tongue. "*What?*"

"No," he breathes, as thunder rumbles above us. "I'm saying no, Ophelia."

"We don't get a happy ending."

"Says *who*?"

"The universe!" I shout back, over the storm that whips my hair around my face. I turn away, anything to not have to see the look in his eyes. "Do you see the way they stare in there? We're a car crash."

A warm hand shoots out to grab my biceps before I can walk into the woods, away from him. "That's bullshit, Ophelia."

I spin to face him, snatching my arm from his grip. All I've given him so far is anger, but when my voice cuts through the howling of the wind, what I hear in it is the hurt and the insecurity that he put there on that miserable January morning. "You left me!"

"I know."

"I never want you to have to choose again. I never want you to be split in two again. I never want to feel the way I did when you left again."

"It won't happen again."

"How can you know that?"

He pulls me to him, sheltering me from the rain. His voice is softer now, barely audible over the howling wind. "Because every day that you're not mine is knocking another year off my life."

I rest my forehead against the soaking fabric of his shirt, feeling the thundering heart beneath. I'd do anything to protect that heart. "It's not just what happened last month. It's everything. It's what your father did to me. It's the distance between us. I am a student, Alex. You're a CEO. We are worlds apart. I'll hardly see you for the next few years. I can't get on a plane to see you, and I can't ask you to spend time away from the girls."

I feel his cheek rest on the top of my head, the two of us standing outside Sorrowsong's lichen-covered walls in the driving rain.

I wish that being in his arms didn't feel like coming home. "I'll still see you."

A couple times a year, if we're lucky.

His hands slip beneath the low back of my dress, over my frozen skin. His shaky exhale warms the top of my head, voice ragged with desperation when it splinters our silence. "I need you. I can't live without you."

I sigh into the curve of his neck, a warm, dry haven in the violent storm. "*Alex.* We're young. We don't know what we need. We don't know anything about anything."

"Is that what this feels like to you?" he asks, hands sliding down to my hips, pressing my body against his. "A young, foolish fling?"

No. This feels like the beginning and end of the world. The unbridled hope of a sunrise and the regret and closure of the sun sinking behind the horizon. It feels like he's holding the needle and thread to stitch up my broken heart. If I let him in and he pulled away again, the thread would rip through the delicate flesh and leave me to bleed out on the floor.

But my judgement is clouded by lust, emboldened by the whisky I can still taste on my tongue. Desire is a potent drug, and Alex seems to inject me with it. He plants his soft lips at the point where my pulse drums in my neck and gently sucks, sending my head dropping back involuntarily. His hand slips down the low back of my dress. The thunder covers any noise he makes, but I feel the rumble of it in his throat. "*Please.*"

I walk him toward the wet stone wall behind us, legs wobbling.

"Give me until midnight. Three hours. Just give me three hours."

Three hours. One hundred and eighty minutes to remind my lonely heart of what it feels like to be loved again.

I don't know how anyone could be strong enough to resist.

His next kiss on my neck makes my knees buckle. He pulls away, waiting for my answer with bated breath. His wet hair tumbles down in tousled strands, the black ink on his chest peeking through the soaking fabric of his white dress shirt. A fat raindrop seems to drip from his clumped lashes in slow motion as his gaze drops to my lips, asking, begging, *wanting*.

"Midnight," I choke out, and his lips come crashing down on mine.

Nothing about the kiss feels young or foolish. His touch is rough and reverential all at once, spanning my neck and jaw to hold me in place. My skin turns to gold wherever his fingers sink into my flesh.

I push his blazer open, feeling the muscles of his abdomen tense beneath the crisp white cotton. The hand on my jaw squeezes gently, forcing my mouth to open just wide enough for him to deepen the kiss. Desire trickles down my spine, pooling in my lower stomach like warm honey.

God, I've missed this. But it's not just this—I've missed *him*.

He spins us so it's *my* back against the stone of the castle walls, hand grabbing the back of my thigh and hooking my leg over his hip as he swallows my frantic moan. His mouth is hot and heavy, demanding and possessive on mine as his fingers find the sensitive skin beneath the skirt of my dress, trailing inwards from my hip.

He breaks the kiss with a gentle bite of my lip, broad chest heaving. His pupils dilate, inky black pools of need when he realizes just how much he turns me on. "Can I?"

I nod, desperate for his lips on mine again. "No strings."

His fingers sink into me, sending my head falling forward into his chest and my eyes to the back of his head.

It'll never be like this with anyone else.

"Strings, Ophelia. So many fucking strings. Strings in every cell of my body."

My strangled cry gets carried away on the wind, wishing so badly that he wasn't right. I am tied to Alex in a way I cannot explain, hoping like a fool that the threads will dissolve in the rain like week-old stitches. "*No strings.*"

"If that's what you have to tell yourself," he concedes, gazing down at me lazily like his fingers don't have me clawing at the stone behind me. His other hand slips beneath the neckline of my dress, thumb skating over my nipple. Frantic pleas tumble out of my mouth, my hips starting to move in time with his thick forearm.

"Does this feel *no strings*, to you?"

My leg gives out, but his body holds me upright against the wall. Each labored thud of my heart sends another torturous wave of *him* into my bloodstream. "*Alex.*"

"Do you think a man with no strings attached could make you feel this way?"

My heel digs into his lower back, hand shooting out to grab his arm like there's a chance he might stop. "*Please.*"

"You don't need to beg me for anything."

My chest rises and falls beneath my dress. Stupid, angry, love-sick, ecstatic tears spill from my eyes. "I'm going to—I'm gonna—"

He drops to his knees on the wet cobblestone, moving my thigh from his hip to his shoulder and burying his head beneath the lush satin of my skirt.

My back arches. His hand comes to steady me at the waist. I shout his name at the swirling sky just as a furious bolt of lightning splits it into two.

And I fall apart.

Physically. Metaphorically. In every way.

The world melts into a flat, white sheet until all that exists is him and me and the endless mass of strings that tie us together in a hundred different ways.

He rises to his feet and catches me in his arms, brushing the hair from my face. His lips are a little swollen, vibrant green eyes watching me intently. "Okay?"

I shut my eyes. That was . . . *okay* doesn't scratch the surface. I nod weakly, limp in his arms as he carries me past the entrance to the hall and onto the forested path to the mansion. I put a hand on his chest, trying to get to the ground. "Put me down."

"You need to get warm and dry."

"But my friends . . . I ditched them."

"Colette and Vincenzo know I'm here. They helped set this up."

"Put me down," I repeat, but there's zero conviction behind the words. My head leans into the hard wall of his chest, fingers curling around the fabric of his shirt.

He hurries us along the path, the mossy cobblestones borderline underwater at his feet. The mansion looks dark and deserted when I swipe my access card beside the double doors, hyperaware of every shadow, every noise, every open door.

He climbs the stairs in silence, save for the chattering of my teeth and the dripping of water from our clothes onto the polished steps. I drink in every inch of him and pretend that the way his thumb gently strokes my back as he walks doesn't fill me with hope for our future.

In my room, Alex heads straight into the bathroom to get a towel, and I fish my phone from Colette's borrowed purse to tell her I'm at the mansion.

My eyes zero in on the lone notification on the lockscreen, my blood turning to ice in my veins.

The photo of Alex and me is hazy from the rain, but I know it was taken no less than ten minutes ago, the two of us huddled together as we jog toward the mansion.

Unknown
What makes you think you get a happy ending?

Unknown
Leave him, or he'll be dying with you.

I open my mouth to tell Alex, but then the second message comes through.

A photo of an airport. And beyond a wire fence, a Green Aviation jet.

Unknown
Wouldn't want something to happen to his plane, would you?

No, no, no. Please, no.

I'm at the window in half a second, scanning the brambles and the hedges of the mansion's unruly gardens. I brace myself with each startling flash of lighting, just waiting to see a shadowy figure standing alone on the lawn. Cain, Carmichael, Shawn. I'm simultaneously terrified and desperate to catch a glimpse of something, anything that might identify who is doing this.

"Ophelia," Alex sighs, coming out of the bathroom with a towel for my hair. The exasperation is evident in his tone as he begins meticulously drying each strand. "You cannot be serious with this no strings thing."

My heart is hammering in my chest, tongue tied in a knot. His eyes flick to the window, at my ghostly white reflection in the thin glass. The next gust of wind sends a branch of ivy into the window, and I jump out of my skin.

Alex frowns beside me, a steady hand landing on my lower back. "Are you all right?"

"I . . . I don't think you should be here. You need to leave."

His lips drop to my shoulder, but fear is like a blanket starving the flames of my desire. "I disagree."

"Alex, you'll leave tomorrow morning and then we probably won't see each other for eight months." I lay out the excuses as the text burns through my mind. "And I can't handle you leaving me every time you convince yourself you're not worthy of a relationship, and you're so many miles away, and you have your sisters, and—"

And he's always afraid that his presence in my life puts me in danger, but now I'm wondering if it's the other way round.

"Ophelia, *breathe*."

The blood is rushing in my ears, a deafening roar like the rotors of a helicopter spiraling down toward the forest. "I can't."

"You can, baby. You definitely can."

I can't drag my eyes from the window. I inhale to tell Alex about the text several times, but nothing ever comes out. What if someone's hovering outside the door, if someone has bugged my room, if someone's watching us from the window?

I need to call Mack.

A steaming mug of tea appears between my hands, delivered with a gentle kiss to the top of my head. "I can't do no strings. Not with you."

"Then let's just . . ."

"If you're about to say *be friends*—"

"You should go, Alex. I'll call you tomorrow."

"Is that really what you want?"

No.

I turn to face him in the quiet darkness of my room and give him half of the truth. "I don't trust myself to share a bed with you and just sleep."

His eyes soften between wet, clumped lashes, like he really does understand. "Tell me we still have a chance, Winters."

I flick a nervous glance to the door, voice barely audible as if there's an invisible third person in the room who might be listening, waiting to take him from me. "We do. I just need . . . I just need time, Alex. I have things to . . . sort out."

The fierce green of his irises seems to dilute with relief, a small smile on his lips. "I'm gonna roll a double."

Were his lips always this tempting? How did we ever get any studying done last term?

He cups my face in his hands and plants a searing kiss on my lips. What happened outside Achlys's Hall was pure, unadulterated lust, but this? This is something else entirely. A soft, tender sort of love that's melting all my broken pieces together.

"I'll walk you back," I blurt out, panicked for his safety.

But what if my presence only makes him more of a target?

I've not had someone to worry about for a very long time. I'm out of my depth.

"I think I'll survive." His unbothered smile only makes me more uneasy. The pad of his thumb skates a lazy line along my bottom lip. "Stay out of trouble, Twist."

And then he's walking backward, away from me. Away from harm, I hope. I'm relieved and disappointed in equal measure, watching as he pulls open the door and leans against the doorframe and *oh god, why does he have to do that?*

I'm blushing like he's just done something unthinkable, looking anywhere but the inch of exposed skin where his shirt has untucked beneath his jacket. He's fighting a smile when I finally manage to make eye contact, like my thoughts are projected onto the wall behind me for him to see. "Four letters, first letter *F*—"

I splutter, squeezing my thighs together beneath the skirt of my dress. "I . . . we . . . *no*, I wasn't . . ."

"Such a dirty mind, Winters, I was going to suggest you get some food."

And then he's gone, taking this ridiculous sexual tension with him. I catch sight of my reflection in the mirror. If *horny and anxious* was a facial expression, I've really nailed it.

Pull yourself together, Winters. Jesus Christ.

Pressing my phone to my ear and my forehead to the window, I watch Alex's oversized silhouette pace up the path away from the mansion.

The voice on the other end of the phone is *way* too cheerful. "Joe's Pizza."

"I . . . what?"

"It's Mack. You might be the first person to fall for that. You're in luck; I'm with Brendan. What can we do for you?"

"Can you have someone check, double-check, and triple-check Alex's plane home?"

I hear fingers against a keyboard. "They do that anyway."

"Quadruple, then."

"On it." I hear muffled voices. "Oh wow."

"What?"

"The picture of the plane."

"How did you . . ."

"Even if Brendan *wasn't* capable of hacking into almost any system anywhere in the world, I think I would've guessed Gandalf1 was your password in my first three tries. Did you tell Alex about this?"

"No."

"You know, if you guys went to couple's therapy, the first rule is always communi—"

"Alex cannot be in danger, Mack. I can't let anything happen to him."

"We're in agreement, then."

"I don't understand why you can't trace—"

"The texts to a specific person, yes, we know," comes Brendan's voice. "You've said that twelve times. Ophelia, if you were going to send someone anonymous texts, would you do it from your phone?"

"No," I grumble.

"No. Exactly. You'd buy a burner phone. The issue is not that we can't hack the phone. It's that it's a cheap burner phone with nothing on it. No email address, no bank details, no addresses, nothing. All I can tell you is that the texts are coming from Sorrowsong and that we—"

"Think it would be below Cain to stalk me, yes, I know. You've said *that* twelve times."

Brendan interrupts me with a victorious-sounding laugh. "It's from the internet, the airport picture. It's just taken from a plane-spotting website."

Relief washes over me, but it leaves plenty of unease behind. *What are they playing at?* "Just because they used an old picture, doesn't mean he's not in danger."

Mack sounds like he wants to block my number. "We are being paid to keep Alex and his family safe, and that's exactly what we're doing. As soon as you have any evidence to suggest we're not doing that well enough, we'll gladly accept this miserable attitude of yours—"

Alex disappears from my view, lost to the ominous darkness beyond the mansion's gardens. "I liked Joe's Pizza better."

I hear Brendan's laugh. "You ever been to New York?"

"I've never been on a plane."

"Great pizza."

"I'll have to take your word for it. Goodnight."

They hang up, but I don't move, stood with my breath held and my phone in my hand until it finally pings with a text.

Alex

Made it to my car in one piece.

Alex

You were beautiful tonight.

Chapter 8

ALEX

[DRAFT]

From: Alex Corbeau-Green

Subject: Breathing (verb) *Harder than they'd have you believe*

To: Ophelia Winters

Twice in my adult life, I've forgotten how to inhale. Both times involved you in a backless dress.

THE SHOWER HAS been off for so long that the water on the glass door is dry. The rhythmic *drip*, *drip*, *drip* of my wet hair stopped at least twenty minutes ago.

My fingers flex and unflex around the sides of the sink, a shaky exhale clouding the mirror.

Everything is gray today. Worse than usual.

It's been nine days since I got back, ten days since Ophelia rearranged my universe with a single kiss and then told me to leave.

I can't make sense of anything. Can't understand why my six funny, clever girls and our loving mother downstairs aren't enough to make me happy.

Behind my reflection, I practically see the word *ungrateful* flashing above my head.

I woke up, I exercised, I ate breakfast with my sisters. I did everything I was supposed to, and I still feel like shit.

But if I die today, I won't get to try Mia and Éléanor's stupid two-day-long focaccia recipe that they've been going on about for a week.

My phone buzzes as I slide my rings onto my fingers and tame my unruly—but trimmed, at long last—hair. *Mike Wilson.*

My second-in-command is probably wondering what the hell I'm doing.

I hit decline and pull on a shirt and slacks.

"*Alexandra*," says Mia, spoken like one of the royals in those regency romance shows she watches. I pretend not to watch or care about even though I'll put the TV in the trash if the maid doesn't end up with the duke.

"Come in."

Mia cracks the door open, peering in. "Hey."

"Hey."

"Are you planning to go to work at any point?

"Shut up."

"Great comeback. What else you got?"

"Shut up."

"This is good material. Do you do weddings?"

I shrug on a jacket. "Funerals and divorces?"

"Great. I'll book one of each."

I smile and ruffle her dark hair. "You should be studying."

"I am. But I thought I'd come and check on you. Worried for the family millions, you know?"

My phone lights up with an incoming call. "So is Mike, it seems."

She's right behind me as I head down the stairs. Did I have this much joie de vivre at fifteen? Doubt it.

"I'm surprised you kept him."

"Mike?"

"Yeah. I mean, he was always up Dad's ass, so—"

"Thanks for that visual, Mia. Mike is good, he knows his stuff."

She gags behind me, following me to the door. "What happened on your London trip?"

"Nothing."

"Well . . . something did. You've been weird since you got back."

"Nope."

"Did you go to Scotland?"

I wince. "Mia."

"Well, Beatrice Jones said that you showed up at the Sorrowsong Ball and then I saw someone posted a photo of you and—"

I hate that everyone seems to care what I do. Hate that my appearance at the ball has only prompted more unkindness toward Ophelia. It's not exactly helpful when I'm trying to convince her that things are better when we're together. "By engaging with that content you're only perpetuating the cycle we're in."

Her tone is more serious now, and she looks a lot more like her twin sister all of a sudden. Evie has always been the more pragmatic of the two. Mia . . . well, Mia once threw a boiled egg at Dad, so . . . not so pragmatic. "Well, maybe if you talked to us more, we wouldn't be forced to look for details of your private life on random websites."

I turn to face her, but she's already stomping back up the stairs.

BRENDAN VIDEO CALLS me as soon as I've sat down at my desk and accepted a steaming coffee and a concerned glance from Jacqueline. "Hello?"

"Hey, one sec, bear with me. I'm on *Minecraft*." His eyes are focused somewhere else, mouth in a determined line.

"At eleven a.m.?"

"Yeah, at eleven a.m. What time would you rather I did it?"

"Not when you've called me."

"You were a lot less of a dick before you were a CEO, Corbeau. You're all the same. If you didn't pay ridiculous money, I'd be long gone."

I wince at that. Was my father like me before he became the man he is now?

"Tell me what you know."

He ruffles his hair beneath his black hoodie, looking a bit uncomfortable. "I've traced the article leak."

Fuck. I've been so hyper-focused on my father's whereabouts, I almost let myself forget about the article. "And?"

"It's a college buddy of mine."

Confusion and frustration swamp me in equal measure. "Who?"

"She works in tech, like me. She knows what she's doing. Buried her tracks so well that it took me months to find her."

She's a hacker, basically.

"Who paid her?"

He throws up a hand, lips pressed together. "She won't say. It would be a real breach of the unspoken code for me to keep asking. You wouldn't want me disclosing that I work for you to strangers. We all respect each other's work."

My life is being fucked over by some hacker bro-code. "We need to find out who it was."

"I'm working on it, but *man*, her drives are hard to get into."

If I was my father, I'd have the information tortured out of her.

But I'm not.

"I have one lead. She's not really in this for the money. All her jobs follow a trend."

"Like?"

"In college she hacked into someone's bank and wired the money to his wife. Turns out he'd been abusing her real bad. She mostly works for vulnerable women, women who've been let down."

Like Ophelia. "Do we even know this was a request? Could she have stumbled across what happened to Ophelia's parents and done it to get revenge for a mistreated woman?"

"It was a request. She's told me that much."

"It's got to be someone we don't know. That's the only possibility I can imagine."

Mack appears on the other half of the screen, a baseball cap pulled low over his tanned face. "What have I missed?"

"Alex thinks I'm a dick for playing *Minecraft*. And I've filled him in on the article leak."

"Any ideas on who it could be, Alex? We're tentatively narrowing it down to female, but it could still be anyone."

"No idea. I'll have to call Ophelia. Could be someone from her past."

"Otherwise, the possible sighting of your father in the UK was false. It was some other guy on the run. I have a lead that would place him in New York."

My nails dig into my palms beneath the desk. I'm furious, but I'm not surprised. My father has been expertly dodging the law in so many ways for so many years. He's only doing what he does best.

There's a small part of me that prays my father is here, far away from Ophelia, but another part of me wants him a long way from my family.

I hate that I can understand her logic, can understand why she suggested no strings.

Ophelia has known nothing but loneliness and isolation for her entire adult life. The man she deserves would be at her side right now, holding her, protecting her.

That isn't me. I can't be that man.

But I'd die trying to make it our reality.

I hang up on them and let my head rest in my hands. I'm surrounded by great people, and yet I'm desperate to feel anything that isn't gray.

Orange would do.

Alex

Where are you?

Ophelia
Just got back from the pool. About to shower, why?

A sparse but steady string of texts between us has formed since I got back. She isn't icing me out, but it's going exactly how she predicted it would, an endless loop of: *sorry, call you later*s and *something came up, let's do tomorrow*s. I call her while she's in a lecture, she calls me back while I'm getting Josie to bed, I call her back and she's swimming.

A tempting sort of torture that I'd take over her silence any day.

I hit FaceTime on her contact, and her concerned face fills my screen after a few rings. She's naked save for a towel that wraps over her chest. "What's wrong?"

My brain short-circuits at the sight of her. "Nothing."

"Tell me."

"You look beautiful."

"And that's what's wrong?"

I laugh. "Yeah."

"You know you can still talk to me about anything."

"Turn the camera."

She purses her lips, but her eyes flicker with something that makes me feel drunk. "Alex, we're . . ."

"No strings, taking it slow, whatever you say," I drawl, like it's all boring semantics I don't care for.

She does as I ask and turns the camera toward the mirror, exposing every dizzying inch of her reflection. My fingers postpone my next meeting without my brain even having to ask them to. Copper hair tumbles over the pale skin of her breasts, messy waves licking her stomach like flames. I press the knuckles of my free hand to my lips to try to keep my errant mouth shut before I scare her off again. "Good girl. Put your foot up on the sink."

She does as I ask, I'm convinced the world starts spinning westward. "Next?" she breathes, and my heart stutters.

"Fuck, Ophelia. Let me see you touch yourself." Her eyes drift shut, mouth dropping open as her hand moves off camera. My fingers curl around the edge of the desk, like I might start levitating any moment now. "You drive me insane."

She tilts her head back in a slow, languorous movement, and I think she's trying to finish me off, because her tongue darts out to wet her lips before she says, "You too. *Please.*"

I have my office door locked and my belt unbuckled in half a second, and the sound she makes when I groan her name feels so much more significant than anything else I could achieve in this office.

And it's just so easy to pretend. When she breathes out my name, it sounds no different than it did when she was sure she wanted me.

A little orange thread ties itself in a stitch somewhere inside my rib cage.

What's one more string in a sea of ten thousand?

I BLOCK OUT fifteen minutes in my schedule every afternoon for the rest of the week, just in case Ophelia wants to repeat what happened earlier today.

Then I reluctantly text Mike and Luis and tell them I'm free for our meeting, swiveling to face the city. The rain is a fine mist that turns the sidewalks dark and the roads shiny.

Where are you, Cain?

Mike knocks and enters, juggling his laptop, phone, notebook, and a steaming cup of coffee. "How was your call with the French?"

"Good, actually. Reminded them that five airports have cut their contracts with Vortex this year alone. We're a no brainer, even with the drama around my father."

"We've got to land Nice. There's *so* much business from Monaco at the moment."

"Yeah," I agree, genuinely *trying* to care.

I don't hate running a business. I'd do it again, but maybe when I'm older and wiser. I like negotiating, like analyzing the numbers, but private jets and airports don't interest me in the slightest.

In some twisted way, every bit of profit I make here feels like a favor to my father. *Look at me, Cain, doing exactly what you always said I'd do.*

I took on Synx, the cybersecurity firm, purely to have leverage over Rocco, a way to force him to agree with my plan not to let him use Green helicopters as a tool anymore. No more hits, no more bugging helicopters with listening and tracking devices. But now I'm considering keeping it, even after I leave Green.

Luis comes in, nodding at us both. "Fucking LAX."

"What about them?"

"Three jets in the hangar for maintenance. *All* delayed. Staff shortage."

"I'll talk to them straight after this," I say, tapping my pen on my thigh. So much of this job is just being angry over the phone.

Maybe Ophelia should do it.

My phone buzzes.

Vincenzo

Guess who's nose I just broke

Alex

Your own?

Vincenzo

Not this time. Hugo from the Sorrow-song soccer team

Alex

Wow. That's a nose on my dream bucket list of noses to break.

Vincenzo

He said something to Ophelia that made her throw a tiramisu at his head at dinner.

My stomach sinks. It would have to be something terrible for her to waste a good tiramisu.

Alex

When it heals, break it again for me.

Vincenzo

If it heals, I haven't done a good enough job.

I tune back into Luis and Mike's conversation, dropping a few *let's touch base on that laters*, a couple of *let's not reinvent the wheels*, and a *blue-sky thinking* for good measure. They nod in agreement, moving on to some sales figures we got earlier. I flick to my calendar while the two of them talk, eyes scanning over the next two weeks. *Mia college open day. Evie dance solo. Boston Aviation Conference. Mom hospital appointment. Élé teacher conference.*

Alex
Want me to ruin Hugo's father's life?

Ophelia
No, it's okay. Thanks for the offer though.

Alex
I can't come to you this week. I'm sorry.

Ophelia
Don't be sorry, I don't expect that from you.

And that right there is the issue.

Chapter 9

OPHELIA

Professor Maguire is Professor Bancroft's replacement, and though they both look like the kind of people who stay up late, excitedly counting down the days until bin collection day, the similarities end there.

The new childhood social psychology lecturer seems to enjoy his job, waving a stick in front of a chalkboard like an orchestra conductor who's taken something.

With any luck, I won't murder this one.

The lecture hall is comically dark, the brass sconces kicking out a soft orange glow that doesn't touch any of the corners of the room. The wind is whistling through the rafters above us, and I'm sure the entire back row is asleep.

I type away at my coursework essay while Maguire talks, wrapping up the final lecture of the day. For all Sorrowsong's ugly parts, I love the work, and when the teachers aren't trying to kill me, they truly are the top of their field.

A notification pings through on my lockscreen.

Unknown
Nice laptop. Did your rich boyfriend give you that?

What?

I spin around where I sit, surveying the faces illuminated by screens. I bounce from person to person, waiting for someone to meet my eyes, to slip up, to give themselves away. I turn to face the front, but every open laptop I can see is open on the course notes.

My eyes drop to the only other way someone could've seen me: a huge arched stained glass window at the front of the room. The world beyond is too dark to make anything out.

Did your rich boyfriend give you that?

They sound almost . . . jealous. Jealous of Alex? Jealous of our relationship?

Or . . . jealous that I *chose* Alex? My breath catches in my throat as I shut my laptop, haphazardly tossing my things into my bag and hurrying out of the lecture hall and into the tunnels beyond.

The door to the Cortinar halls is ajar when I reach it, slipping through the gap and into the warm, rich interior of the common room. Shawn Miller is exactly where I hoped he'd be, laughing with his finance buddies whose foreheads are all as shiny as their loafers.

"Who's your victim this time, Winters?" asks a girl by the door.

"Fuck you," I bark back, just about ready to leave this castle and never return.

Shawn's smile fades when he sees me approaching, the chatter around their little circle of chesterfield sofas dwindling to an awkward silence.

He manages to find his smug expression again, running his eyes up and down my muddy boots and oversized track pants. "Wow, Winters. You look . . . you know Halloween isn't until October, right?"

I give him a sweet smile, silently hoping his snickering friends burst into flames. "Weren't saying that when you were begging me for a second date, were you?"

His smirk melts into a snarl. "What do you want?"

"To talk. Alone."

He laughs. "And end up in a trash bag in the trunk of your car?"

"With all these witnesses, Shawn?" I ask, like he's three years old. My patience has frayed beyond its limit. "Not the sharpest crayon in the box, are you?"

He scoffs, muttering something to his friends that has them howling with laughter. "We can talk in here."

"In private," I grit out, and someone wolf whistles behind us.

"I'm not going to take you back," he says, crossing one ankle over his knee and leaning farther into his seat.

"Investment advice as foreplay doesn't really work for me, so the feeling is mutual."

"If you want to chase the market and miss the best entry points then be my guest," he says, his mouth tipping up like he's just landed a great burn.

He's even more hopeless than I thought.

"Are you following me?"

"You're a psycho. Anyone ever tell you that?"

"Are you texting me?"

"How much spare time do you think I have?"

"Your father is friends with Cain, right?"

His eyes narrow on me. "What are you accusing me of?"

"Are you sending me anonymous texts?"

"You're beyond hope, Winters," he mutters, knocking back the whisky in his glass.

"And you're pissed that I chose Alex."

"Delusional," he snorts, but I'm distracted by the unmistakable sound of a helicopter flying over.

God, no. Why now?

Whatever I wanted to say back gets stuck in my throat, blocking my airway.

I vaguely hear declarations of "Oh my god, she's really going to do it. She's going to lose it" and "Shawn, you're a dead man, mate."

It rattles my bones, that awful, jarring sound.

I stumble back through the ring of students watching us, trying to drag air into my lungs. My heart is beating so fast that it feels like it might give out, like it can't keep this rhythm for a minute longer.

Someone is filming. Someone asks me if I'm okay.

I stagger out the door and collapse against the wall outside. They're right about me. I am losing it. This place is my downfall. These people are my downfall.

I just want my dad.

* * *

I'VE HARDLY LEFT my room in two days. I've hardly moved a muscle. I haven't really eaten anything, either, except the four stale biscuits I found in my tote bag.

Instead, I've discovered *scrolling*.

Turns out, I can get off my high horse, because I'm not above getting addicted to short form content, after all.

I don't know how long I watch people making slime, falling over, cooking on weirdly big outdoor grills, making depressing, low calorie versions of my favorite foods. *Craving a cinnamon roll? Add a teaspoon of cinnamon into cottage cheese, it tastes the exact same*, the cheery blonde on my screen says to me.

Jesus Christ, life is bleak.

I'm halfway through watching a man trim a horse hoof when Colette calls, interrupting my fun.

I hit decline, opting instead to search Alex's name on various social media platforms to see if he's gone outside in short-shorts recently. Humble enough to scour the internet, too proud to say, *Hey, Alex, I need a picture of your thigh tattoos for scientific purposes.*

But when I search, it's me that comes up. My least favorite photo of myself, climbing out of the pool at that stupid swimming meet in Manchester.

At least the videos of my spectacular meltdown in the Cortinar halls have vanished.

I zoom in on the picture again, into the backs of my thighs. I'm convinced I don't really look like that. *Surely* I don't look like that.

The caption of the post says it better than I could.

Alex Corbeau-Green and this thing???? make it make sense.

I hate them. I hate everyone. My tears are angry, sliding down my cheeks that I'm sure must have valleys carved into them by now.

I forward it to Colette.

Ophelia

Help me to not look like this, please.

Colette

Pick up the phone, you idiotic fool

Ophelia

Let me wallow in peace

I hear rattling from the door a few minutes later.

I stay silent, refusing to escape the warmth of my duvet.

Except it just keeps going on. And I hear the handle being pushed down. More rattling. Handle again. Some frustrated cursing. Handle *again*.

But I just cannot be bothered to move. *Rest in peace, Ophelia—killed by the world's shittest burglar.*

Finally, the door unlocks, and I grab my mug, ready to throw it at the head of whoever comes through the door.

The door swings open, and I draw my hand back.

Colette shrieks, and I drop the mug onto the side table just in time. "Whoops. Sorry."

Concussion avoided, she crosses her arms and takes in the state of me. The biscuit wrapper, the pile of tea mugs. The tissues on the side table, the screwed-up cardboard from when I ran out of tissues and just used the box. "Good grief, Ophelia."

"Leave me alone."

"No. Absolutely not. Get up."

"Leave me alone!" I shout, and the false humor I try to inject into my voice doesn't even begin to cover the sadness.

Colette starts swanning around the place in her long, white trench coat and white fluffy hat, stuffing my belongings into a bag.

"What are you doing?"

"We're going for a girls' weekend! In London! It's going to be so fun. We'll get you some clothes, eat nice food, get away from Sorrowsong for a bit."

"No."

"Please? I'd love it, too. And it gives me an excuse to miss my weekend visiting my stepdad. He's . . . he's really found a second wind on the whole *choosing me a husband* thing."

"I'll be your husband."

"I'm very expensive," she says, putting her twenty-thousand-euro handbag onto my desk as though to prove her point.

"Count me out of the running, then."

She perches on the bed and opens up my phone, quickly deleting the screenshot of the nasty post about me, and closing down all my apps.

"Where will we stay?"

"I picked the *best* hotel, don't worry. I wouldn't put us up somewhere bad. The spa is one of the best."

"That's really, *really*, not what I'm worried about."

"It's my treat."

"*Colette.*"

"We're sharing a room, so it's like a sleepover! And we're stopping at a cute hotel in Sheffield, too."

She holds out her hand, all smooth, moisturized skin and baby pink nails. Reluctantly, I slide mine into hers and let her pull me out of my pit of despair.

Chapter 10

OPHELIA

I doubt any man has ever felt the relief that Eike feels as we pull up outside a posh hotel on the busy streets of central London.

He cuts the engine, and with that, his twenty-four-hour nightmare of two twenty-something-year-old women screeching the *Mamma Mia* soundtrack has come to a close.

For the millionth time, I wonder why he stays in this job. He can't be older than thirty-five, he's smart, good-looking, could probably get a job anywhere he wanted. And yet, he's spending his early thirties in a cold, damp castle with no social life, no family nearby, guarding the estranged daughter of some Luxembourgish billionaire.

But here I am, lingering at the very same castle for no real reason, so who am I to judge?

The hotel looks *nice*. The kind with smartly dressed men in earpieces stood on the steps and double doors that look straight out of a fairy tale. Eike rounds the car to open Colette's door, and a hotel employee clutching an umbrella opens mine, shielding me from the London drizzle. I go to grab my duffel bag out of the trunk, but Eike already has it, along with Colette's suitcase—large enough to fit a small elephant inside.

Eike ushers us into the lobby, all polished marble floors and soft velvet furnishings. I vaguely hear him tell us to stay put while he checks us in, but I'm distracted by my lavish surroundings. If there's one thing my lonely life has made me, it's nosy, and a hotel lobby is a feast for the senses. A couple argue at the check-in desk. An influencer is setting up a tripod in front of the lobby's water feature. A man with three bodyguards exits the lift.

Who are they all, and how do they have enough money to drop several thousand on a hotel night stay?

Colette comes from *old* money, Alex informs me. Like that matters. Everyone at Sorrowsong is preoccupied with exactly how old someone's money is. What they're not worried about is how someone's money came about. *It's fine if you did something heinous to earn your mansion, as long as you did it before color television was around*, seems to be the rule.

Eike materializes in front of us, his gruff voice drowning out the couple's argument I was straining so hard to hear. "Room is ready."

The journey to the hotel room is an adventure in itself, past not one, not two, but *three* restaurants, and the entrance to a huge gym, furnished in garish shades of gold. Colette doesn't seem fussed, typing on her phone as the click-clack of her heels comes to a stop outside four elevators. I take a leaf out of her book, snapping my mouth shut and giving my best nonchalant face.

I'm not in the right tax bracket to understand why we need an immaculately dressed man to press the elevator buttons for us, but it's a nice touch.

Our bags are already in our room when Colette swipes her key card and pushes the door open, kicking off her heels and diving onto the enormous bed. "Ooh, champagne in the mini fridge!" she cheers, starfishing over the crisp white duvet. "Shall we eat out? Or get room service? I haven't had a girls' weekend in *so* long."

I'm busy exploring the ridiculous suite, sniffing all the free toiletries. There are two rainfall showerheads, and my traitorous mind wanders to what it might be like to share a room like this with Alex.

I squash my errant thoughts down and step back into the bedroom, where Colette is pouring two flights of champagne. "Is Eike staying here, too?"

"Yeah, he has a room somewhere."

"How long has he worked for your stepfather?"

She takes a long sip and exhales like she's in heaven. "Umm . . . a year and a half. He used to do more . . . high-stakes stuff. I think he wanted something quieter."

I don't pry further. I don't think Eike is the sort of person to share much of his past with anyone, even Colette. I swipe the other champagne glass from the side table and join her in bed, taking a sip.

It's nice. Not as nice as orange juice or hot chocolate, but it's nice.

"We could get a pedicure?" she says, reeling off an endless list of details from the hotel's website while I switch on the TV to some trashy reality show that Vincenzo probably loves.

"What's going on with you and Vincenzo?" I blurt out.

"We're just friends," she says, easily.

"Right," I say, doubtfully. Her and Vincenzo seem to have some kind of agreement going on where he comes over and fucks her seven ways to Sunday most nights, and then they both pretend it didn't happen the next day. I know for a fact it's her who's holding it back, because Vincenzo is obsessed with her.

Her expression turns scandalous. "Like *you* can talk. What about you and Alex?"

"Umm . . . friends also."

Friends who do unspeakable things on FaceTime.

She nods slowly, tone sarcastic. "Yeah, sure."

"If you and Vin are just friends, Alex and I are, too."

She shakes her head at me as she finishes her first glass of champagne, grabbing the bottle to top us both up. "Nope. Vincenzo and I aren't in love. You and Alex are *soulmates*. You can't be friends with benefits and also soulmates. It doesn't work."

I watch the bubbles cling to the edge of my glass, heart sinking. She's not wrong. Alex and I both know this only ends in disaster, but neither of us has the willpower to stay away. "We can't be together; we can't be apart. I don't know what we're doing. Maybe in a few years we could work."

"You could be together."

"How?"

I watch the cogs in her brain turn, playing out each scenario. I pack up my whole life, give up on my degree and my new friendships, get on a plane, and move to New York? *No.* He moves his entire family to Scotland? *No.* He moves to the UK, leaving his family behind? *No.* We do it long distance, only seeing each other occasionally? *No.*

Her chest deflates. "Look . . . if there's no way for you to be together, whatever it is you're doing now is just going to make life harder on you both."

"I know. I tried to tell him that," I grumble, just as a text from Alex pings through on my phone.

Alex

Hey, Twist. How are you feeling? FaceTime?

With Colette's wisdom still fresh in the air between us, I type out a reply.

Ophelia

Sorry, I can't.

His reply is immediate, as always.

Alex

You okay? Did you sleep better last night?

I switch my phone to silent, pushing him out of my mind. I did sleep better last night, as I have every night since he started calling me right before I go to bed, reading aloud until I drift off into some lustful dream. But Colette is right. Alex's heart is broken enough, *my* heart is broken enough, and I'm playing with them.

No strings attached is the stupidest lie I've ever told.

I toss my phone across the room, finishing my second glass while Colette books us a pedicure each and orders two mimosas.

IT'S TWO IN the morning, and I am *easily* drunker than I have ever been in my life. I might throw up in this super luxury room.

My toenails look cute, though, and my feet are *so* smooth.

Colette slaps my phone out of my hand before I send a photo of my feet to Alex. "Girl, what are you doing?" she slurs, the end of each word melting into the beginning of the next.

"Fishing for compliments," I say, trying to grab it back. When I bend over, the whole world tilts on its axis. "Was that an earthquake?" I shriek.

"A drunkquake," she says, changing into her pajama shorts. "You don't need compliments; you're so pretty."

"Not according to everyone at Sorrowsong," I say, sticking out my bottom lip. The room service guy arrives with two pizzas, and I can't decide if I want to inhale them or gag.

She opens her box on the bed and folds a slice in half, eating it in one massive bite. "You're *so* pretty. They're just mean."

Oh no. I think I might be crying. Another text pings through from Alex.

Alex

I saw you last night, in my dream.

Ophelia

What was I doing?

Alex

I'd better not say.

My teeth sink into my bottom lip. Horny and sad has become the baseline for my moods of late. And Alex's, too, I imagine. I flop back onto the bed and shut my phone off before I can say something equally romantic back.

Alex

Don't go all quiet on me. If I've done something, let's talk about it.

The sob I let out is watery and embarrassing. I've never given my appearance a second thought, never cared about my eyes, my nose, my hips, my lower stomach. Not until the last few weeks, where I stand in front of the mirror and pick myself apart in a way I wouldn't dare to do to anyone else. "They say I'm bland and boring . . . I can't believe how I look in that photo."

"People say you're bland because they don't know the first thing about you." She's scrolling on her phone, pizza crust dangling from her pink lips when her face lights up. "Oh my *god*."

"What?"

"You should do this! It's in two days. It'd be perfect for your confidence!" She claps her hands, looking ten times more alive than she did a minute ago. She leaps out of bed like Charlie Bucket's grandfather, passing me the phone. I'm so drunk, the Instagram story looks like spaghetti to me.

I blink twice, slowly letting the letters shift back into a line.

Last minute life model needed due to cancellation. Paid opportunity.

"Absolutely *not*."

"My friend Jas did it, she said it literally *transformed* her confidence."

"I am not standing naked in front of a load of people. I have no idea if my nipples are normal. What if I have weird nipples, and *this* is how I find out?"

She crosses her arms, eyes dropping to my tank top. "Show me them."

"No!"

"You would be so good. You have that Aphrodite figure." Her eyes are so wide they might pop out of her head, nodding like a dashboard figurine. "I'll go with you!"

Six cocktails have me thinking maybe it's not the absolute worst idea. Maybe it *will* be empowering. Maybe my nipples *are* normal. Maybe they're particularly good ones.

This is the kind of thing every woman should do once in their life, I tell myself. Be a muse. So what if your nipples aren't normal, normal nipples are probably boring to draw. *Let the good people of London draw your weird nipples!*

"It *heally* relped . . . no . . . *really* helped . . . your friend?"

"Yeah!" she says, enthusiastically.

I blurt out a giggle of disbelief. "Okay, *fine*."

She cheers, dancing round the room like she's won the lottery. "I'll come with you! I'll cheer you on from the back. Maybe I'll meet a really hot artist!"

"And you can both live in the Loire Valley and run a painters' retreat!"

"And have cute babies," she adds, stumbling over.

I take a giant bite of the pizza. It's *incredible*.

This is a horrific idea.

Chapter 11

ALEX

I've never been a violent person, despite my father's best efforts. He tried to make me as angry at the world as he was, tried to make me turn my own self-hatred into little bullets to fire at others, but it's not really my style.

And yet, here I am, approximately two seconds away from putting my fist through my laptop screen.

I don't understand how, in this day and age, in this era of technology, of CCTV and electronic banking and border controls, my father can have been completely untraceable for two months.

We were homing in, we thought, we had two possible sightings and a blurry CCTV of someone checking into a cheap bed and breakfast in Boston, *not* New York, with fake documentation. But no. Neither turned out to be enough to determine whether it was him or not, and investigators found the bed and breakfast room empty, the fees paid in cash.

And now it's been six days since we've had anything at all, widening our search once more to the entire fucking globe.

I shouldn't be surprised. My father may be a nasty piece of work, but he's a clever one, a resourceful one, a wealthy one—frozen bank accounts or not. All he'd need to do is pawn off a couple of his rarest Breitlings and he'd be able to pay his way out of anything.

"This is *such* bullshit," I say, leaning back in my office chair. "Such a load of shit."

Mack rubs his stubble, shakily holding his phone in a car somewhere in Massachusetts. The FBI agent heading the case rubs her forehead. "We're going to get him."

She's said that on every phone call since early January, as has Mack. Each time they do, there's a little less belief in the words.

"What about the lead you had with Gerry Suarez?" One of my father's slimy buddies moved a private jet from New York to Boston two days ago, seemingly for no reason at all.

"The jet hasn't moved. They might know we're onto that trail. I'd guess they're holding their breath somewhere at the moment, but they'll have to surface."

I watch the time hit 2 p.m. in the corner of my screen. I'm going to be late to a hospital visit with my mother. She was admitted a few days ago, after one hell of an episode. The psychosis and the delusions we're getting better at managing, but it's the lack of eating, the painkillers, the pills, the side effects that have her shrinking into an unrecognizable woman.

Years of being picked at, poked at, told to be thinner. Catwalks and drug addiction and a son that appeared in her life earlier than she'd ever planned. A husband who let her down at every turn, six daughters in his desperate hope for a second son, a *better* son.

Maybe if I wasn't so—

"Alex? You with us?"

I scrub a hand over my mouth, steadying my breath. "I have to go. The next time we speak, you better have something more useful to tell me."

I cut off their *yes, sirs* by slamming my laptop lid shut, my mood sinking lower than I ever thought it could go.

Why am I in the office on a Saturday?

Depression may be a mental illness, but days like today it feels physical. Like it's tied heavy weights to my limbs, dulled the nerve endings in my brain, shrunk my rib cage so it's just a *little* too restrictive for my lungs.

But I have my mother's appointment today, and spaghetti night with the girls tomorrow, so I know I have to survive the next two days at least. Then I'll reassess.

I've never been a particularly anxious person, but I'm a nervous wreck as I make my way through the streets of lower Manhattan, sidewalks glossy with rain. I've never been religious, either, but I still find myself begging someone, anyone who is listening, to let my mother's days get easier.

I'm running late, but I'm also about to fall asleep standing up, so I swing into the café beside the hospital, hoping my sunglasses are enough to not have someone's phone pointed in my face and photos online by the time I pick up my order.

I bring up my emails and wait, staring at the long stream of unsent drafts to Ophelia.

I've got it *bad*.

A disturbance distracts my attention: a hooded figure shoving his way out the door.

He's tall. My height. Lean and athletic, and when his head turns to the side for just a second, I catch a glimpse of graying blond hair and *holy, shit, it's him.*

Discretion long abandoned, I push past the line of people waiting to order, flying out the doors and onto the street outside. It's Saturday afternoon in Manhattan; the streets are busy, faces obscured by umbrellas. I look left, right, left again, scanning over what feels like an endless sea of people.

I spot the figure hurrying across a crosswalk and make a run for it, barging through groups of tourists and shoppers, and it all comes to the surface, the anger, the disgust, the bitter hatred. I clamp a palm onto his shoulder, forcing him to face me, forcing him to look me in the eyes when I—

Fuck.

It's not my father.

He has blue eyes and an eastern European accent. His hair isn't really graying at all. "What the fuck, man?"

Back to square one. I open my mouth to reply as horns sound from the waiting traffic, but I have nothing to say. He yanks himself away from me, disappearing into the busy street and leaving me and my thundering heart in the middle of the road.

I'M STILL SHAKEN when I reach the hospital, but I force my panic into a box for my mother's sake. She's sitting up in bed and looks brighter than she did a few days ago, and the relief must be visible on my face because she rolls her eyes at me. "You saw me *last night*, Alex."

"I know, it's just good to see you."

I take the seat beside the bed, letting her hand rest in mine while both the doctors talk to me about how she's doing, and about the new antipsychotics they're trialing. And though my mother and I promised ourselves we'd stop getting our hopes up a long time ago, it does all sound positive.

A dangerous little seed of hope plants itself in one of the holes in my heart.

I watch my mother complete some simple exercises, sorting blocks into color groups and some memory tests. She swallows her pills and rests back on the pillows, squeezing my hand. "How is Ophelia?"

The doctors leave us to it, happy that my mother can continue her recovery from home after dinnertime. "She's . . . good, I think. I don't know. She's gone silent on me. I guess I haven't exactly given her the impression of a reliable boyfriend these past few months."

I'm trying to convince Ophelia not to give up on love, to give us a chance. I FaceTime her in the evenings, read too far into every little word she says, get my hopes up every time she laughs.

My heart builds castles out of the little crumbs she leaves me, spins whole futures out of the smallest of smiles. I bend and shape the things she says into what I want to hear, because a future without her feels unmanageable.

Mom shakily picks up one of the raspberries I brought for her. "Oh no. Silence means she's overthinking."

"Ophelia is always overthinking."

"Better than underthinking. Your father is an underthinker."

I grin down at her. "That man hasn't had a solid thought in years."

Then we're both laughing at a situation we really shouldn't be laughing at, exchanging increasingly creative insults for my father.

My phone lights up with a FaceTime call from Vincenzo.

"Pick up. I don't mind."

His face fills the screen, complete with a shit-eating grin. He's up to something. He's in his Sorrowsong rugby jersey, a heavy black sky hanging low over his head.

I miss rugby. I only started it because Vincenzo asked me to, but now I find myself wanting to get back to it. He peers in closer. "Where are you?"

I pan the camera around the room, and my mom gives Vincenzo a little wave.

"Woah," he says, when I turn the camera back around so he can see us. "Is that . . . surely it can't be . . . is that the most beautiful woman in the world?"

"That's my mother, you dick," I say, but *Maman* is laughing. Her cheeks are pink, like Vincenzo might have just made her whole month.

His chest shakes with laughter, enjoying riling me up. "How's it going, Elise?"

"Apparently, I'm doing good. You look suspicious."

"It's because I have some information Alex is *really* going to want."

I tilt the phone back to me, mind racing. "What?"

"What's in it for me?"

"What is it about?"

"A certain ginger girl."

"Tell me."

"Fine, but you have to put in a good word about me to Colette, okay? She's still not sold on us."

Terrible idea, but I nod. I'd probably give him my left ball for a snippet of information on Ophelia if he wanted it. "Deal."

"She's in London on a girls' weekend with Colette, and she's doing that naked modeling thing at an art class tomorrow night," he says, practically hopping from foot to foot with excitement.

The sounds of a busy ward outside slow to a dull ringing in my ears. "She's *what*?"

"Colette rang me, absolutely *wasted*, last night and told me all about it. It's called *life* drawing, apparently."

"I know what fucking life drawing is," I snap, knuckles white around the phone. "Where is the class? What time?"

Vincenzo howls with laughter. "I *knew* you'd lose your shit over this. *Just friends*, my ass."

"I'm not losing my shit over it," I grit out. I am absolutely, categorically, most definitely losing my shit over this, for no good reason. Ophelia is an adult. She can try new things. I've sketched from a live model several times. I know better than anyone that there's nothing sexual about it.

Yet, the idea of a room full of people looking at her, taking note of the small intricacies of her body, the soft smattering of stretch marks on her outer thighs, the gentle dip of her hips . . . it's turning me into a different man. A jealous man. An *unreasonable* man.

It's so unlike her. In fact, I'd say it sounds like her worst nightmare.

"Tell me where it is, Vincenzo."

He strokes his chin. "Elise, what do you reckon? Are they *just friends*?"

My traitorous mother hums beside me, tone so sarcastic that it's very obvious where Fleur gets it from. "I'm not sure, Vincenzo, it's just *so* hard to tell."

I'm one second away from raising my voice—which I *never* do—when a link pings through from Vincenzo at the top of my screen, saving his life. "Gotta go," I say, hanging up.

"I *knew* it."

"Don't you start," I say, to my very smug mother, opening up the link to the event. "I'm just . . . making sure she's not made a mistake is all. Looking after her."

"Is that what you kids call it nowadays?"

I grind my teeth, staring down at the event description. It's tomorrow night in Camden. I'd barely get there in time.

I shut my eyes, trying to be rational.

There is absolutely zero reason for me to fly to London. Or intervene. Or even be bothered about this.

A soft hand lands on mine. It's a hand I know better than my own. It has rested on top of my fingers at every twist and turn of my life. When my vision has blurred from tears, when life has felt unlivable, when I've bled at the hands of my father, when nightmares rocked my sleep as a child. "You should go, Alex."

I pull my hand away and let my head drop to the crook of my elbows, fingers interlacing behind my head. "I really shouldn't."

"Your brain deprives you of the best things in life."

"I won't be able to make her happy. She wants someone present, not someone like me."

"Who wins the Super Bowl next year? I'll put a bet on them."

"What?"

"Tell me who'll win the Super Bowl, since you seem so confident you can predict the future?"

"*Maman.*"

"No, Alex. I'm sane enough to know she's right for you. You're depriving yourself of a chance at something beautiful because there's a possibility it won't work. And all the while, you're always asking me to try new pills even though we both know the odds are stacked against me."

Fuck. She's right. I'm not setting a good example for her. "I'm scared," I whisper, finally admitting it out loud. "Scared I'll lose her all over again, scared I won't recover from it."

"Love is maddening, Alex. It's sickening, frightening, embarrassing, depressing. It turns us into the people we swore we'd never be. When I first held you in my arms, I felt terrified. I felt like my heart was walking outside of my body, and I'd have to send that heart to school, to football practice, to Vincenzo's house, and trust it would come home to me safely. If you're not absolutely terrified, you're not doing it right."

"But we'd have to be long distance, and if she gets hurt and I'm not able to get to her, I'll lose my mind."

"You haven't proved to her that you can manage long distance very well. She's probably worried you'll run if something bad comes up again. You need to win her over. We want you to be happy. We want you to choose yourself, to go to her. You don't have to drop everything and run to us all the time. We have staff to help."

Her fingers tangle in my hair, and oh *God*, I can't imagine how I'll survive my mother's death when it comes.

"Back in five," I grumble, through the stinging behind my eyes, leaving my mother's triumphant smile behind to step into the hallway.

"If I had any updates, I'd have called you," Brendan grunts, picking up on the first ring.

"I need a favor."

"Is it legal?"

"No, probably not."

"Color me intrigued. Is it a hacking job?"

"There's an event in London that's sold out. I want everyone's tickets refunded, canceled, then I want all the tickets for myself."

"How big are we talking? If this is a concert, you'll never get away with it."

"It's small. It's . . . Ophelia is . . . don't worry about what it is, I'm sending you a link now."

He's silent on the other end of the line, but I can imagine him shoving his too-thick glasses up his nose, leaning in.

He hums cheerfully. "Man, this is a shit website. Yeah, easy enough."

"Thanks. Bill me for it now."

"On the house."

"Not your usual style."

"Yeah, but you need a girlfriend, and I'm a hopeless romantic."

This is news to me. I don't think he's ever been on a date in his life. "Are you?"

"Nah. Just sick of your shitty moods. I'll text you when it's done. Bye."

The line drops before I can say goodbye. I text my team to tell them I'll be in London for a couple of nights, then call the housekeeper, nannies, and security team, too.

My mother is asleep when I get back to the room, and she looks so peaceful that I don't dare wake her. I text the sibling group chat.

Alex

I'm heading to London overnight tonight. I'll be back as soon as possible. Ingrid, Erin, and Emily will all be with you, and the security guys, obviously.

Evie

What's in London?

Mia

Does it rhyme with schmophelia?

Élé

WE KNEW IT!!!

Mia

CEO of an airline and he's completely in shambles over a girl

Evie

loool so true

Fleur

Are we talking about the girl who put so much shit about us into a news article? Don't you guys care about that?

My stomach sinks. Fleur couldn't be any less approving of Ophelia.

Mia
Hey, if Ophelia's article is what it took to finally get Dad to fuck off, I'll take it.

Evie
Agreed

Alex
Watch your language in group chats. M. Élé is twelve.

Élé
I know WAY worse words than fuck

Fantastic.

Alex
Bringing Mom home in a couple hours. She'd love to see you all.

I lean back in the uncomfortable chair, book myself a flight for late tonight, and attempt to pull together some kind of speech to give to Ophelia.

My mom's words have batted away the fog of doubt that's kept me holding back. Ophelia is mine. She's mine in a way that has made me start to believe in fate. In a way that makes me think that maybe, *just maybe*, there's a brighter future laid out for me that runs alongside the darker one.

I have a strong feeling I'm at the crossroads where I choose one.

I call Ophelia, but it goes to voicemail, so I fire off a shameless sixth unanswered text.

Alex

Call me

Finally, I get a reply.

Ophelia

We should talk, but I'm not ready for it yet. I'm at a Colette with bar and Eike.

Ophelia

Hahaha

Ophelia

I meant I'm at a bar

Ophelia

With Colette

Ophelia

And Eike

No, no, no.

Alex
Call me, sweetheart.

Ophelia
Does this hurt your heart more than it feels good?

Alex
Call me.

Ophelia
We're doomed, Alex

My sweet, lonely, pessimistic, drunk girl. I want to be the reason she learns to have faith in the world again. I feel like I've turned a corner. Like we can be together and figure out the distance and the baggage later.

Alex
We're fated, Ophelia.

Ophelia
Fated for dooooom.

Alex
Fated for an old dusty cottage, where I can watch you do crosswords until your hair turns white.

Ophelia

There aren't cottages in New York City

Alex

Who said anything about New York?

Ophelia

I'll call you on Monday when I'm back at
Sorrowsong, ok????

I pack my mother's things into a bag, wondering why, after a life in a house with seven women, I'm no closer to understanding what goes on inside their heads.

Chapter 12

OPHELIA

Colette's commitment to an iced latte knows no bounds.

She sips hers through a lipstick-stained paper straw while I cup my giant mug of tea, watching the rain trickle down the windows of a quiet café in Covent Garden. The temperature in London may be flirting with single digits, and the UV index might've somehow worked its way into the negatives, but Colette is sporting a miniskirt and sunglasses. She's got those narrow-framed ones that only someone like her could pull off, balanced precariously on top of her head as she sighs happily into her drink.

Eike sits quietly on the table behind us, reading a thriller with his earphones in.

The idea of a shopping day had filled me with dread, but when Colette said she could work with *any* budget, she really meant it. A morning spent traipsing along the racks of London's dustiest charity shops has left me with two pretty dresses, a new skirt, jeans that actually fit me, and two new knitted jumpers, all for less than the single cocktail I bought at the bar last night.

Colette's phone pings on the table in front of us, prompting us both to lean over to look at it. It's morbid curiosity on my part; the texts Vincenzo sends her are beyond filthy. I have to google half the things I see in them. But it's not Vincenzo. It's an address, sent from an unsaved number.

She looks at me warily, and worry trickles down my spine. I turn around and scan the café, just in case. I've had such a busy couple of days, I almost forgot about my stalker. "Don't open it."

"You think it's from . . . oh my god. How did they get my number? What if they know what hotel we're at?"

Eike pulls out both earphones and is at our side in a split second. "What is it?"

"Someone sent Colette an address."

"We're too scared to open it."

Just as I finish speaking, a second text pings through. We stare at the phone like it might be about to blow up.

Here's the address for today. Thanks soooo much for this, cannot tell you how much we appreciate it! It's a sold out event and it'd be so sad to cancel! Clemmie x

Colette picks up the phone, frowning. "Did I book us in for something? Volunteering?"

"I don't know. I don't remember."

Her pink nails tap at the screen, expression pensive. Eike is stressing me out, pumping out tension like a radiator where he hovers over us. Colette's pink flush drains away, her face pale.

"What is it?"

"Okay, Ophelia," she says, like someone trying to talk down a wolf.

"What is it?"

"I need you to not freak out."

Obviously, I'm going to freak out. I've never successfully *not* freaked out. "Tell me."

"Oh God," she says, dragging both hands down her face in a way that is *so* unlike her. She's smudged her makeup, so I know it must be *bad*.

"I'm freaking out."

"Oh God," she repeats. "Oh God."

"Eike, hit her reset button, she's malfunctioning."

"Shit, Ophelia," she mutters, and now I really am worried, because she *never* swears. If it's skydiving, I'll lose my shit. "It's all coming back to me."

I place my clammy palms on her narrow shoulders and give her a gentle shake. "What is it?"

"We signed you up to be the model for a one of those naked drawing classes."

Skydiving would've been alright, actually.

And just like that, little fragments of Thursday night come back to me. Three mimosas at the spa, a bottle of champagne from the hotel room minibar, a cocktail from room service. The pizza. The life drawing.

Eike heads to the counter to fill a glass of water and sets it in front of me.

Colette is staring at me, worried. "Say something, Ophelia."

My voice sounds far away. "Eike, if you could just . . . run me over with the car . . ."

"Okay, I'm sure we can cancel."

I snatch her phone from her hand and dial the number. If I have to conquer my introvert fear of rejecting people to conquer my other introvert fear of literally baring my asshole to a room full of artsy Londoners, so be it.

A bright, airy voice chimes through the speaker. "Hello, Clementine speaking."

Bloody hell. Of course her name is Clementine. "Uhh, hi, Clementine. It's Ophelia, the model for today."

"Hi, darling! It's *so* good of you to volunteer. Every single ticket sold!" she squeaks, delighted.

"Yeah . . . about that . . . I'm so sorry."

"Are you having second thoughts? That's totally normal."

I'm way beyond second thoughts. I'm in double-digit number of thoughts. "I was drunk when I signed up, and I am *really* not the right person for the job."

"It'll be so good for your confidence. It's really empowering."

I don't think me on a table, sucking in my stomach and covered in goose bumps like a raw supermarket chicken is going to be empowering. "I'm not so sure."

Her breathing sounds a bit stressed now. Like she's imagining ringing each guest and telling them not to travel to the event. Now *I'm* overthinking it. What if someone has come from afar? What if this life drawing class is someone's dream birthday activity? "Do I have to be naked?"

"What if we just covered a few bits with a sheet?"

"Yeah, but—"

"Yay! Thank you so much. You're going to be so perfect. I'll see you in a couple of hours."

The line goes dead.

Colette holds both her hands out in a *well?* motion. "Did you cancel?"

"No."

"No?" they both repeat.

Even Eike looks like he's worried I'm having some sort of meltdown. "What now?"

"I dig a hole and crawl inside it, obviously." I fold my arms on the table and drop my forehead onto them, letting out a mangled cry.

"Okay, well, let's look at the positives."

"Such as?" I snap.

Colette comes up blank. Eike peers over at the website listing of the event. "Free cocktail on arrival?" he offers, and it does make me laugh, only because Eike says an average of 2.5 words per day.

I push the wooden chair back and stand. "Let's find a pub. I need something stronger than tea if I'm actually going to do this."

DESPITE MY DESPERATE pleas for just a tiny little non-serious road traffic accident on the way to the event, Eike's driving remains as smooth as ever. He pulls up outside what looks like a smart Victorian townhouse, rounding the car to open the door for Colette and me.

"I didn't even shave my armpits," I whisper, as Eike heads up the three stone steps to open the door for us.

"Like a goddess," chirps Colette, cheerfully. She's offered to do this with me about a hundred times, but I think Colette is famous enough that it somehow might get back to her too-strict stepfather.

"I'll wait in the car nearby," grumbles Eike, voice so deep I can barely hear. "Text me when you're done, Colette."

"Thank you," she says, taking my hand as we walk inside.

The small entryway is dimly lit, a giant pinboard to my left with flyers for all the other events that happen here: kids clubs, Pilates classes, food banks, steel drum workshops. It smells like embarrassment and humiliation and a future viral video entitled "Ginger Life Model Mental Breakdown HD Full Version."

Okay, it smells like some sort of incense, but still.

I feel sick.

A door at the end of the empty hallway swings open, and *wow*, Clementine is exactly as I pictured her. She's in patchwork floaty pants and a sports bra, and the tote bag slung over her shoulder reads *big clit energy*. "Oh my gosh." She spins me around in delight. "You're the *perfect* model. You'll be brilliant."

She ushers me into a small classroom where seven easels are arranged in a circle around a chaise longue.

Oh God. I can't do this.

"It's a very casual event, bring your own drink, play music, that sort of thing. I can stay or leave—whatever makes you comfortable."

"Um, maybe you could leave?" I say, like eight strangers seeing my weird (still to be determined) nipples is somehow any worse than seven.

"Of course!" She leaves a fluffy dressing gown and a sheet for me, turning up the thermostat just a little and lighting a couple of candles.

"I think I might throw up," I say, once we're alone.

Colette folds me into a warm hug. She smells like flowers and clean linen and unwavering belief in me. "I'm so proud of you."

I don't want to undress, but the idea of having to do it after everyone has already arrived, each of them awkwardly watching me hop around while trying to get a sock off and fiddling with the sheet is *so* much worse that I shrug off my cardigan and step out of my boots and dress.

I can hardly even look at Colette, scurrying to grab the sheet as I sit on the chaise and wrap it around my shoulders. "Shall we leave?"

"No. You're doing this, and then we're going out to celebrate. We can get fries."

"Chips. Proper pub chips. Triple-cooked chips."

"Triple-cooked? Like . . . burned?"

"Oh my god. You haven't lived."

"Okay, deal. I'll get us triple chips, or whatever."

I lie back like that girl in the *Titanic* movie, letting Colette tastefully drape white fabric over my hips and breasts. She bites her lip to suppress a grin. "You look *so* good."

"Somehow, I doubt that."

Chapter 13

OPHELIA

When, three minutes past the start time of the class, not a single person has shown up, I should feel maybe a *little* disappointed, but what courses through me is pure relief.

"Maybe no one is coming?" I say to Colette's disheartened expression.

The sound of the main door opening and closing echoes loud and clear in the empty hall. I shut my eyes, a fresh wave of dread engulfing me. "*Why* did I say that?"

Muffled voices sound from outside the door to the hall. I sit there in silence, like I'm awaiting execution.

The door to the hall opens. I can't even bring myself to look, my whole body turning pink with embarrassment. The sheet is too small, my skin too exposed. The goose bumps on my arm are almost painful.

This was a bad idea.

"Um . . . Ophelia," whispers Colette, from behind me. The edge to her voice makes me snap my eyes up.

Green. Bright green, like fresh rain on the English countryside.

It's a shade of green I'd know anywhere.

Alex looks at me from the doorway, dark hair wet from the rain. Seven tickets dangle from the hand at his side. His lips are parted, breathless. The shirt that clings to his frame is damp.

He's *devastating*.

"Alex," I whisper. It comes out like a question, like a request, like a desperate prayer. I don't even know what I'm asking him for. *Leave me alone. Don't you dare walk away. Give me space. Let me love you forever. Don't touch me. Touch me everywhere.*

I don't think he's noticed that Colette is here. He's holding my gaze in such a way that I'm not sure he's even noticed that I'm naked, either.

The silence unravels between us like a thread pulled too tight until, finally, he snaps it. His voice is hoarse, thick with emotion. "I'm really, *really* in love with you, Ophelia Winters."

I love him so much it feels like a sickness.

Colette slips out the door behind him. The hinges creak closed, and then we're alone.

"I was going to call you."

"You were going to end things."

"I just . . . you have enough things, Alex, and I'm just one more thing. A long-distance relationship is just one more thing."

"You're *everything*."

He's got it the wrong way round. *He* is everything. He's the light at the end of the tunnel, the fireplace in a cold house. He deserves better than *bland and boring* and never-ending jet lag for a girl he'll only see a couple of times a year.

I go to move, but he shakes his head. "I've paid for this session."

"You have to be kidding."

"London is expensive. I want my drawing practice."

"Alex, you could buy this whole building if you wanted to."

"Good thing I don't want to, then," he says, dropping his duffel. My heartbeat is a dull, syrupy thud in my chest as he strides over to the table of cocktails, picks one up, and walks over to me.

The few precious inches between us don't stop the heat from his skin from warming my own, his presence a balm over my tender flesh. The rim of the glass is ice cool when he presses it to my bottom lip.

I say nothing. I *do* nothing, stunned speechless by his arrival, his appearance, the hunger in his eye unlike anything I've ever seen before. "Now, now, Ophelia," he drawls, hooking his thumb between my lips to part them. "Closed mouths don't get fed."

Holy *shit*. I shut my eyes, trying to block him out. I need to keep my head together around him, and whatever it is he's doing here has scattered it into a hundred pieces between here and Tower Bridge.

A drop of sweet, sharp liquid lands on my tongue, passion fruit and vodka and undiluted lust. His familiar scent wraps around me like a cocoon, warm and welcoming. He leans in, so close I think he might be about to kiss me, but his lips bypass my own, stopping at the shell of my ear. The only solace I have from the embarrassment of being more turned on than I have ever been in my life is the fact that I can see that he is, too. "I paid one hundred and forty pounds for the privilege of drawing the most beautiful woman in the world, and I *hate* wasting money."

With that, he's gone, cold air rushing in to fill the void he left. I stare at his muscular back, watching him pick out colored pastels from the boxes beside the cocktails.

"You live in New York now," is all I can choke out, once I finally find my voice. He straddles a stool in front of the first easel, rolling up the sleeves of his white shirt, and *Jesus Christ*, I have to look away. I could get lost in those thighs.

"I'd live anywhere with you," he says, over the soft sound of pastel on paper.

"But you can't."

"No, not yet. But once I've left Green."

"You have enough on your plate. I can be difficult."

"You're the easiest decision I've ever made."

"You deserve better."

"We deserve each other."

"I'm bland and boring."

"You're every color I've been missing."

I stare down at the white sheet that covers my pale chest, licking a salty tear from my upper lip. "I'm scared we'll lose each other again, that the distance will eat us alive."

"So am I."

"And that doesn't bother you?"

"It bothers me less than the idea of a life without you."

I stew on his words while he sketches. That's it in a nutshell, so succinctly put. I've overthought it so much, I've forgotten that all of this boils down to a simple decision. Life without him in it, or a future together.

And I don't know whether it's the look in his eye, the vulnerability of my position, or the fact that he's here in front of me, but I feel the churning cogs in my mind slow down. I feel my overactive brain roll toward a decision.

I'd rather be terrified at his side, than fearless and alone. My smile is watery. "You really want to watch me do crosswords until I'm old and gray?"

His hand flies across the paper, but he's looking at me. "It's everything I want, Twist."

"I want it, too. But—"

"We'll figure out the logistics another day."

"I get stalked like it's an Olympic sport."

He stifles a yawn, the corners of his mouth tipping up in a boyish grin. "Boring. Stalkers are boring."

"Not when they're trying to stop us getting a happy ending."

"They're *especially* boring then. Your stalker, my mom, the girls, your fear of flying, the distance, my father, the media. We'll figure it all out."

I wave my hand, like these are just tiny things and not the giant obstacles most couples split up over. "Minor semantics."

He laughs. It's hoarse and genuine and happy. "*Now* you're getting it. We're young and stupid, but I know we'll work it out."

He stands, admiring his handiwork. I sit up, but he pins me with a glare, sliding onto the stool for the second easel. "What are you doing?"

"Seven tickets. Seven drawings."

"There's only so many times I can watch you straddle that stool and keep breathing."

He sketches the next one in silence, and the next. I understand why he'd watch me do crosswords until we're too old to remember each other's names, because I could watch him do this until the sun sets on this miserable planet for the final time.

He swipes the excess white chalk on his finger over the corded muscle of his forearm, a muted rainbow of oranges and blues and pinks across his raven tattoos.

We're doing this, giving this a real try. The excitement outweighs the terror.

The moan that slips past my lips when he sits on the stool again has him adjusting his slacks, eyes blazing. "You're dirty, Ophelia."

"And the thoughts running through your head right now are perfectly innocent?"

"If I spoke my current thoughts about you out loud, that church across the road would burst into flames."

I press my thighs together, praying he won't notice. Obviously he notices; I'm fucking *naked*. "So fuck me then."

His hand freezes on the fifth sheet of paper, like he didn't expect that from me. But I'm desperate, wanting, yearning to feel his callused palms skate along my hips, the gentle nip of his teeth over the skin that covers my pulse, the unthinkable things he whispers when he's buried deep inside me.

It's been *months*.

"And waste two tickets?"

"Fuck the tickets."

He kisses his teeth, humming thoughtfully. "Might not feel as good as you."

"*Alex*."

He smiles fondly, sketching as though he has all the time in the world. "Seven letters, first letter *O*. *The sun, the moon, the world, and everything in it.*"

I'm so breathless, so needy that it's embarrassing. "Four letters, first letter *A. Somebody help, he's torturing me.*"

"The torturing part comes later."

I slide my hand down my lower stomach, sick of waiting. He puts down the chalk. "Don't you dare. I'll draw twice as slow."

My cry of frustration is strangled, head tipped back against the red velvet.

After fifteen minutes that feel like fifteen hours, he takes pity on me and stops after the sixth drawing, pacing a slow circle around the easels. He spins the first one, and there I am, formed of messy, muted lines. My skin is pale, but my hair is a fiery red. I'm draped across the chaise, and maybe Colette was right, maybe I *do* look beautiful, because he's certainly made it look that way.

"Alex," I whisper, swallowing the lump of emotion in my throat.

He takes my hand, tugging me to my feet. The sheet drops to the floor between us, and I fight the instinctive urge to cover myself. He sucks in a sharp breath, both hands in his hair like he has to touch something, *anything*, that isn't me, and suddenly, I'm on Clemmie's side.

This *is* empowering.

He tugs me to the second easel, and there I am again, but not on a chaise, not in a hall in rainy Camden. I'm in the back of a car, holding a cup of noodles between both hands beneath a string of Christmas lights.

My breath is caught in my throat, any clever comments I had planned long forgotten as he walks me from easel to easel. I'm floating on my back in water, hair spread around me like swirling flames. I'm sitting on a bed, facing away from him. I'm biting the end of a pen, frowning down at a crossword. I'm showering, head tipped back against the spray. He's left in the soft swell of my lower stomach, the pale stretch marks on my hip.

And then I'm blurred through my own tears, a soft hand cupping the back of my neck as I stare at the artworks in front of us.

"I know you're worried I'll panic and leave you again when things get hard. I haven't exactly proved otherwise," he says, thumb tracing a line between my shoulder blades. "I know you're worried about long distance, that it'll stretch our strings too far. I'm so sorry I let you believe that."

I drop my head, but a gentle finger tilts my chin up and to the left so I'm looking at him when I speak. "I just don't want this not to be enough. I don't want you to forget me."

"I don't need you in front of me, Ophelia. I don't need you as a model. I know the curves of your waist better than the hallways of my own home. I could draw you in any lifetime, together or apart. I haven't produced a drawing since January that isn't you in some way or another. If we have to be long distance, I know I could do it, because you're never further from me than my pencil."

I bury my head in his chest and let an unapologetic sob hiccup its way out of my throat. I've never needed to thicken my skin around him.

To be loved by Alex Corbeau-Green is unlike anything I've ever known.

He steers us to the final easel, lowering onto the stool. He pulls away, those tortured eyes regarding me through messy hair in need of a trim.

His eyes drop down to my lips, his tongue running a slow line behind his teeth. We haven't kissed yet, but he's hard beneath his dark jeans, practically vibrating with want.

It's too much, too hot, too tempting. I've lost control of my pulse, my self-control is abandoned at the bottom of the Thames. I thread my fingers through his hair and straddle him where he sits. His groan is animalistic. "I think Tangerine is standing outside."

"Clementine?"

"Satsuma?"

I wriggle my hips against his, impatient. "Are you gonna keep naming soft fruits all evening?"

I can't remember the last time he smiled like this. Like the weights that burden his shoulders all day have been temporarily set down. "I wouldn't go *raisin* your blood pressure like that."

"Alex!"

His laugh echoes around the hall, a little blush forming on his cheeks. I fall in love all over again, ridiculing the girl inside me who thought *no strings* would last. He sighs, expression sobering as he regards me like I put the moon in the sky and arranged the stars around it, just for him. "I'm pretty sure she's listening outside."

I run my fingers over his chest, worried he's not real. Maybe Clementine murdered me with her giant kombucha bottle, and this is the afterlife. Maybe Eike *is* a dangerous driver. "I don't care."

His hands on me are shameless and clumsy, flying from my waist to my hips to my breasts to my thighs like he can't quite believe I'm here, either. His thumb traces over my lips, pupils so dilated that his eyes are an inky abyss. "Can you be quiet, Ophelia?"

"Can *you*?"

A breathless laugh tickles my throat. His hands move dangerously close to the top of my thighs, scorching a path across the freckled skin. "I wouldn't have thought so, no."

His fingers dip between my legs, spare hand steadying my waist.

My head tilts back, his name a desperate gasp between my lips. He guides my legs farther apart, skillful fingers sinking into me to ease an ache that has plagued my nights for so long.

It's different now; there are no secrets weighing down the back of my mind; we're not trying to cram too-big feelings into a friendship-sized box. My heart is in his hands, and his in mine.

His fingers brush my clit, lips tracing my collarbone, and while his actions may feel sinful, his words feel anything but. His words are worship.

"I can't live without you, Ophelia," he breathes, against my pale skin. "Not in this lifetime, not in the next."

"You've gone all philosophical on me."

His tongue grazes my nipple, and there's no way Clementine doesn't hear the soft moan that echoes around the empty hall. "Well, you've given me hope for the future."

My fingers fumble with his top few buttons until more of his skin is exposed to me. I breathe in his scent, letting him fill every inch of my lungs. The rush of euphoria that follows is dizzying. "And you've made me stronger than my past."

My fingers flex over the zipper of his dark jeans. His breath catches in his throat, giving way to a quiet whimper. It's my undoing. "And you're going to make me a one-minute man."

I laugh, slightly grateful for the turn to less emotional conversation. The last thing I need is to start crying during hot makeup sex. There has to be at least *one* event in my year that I don't cry through.

His fingers move faster inside me, thumb circling my clit. A long thread of warmth unravels in my abdomen, forehead dropping to his shoulder. His spare hand splays over my stomach, both of us covered in differently colored streaks of chalky pastel.

"This is how my dreams go," he whispers. "Every night, this is how they go."

We're an artwork of his creation, messy lines that form something wonderful in all the chaos.

"Fuck, fuck, I'm gonna—"

He stops abruptly, pushing me off the stool, and I think maybe he's as close as I am, just from a few touches. "Jesus *Christ*, Ophelia. Turn around."

I do as he says, turning to face the blank canvas. His breaths are heaving when he reaches around me and grabs two of the pastels. The fabric of his jeans is rough against the sensitive skin at the back of my thighs, every graze of his shirt against my arms sending a jolt of electricity down my spine.

He swipes the colored pastels over my hands in long, languid strokes, unhurried even as the evidence of his desire presses into my lower back. A shudder racks my body, the sheer weight of the anticipation between us almost too much to bear.

A soft kiss lands on my neck; a strangled curse floats over my shoulder. Two large hands drag my hips back just enough that I have to splay my hands over the blank paper to steady myself. Brown and orange handprints mar the pristine white page.

Alex's voice is husky in my ear, breath thawing the cold shell I've spent so many years building around my skin. "Paint me a picture while I fuck you, Ophelia."

The noise that escapes me is embarrassing: a moan and a garbled version of his name trying to escape at once. Orange claw marks rake over the paper as I fight to keep my balance. Alex traces his thumb down the dip of my spine, murmuring a string of muttered French.

He seems keen to take his time, to drink in every detail of this moment, hands kneading the skin of my back like he's a sculptor and I'm the prize in his collection.

But I'm more of a *fuck now, examine each other's vertebrae later* sort of girl.

"What's the hold up?" I demand, voice edged with desperation. He's dragging this out just to watch me squirm. "Stuck in traffic, or something?"

He laughs in disbelief, wrapping a handful of my hair around his fist, forcing me to look up at the mess I've already made of the paper. Tears prick my eyes, every sense on high alert. His hands on my waist are red hot, branding his fingerprints into my skin, and suddenly I'm delirious with need, a frantic longing to be *his* again. The word *please* slips through my lips like a chant.

"Ophelia, baby. You've got yourself all worked up."

One more *please* slips past my lips, and then he slams his hips forward, one hand on my waist, one on my shoulder to stop me flying into the easel in front of us.

He's everything, *everywhere*. The eye of the storm, the calm in the chaos. The pleasure in a lifetime of pain. Neither of us is quiet. I cry out his name, he whispers a broken *thank you*, like he's been drowning for weeks, and he's just been given a lifeline.

And for the first time since the beginning of the year, I can see land after so long at sea.

Chapter 14

ALEX

If Ophelia wasn't so worried about Clementine walking in, I'd have kept her in that hall all night.

"One down, eleven letters, first letter *M*," I straighten her up to place a kiss between her shoulder blades. She smells like coffee and fireplaces and something so uniquely *her*. "*An outstanding piece of art, our finest creation.*"

"A masterpiece," she breathes, on a laugh. The paper in front of us is damning evidence of our transgressions, littered with orange and brown handprints, smudges, *claw marks* from Ophelia's delicate fingers.

It's priceless.

I divert my eyes from it before I bend her over all over again. I turn her to face me, tucking a wayward copper wave behind her ear. Her freckles are lost in her flush, whisky-brown eyes wide and watery when she breaks the tranquil silence. "I love you."

"I love you, too."

I gather all seven drawings, treating the final one with extra care while she quietly dresses behind me. The silence isn't awkward; it isn't full of unspoken words and stifling tension like that day in my car. It's contented and comfortable, like we're right where we should be.

When I turn, Ophelia is in some sort of long, strappy sundress, green and floral and paired with thick tights and boots. The straps are thin, neckline low. I rub a hand over my mouth, trying to think of something to say that isn't wholly inappropriate for such a sweet moment. "That's a new dress."

My voice sounds strained, cracking on the final word like I'm fourteen years old. She notices, of course, laughing at me like I'm an idiot. I *am* an idiot. "It was two pounds from the charity shop."

She bends to tie her laces, stretching the thin cotton that covers her ass. I almost lose my mind. "It looks good. *You* look good."

A little smile creeps onto her face, and she swishes it at me, doing half a twirl like she might be starting to see herself the way I see her. Her confidence is recovering, small but steady. It makes my mood buoyant. "Colette picked it out for me."

I'm going to have to start paying that woman a commission.

She pulls her phone from her pocket and reads a text. "Eike took Colette back to the hotel."

"Do you want me to drop you off there?" I offer, even though I'll probably put one of these pastels in my eye if she says yes.

Lucky for my retinas, she shakes her head with a soft smile. "Shall we get dinner? I'm fifteen minutes from hangry."

Shit. Ophelia when hangry is a force to be reckoned with. "Better go get pasta before you start punching members of the public, then."

"It's when the car smashing starts that you really need to worry."

I tame my hair and smooth out my shirt, trying to retain just a modicum of discretion for Ophelia's sake, even though there's no universe in which Clementine didn't hear her not-very-politely asking me to fuck her faster about five minutes ago.

But Ophelia seems convinced we can maintain our innocent facade, so when I tug open the door and find our brightly dressed host in the hallway, seemingly battling it out with my girlfriend for who can blush the hardest, I fight to keep the ridiculous grin off my face.

Tucking the drawings under my arm, I give her my most charming smile—the press conference smile—and toss a forty-pound tip on the side table in the hallway. "Fantastic event, Clementine. Thanks *so* much." *And sorry for fucking the model.*

"You guys have a good sleep . . . sleep together . . . night together . . . have a good night," she chokes out, all hot and flustered. Ophelia manages a mangled *thanks very much*, and I think my lip might actually be bleeding from my pathetic attempt to bite back my smile.

God, I've missed her.

THE FIRST THREE restaurants I stopped at were full, and the fourth offered me a table in return for a social media post about how good the food is. Then Ophelia's mood slipped from ebullient into hangry. She was annoyed at the rain, annoyed at her bra straps, annoyed at the traffic.

Fancy dinner plans long abandoned, she's in the passenger seat of my car, hugging two steaming pizza boxes to her chest, sneaking tiny corners of crusts every thirty seconds when she thinks I'm not looking.

Her miserable music plays through the speakers, her thigh drumming beneath my hand. The darkness inside me has shrunk enough to let me take a full inhale.

"Saw that," I say, as she sneaks a piece of pepperoni from my pizza and eats it.

"Saw what?"

"You're stealing my toppings."

She frowns over at me, face illuminated by the red light we're stopped at. She's ethereal. "You really are getting old. Let's book you in for an eye test."

I squint at her. "Who said that?"

She giggles as the light turns green, humming softly as I steer us through the driving rain and busy evening traffic to my father's house in Kensington. It's a five-bedroom house at the end of a terrace on a well-kept road, furnished as tackily as you'd expect from a billionaire CEO who thinks gray crushed velvet is still on trend.

I park on the street, glancing around as I do. I have zero doubt that my father would love to get his hands on Ophelia. The street is quiet, neatly manicured hedges perfectly still. No sign of anything amiss.

I walk over to open the car door for Ophelia, taking the boxes from her lap. She's quiet as we walk up to the front door, as she always is whenever she's taking in how people like me live. I know she's disgusted by the excess of it all.

"Another spare house," she mutters, as I turn the key in the lock and enter the security code into the pad. "It's like real-life Monopoly for you people."

"And you're the best Chance card I ever drew."

She rolls her eyes, but her face flushes pink. "All right, Corbeau. Calm down."

The house is cold and still, and I try to remember the last time the eight of us stayed here. Paris, we've spent a lot of time in, but London was a place we stopped visiting when my dad stopped caring about being a parent.

"Show me your bedroom!" she says, excitedly. "Have you got posters up? Embarrassing childhood pictures?"

I laugh, but it's slightly strained. "It's not that sort of home, love." *It wasn't that sort of childhood.*

I don't bother with a tour, nor does she ask for one. She follows me up the stairs and into the bedroom I usually sleep in. The walls are white, the bathroom is marble. The bookshelves are full of those clothbound coffee table books that no one would ever read. *Luxury Handbag Collections of the Nineties.* That kind of thing. There's not a photo, poster, toy, or splash of color in the whole house. "Oh."

"Yeah."

She flops onto the bed, taking her pizza from me. "We can stick your drawings up."

I lie down beside her, flipping the lid of my pizza box. It looks like a mouse has been at it. "Your drawing is going in my office, where I can stare at it all day."

She folds a slice in half and eats it in one bite. *That's my girl.* "Sounds inappropriate for a corporate environment."

"So is having phone sex with you while I'm sitting at my desk."

She turns bright red. "Oops."

"Yeah, *oops*."

We lie on the bed, sprawled out over the duvet while making light work of two extra-large pizzas.

I pull my phone from my pocket, catching up on the sibling group chat. Mia has very thoroughly documented the baking process for her pistachio cookies, complete with a selfie of her and Evie at the end, cheeks full like hamsters.

Mia

You're missing out, Alex

I look at the girl beside me, hair still messy from our time in the hall, a smudge of pizza sauce on her pink bottom lip.

I think I'll manage.

Alex

You guys all okay? Save me a cookie, M.

Mia

All good here. Mom is currently telling the gardener that you've got a girlfriend again.

Evie

Breaking his heart, no doubt

Alex

I'm sure George is happy with his wife of twenty-five years.

Mia

Did Ophelia forgive you for being an ass?

Alex

Might've gotten away with it

Evie

Pics or it didn't happen

I laugh, sending a blurry photo of the two of us on the bed.

Élé

Cute dress

Mia

Send that to Mom. It'll make her entire year.

I do just that, and then I toss my phone aside so I can make love to my girl.

I WAKE UP with a jolt, like something might've startled me.

Ophelia is sprawled out on top of me, naked limbs tangled with my own. Her hair fans out, fiery and wild in the strip of moonlight that bleeds through the white curtain.

I trace my finger over her cheek, waiting for my racing heartbeat to return to normal.

She's here. We're safe.

So why do I feel on edge?

I grab my phone from the bedside, careful not to wake Ophelia, and text Fleur a message.

Alex

Is all good at home?

Fleur

Isn't it like 2am for you?

Alex

Woke up with a bad feeling

Fleur

Might be the clinical depression??

I snort quietly in the silent house. *Yeah, might be.*

Fleur

We're all fine. The others are watching a movie before bed

Alex

How's Freddie?

Fleur

Do you actually care?

I couldn't summon two shits to give about her idiot boyfriend even if I spent all night trying my best, but I *do* care about Fleur, and should she find a man who makes her happy, I'll try to get over my irrational fear of my sisters growing up.

Alex

I care about every element of your life, Fleur.

Fleur

Except my safety when Dad is on a rampage, of course.

I shut my eyes, letting out a slow exhale. If I apologize again, it'll be the one thousandth time. But I'd do it again. My father while at the head of a billion-dollar company is completely bulletproof. Now, he has nothing.

Fleur

Freddie's fine. Maybe you were right about him.

My phone is pressed to my ear in half a second, Fleur's exasperated sigh in my ear. "What did he do?"

"Why are you anger-whispering?"

"Because I'm angry but Ophelia is sleeping. Tell me what he's done."

"He's just . . . funny about my outfits."

Nope. He has to go. I won't have one of my sisters falling into a relationship that'll end up like my parents', where the honeymoon phase rots into a twisted dynamic where one of them sucks the life out of the other. "That's a slippery slope, Fleur."

"His dad is a really great modeling agent, though. He landed a Dior campaign for Bea."

"And our mother is one of the most famous supermodels of all time. You don't need to stick around with him for industry connections."

"I'll see how it goes."

"And if one of Rocco's hitmen accidentally pushes him off a bridge?"

Her laugh is so rare nowadays, sometimes I wish I could bottle it. "Don't you dare. Night, Alex."

She hangs up before I can rant about her boyfriend anymore, but I text Brendan and ask him to find me Freddie's phone number, just in case.

Now I'm even more stressed than I was when I woke up. I slip out from beneath Ophelia, drape a blanket over her sleeping form, tug on some sweatpants, and gently pull the door shut behind me.

Scrolling through a few work emails in the darkness, I pad down to the kitchen for a glass of water.

The house is quiet. Everything is eerily quiet, especially for a busy London borough. I'm tempted to check under all the beds, but I'm wary of giving in to paranoia. I don't want to fall onto the same road my mother fell onto.

I flick the lights on in the ostentatious reception room, and in the home office. My father's oversized poster of a Green Aviation helicopter behind the desk makes my stomach churn.

In the kitchen, I pull a pint glass from the cabinet, rubbing the sleep out of my eyes. In the window above the sink, I glance over the shoulder of my reflection to check no one is there, like when I'd stayed up too late watching horror movies as a kid.

I turn the cold tap on, and then the glass window in front of me shatters with a nauseating *crack.*

The whole house is drowned in a deafening alarm that's so jarring, it sounds like it's coming from inside my head, rattling the bones of my skull.

I snap my head to the side in an effort to avoid the thousands of glass shards that fly toward me. Light burns behind my closed eyelids, and when I swing them open and make a break for the door, the floodlights on the security system drown the small garden in a harsh white light.

At the far end, a black-clad figure is scrambling up the trellis on the brick wall.

I yank open the glass door, hurtling across the garden just as the hooded figure drops down the other side of the wall. I climb it with ease, but when I push myself up onto the cold brick, the overgrown alleyway beneath me is deserted and quiet.

Fury burns beneath my skin, chest rising and falling with badly contained frustration.

If Ophelia wasn't in the house, I'd search the streets. I bite out a curse as I drop back into the garden, gaze snagging on the black glove that hangs on the trellis, tangled in the ivy.

I pluck it free from the inky green leaves and head back into the house with one person on my mind.

She's pale and wide-eyed in the threshold to the kitchen, the security alarm so loud that it's hard to form a thought. Her small feet are bare on the tile, too close to all the broken glass. I slip past her and reset the system in the hallway, and the silence that follows has my ears ringing.

"This is my fault," is what she eventually says, the two of us standing and staring at the glass that looks like a layer of snow all over the kitchen counter. There's a brick in the kitchen sink.

"No," I manage, but I'm too angry to say much else. I fire off a rapid string of texts to Mack and Brendan.

Whoever that was, they'll die for scaring her.

I grab our jackets from the door and pocket my wallet, slipping my hoodie over her head. "Brendan is sorting us a room somewhere."

She shakes her head. "I should get back to Sorrowsong."

"No."

"I was warned so many times."

"*Ophelia.*"

"It's not safe for you to be with me. Not until I've found whoever is doing this."

"This was probably a teenager trying his luck with a burglary. This has nothing to do with you," I say, though I'm not even convincing myself. Whoever this was clearly waited for me to be in the kitchen before . . . what? I don't understand their motive.

They didn't anticipate the security system. That much is clear.

"Let's just get some sleep, let the cops search the place."

There's a distant look in her eye, her shoulders drawn up like she's just waiting for something else to hit us. I exhale a slow, steadying breath, tugging her into my embrace. I bury my nose in her hair, and no matter how hard I hold her, it doesn't feel hard enough. Her heart is a thundering, galloping beat in her chest. "You're okay, Twist."

"I wish I had a home to run to."

It's a whispered confession, perhaps not meant for me to hear, but it's a red-hot poker to the chest, because she's right.

I'll get off the plane home, and the house will be busy and full. My mom will be waiting for me; my sisters will be ready to insult whatever public appearances I made this week. My bedroom will be warm, and Josie will be snoring in the room next door.

I'd do anything for her to have that feeling.

I curl my fingers into the hair at the back of her head like maybe I'll be able to hold her together, even a little bit.

"I should call Colette."

"Ophelia, you—"

She pulls away, eyes on the small cut I can feel just below my bottom lip. Gently, she runs her finger just beneath it. Her eyes are a boiling, swirling sea of emotion. "They threatened *you*, Alex, they almost . . . you almost . . . If something happened to you because of me, I wouldn't survive it."

"It didn't. It won't."

She flips my palms, grazed from the broken glass and the brick wall. "I was *warned* to stay away from you, but everyone told me to ignore it."

"As you should. Don't let whoever this is strip your life of all the good."

"You are the good in my life, Alex. I could've lost you. Your sisters could have lost you."

I pull the glove from my pocket, draping it over my palm. "They dropped this."

She frowns, seeing what I see. I don't think my hand would fit in that glove even if we had half an hour to try. "Are you sure?"

"Yeah."

She hovers her hand over the black fabric. It looks like a perfect fit.

"It's not my father, Ophelia," I say, telling her what she's been told a hundred times before. "I know you think it could be him, but it isn't. This stalking is sloppy, disorganized. Weak threats, as though they want to hurt you but can't pull it off. That isn't Cain at all."

Her shoulders sink, like she's been knocked back to Go on this fucked-up board game we're playing. I know it's not that she's desperate for her stalker to be my father; it's that she's desperate for something, *anything*, to suggest we're making progress.

"Don't do whatever they ask you to do, Ophelia. Rocco's men will catch them in Sorrowsong."

"They won't, clearly," she says, wiping her nose on her sleeve. "It's like this person is invisible, forgotten and left off all records."

"Tread water a little longer. And come to a hotel with me."

"Go back to New York."

"No."

"Please. Until we've caught this person, until I know they can't hurt you."

Her lips are pillow soft, her face warm between my palms. I drag an inhale through my nose, trying to drag enough of *her* into my lungs that the next however long without her feels more manageable.

I love you, her gaze says.

You're the reason I'm grateful to be alive, I hope mine says back.

I brush a lock of hair from her forehead, holding her gaze so intensely in the quiet, dark house that it feels more intimate than anything else we could do. "Don't go all *no strings attached* on me again."

"Our strings are stitched through my heart, Alex. I can't get rid of them even when I try."

Chapter 15

OPHELIA

Sorrowsong has this way of convincing you that you're losing your mind, like the fog that constantly hugs the turrets has infiltrated your brain and clouded your judgement.

Did someone really try my door handle last night, or was that part of my dream?

I clutch my phone to my chest, knife in my pocket as I climb the steep hill from the tarn to the thick stone walls of the castle.

Don't let whoever is texting you stop you from living a normal life.

It's advice that's been given to me by Alex, Colette, Mack, Divya, Magda.

It's advice that's easy to give when you're not the one in my situation.

When I found Alex in the kitchen of that ridiculous London mansion last weekend, blood tricking down his jaw, my willingness to listen to that infuriating piece of advice dwindled and died.

If it was Alex being texted, *my* life being threatened if he dared to spend time with me, I'm sure it'd be a different story.

My boots squelch in the mud beneath me, glossy ferns reaching out for my shins.

It's been a week. I wonder what he's up to. What he had for breakfast, what he did at work. I wonder what his mood is.

I wish so much that we'd been dealt a different set of cards. That we could spend weeknights together and go on a holiday and that I could take him home to meet my parents.

I wish I wasn't scared he'll get hurt because of me.

The clouds seem to cast a gray filter over the landscape, and over my mood. The campus around the castle is quiet, everyone either hungover, headed home early for the Easter break, or buried in textbooks ahead of the end of term exams next month.

Colette heads to Bora Bora next week, and Divya is off to some fancy beach resort in Sri Lanka a few days after.

I try not to think about going back to my parents' house. I need to call the nursing home and beg for a job. My bank account is barreling back down toward zero.

A bush rustles somewhere behind me, too much to be caused by the wind. I wait for a deer to emerge from the foliage, but everything falls still.

A prickly sense of unease slickens my palms.

I glance over my shoulder for the third time in as many minutes, willing my tired legs to move faster.

I swear I hear a sharp inhale behind me. I whirl around to face the forest, fingers tightening around my knife as I scan the trees that shroud the path to the castle.

My voice sounds surer than I feel when I break the silence. This has always been my plan, hasn't it? To keep this between the two of us? I'm tired of waiting around for other people to fix my problems for me. "Isn't this what you wanted? Me, alone?"

I step into the dense foliage, trying to catch a glimpse of anything moving.

"Let's do this like adults," I say, into the dark shadows of the forest.

I can feel someone listening, feel someone's presence.

My phone pings, echoing between the gnarled tree trunks. I scramble to turn it on silent, my pulse a hammer in the side of my neck.

Unknown

Tag, you're it.

Somewhere through the trees, a figure clad in black takes off running.

Before I can start to chase them, three silenced gunshots fire from my right. The figure falters for a moment before sprinting deeper into the woods, out of sight.

One of Vincenzo's men steps out of the greenery to my right, a pistol in both hands as he fires two more shots into the trees. He lowers the gun with a sigh of frustration, like it's not often he misses a target. "Are you all right?"

"I . . ."

I'm not built for Sorrowsong. I'm not built for any of this.

My friends may not be disgusted by the guns and the danger and the fame and the wealth, but I am.

The man—I think his name might be Luca—plants a heavy hand on my shoulder, jolting me out of my trancelike state. "Are you hurt?"

I shake my head, but he doesn't look convinced.

"You saw him, right?" I ask, desperate for confirmation that Sorrowsong isn't snatching my sanity.

"Didn't get a look at their face," he grunts, pressing a phone to his ear. I take a step farther into the woods, but he grabs my arm and shakes his head.

The air isn't freezing, but my teeth chatter violently, the inside of my jacket like sandpaper against the goose bumps over my skin.

"Why did you have to do that?" I snap, suddenly frustrated that I wasn't alone, that I couldn't chase my stalker into the woods and finish this once and for all.

Luca stares at me for a beat, realizing I'm serious. "Save your life?"

"Intervene." I sound manic, one hand flying up in the air as I turn to face the forest, but it's no use. They're long gone.

He pinches the bridge of his nose and curses in Italian. "Belladonna wasn't lying about you."

"What?"

"Survival instincts of a moth."

I stand on the forest's edge for what feels like forever, until more of the Morello's men have vanished into the trees to search and my anger has stewed and stewed until it's reached boiling point.

I'm in a trancelike state as my legs carry me up the hill, storming across the overgrown lawns and back to the mansion with a plan taking shape in my mind.

Every other emotion inside me has been replaced by rage. I open up my texts and fire off my first reply.

Ophelia Winters

You wanted me to hand myself over?

Unknown

This could all be so simple.

Ophelia Winters

Tomorrow?

A location pings through, a small patch of woodland not far from a petrol station near Lochinver.

Unknown

5am. Leave the gunman behind, this time.

Ophelia

It's a date.

Obviously, I'm not going to go alone. That's literally the first mistake that every horror movie heroine makes. Instead, I dial the number of someone who is most likely going to ignore my call.

The line rings for so long that I think I'm right, until Belladonna's smooth voice comes through the speaker.

I don't think she likes me. I'm just hoping she likes Alex enough to help me.

"I really don't think we're close enough for you to start calling me, Winters. You're more of a text contact."

Charming. "Did you tell your men I have the survival instincts of a moth?"

"That's the least of your worries. I've said much worse."

"I need a favor."

She must detect the seriousness in my tone because the background noise melts away, a door clicking shut on the other end of the line. "What is it?"

"I just need you to drive me somewhere tomorrow."

"Do I look like I'm running a taxi service?"

"I just want you to drive me somewhere in the morning and be on standby. I can pay you for petrol."

"Don't insult me." She sighs, like I'm a toddler asking her for another round of a game. "Ophelia, if you need someone to die just leave it with us. You'll make a fucking mess of it."

I must be hormonal, because Belladonna being willing to kill for me shouldn't be making me emotional. "I'm just meeting someone is all."

"Who?"

"I . . . don't know exactly who it is."

The silence drags on, and I can practically hear her trying to make her mind up.

"Does Alex know about this?"

"No. That's why I'm asking you and not your brother. Listen, last week . . . last week I stayed a night with Alex in London, and someone smashed into the house."

"Were either of you hurt?"

"I was upstairs. It could've been bad for Alex. Whoever has been sending me these messages . . . they told me they'd hurt him, and I didn't listen."

Her voice carries a lethal edge when it next comes. "Okay, and your plan is . . ."

"Can you shoot?"

She laughs like she's offended by the question.

"Whoever it is, I don't want them dead, but I want them captured. But I'm supposed to be going alone, and . . ."

"If you contact the police, they won't show."

"Yeah."

"This is a bad idea, you know that?"

I do know that, but I also can't keep going on like this.

"It's like my life is being dictated by someone else. I just want to know that I did what I could. Whoever is texting me clearly isn't traceable. Alex's investigators would've found them by now."

Her voice quiets, softens around the edges. "I understand that."

"I'm not asking you to put yourself in any danger. If it looks unsafe, just leave."

"I won't be in danger. I *am* the danger. I'll swing by your room when I'm back from Raigmore later."

SORROWSONG'S WILD GARDENS are glistening in a thin film of dew when I meet Belladonna outside the Nightshade mansion at four in the morning. She's in black sweatpants and a hoodie, car keys dangling from her pinky as she types something on her phone. She doesn't even look up, just bites out a frosty "Let's go" and starts to lead the way up the gravel path.

We walk silently through the shrouded paths to the car park south of the castle, but I'm jittery, teeth chattering and hands clammy in my pockets. If there was any tiredness left in me when my alarm went off this morning, it's been swallowed whole by the adrenaline that has my heart pounding beneath my ribs.

Belladonna unlocks her Bronco and slides into the driver's seat, putting a steaming flask of coffee in the cupholder. "Still sure?"

"Yeah."

Her fingernails tap against the large screen on the center console, the interior a combination of black and dark red. It's a little over a thirty-minute drive when she presses the green button to start the route, pulling out of the parking spot and up the bumpy track to the gates.

I drum my fingers on my thigh, nervous in the awkward silence. I could do with a guidebook right about now. *How to Make Small Talk with the Daughter of a Notorious Mob Boss For Dummies.*

"How's your family?" I try.

"I'm supposed to report anyone who asks about my family as suspicious."

"Alright, then."

Silence resumes, Belladonna's icy gaze constantly flicking to the mirror to make sure we're alone.

I wipe my sweaty palms on my leggings, puffing a slow breath from my cheeks.

I just cannot cope with silence when I'm nervous.

"How's Raigmore?"

"Fine."

"Do you have a favorite . . . area? Of medicine?"

"Neuro."

That makes sense, somehow. I can imagine her doing that. "Is that what you're choosing?"

Her jaw tenses, lips press together. "No. Emergency medicine."

"Oh." It's not often I see emotion from Belladonna, but I sense it now. I don't pry further, even though I'm desperate to be distracted from whatever may happen in thirty minutes' time.

"It's better for the family business," she says, eventually.

"Emergency medicine?"

"Yeah. I'll work as a doctor for the family."

I wonder if she has much choice.

She clamps her mouth shut as we turn onto a less overgrown road. I take it as a hint that I am not someone she wants to open up to.

"How'd you get your hair so glossy?" I try.

"Genetics."

"So, you're telling me I shouldn't be smearing flax seeds and bananas and coconuts on my head like that YouTube video told me?"

She bites down on a smile, glancing over at me. "Making granola on your head won't fix shit." She rubs the muscle in her shoulder and winces. "The beauty industry capitalizes on the stuff you can't change. That's why it's still an industry."

She may see me as an irritating fly, but I think my attachment issues and I are starting to see her as a big sister.

"Why don't you like me?"

"You looking to do some self-improvement, or something?"

"I am," I say, genuinely.

She laughs, rubbing her hands together like, *Where do I even start?* "I think you're immature. And that's probably harsh, because I think I was like you at your age, too. But it's still annoying. And you're selfish, ignorant to the way your actions affect others."

"Like what?"

She sweeps her hand around her. "Like *this*. Doing this with seemingly zero thought on how it would affect Alex if something happened to you. I'm only going with you because if you went alone, you'd do something stupid like slip over and immediately get shot, and then he'd be moping around for the rest of his life."

She's probably right.

I'm not used to having someone who cares.

"Maybe I'll do something really cool, like . . . drop-kick them in the head."

She laughs. "You're literally that character in the movie that just fucking . . . *dies*."

Great. Really filling me with confidence.

Oh God, this *is* a bad idea.

"I hope you and Alex can work it out," she says, after a few minutes of silence, and I know how important he is to her, so it just might be the kindest thing she's ever said to me.

"So do I."

"By the end of tonight, you'll feel ten times lighter," she says, with the same easy confidence Alex has about his own safety. Maybe it's a byproduct of the dizzying combination of both money and power, but everyone at Sorrowsong seems to believe they're invincible. "So what's the plan? We deal with your stalker, and then you and Alex are fixed? Just like that?"

Not fixed, but maybe we'd have a chance to start to fix it, to begin building the giant ladders we'll need to overcome the obstacles between us. It feels like we have these great big boulders blocking our way, that there might be a happy ending for us somewhere down the road, but neither of us can see it.

We just have to believe it's there.

"That bad, huh?" she says, when the silence stretches on.

My fingers tighten around my seat belt when she skids round a bend *way* too fast. "We have a lot to adjust to. A lot of things that'll make it difficult. But we'll make it work. I know we will."

The screen in front of us lights up, casting her frown and the flowers tattooed up her left arm in a blue glow. The sound of her phone ringing blares through the car speakers, cutting off whatever she was going to say.

"Dad," she says, affectionately. "Always lovely to hear from you."

Her father's voice is deep, rough like he's spent too many years smoking cigars. "Belladonna, my darling," he begins, tone sickly sweet. "Luca has just informed me that your car isn't in the castle parking lot."

"He's always been observant, that one."

"What are you doing at four in the morning with no guards?"

"Just a favor for a friend. If we have an entourage, it won't work."

I try not to linger on the word *friend* for long, in case she takes it back.

The undercurrent of frustration in his voice is outweighed by the affection. "You turn my hair gray, *Piccola*."

"I'm safe, I promise."

"Who are you burying?"

She laughs, her usually sullen face brightening the same way Vincenzo's does when he talks about his family. "I'll tell you in about an hour."

"*Belladonna Luigia Francesca Morello.*"

"What?"

"If I tell your mother, she'll have your head on a platter."

"Whoever it is, they tried to kill Alex last week."

There's a loaded pause, and maybe Alex's stories of how his father treated him have scarred me, because I wait for the string of expletives, the cutting remark. But Rocco just sighs, like this is the third time this week that Belladonna has put her life at risk. "Don't try anything clever. Just shoot for the heart and I'll clean up the rest."

Oh God. I think I'm having a panic attack.

I tune out for the rest of their conversation, staring at the inky landscape that juts above the bushes. The hills, fields, and pines of the Highlands are stained in dark shades of juniper and slate, ruffled by the wind beneath a cloudy, black sky.

Belladonna is watching me out of the corner of her eye. I'm sure she can see the panic on my face because she says, "Do you want me to turn around?"

"I don't know."

"I won't let anything happen to you. Alex is family, which makes you family. I think you're a dumbass, but he clearly doesn't."

"Thank you," I whisper, picking my nails. "I'm just so tired of having this looming over me. I can't remember the last time I actually slept. Like, properly *slept*."

"So we're doing this," she says, finality in her tone.

She dims her headlights on the deserted road, I know we're not far from Lochinver, because I can just about make out the lonely curve of Suilven jutting out over the hills and lochs.

The screen says we're a few minutes away, so she slows the car to a roll, leaning forward slightly to scan every shrub, rock, and tree that we pass.

It's eerily quiet, eerily deserted.

The location from the text takes us off the narrow road and onto a grassy plain that looks like it leads to nowhere. The wind whips around the car, churning the sea of sharp brambles and browning bracken that carpet the earth beneath us.

She turns all the lights off now, tires sinking into the marshy earth as we roll blindly toward a dense thicket of pines in the distance.

God, I hope the car doesn't get stuck.

I don't like this, and I can tell by the way Belladonna leans over me to open the glove box for her gun that she doesn't like it, either.

She stops the car in the soft earth, pointing to something in the distance.

A car is parked at the edge of the trees.

"At least we haven't been stood up," I breathe, on a nervous laugh. I try to make out the silver car in the dark. It looks cheap, dented, and damaged. "Can you make out the license plate?"

"No. Looks like a piece of shit car. They might've stolen it."

My shaking hand pulls the door handle as quietly as I can, the soft whistle of the wind infiltrating the car. "I'm scared," I whisper, as I push the door open. The thought of standing face to face with my tormenter is suddenly overwhelming. The list of suspects parade through my mind, a little procession of everyone I've ever pissed off.

"I'm not," she replies, calmly. "We'll handle it."

"If it's Cain?"

"It's not. But if it is, we'll deal with it."

"If it's Carmichael?"

"It won't be. That'd be miraculously stupid of him. He loves this job."

"Who do you think it is?"

Her eyes widen, like she's one annoying question from leaving me to die in some thorny swamp in the Highlands. "How the fuck would I know? I hardly know you."

"Could it be Shawn?"

"I could snap Shawn in half. Are you gonna keep naming people all morning?"

"Right. Uhh . . . no. I'm going."

My boot sinks into the ground, the merciless cold sinking its fingers beneath the neck of my hoodie. "Wait here."

Then I clutch my pen knife in my fist and push the car door shut.

Chapter 16

OPHELIA

Walking away from Belladonna feels like an awful idea, but I can't drag her into this any further than I already have. This is my mess.

The short walk to the trees feels like a marathon. So much time to overthink, so much time for my heart to accelerate into a rapid rhythm. Each whisper of the wind in my ear or bare branch reaching out for my legs has me spinning around to face a person who isn't there.

By the time I reach the abandoned Golf, I can barely make out Belladonna's vehicle behind me.

I glance around, the world silent enough that my breaths are deafening and my footsteps sound like they could be heard for miles around. I dare to turn on my phone flashlight, peering through the yellowing windows. The car is filthy, inside and out. The driver's seat is empty, passenger seat covered in empty water bottles and food wrappers. The small back seat has a stained pillow and a blanket.

Whoever is here, they're living in this car.

The coordinates I was sent lead into the mass of pines in front of me, but when I scan the tree line, there's no trace of anyone or anything.

I pace around the vehicle, knife clutched between my clammy fingers. I can't find any clue in the car, but my eyes land on the license plate, so thick with dirt that it's almost unreadable.

I take out my phone and cringe at the brightness of the screen, scrambling to turn it down before I'm seen. I half expect Mack's tech guy not to pick up, but he does. God knows what time it is wherever he is.

"Brendan?" I whisper, so quiet I can barely hear myself. I glance over both shoulders, crouching down to hide behind the car. "It's Ophelia. If I give you some plates, can you tell me who's driving a car?"

He must notice the fear in my voice, because he doesn't ask me why I need it. "What country is the car from?"

"The UK."

I hear a drawer open and shut on the other end of the phone, then the sound of him typing. "Why are you in the middle of nowhere?"

I look beneath the car and at the cluster of trees beyond, finding no one. "It's a long story."

He sighs. "Tell me the plates."

"MG01 ARJ."

"Hold on."

Somewhere in the trees, a twig snaps. Panic cuts through me. I can hear Brendan muttering under his breath, like he's having trouble on his end. "Um, how long until you get a match?"

"Are you in danger?"

I suppose now's not the time to sugarcoat the truth. "I think so."

"Who does the car belong to? The person sending the texts?"

I look down beneath the car again, watching the tree line like a hawk. "Yeah."

"Ophelia, get out of there and leave it to us."

"I've been leaving it to you guys for months. I can't just sit around and wait for someone to kill Alex."

"Okay, well, let me know who the stalker is, if you survive. The car has an expired MOT. It isn't taxed, either. It's likely stolen."

I curse in frustration, keeping him on the line as I pace over to a small, round shrub, watching, waiting for anyone to appear. No one does.

It leaves me no choice but to head over to the trees, wincing at every twig and leaf that crunches beneath my Doc Martens. My teeth chatter together on an exhale as I'm plunged into complete and total darkness. Brendan's steady breathing and typing on the line are the only things keeping me company.

Just like in the Solemn Woods that surround Sorrowsong's crumbling walls, the forest snatches all five of my senses from me. I lose my sense of direction, fumbling blindly through the cracked tree trunks until I hear a second set of footsteps in front of me.

Or are they behind me?

Every sound reverberates through the forest, coming at me from every direction.

I head toward the footsteps, knife in hand, and just when they sound like they could be walking alongside mine, the forest falls silent and still.

A cold sweat sticks to my skin.

I feel it again now, just like I did in those woods with Bancroft: a nauseating, crushing sort of dread.

But somehow, I feel stronger than I did then.

"Gotcha," mutters Brendan, making me jump. "Last year, the car was registered in Inverness to one Ms. L—"

Something—some*one*—slams into my back, sending my phone flying. The earth comes to greet me with a hard thud, the taste of blood and damp earth invading my mouth. I hold on to my knife, slashing it behind me as a pair of knees come crashing down on my lower back.

But I know as soon as those knees land on my back that this isn't a fair fight.

No weight accompanies them. When my hand encircles the forearm that snakes its way across my neck, it's nothing more than skin and bone.

The voice that comes is hoarse with sickness and frailty, but the Scottish accent is familiar. "I hate you, Ophelia."

I shut my eyes against the thorns and the dirt and curse my own stupidity.

I don't know why I didn't see it before.

There is only one person I know who wanted Green to crumble with the same intensity that I did.

"Laura," I choke out.

"I gave you my father's tape," she hisses, the thin line of her forearm pressing harder into my neck. "You tricked me into giving you my final piece of him."

I remember her home, her desperation as she handed me the confession tape that would give us the vengeance we'd both dreamed of for so long. It was crucial information in my case against Cain Green. It was her prized possession, and I promised her that giving it up would be worth it.

But I chased a happily ever after instead.

And barely thought about her again.

"It wasn't like that," I wheeze, through my compressed airway. I clutch my knife, but I might as well throw it into the bushes.

I won't kill Laura. I can't kill her.

"How did your boyfriend bribe you to steal the final piece of evidence against his family? You begged me for it, pretended that you hate the Corbeau-Greens." She laughs maniacally, bony knees digging into my spine. "I sent you that tape, and you went *silent*. And I thought maybe you'd forgotten about me, like everyone does. But I found Alex online. Laughing with you, spending Christmas with you."

"No, no, no," I plead, trying to get her to see, trying to starve the flames of guilt that are burning me alive.

"I came to you. I watched you. I came to Sorrowsong because surely, *surely*, that girl who came to my house wasn't truly bad. Surely it was all a misunderstanding. And what do I find? You and him, burying that man. Was he like me, too? Did you trick him?"

"Laura, please," I choke out "I wasn't trying to trick you, I fell for him after, I swear. I always intended on bringing Green down."

"All you ever do is *lie*."

I buck her off me just enough to roll onto my back. It's too dark to make out her features, but the silhouette of her greasy hair is lank and limp against the moonlit treetops. "I posted it back. The tape." I pant. "You can have it back."

"I sold the house to pay a hacker to finish what *you* promised me you'd start!" she shouts, hands grappling for my neck. Thin fingers dig into my flesh, but there's no threat, no strength behind her movements.

I hear a mechanical *click* somewhere beside us and freeze, eyes widening in dismay. "Belladonna, don't shoot!"

A mottled ray of moonlight catches on the distinctive metal lines of a gun, aimed right toward us.

But this only panics Laura, hands flying in a frenzy.

"She has a knife, Ophelia."

"*Don't. Shoot,*" I beg her, trying to catch one of Laura's arms. The knife settles at my neck, my hand on her wrist preventing it sinking into my skin. "Laura, listen to me."

"Listen to you? Listening to you was my final hope."

"I am so, *so* sorry."

And I am. Sorry doesn't cover it. The guilt makes my breaths labored, turns my blood to ice.

Laura is me, and I am Laura. Two women let down by the same man. Two women united by the same trauma. Two women forgotten by the law.

And then I forgot her, too.

I wrap my other hand around the blade, and it bites my palm as I carefully push it away from my neck. Blood trickles onto my clothes. "I'll get you some help. I'll help you."

"You made me *believe*. But you're just like the rest of them."

"I'm so sorry. I never intended to fall in love," I plead, desperate for both of us to make it out of here alive. It doesn't take much effort to push her upright and away from me, for me to see from her outline just how skeletal she really is.

I did this.

I am no better than the people I swear to destroy.

Her breathing calms just a fraction. My thumb strokes small circles on her knuckles where I hold both of her hands in mine. "That's it," I whisper, like I'm taming a wild animal. "Breathe. I'll help you. I'm *so* sorry."

She backs off me, and for a second, I think it's working.

But then she makes the fatal mistake.

She lunges toward Belladonna.

"Don't!" I shout, but I've always admired Belladonna for her ability to put herself first. One single gunshot slices through the dense air, ruthless and efficient.

It casts the forest in an orange glow for the briefest of seconds, and then Laura crumples to the ground in a heap of stained clothes and gangly limbs.

"No," I croak, crawling over to her. Even in the dark, with a moving target, the shot couldn't have been more accurate. I press my hands over the blood that pumps out of the wound just above her heart, like that'll fix anything, like I didn't kill Laura five months ago when I chose love over revenge.

"I'm so sorry," I whisper. *Oh God, I'm so, so sorry.*

The whites of her eyes seem to glow in the dark, wide with shock. Her blood is a crimson river that trickles into the earth, and if she'd been offered the scholarship, if she'd met someone she loved, if our roles were reversed, it'd be mine.

"I don't want to go to prison," she whispers, like she believes she might survive this.

I clutch her body to mine, my hand a steady support beneath her head. "You won't. I won't let that happen."

"Promise?"

"I promise," I say, holding her emaciated hand in mine. Something splinters inside my chest. "Belladonna is really good at hiding evidence."

"Yeah?"

I brush the hair from her face, a tear trickling down my upper lip and bursting on my tongue. "Yeah."

She dies quickly. Quicker than Bancroft. She dies with her hand in mine and my hoodie draped over her shivering frame.

I think part of me dies with her.

"I'm sorry she died," says Belladonna, after five silent minutes of me kneeling beside her with my head in her hands.

My voice sounds alien, distant and muffled. "I wouldn't have wanted you to put yourself at risk."

"She's probably better off this way," she says, and it fractures this illusion I've had that I want to be exactly like Belladonna one day, because it's such a cold and callous thing to say. If being strong means dulling your emotions to things like this, I don't think I want to be strong at all.

It's only another few minutes before a few of Rocco Morello's men arrive, shining flashlights on the ugly scene in front of us, shining a flashlight on what I did to a woman who deserved so much more, and as they start to clean up the remnants of her existence, only one thought rattles through my brain.

It should be me.

Chapter 17

OPHELIA

The house isn't much different than when I left it just after New Year's, save for the overdue bills on the doorstep and the fresh layer of mold on the damp windowsills.

It's eleven degrees outside, but somehow inside feels even colder. I wrap my flimsy brown jacket tighter around myself, the thick white socks that sit over my tights doing nothing to dull the sting.

It hurt coming back to this house before Christmas, with its empty bookshelves and dusty furniture, but now, where memories of Alex and me sit between the grief and the decay, it's somehow even worse.

I didn't see what Morello's people did to clean up the scene; I just walked, mute and stiff back to Belladonna's car.

I let their questions wash over me. *Are you hurt? Would Laura have been working with anybody? Does she have family we need to silence? Where do you want to go now? Can we clean the cut on your hand?*

I only had one answer: Please don't take me back to Sorrowsong.

Instead, I had Belladonna's men bring me some clothes and my laptop and drop me here, not that I've bothered to change. My leggings are caked in mud and there's blood beneath my fingernails that I don't think I'll ever be able to truly erase.

I'm *disgusted* with myself. Disgusted at what I did to her. Disgusted that I was so desperate to leave the snake pit of loss and loneliness and anger and despair that I climbed out of it and took the ladder with me.

I ignore my phone ringing incessantly on the chipped laminate worktop in the kitchen. It takes one, two, *three* tries for my shaking fingers to plug in the kettle, another two tries to prize open the rusting tea bag tin and throw one into my dad's favorite mug.

I don't know what to do.

Sorry wouldn't cover it, even if she was still alive for me to apologize to.

My tears drip onto the white envelopes as I slice them open. Water, gas, electricity, tax. They amount to almost nothing, but so does my bank balance.

And I'm currently in no state to call the care home and ask for a job.

I hiccup a sob as I bring the mug to my lips, the steam scalding my nose, red and raw from crying.

Tea is pointless without milk.

I flip my phone over, daring to look at the screen. Ten missed calls from Colette. Ten more from Divya and Magda. Four from Vincenzo. Three from Mack, two from Brendan. One from Belladonna.

Endless calls from Alex.

It should warm my heart. It's all I've hoped for.

But it's a reminder of Laura, of what her phone must've looked like: empty, save for anonymous messages to a girl who let her down.

I put down the phone before the tears *really* come. Before the regret and the desolation and the self-loathing that I've held in for the past eight hours finally hit. It reduces my knees to jelly on the small, square landing at the top of the stairs, folds me at the middle, spreads a migraine like hot oil through my skull.

For the first time in four and a half long years, I stagger into the larger of the two bedrooms and pull back the pristine covers, slipping beneath the duvet with puffy eyes and a broken heart. My scream of frustration is muffled by the pillow. "I need you," I sob into the dusty fabric. "I need you both, and you aren't here."

I AMBLE THROUGH the council estate, corner store bottle of milk dangling from my pinky and lollypop hanging out my mouth. I lasted four hours without a decent cup of tea before I gave in and shuffled my way down the street in what I am sure is a flattering combination of Alex's sweatpants and my mom's old sandals.

For the first time since my parents died, I find myself free of questions.

I know that my parents died as the result of some cheap, heinous deal to keep one of Cain Green's many affairs under wraps.

I know Bancroft and my mother had an affair.

I know who texted the photo of Alex and me and Bancroft's body.

I know that Brendan was able to recover Laura's phone and erase all traces of it.

I know *everything*.

So where is the satisfaction? Where's the sense of victory I've chased incessantly for five years?

I've filled the answers to all my unknowns like the potholes on these shitty Scottish roads, but it feels like they're only in worse condition.

I just need to get through today. Tomorrow I'll tackle things like showering and eating and studying.

I nod at Mrs. Smith who lives on the corner, standing in her dressing gown with a cigarette between her lips. She nods back, setting her cup of tea on top of the green wheelie bin beside her. "You got any dishwasher tablets spare, Winters?"

"Haven't got a dishwasher, Mary."

She coughs, a heaving, wet cough that racks her whole body. "You should get one."

"Probably."

"Is it true? You went to that posh castle school?"

"Yeah."

"What's it like?"

I pause just past her house, in almost as much disrepair as mine. A heavy sigh has my shoulders sinking. "The food's good."

"I bet." She exhales a thick plume of smoke. "If you see Steve, ask him if he has a dishwasher tablet spare."

I don't know how I did this for four years, survived off petrol station bread and my own tears. When I round the corner onto the gray pebble dashed terrace that I call home, my feet come to a stop.

I should be pleased to see him, to discover he hadn't flown back home yet, but there's something about that car being here. A hundred-thousand-pound car parked between houses that cost the same. Wheels that probably cost a month's rent each while Mary is trading the items in her kitchen cupboard for dishwasher tablets.

When I reach the ridiculous Land Rover, it's empty, but the lights are switched on inside the house, something I didn't bother to do.

The door is unlocked. I kick my sandals off on the peeling vinyl flooring and drag myself into the kitchen.

Alex turns to face me, the room plummeting into silence. He looks tired. He rakes his eyes down my body, and whatever he sees is enough to fill them with something that looks a lot like sadness.

Great.

"For the sake of my carbon footprint, Ophelia, we are really going to have to work on our communication issues."

I kneel to place the milk in the fridge, but it looks ridiculous now, surrounded by fresh fruit and yogurt and cheese and ready-made meals that Alex has already put there.

The yellow light from the bulb in the fridge swims from the tears I can't keep at bay, the guilt that sits on my shoulders too heavy for me to stand.

I brace a hand on the bubbling floor in front of me, curling my other against my heart, because it *hurts*. If it were anyone else stood behind me, I'd be embarrassed about the mangled sob that tears its way out of my throat.

"You can't just switch all my lights on," I cry, like that's the issue here. "I'm trying to keep my bills down."

A hand settles on my lower back, rubbing a gentle circle. "Let me help with—"

I sit back on my heels, the two of us kneeling in front of the fridge in this tiny kitchen. "You can't just throw money at everything to fix it," I snap, even though it's harsh. He's exceptionally good at not throwing money at me, at not making me uncomfortable in that way.

"Tell me what happened."

"I forgot," I hiccup, through my tears.

"Forgot what?"

"I forgot *this*." I wave my hand around the house, then toward the faded picture of my parents pinned to the door. "I forgot them. I forgot Mary from down the road, and I forgot Laura. And you're all just so out of touch, and I got so used to all the luxuries that I fell out of touch, too."

"Ophelia, you're not someone who's used to luxury things."

"That's not what I'm referring to."

I don't mean the cars, the handbags, the shoes. I mean *real* luxuries. Friends who care, who show up with chalkboards and snacks whenever something needs to be planned, friends who will drive you places at four in the morning just because you ask. Alex. Alex who loves me so much and so deeply that the chains of my past feel looser now.

Luxuries Laura might've had, if I hadn't deserted her.

His eyes soften with understanding. "Being loved and accepted for who you are isn't a luxury you don't deserve."

"Someone *died* because of me."

"I don't know who Laura is, but I know that you are not the villain in her tale. You didn't decide her fate. You're giving yourself way too much power in her life."

"Stop it."

"We're not doing that. You're not depriving yourself of kindness because you think you don't deserve it."

My shoulders shake, chest aches. "Please stop."

"Tell me what happened."

"I gave up on revenge for a relationship with you is what happened," I bite out, angrier at him than I really mean. There's only one person I'm really angry with. "I let myself get consumed by you."

"Who is Laura?"

Self-loathing is a dull blade somewhere inside me, clawing its way from the inside out. "She's *me*. She's me if I hadn't met you."

He rises to his feet, and I hear the clatter of a mug against the counter, the spluttering of the kettle. And then he's gone, footsteps sounding upstairs before the sound of water filling the bath.

It only makes what I've done feel worse.

I'M ON MY third episode of *MasterChef*, ridiculing the way Clare from Birmingham has made a roux even though I haven't got a single idea what a roux is, when Alex finally joins me on the sofa after what felt like a hundred work meetings. Fresh out of contact lenses, he's in those reading glasses, the ones that appear so rarely and yet feature in almost every single one of my daydreams.

Following what can only be described as a catastrophic breakdown overnight, today I feel all out of fight, like the still quiet after the storm when the sky couldn't possibly rain anymore.

"She's put rosemary in a roux," I say, because I don't want to talk about anything else.

His legs join mine on the coffee table in front of us, lifting my hoodie to check on the bruises that stain my ribs from my fight with Laura. "What the fuck is a roux?"

"Dunno. But I bet you're not meant to put rosemary in it."

"What an idiot."

"Literally."

He stares at the TV with mild disinterest, watching a contestant putting potatoes through a sieve with so much gusto that sweat is beading on his forehead. Alex is restless, the muscles beneath the ravens on his forearm flexing as he spins the gold ring on his index finger. There's a darkness about him that reminds me of that first day we met outside the Sorrowsong gates, like there's a storm brewing just beneath his skin.

I lean over to scratch my fingernails through his hair, watching his eyes drift shut and the tension dissipate from his shoulders just a little. "Talk to me."

"We're never going to catch my father."

"You will. He's just slimy."

"He's too smart. Too well connected. I don't think there is a police force, airport, government authority, or crime group anywhere that he doesn't have a contact in . . . Why are they mashing potatoes through a sieve?"

"I gave up trying to understand this TV show when you were on your first cigarette. That ginger guy just compressed a tomato."

He sighs, like it's genuinely the TV program that's distressing him, and not everything else. "What is the point of it all?"

"Dunno," I say, putting a biscuit in my mouth. "You'll get your father, Alex. It's a waiting game."

"I just want to be done with him. We've been through enough. We've waited long enough."

"It feels like that, but three months isn't that long."

"When you had to wait three months for a new book to release you said three months was the longest time period imaginable. And when I said, 'What about four months?' you told me to mind my own business."

I *did* say that, but I don't admit it. "Oh dear. Deteriorating eyesight *and* memory. You're a lost cause, Corbeau."

"I am."

Somehow, we've ended up horizontal, spooning on the too-narrow sofa with the TV blaring. A contented silence settles in the dated living room as we watch Clare make a mess of plating her dauphinoise and pretend the world isn't burning around us.

When the judge says he appreciates the rosemary that went into the roux, Alex turns the TV off like a disgusted football fan, covering my ears until the sound stops, like I'm a child and he doesn't want me to hear something inappropriate. "That's bullshit. Don't listen to them, baby. You were right about the roux; they were wrong."

"I'm going to email in and complain."

He sighs, his body tense behind me. I rotate where I lie on the sofa, so we're almost nose to nose. I think we're both delirious from lack of sleep. "We'll get through this, Alex. And then we'll get through the next thing. And the next."

He smiles, and it makes my heart skip a beat. "I'm tired of *things*."

"Tough luck. Life is full of *things*."

His smile is soft, finger tracing down my nose. "Thank you for being mine."

"Thank you for coming to that life drawing class."

"I'm irrational. I can't bear the thought of someone else drawing you."

I bite my lip. "Jealous, Alex?"

His hand moves down, thumb pressing against the spot where my pulse hammers in my neck. "I'm sick with envy at the wind that slips through the holes in your knitted sweaters, Winters. Jealous doesn't cover it."

"You don't need to be." My grin is involuntary, but it feels so good. I like jealous Alex.

His eyes are alight again, no longer endless pools of desperation. I run my finger over the scar beneath his eyebrow. His father's handiwork.

I hate Cain Green for so many reasons.

His throat works with a swallow, stare fixed on the world beyond my yellowing curtains. The sun is setting outside, copper shards of light illuminating the crumbling terraces on my street. A plane cuts through the haze, and like he's reading my mind, he says, "I have to fly home soon."

"I know."

"I have no idea when I'll next have time to come to see you."

"You deserve so much more than what I can give you." I've been trying to listen to fear-of-flying podcasts so I can come visit him, but my fear runs so deep, braided with so much trauma, I'm getting nowhere. "The distance is just another *thing*, Alex. We'll get through it."

He's tense, muscles taut as though he's holding something in. "You should know what you're getting yourself into with me. I need you to be sure."

"I do know."

His lips brush mine, soft and tender. "I come with an unwell mother."

"I know."

A kiss lands on my jaw. "And custody of six girls who are really great but also really, really mean. After you graduate, when we're finally able to be together, the youngest girls will still be with me."

"I know."

Another kiss, this time on my collarbone. "And a tired, miserable brain."

"I know."

"I'm not sure if I ever want kids."

"Neither am I."

"I'm exhausting to be around on my lowest days."

"I want you. I want all of your baggage, too. I love your mom. I love the girls. I want everything about you."

The relief on his expression almost brings me to my knees. He really thinks I don't understand. That I'll run when his homelife gets too hard, or when his depression gets worse.

"I want the messy life, Alex. The big fights, the small ones, the leaking washing machines and the car breakdowns and the grumpy teenage girls. I want a normal life, full of people and all their issues."

Now he's full-on smiling. "I want that, too."

"Yeah?"

"Yeah." He swallows, brushing a tear from my bottom lashes. I didn't even realize it was there. "I want a cottage, and an overgrown garden. I want long, lazy afternoons between your thighs. I want to watch you go gray. I want fresh flowers, and an old wife. And if we did have children, they'd never fear the sound of their father's footsteps."

I feel a second tear fall, slow and silent as it trickles across my cheek. For someone who refuses to think about his future because he struggles to believe he'll have one, the magnitude of his confession isn't lost on me. "We can have all of that. We just need to get through the *things*."

"I can hold on."

"Hold on until midnight. Tread water until midnight."

I feel his smile against the top of my head, arms tightening around me. "Until midnight."

WHEN I WAKE, Alex is sitting on the end of the bed in a black hoodie and *those* rugby shorts. His bags are packed at his feet, and disappointment I have no right to feel swirls within me.

I'm exhausted. A night of dreams about Laura and the forest have left me feeling worse than I did when I went to bed.

"I have to leave in half an hour for my flight."

"Okay," I croak, trying to keep my tone cheerful. "That's okay."

Something in his expression tells me there's more.

"Brendan has my father on CCTV about five hundred yards from our house."

Dread punches me in the gut.

"In New York?"

"Yeah. Last night. He's masked, but it's definitely him."

"Shit, Alex."

"There's security at the house, but . . ."

"I'm glad you'll be there soon," I say, heading into the bathroom to brush my teeth, trying to process this snippet of news.

I really, really need Alex and his sisters to come out of this unharmed.

I splash my face with cold water, mildly horrified by my own reflection. If I was being kind, I'd say Alex and I have both looked a little . . . disheveled, lately. Only, he's pulling it off. His hair is messy in a hot, bedhead kind of way. The tiredness on his face makes him look older—sexier—and the whole grumpy, broody vibe he has going on is only making me more flustered.

Me? Not pulling it off so nicely. The color of my skin has gone beyond paper white and into the blue spectrum, and I've prodded at the lonely hair on my chin for so long it's now a spot.

But when I return to the bedroom and sit against the pillows, Alex looks at me like I'm everything he's ever hoped for and more.

The mattress dips under the heavy weight of him, and his hands land either side of my head. He hovers over me, all parted lips and long, dark lashes as he drinks in the sight of my tired, too small camisole.

I'll never get bored of this view.

His work laptop chimes nonstop from the side table, until he leans over and slams the lid shut with so much enthusiasm that I can't contain my laugh.

"How is the world of private jets and stock market crystal balls?" I ask, while my pulse drums in my throat. I wonder if I'll ever stop having this visceral reaction to him, the same reaction I had the first day I met him. Like I've wandered right into his trap but never want to leave.

I'm putting wallpaper and ugly furniture into this trap, making it a home.

He's playful despite the tiredness around his eyes and the darkness that weighs him down. He tugs his hoodie over his head, tossing it aside and falling back down onto two thick forearms. My brain has left the building. "My crystal ball is proving quite useful."

"Oh yeah?"

He nuzzles my neck, inhaling my scent. He's hard against my thigh. "Mmhmm."

"And what does it say?" I ask, expecting him to tell me some mind-numbing shit about supply chains and staff turnover rates.

"That you should ride my face."

I laugh in surprise, looping my hands round the back of his neck. A fire burns somewhere in my lower stomach. "And?"

"And then my dick."

I wiggle my hips beneath him, turning his next exhale into a quiet growl. "Hm. Doesn't sound like it's very helpful with the stock markets. Might be broken."

He hooks his leg between mine, flipping us so I'm straddling him. "Baby, I haven't given a shit about the stock market—or anything else for that matter—since the day I found out you own stockings."

His hands encircling my waist, he slides me back a few inches and bends my knee so that his thigh presses, hard and firm, between my legs. I can't help my smile. It's like our first night together, the first time we finally gave in.

It feels like we've come such a long way, and somehow no distance at all. Still in love, still just out of reach of a happy ending.

Oh *God*. I'm going to miss him.

I'd take Alex in any form I can get him; if it has to be video calls and nights stolen from his airport layovers, then so be it, but I won't pretend it doesn't gut me that we won't get to wake up beside each other like all our friends in relationships do.

He runs his thumb across my jaw, tender and reverent like he always is with me. "What's going on in that head, Twist?"

I let out a shaky exhale, pushing out all my negative thoughts with it. I don't want to sully our last half hour with my God-given pessimism. I roll my hips against him, pulse sticky, stomach clenching. "I'm thinking it could be *really* dangerous to disobey the crystal ball. Don't want to tempt fate."

He sucks in a sharp breath, hands gripping my thighs so hard that it sends a delicious, warm pain through my lower half. "Sounds sensible," he drawls, playing along. "For *safety reasons*, you should come on my face."

"And your dick."

"You're a real beacon for the community."

"Exactly," I say. My laughter turns into a yelp as he slides his hands under my thighs and drags me toward him until my knees are either side of his head.

He pauses slightly, before a soft laugh tickles my inner thigh. "You know, when Harwood has me picturing my happy place, it's right here."

And with that casual comment that feels anything *but* casual in the way it buries itself deep into my heart, he tightens his arms around my thighs and makes me forget *everything*.

Chapter 18

ALEX

"Alex."

This house has Tudor windows. Maybe they're the original windows from when it was first built, the glass slightly warped. There's a glass conservatory with sweeping views of rugged green landscape and the North Sea beyond, a pond that looks straight out of a fairy tale.

I hit Save. You know, *just in case.*

The next one has nine bedrooms. An old manor house nestled in acres of trees and grass and glittering streams. An art studio that Evie might like. A room overlooking the garden that I know Fleur would love.

Save.

"*Alex.*"

"Huh? Shit, sorry."

"I have other clients who actually make use of my time."

I close the property website on my laptop, where the location on the filter drop-down has accidentally ended up in Scotland, rather than New York City.

It happens.

Robert is looking at me over his glasses like he'd quite like to throw his notebook at me. "Sorry. Distracted."

"Has something in particular happened this week?"

"Something in particular happens every week," I grumble. He raises an eyebrow, like he's not accepting that as an answer. "I thought I saw my father."

"When?"

"Before London. I was in a coffee shop and . . . I was *so* sure. And I felt like he'd come to the café to . . . I don't know, taunt me . . . and I ran out and I confronted this guy in the middle of the fucking street, and it wasn't him, obviously, and I just felt like . . ."

"Felt like your mother."

I nod, swallowing thickly. "Doesn't that worry you? That I'm turning paranoid? Isn't that how it all starts?"

He blinks, shoulders sinking on a long exhale. "No, Alex. I'm not worried you're on that path. Stress can do incredible things to a brain, and you're under a lot of it."

"Do you think it's genetic?"

"What?"

I sweep a hand over myself, at how exhausted I must look. "I don't know . . . this. If I had kids, would they be miserable, too?"

I'd hate that.

"Is that something you worry about? Your future children?"

Jesus Christ. "Does the final exam for being a shrink involve answering every single fucking question with another question?"

He laughs, sipping his tea. "Pretty much. You've never mentioned kids before."

I've never considered I might have a future before. I shrug. "If Ophelia wanted kids and I . . . if I'd make them . . . I think I got issues from my mom and my dad. I don't want her to . . . I don't want to . . ." I trail off, unsure what I'm even asking. I don't want to end up like my parents. *I don't want her to end up with a son like me.* I don't want that future for Ophelia.

"I think your struggles have a lot to do with your environment and experiences."

I swallow thickly. Force out a nod. "Okay."

Emails ping through on my laptop incessantly, but one sender catches my eye. *Harris Carmichael.* Before I can read it, Robert steals my laptop from my desk and shuts it.

"I was reading an email."

"Do you want to keep paying me almost four figures a session to watch you read your emails in silence?"

"Why is it my problem that you're massively overcharging?"

His smile is genuine, mustard-colored socks appearing as he stretches his legs in front of the sofa, hooking one ankle over the other. I trace over a squiggle across my notebook for the millionth time. "Bad day?"

It is a bad mood day. One of the lowest. One where I don't understand how I'll make it to midnight. One where money has lost all meaning, food has no taste, and work issues don't drum up a single reaction out of me. The world feels like a wildfire chasing me down, and dying feels like a crisp, cold swimming pool. "I don't understand why I want to die."

"When you've finally got Ophelia back?"

"Yeah."

"A relationship won't fix your depression, no matter how much you love her."

"It does in the movies."

"Mice cook meals inside chefs' hats in the movies, Alex, that's not a good frame of reference."

"It's a rat. It's literally called *Ratatouille*."

He waves his hand like it's an inconsequential detail. Ophelia would have something to say about that. "You're depressed, Alex. Ophelia might not fix it, your mom getting better might not fix it, leaving Green might not fix it, your father being caught might not fix it, either."

"That's reassuring. Thanks."

"Your view of Ophelia is not particularly healthy, as we've spoken about a hundred times before. She is not the cure to all of your problems. But feeling supported and loved will make it a lot easier for you to support yourself. You can't look after yourself at the moment because every waking minute of your life is spent thinking about your father."

"I just can't keep treading water forever." I'm *tired*.

"Sooner or later, the first domino will fall."

"No matter how the final domino falls, it'll be shit for the girls. Josie still thinks her dad is a superhero. She's convinced he's coming back home. I'm trying to prepare them."

"For having their father die? Or put in prison?"

My pen draws a long, looping line until the sketch on my page resembles Ophelia's hips. I hope she's okay. I hope she never knows a mood as low as this one. "Either. *Both*."

Fleur is heading the same way I've gone. The last thing she

needs is more drama, but she'll get it. She'll probably get it for the rest of her life.

The rest of my session with Robert is the same: me despairing, him offering sensible and rational answers that I refuse to listen to. The only highlight was discovering he went on a date with Jacqueline last week.

My phone buzzes to life as he leaves. Ophelia. I decline and fire her a quick text.

Alex
I'm bad company today, baby.

Ophelia
Not to me. Just calling to say I'm back
at Sorrowsong safely.

Alex
Evidence?

I'm rewarded by a picture of her in her shitty Sorrowsong bedroom, my hoodie pulled tight around her face like it was when I left. Her face is smiling and freckly.

It's the perfect reminder of exactly why I'm still treading water.

Alex
Cute

Alex
I'll call you later.

Ophelia
I'll wear stockings.

Oh, that's *it*. I've been teased by stockings long enough. I hit FaceTime on her contact. She picks up but hangs up right away—just long enough for me to hear her cackling on the other end.

Ophelia
I gotta go to an evening lecture. Later.

Alex
Great, now I'm depressed and hard.

Ophelia
When are you not?

I'm smiling at my phone when I lock it. She's a nightmare. *My* nightmare. But she's lit a copper spark in an otherwise charcoal day.

I bring up my emails again. Carmichael has ended his months-long silence with me to forward me a news article from three years ago, like he's trying to remind me of something.

Sorrowsong University Adds Architecture to Its Limited List of Course Offerings in Rare Break from Tradition.

From Carmichael, it feels like a slap in the face.

No apology for how he treated me, for how he treated my girl, just this.

He picks up my call almost immediately. "Alex. It's been a while."

"You're a real piece of shit, Harris."

"I wouldn't delete my email without giving it consideration." He's calm. Friendly, almost. Like he's my father, giving me a man-to-man chat about my career. It only makes me angrier.

"You've got a lot of nerve emailing me."

"I'm genuinely sorry for the way it all played out, Alex."

"You voted against me," I bite out, pushing back my chair and pacing my office, the sky so full of black clouds that it's almost the same shade as my mood. "You almost cost me the CEO job. After *everything*. I came to Sorrowsong for no good reason. You were never going to vote in my favor."

"I was."

I laugh bitterly, and he must sense I'm about to hang up, because he carries on. "I was, until I really got to know you. I could not, in good conscience, agree to elect you as CEO of Green."

Well, that's rude. I haven't dragged the company into liquidation just yet. "I'm doing fine."

"It's not a matter of competency, Alex. I knew you'd manage fine."

"You better start making sense soon, before I get one of Rocco's men to knock you out."

"Ask your mother."

"My mother can't remember what day it is half the time."

"She asked me to vote against you, Alex. The same day you left for Sorrowsong. She knew exactly why you were going, and she asked me to, if it came to it, do anything in my power not to let you take your father's job."

I open my mouth and shut it again. Confusion, hurt, betrayal, *denial*. They all make their steady way through my mind. "She wouldn't."

"She made me promise."

"You're lying."

"How is she?"

"You have absolutely no right to ask about any of them."

"Our architecture program is already widely renowned, Alex."

I hang up, blood boiling. If I could grip him by the purple waistcoat and toss him off Sorrowsong's tallest turret, I would.

But that would make me my father.

So I delete his email without responding and put my head in my hands at my desk.

MY SISTERS ARE at school when I get back to the house. I left work to finish the day from home, too rattled to do anything else.

It's odd when they're not home. Too cold, too quiet in this modern monstrosity of a house. The white walls are clinical, the lights are bright and harsh, the mirrors make me miserable.

I can't wait to leave this house, these memories, behind. I make a mental note to email my realtor.

My mom is in the small garden with one of her caretakers, picking flowers and putting them into a vase. She's coming out the other end of a real low. Every day she eats less, looks frailer. I open the sliding doors noisily so as not to startle them, stepping out into the chilly breeze.

My mom's face lights up when she spots me, as it always does. Her carer heads inside to give us a moment. "You're home."

"I'm home."

I take a seat on the bench beside her, huffing out a long breath.

She tips my face toward her, scrutinizing me. "Something's happened with your father."

"How'd you know?"

"You and Ophelia are fine. I'm circling the drain, but that's not new. The girls are okay. I don't know what else could make you look so exhausted."

"He's nearby. He's circling us, I can feel it."

She sighs, opening up the petals of a flower gently before she slides it into the vase. "He has an awful lot of contacts in the city, and in the travel industry."

"Yeah. Shame he didn't get into something like bakeries."

Her laugh is melodic, eyes bright and alert above the dark circles below. "If he was into bakeries, he'd have been smuggled here in a bag of flour. You know what he's like."

"I feel so useless."

She trails her fingers over the gold band on my index finger—her father's ring. "I said the same thing to my mom at your age."

"And she said?"

"You're not useless; you're just twenty-three. They can feel similar sometimes. I couldn't be prouder of you if I tried. And I'm not scared of your father."

"I am."

"Tell me about your time with Ophelia."

I pull out a photo of my girl holding the pizza boxes in the car, her face the embodiment of a thundercloud. My mom laughs. "Make her bigger."

I zoom in and hand it back. Mom's joy is almost childlike. The women in my life are *way* too invested in my love life. "Isn't she just wonderful? She has such incredible hair. So many freckles. And what a pretty dress."

"She just bought it from a charity shop. It was two pounds," I say, swiping to the next photo. Ophelia's on my bed at our London home, hugging her knees as she eats a slice of pizza. She looks much happier in this one. My mom's smile broadens, if that was possible. "Alex! Eating pizza on white bedsheets. I didn't raise you to be a caveman."

"I think you must've."

I swipe again, to a picture of Ophelia bundled up so tightly in the duvet that only her eyes and nose are visible. Mom presses her hand to her chest and sighs. "Oh, Alex. I'm just dying to meet her. She must love you so much to be able to see past what your father did."

That isn't lost on me. It stuns me every day she spends with me. "I know."

She looks at me with so much warmth. "How was the house in London?"

"Fine," I say, shutting off the phone. I leave out any details of the break-in. It won't do her any good.

I know my mother is not particularly fond of New York. "Do you like that house?"

She picks at a scab on her cracked bottom lip, lost in thought.

"Would you move there?" I clarify, before she gets triggered by some old memory. "When all this is over?"

She shifts her knees up onto the bench, hugging them. "Maybe. I do want to get out of this city, one day. I've never really loved cities, anyway. I prefer the countryside."

"In Scotland?" I say, half joking, half hopeful.

"I'd love that, Alex. But the girls might be a harder sell."

"That's true." Convincing Fleur to leave New York would be the achievement of a lifetime.

"Don't give up on it, though. Those girls know how much you've sacrificed for them; I wouldn't be surprised if they'd live there for you for two years while you study. We've been through a lot here in New York."

I wonder if the glitz and the glamour and the memories that fill these walls have tarnished into something rotten for any of the girls. If my father's footsteps echo in the hallways, my mother's screams rattle the windows for them, too.

I grew up between Paris, London, and New York. This has never felt like home to me, but I'm sure it does to Josie, who has only *ever* lived here. I need them all on board before I can move us.

"Besides, there isn't much Mia wouldn't do for you."

I smile when she sets the vase of flowers on the stone patio at our feet. "I love that little idiot."

"She's got the best bits of your father." She fiddles with her fingers. "Maybe in a few months, when I'm not on some horrible low, I could fly to meet Ophelia."

I'm not sure it's the best idea, but I don't shoot it down. "I'll have a chat with the doctors."

She sighs, contented and happy with the mottled sunlight on her bare toes, and drifts off to sleep with her cheek against my shoulder. I slip my jacket around her narrow shoulders and promise myself never to forget the quiet moments like these.

Chapter 19

OPHELIA

Knowing Cain Green isn't in Scotland would be relaxing if I didn't know he was in New York. Alex must be tired of me texting him every five seconds for confirmation that he and his sisters are still alive.

His latest update comes in the form of his arm, covered in eyeshadow swatches while three different hands swipe varying shades of purple onto the remaining bits of space on his forearm.

Alex
Help. It's 3am.

I grin, typing out a reply on my laptop from one of the Nightshade library's dark, dusty corners, where I study opposite Divya.

Ophelia
Purple might be your color.

He sends back a zoomed in photo, and though it's blurry, I know it's a closely cropped photo of my hair.

Alex

This is my color.

Ophelia

Careful, Corbeau. Wouldn't want to come on too strong.

Alex

This crush I have on you is getting out of control.

Alex

FaceTime me when you shower later.

My bottom lip almost bleeds from the effort of biting down on my smile. Over a *man*, no less. How far I have fallen.

I close the tab before I add *failing all my exams* to the list of things I'm doing over a man. Divya gives me a knowing look, teasing but smiling ear-to-ear as she sits with her headphones on, poring over a cardiology textbook.

I think she's been sitting here for thirteen hours. Medical degrees aren't for the weak.

It's gloomy out, as it always is. The sky has a dark, rumbling underbelly that's rolling its way over the unkempt pines. A fine mist of rain obscures the spires of the castle, but inside, the fireplace beside the library bar is kicking out a steady warmth. A cozy glow from the brass wall lamps casts the dusty shelves and creaky desks in a soft light. It's quiet in here, thanks to some party that went on way too late last night, so the sense of foreboding that looms over my shoulder while I write my notes on grief in childhood makes no sense to me.

I hate the distance. It feels like helplessness a lot of the time. Whenever Alex has a bad day, all I can do is text him.

I just hope it's enough to get us through the next two years.

DIVYA IS ASLEEP on her laptop keyboard when I get back from swim practice, exactly where I left her.

I drape my jacket over her shoulders and leave her to rest.

I work in the library until the lines of my multimodal perception essay don't seem to make any sense anymore, until I've stared at the word *cognition* for so long that it looks like a weird assembly of letters with no meaning.

It's then that I notice the strange looks starting.

Actually, they've never really stopped. I can't walk across this campus and not catch a few death glares, but they definitely seem to intensify.

The two girls on the brown chesterfield by the fireplace, dressed like they're off horse riding and not sitting in a dusty castle in the Scottish Highlands, swivel where they sit. One of them whispers something to the other, which isn't uncommon. Something about my outfit, usually, or my slightly wonky teeth, or my freckles. I'd hoped to keep myself out of the spotlight this year, but getting back together with Alex has shattered that plan. Everything I do now seems to be publicly debated, sorted into *worthy of him* and *not worthy of him.*

But this time, no one seems to be laughing. If anything, they seem . . . sympathetic? Worried? *Angry?* I'm not sure; I'm terrible at reading people.

When I glance around the sagging wood shelves and dusty vaulted ceilings of the room, a lot of people are staring at me. I open the camera app on my MacBook to see if I have leftover pasta sauce on my chin, but it's got some dumb filter on it that makes me eyes bigger than the rest of my head.

In the photo gallery on the bottom left, photos of Alex and me in bed at my parents' house with giant bug eyes and tears of laughter glistening on our cheeks stare back at me.

The ache in my chest is hollow and heavy all at once. Long distance is *hard.* Especially on afternoons like this one, when I can't get hold of him and I'm left wondering if he's in a million meetings or lying in bed, grappling for reasons to keep going.

Colette's name appears in the top corner of my screen,

Colette

Hey, honey. Are you okay?

Ophelia

Have I put on a particularly pitiful outfit, or something?

Colette

You don't know?

Alex. A sickening feeling hits me. A hundred images flit through my brain. Oh *God.* A call from Colette has my phone vibrating on the desk, but I hit decline and gather my things.

I can't lose anyone else.

Ophelia

Text it.

I stumble my way out of the library and into the foyer. The walls are closing in on me, the decaying portraits laughing at my panic.

Colette sends a link to a news article.

Former Model and Wife to Missing Aviation Tycoon Elise Corbeau Believed to Be in Critical Condition After Collapsing Outside Her Manhattan Home.

No.

No, no, no.

"Ophelia, there you are." Vincenzo jogs in from the rain, phone pressed to his ear. He pulls it away again, hitting redial. "Come on, man. Pick up," he whispers, a gentle hand wrapping round my arm as he pulls me toward the dark spiral staircase. I have to run to keep up with him, a high-pitched ringing in my ears.

"He's not answering," Vincenzo tells me. "I've been trying him for the last twenty minutes."

I don't have to imagine what Alex is going through. I know it. I relive it every night, every time I'm bored, every time I see burgers, Scrabble tiles, helicopters, anything that reminds me of them.

I have to go to New York. I have to be with him.

"Bella." Vincenzo's voice cuts through the fog, phone on loudspeaker so he can text and talk as he guides us up the steps.

"Did you hear about Elise?" Belladonna's voice is strained on the line.

"Yeah. I'm gonna fly back."

"Your exams, Vincenzo."

"I'll retake them, do an extra semester if I need to. This is bigger than exams."

"Have you heard from Alex?"

"No." Panic lines the word.

"I'll come back with you. Call you back in a minute."

I call Alex while Vincenzo calls his father. I focus on the steady rhythm of his combat boots on the stone floor, trying to not think about what this means.

This means air travel, and even my terror for Alex and his mother isn't enough to distract me from that.

I can hardly breathe.

My call to Alex goes to voicemail. I try not to crumble. *Please, lord, let him be okay.*

Ophelia
Tread water, Alex. Tread water until midnight, and we'll figure it out from there.

We stop at the top of the stairs, and Vincenzo reaches out for the door, hand pausing above the handle like he's forgotten to do something. He drags me into a rough hug. "You okay?"

I swallow thickly, force out a shrug. His presence is comforting, sure and confident as always. I'm grateful Alex has him, has *always* had him. "I'm worried about him."

He pulls away, two giant hands settling on my shoulders like he's trying to keep me together. "He'll be okay. He has you. You two are the real deal."

"He has me," I repeat, with a nod. I *need* to show up for him. I'm not the girl who fell into despair for four years. I'm not the girl who runs away, who closes off her heart. I've grown. "Let's go."

VINCENZO HOVERS IN my doorway while I empty the bottomless pit of junk that is the top drawer of my bedside table onto the bed. My passport is there, stuck closed by a melted Haribo. It'll do.

"I can't bring liquids?" I ask, throwing an eclectic mix of clothes into a bag without really looking. The flight is the elephant in the room. I can tell that Vincenzo doesn't believe there's any universe in which I'll actually set foot on a plane.

Neither do I, but I'm hoping I'll just do it when the time comes.

"Yeah, you can."

"What?"

"It's a private jet. You can bring what you like."

"I . . ." Oh no. A private jet. My hands shake violently as I try to get a hold of the zipper on my bag. "I . . . I can . . ."

"Worry about the whole plane thing later, Pheelz."

"Yeah," I choke out, finally zipping up my duffel. Vincenzo slings both my bags and both of his own over his shoulder, picking up another phone call as we walk.

He leads me out of the mansion and onto the shady path to the car park. I stop beside his distinctive Maserati, but he keeps walking, toward Belladonna's Bronco. "She's the faster driver."

Belladonna arrives, together with Jack, one of Alex's friends from the rugby team whose parents are part of Elise's medical team. I haven't spoken to Belladonna since the night in the woods, though she often makes an appearance in my nightmares, an endless loop of Laura's death and blood on my hands.

It's tense between us. We've not spoken, save for the odd question she texts through from her men to confirm they've cleared up all traces of Laura's existence and buried the final copy of the photo that started all this. I have no right to be upset that she intervened, that she killed to protect herself, but I am. She had every right to be angry that I put her in that position, and by the look she shoots my way, she still is.

Vincenzo tosses all of our bags into the back, and the four of us climb into the car. Belladonna makes Eike look slow. I have one hand pressed to the roof and the other braced on the window as she skids the car out of Sorrowsong's long forested driveway.

On the plus side, it makes me slightly less apprehensive of the flight, because at this rate, none of us are making it to the airport alive.

They all make phone calls, Belladonna to her father, Vincenzo to his security guys, to his mother, to the airport. Jack to his mom, his girlfriend.

They all ring their people, but my person—my *only* person—is three thousand miles away, somewhere I can't hold him or comfort him, like he does so well for me.

All I need to do is get on that plane. I can't get off once it's up. I just need to get into my seat and do the panicking afterward.

But I stare at the journey time ticking down on Belladonna's dashboard like it's a countdown to my demise. I scrub clammy palms over my tights, trying to think of things I can see, smell, hear, taste.

The gray water and foggy hills of Loch Glascarnoch are vanishing in the rearview mirror. I have a horrible fear that I'll turn back around when the time comes and let Alex down.

Just over thirteen seconds. That's how long my parents were in freefall. It doesn't sound long, but I bet it was. I wonder if they were conscious. If they knew what was coming. If it felt like the longest thirteen seconds of their lives.

It's probably even longer in a plane.

This is not a helpful line of thought.

By the time a warning light forces us to stop for gas about fifteen minutes from the airport, I'm paralyzed by fear.

Vincenzo hops out to fill Belladonna's car for her, tugging my door open to poke his head in. "Want anything for the . . . umm . . . the bus ride?"

"The bus ride?" I say, voice distant and gaze focused straight ahead through the windshield. My teeth chatter, hands shake, pulse hammers.

"I'll get you some chocolate," he says, but he sounds far away.

I don't think I've ever felt this scared.

"Ophelia, hey," says Jack, like he's trying to distract a child. He drapes his hoodie over my legs. "Get her some activities to do, Vin. Like a puzzle book. And a pack of gum."

"Will do." He slams the door.

Jack turns to me. "Download a film and some music, or a podcast or something for the flight. It'll help."

Belladonna scowls at me but says nothing.

When Vincenzo gets back to the car, he has what looks like a weekly food shop for a family of four. He dumps a plastic bag on the back seat between Jack and me. "Got you those gross Wine Gums you like, Bella. And a Red Bull."

"Thanks, Vinnie."

"It's just a seven-hour bus ride, Pheelz. Nothing more."

"Forty thousand feet in the air."

Vincenzo turns in his seat as Belladonna pulls the car away, giving my hand a gentle squeeze. Their security guys follow suit in the black SUV behind us. "You got this. I know you do."

Like Colette, I have some twisted affliction where people being soft and kind to me makes me sad. "Don't."

He rummages around in the bag, seat belt almost strangling him. He drops a packet of Werther's Originals in my lap. "Apparently these are old person candies. You love old person shit."

"That's rude," I grumble. It's not rude at all. It's friendship and its companionship and it's everything I've been missing.

Vincenzo's grin is lopsided, all sparkling eyes and chipped teeth. "Well . . . you like custard and crosswords. And peace and quiet. You think portable phone chargers are the pinnacle of technology."

Somehow, he's dragged a reluctant smile out of me. "These are my favorite sweets."

He cackles victoriously, sliding back into his seat to face the front. "Fucking knew it." He sticks his hand into the back of the car like my dad used to do whenever he heard me rustling a packet in the car. "Gimme one to try."

I drop one into his palm, watching his oversized hand struggle with the wrapper. He drops it into his mouth and immediately inhales it. The other three of us can't stop laughing, even Belladonna. I half wonder if he is going to choke to death, but he does manage to swallow it and clear his airway. His hand reappears immediately, fingers moving in an impatient beckoning motion. "Another. Didn't get to taste that one."

"Are you going to lodge this one in your windpipe, too?"

"I'm not planning to, no."

I give him another, finally understanding why Alex is so determined to keep Vincenzo around, despite wanting to cut ties with that world entirely. In any situation, he's the one that keeps everyone going.

He must like the sweets, too, because his hand periodically appears in front of me all the way to the airport.

The past fifteen minutes have been a lot better, but the first thing I see when Belladonna steers us into the long-stay car park is a helicopter taking off.

"Shit," breathes Vincenzo. He slides his headphones over my ears in half a second, music deafening, but it's too late. I curl in on myself, waiting for the crash, waiting for the almighty boom. I count to thirteen, and when it doesn't come, I count again. I picture the helicopter spiraling down toward the rugged Scottish Landscape.

In my nightmares, it's *my* name that my father screams as he falls.

If I hadn't told them to rush home for burger night, maybe they'd still be here.

I stumble out the car, eyes fixed on my muddy Doc Martens.

I've come here for no reason.

There's no way I can get on a plane.

I type Alex an apology and then decide it's the last thing he needs. I hit backspace furiously, all outside sound muffled by

Vincenzo's music. He and Jack grab all the bags, and Vin lifts one of my headphones up to speak to me, cocking his head toward his father's men. "They wanna search you separately before you get on, I'm sorry. They're not fully convinced you're stable."

A laugh bubbles out of me, imagining my disheveled outfit, mascara running down my face, static hair. "What could've possibly given them that impression?"

He smiles ruefully. "Still, I'm sorry."

We walk into the airport. It's quieter than when I was last here. It's a day I can't bear to think about. A day when Alex and I both thought being apart could be less painful than being together.

"Miss," says one of Vincenzo's men, pulling me aside. I snap my eyes up to Vincenzo, wide and panicked.

He gives me a wink and a thumbs up. *You'll be okay.* "I'll meet you out the other side."

It's different for private planes, or at least for the Morellos. We skip the short security line. Vincenzo's men and an airport employee search me in a side room, emptying out my duffel and my tote into trays.

"You scared of flying?" the airport employee asks, as my shaking hands try to relace my boots. I nod, feeling worse by the second. Why did I think I could do this?

"It's a breeze. Safest mode of transport. No one *ever* dies," he says, popping his chewing gum. I almost throw the boot at his head.

True to his word, Vincenzo is waiting for me outside. "The bus is just refueling, then it's ready."

I nod, swallowing down bile that rises in my throat. "Okay."

"Them candies are really good."

"Yeah."

"Would you rather have them for fingers, or every time you buy a bag of candy, there's a finger in it?"

He drags yet another smile out of me. "Vincenzo, I have no idea."

"I'd rather have them for fingers."

The shaking seems to have spread from my hands to my entire body, every breath a labored effort. "Same, I think."

"You want to know a secret?" he asks, and something about his tone forces my gaze up to his.

"No," I grumble, shivering again. I'm sick of secrets.

"I'm scared of gunshots."

A soft laugh escapes me, before I realize he's serious. "You?" As kind and funny as he may seem to those he loves, he lives and breathes violence.

"Yeah, me. My mom took a bullet in the back for me when I was ten. Jumped in front of me and it caught her spine. My mom is alive and thriving, but guns lost their appeal after that."

And just like that, I learn Vincenzo isn't quite the happy ray of sunshine that he lets us all see. "You do shooting practice most weeks."

"If feeling scared is what I have to do to keep my parents safe, to keep *her* safe," he tilts his head in Belladonna's direction where she picks up a takeaway coffee, "then I'd spend the rest of my life terrified."

"Feel the fear and do it anyway," I whisper, nodding.

I can do this. I can do *anything*. Especially for Alex.

"Fuck yeah, Winters."

I feel like we just made an unspoken pact. *I'll keep being brave if you do.*

One of the men in black suits and earpieces taps Vin on the shoulder. "Jet's ready, Mr. Morello."

We step out onto the tarmac. I wish it wasn't windy and rainy. I wish the clouds weren't so thick. None of it eases my nerves.

I manage the weather better than I expected. I manage the quiet whir of the idling engines, and the employees in high-vis jackets holding things that look like tennis rackets.

I manage it all, until I read the black logo that runs down the side of the white private jet. *Green Aviation.*

My feet slow to a stop.

Any bravery I'd had dissolves into the frigid air. Pure, undiluted terror seeps in to fill the void.

Thirteen letters, five syllables that mark my parents' forested grave. Possibly the last two words they ever read.

The metal blades on the engine look vicious. The windows of the cockpit curl into a snarl. The wings look too thin, too fragile to withstand takeoff.

Vincenzo turns around a few paces ahead, beckoning me forward. "Come on. Can't miss our takeoff slot."

Panic overtakes my chest, all other rational emotions losing out.

Thirteen seconds for them. Endless agony for me.

"I'm sorry," I say, taking the first step back.

Belladonna swivels where she's stopped, halfway up the steps into the jet. Her face is stormier than the skies above us. She hands her laptop and coffee to the flight attendant and marches back down.

"Backing out?" she asks me, like it's a challenge she thinks I'll have to take her up on.

"It's—my parents died in a Green helicopter." I stutter over the syllables, can hardly get the final word out.

If looks could kill, I'd be bleeding into the tarmac. "Under a different CEO."

She looks at the hesitation in my expression and casts her eyes up to the cloudy heavens, cursing in Italian. There's no kindness in her eyes, no patience remaining. "So help me God, Ophelia. Your man is having the worst day of his life over there, and all we're asking of you is that you'll go to him. For once in your shitty life, we're asking you to put his issues ahead of your own. *One time.* Just get on this fucking plane and go back to moping another day."

And then the strangest thing happens. I . . . get on a plane. The one thing I swore I'd never do, a lifetime of scaring myself and accepting my fate just seems to splinter in two as my boots carry me up the metal steps.

It's like an out-of-body experience, watching someone who looks like me step through the doorway and into the jet. I'm on the sidelines, flipping violently between cheering and clapping, and begging her to come back.

I'm so stunned that I don't fully register what's happened until my boots come to a stop on a plush, pale carpet and Belladonna has asked the staff to close the door.

Vincenzo sinks down on one of the four cream leather seats around a small table while I stand in the center of the aisle, frozen still. "You were harsh, Bella."

Belladonna sinks down beside him. "No one has ever smacked any sense into her, and it shows."

My eyes dart around, frantic. The interior is furnished in soft creams and natural wood. The carpet is soft. There's a screen folded into the wall at the table that Bella, Vin, and Jack have seated themselves at. There's a sofa along the right-hand side, and two more empty seats farther down, each with a screen of their own. Four security guys are sitting around a table at the far end. Two flight attendants busy themselves by the door.

It's quite comfortable, for an aluminum death machine.

I run to the window like a dog watching people play outside, nose against the glass. There are patches of silver on the wings that have the contents of my stomach roiling. "Oh my god," I choke out. "It's being held together with fucking *sticky tape*."

They glance out the window and laugh, bucking their seat belts.

"No one is worried about this?"

"It's speed tape," says Jack, watching me self-combust.

"I don't want extra speed. I just want a safe, regular speed."

A pair of navy heels stop behind my feet. "You'll need to sit down for taxiing and take off, miss."

I turn to face the flight attendant. Her name tag reads *Caroline*, and her tone is polite and patient. "There's tape on the wings."

"It's just for securing any minor repairs."

I drag my palms down my cheeks, voice a quiet squeak. "Minor repairs?"

"Nervous flyer? We'll get you a drink as soon as we're airborne."

A pint of vodka might do it.

I lower into the seat beside Jack and opposite Belladonna, the four of us around the table. It feels like we sit there forever, the plane moving forward at a snail's pace.

Strange noises sound below us, beside us, behind us. Vincenzo just repeats the word *normal* over and over after every noise.

And then I'm thrust back in my seat, a deafening roar in my ears. I scramble to cover them, turn the music up to full volume, but I can still hear it. My eyes fly open in alarm, landing on the glacier blue of Belladonna's.

We're hurtling down the runway. Too fast, too loud, too out of control.

She's calm. Composed. *Bored*, even.

The plane speeds up even more, my head tipping back against the seat. I screw my eyes shut, squeezing two hot tears out. They scorch a path down my cheeks, fists curled tight.

I'm silent and still, breath trapped in my lungs, every muscle bunched tight.

This is awful. Worse than I ever imagined. I cannot believe Alex did this almost weekly at the end of last year. *Alex. I'm doing this for Alex.* I hope he's okay. I hope his mother is okay.

A cold hand encircles my own. Belladonna's fingers thread through mine. A warm hand settles on my other, and I dare to crack an eyelid. Jack holds my left hand, Belladonna leans forward, clutching my right. Her other hand sits in Vincenzo's on top of the table. We're connected in some unlikely circle, the three of them calm and composed, me fighting for air.

It almost makes me break down, but I'm distracted by a sickening sinking feeling, like we're plummeting.

This is it.

Thirteen, twelve, ten.

I grip Belladonna and Jack's hands so hard I worry I might break their fingers.

Nine, eight, seven.

Tears trickle over my jawline, clammy and uncomfortable on my neck. My stomach sinks. *Everything* feels like it sinks.

Six, five, four.

My name, cried out in my father's voice, reverberates in my ears.

Three, two, one.

The crash doesn't come. I open my eyes, finding Belladonna's again. This time, they *are* kind. Proud, even. "That was brave," she mouths, picking up her coffee.

I don't reply, *can't* reply, grinding my teeth to dust when the plane banks left.

And then a single, ominous *ding* fills the cabin.

The flight attendant appears with four glasses and a bottle of sparkling wine, giving me a reassuring smile and a little squeeze on the shoulder.

This so twisted. We're going to fall out of the sky any second now, and she's popping the cork out of a bottle of wine.

But I guess I'd rather die drunk than sober, so I gratefully accept the glass when she offers me it.

Chapter 20

OPHELIA

Shockingly, and against all the statistical odds, the plane landed. After seven hours—the hardest, most draining seven hours of my life—I find myself in New York.

As a girl who hasn't ventured outside of rural Scotland much these past few years, I can't help but find it completely *wild.*

The buildings are bigger, cars are bigger. The taxis are yellow. The city is a never-ending square grid of fancy looking cafés, hotels, and restaurants. Bustling pizza joints and leafy green parks. Tacky sports bars and luxury boutiques.

As we make our way across a bridge over a glittering river, I stare out at the dense mass of skyscrapers beyond like I've somehow landed on the moon.

No wonder Divya finds Sorrowsong boring.

Rocco sent a driver to pick us up from LaGuardia Airport. Now we're in the back of a huge black SUV, furnished similarly to the private jet. There's a small mini fridge at the back that we've left completely untouched.

No one has heard from Alex. Not me, not Vin, not Belladonna. The mood in the car is grim and downcast.

Whatever condition his mom is in right now, I already know what he'll be doing to himself. Heaping more blame onto his already weary shoulders, overanalyzing everything he could've done to prevent this.

We're stuck in a long slug of traffic ten minutes from the hospital when Vincenzo finally gets through to Fleur.

"Vin?" she asks, crackly through his speaker. She's holding back tears.

"Fleur, where are you?"

"We're still waiting at the hospital. I only just charged my phone."

"Who's we?"

"Alex and I. He's just checking to see if there's any update. He wants me to go home to eat and sleep."

Alex is okay. He's with Fleur and he's okay. The relief that courses through me is overwhelming.

"I'm ten minutes away."

"You're in New York?"

"Yeah. Do you want me to drop you home?"

I hear her side of a conversation, hear Alex convince her to go and rest, promise that he'll call if he finds anything else out.

He sounds strong. Steady and calm.

I doubt that's how he really feels.

"You can take me home?" she asks, sounding so much younger than seventeen.

"We'll stay for the night, too," says Belladonna. "Help the staff with the girls."

There is so much love in this car. It's in the way Vincenzo guides Fleur through some steady breaths. It's in the way Belladonna calls her father to say she won't be coming home tonight anymore. It's in the way Jack has spent the entire journey reading up on how best to help Alex and his mom.

I've never been struck so hard with it, never had it put in front of me so plainly to see.

Alex is bathed in love, swimming in it. And suddenly I understand his internal battle more than ever. How frustrating it is for him to feel so low with such a support network around him, to have family and friends and still feel lonely.

It must be so exhausting.

The car stops outside a hospital near Central Park. "Call us if you need anything, okay?"

I nod at Vincenzo, stepping out of the car and into the busy rush of an unfamiliar city. Cars rush by, honking their horns like it'll make the lights turn green faster. The people hurry around like they have places to be.

For all the trauma in my life, I've hardly ever set foot in a hospital. Before the helicopter crash, my life was very uneventful. Still, everything looks shinier, newer, more luxurious than the tired hospitals back home. It looks more like a technology store.

I go up to three different receptions, passed around like a pinball. The fourth woman looks me up and down, chewing her gum. "You from the media?"

"No, I'm . . . I'm family."

"You that girl who leaked the article?"

My exasperation reaches new levels. "No, that wasn't me. But please just let me see Alex."

"Never really liked Cain Green, anyway," she says. "Have you got our app?"

"No," I say, feeling my final shred of patience slither out onto the busy streets below.

"It's got a map on it."

Why must everything be an app? If I've said it once, I've said it a thousand times. *Everything* is becoming an app. "Please could you just point me in the right direction?"

It takes another ten minutes, but I'm finally taken to a quieter hallway several floors up. I know I'm in the right place, because a tall, stocky bald guy with an earpiece is in the hallway.

He recognizes me, somehow. "Ms. Winters."

"Did Alex leave with Fleur?"

He shakes his head and tilts it toward a doorway to his left.

It's a dim examination room, mostly covered by a paper curtain. I gently push down the handle and step inside. "Alex?"

I round the curtain and find him sitting in an armchair, elbows on his knees and head in his hands.

"Alex."

He looks up, and *fuck*. A sharp pain twists my stomach.

He looks completely broken. And he clearly hasn't seen any of the texts I've sent him, because he looks like he can't believe I'm here. For the briefest of seconds, I see all the questions he's too exhausted to ask flit through his eyes. The *why* and the *how* and the *when*.

"You're not real."

I squat down opposite him and thread my fingers through his. "I'm real."

"You're not here."

For him, I keep my tears at bay. "I'm here."

And like he'd been waiting for me without even realizing it, his head collapses forward, face buried in my hair.

The first silent sob that racks his body sends a hairline crack down the middle of my heart, the second splits it into two. I snake my arms around him and use everything that's left in my tired muscles to hold him together.

"I'm so tired of treading water, Ophelia. I just want to let go."

I scratch my fingers through his hair. "I know."

"I'm all out of fight. I don't want any of this anymore."

"I know. But I'm here to tread water for the both of us."

And so we sit like that. Me on my knees, him on the chair. Him falling apart, me holding myself together. Him convinced the world is ending, and me, for once, convinced we have a place in it.

We stay completely still while the sun sets outside, until he's able to take steady breaths and I'm sure my knees must be bruised. Until he pulls away, runs his hands over my lips, nose, eyebrows, jaw, checking I'm real. He presses a gentle kiss to my lips. "I'm tired, Ophelia. Not the short-term kind."

"That's okay. I am too."

He holds me at arm's length, the ghost of a laugh sneaking inside his next exhale. "You know I love you, yeah?"

"Yeah, why?"

"You look fucking dreadful."

My laughter echoes around the cold, clinical room. "I think it'd be fair to say I didn't handle the flight well." I take in the tired lines around his face, the red tinge to his eyes. He's beautiful. "You look like shit, too."

"I don't doubt it."

"Is your mom . . ." I trail off, unsure what I'm even asking. Obviously, she's not okay.

"I don't know," he says, swiping the back of his hand over his eyes. "They've hardly told me anything. Her heart is weak because she's been so underweight for so long and the antipsychotics she's on make it worse and how the hell am I supposed to explain all of this to the girls when I don't even understand—"

"Hey," I interrupt, running my hands through his hair to try to catch him before he spirals into a panic. I of all people know not to promise him that she'll be okay, or that he'll feel better tomorrow. So I make him the only promise I know to be true. "I'm here for you. I'll always be here for you."

I reach down to my tired-looking duffel, pulling out a bag of Jelly Babies and dropping them onto the cupboard beside us.

The tiny smile on his lips gives me hope. He drags me onto his lap on the armchair. The heat of his body encompasses mine, his familiar smell like a blanket around my shoulders. "Until midnight?"

"A hundred years from now."

"I love you," he breathes, eyes fluttering shut. The line between his brows smooths out, his breathing deepens, slows down. I feel his body relax beneath me as I run my fingers through the mess of his hair. I think he's fallen asleep. So I hold my breath, and the pee I've been needing for hours, content to listen to the steady beat of his pulse.

A doctor in scrubs comes into the room a short while later. She nods at Alex. "Should I come back? It's positive news."

Thank *fuck*. I shake my head and gently wake Alex, rising to my feet.

"She's been awake for a little while and she's alert," the doctor says, before Alex can ask otherwise. His head falls into his hands again, shoulders sinking with relief. I excuse myself to go to the bathroom while the doctor explains everything that's going on with Elise's weakening heart. It'd feel strange listening to it without her permission.

When I come back, Alex is in the hallway.

"I can visit her."

"Would you rather I stay out here?"

He nods, tucking a strand of hair behind my ear. "I think so. She worries about her appearance. I think she'd like the chance to get changed and do her hair and makeup before she meets you."

The world doesn't deserve him.

"I'll go find us coffee."

He stares down at me, the muscles in his jaw relaxing just a fraction. His thumb swipes my cheek, like a sculptor adding his final touch. "I can't believe you're here."

I let my lashes drift shut, lean into his caress. "I'm here."

I'm here, and it feels like I'm exactly where I need to be.

THE CHARGE NURSE was kind enough to let us stay the night, spooning on a too-small hospital bed and surviving off vending machine crisps and energy drinks.

I'm not sure that Alex really gets any sleep, though. Stress radiates off him in waves, to the point where I'm surprised the windows in this room haven't shattered.

It's gone ten in the morning when he wakes me up. Someone from the security team brought him an overnight bag, and he's changed into more casual clothes: a black jacket and loose jeans that have no business looking that good. "Hey."

"Hey."

He traces my bottom lip with his thumb. "Are you feeling jet-lagged?"

"Is that why I feel like shit?"

He grins. "Could be one of ten reasons. You want to meet my mom?"

"Oh God. I should wash my hair."

He rolls his eyes good-naturedly. "You two are alike. She won't care or notice."

I roll out of bed and stretch my tired arms above my head, hoping to send a bit of life to my groggy brain. I give my hair and my teeth a speedy brush, changing into jeans and one of my dad's old sweaters. It's a green knitted number with a hole in the sleeve, and it probably could do with a wash, but I don't really care. I needed it with me, need to feel close to him. In a way, it feels like taking him with me to meet Alex's mom.

"She's going to be disappointed," I say, staring at myself in the small mirror above the sink in the examination room.

Alex appears behind me, hands settling on my waist. "She's going to see what I see."

"Which is?"

"The greatest thing that ever could've happened to me."

I spin away from the sink to face him. "My dad would've loved you."

This makes him smile. I so rarely bring them up around him, around *anyone*. It's a wound that still feels fresh. "Yeah?"

"Yeah. He liked rugby, too. All sports, really."

"Did he watch you swim?"

"All the time. He was a chef. He loved cooking for us, so I was a very mediocre, twelve-year-old swimmer eating like I was two weeks out from an Olympic gold."

His eyes are glittering with amusement. "*Wow.* So cooking isn't genetic, huh?"

"Fuck you, Corbeau, you'll be grateful for my burned toast one day."

His hands tighten over my hips, pulling me flush against him. "Oh, I bet. He must've been a great man, to raise such a wonderful daughter."

"Oh, well . . ." I'm staring at my feet, cheeks flaming for no real reason. "That's kind."

His hand links with mine. "Come on."

I wait outside a hospital room in a different hallway, watching Alex crack the door open. "*Maman*?"

I can't hear the quiet reply.

"Ophelia is here, but no pressure."

Another reply, too soft-spoken to hear.

"Your hair looks good, Mom."

I hear her ask for a concealer, watch Alex shoot me a knowing look before vanishing inside for a moment. I pick at my nails, nervous.

I'm underwhelming.

I imagine things she might ask me. Where have I traveled? Nowhere. What are my grades like? Just scraping passes. What are my career goals? Haven't got a single one.

Alex calls me in, and I peek one eye round, like that'll save me from my terror.

I feel like I already know the woman in the bed. Not just from magazines my mom had when I was growing up, but from the way she shines through Alex.

Though clearly unwell and so, so frail, Elise is exactly as beautiful as she looks in pictures, even in her current surroundings. She's in a white satin gown that she must've gotten from home, her hair brushed to a soft shine.

"Hi," I croak, floating in the doorway like someone who's never socialized in her life.

"Ophelia," she replies, and I don't know how someone can squeeze so much warmth and so much welcome into seven little letters, but she manages it. Her accent is heavy, like that tiny hint of French that runs through Alex's.

Something about her pulls me forward. She's safe and kind and smiling at me like Alex does. Her eyes are glittering pools of pale green, just like his. "You look so wonderful."

"I look like I've been electrocuted. Twice," I say, sinking into the chair beside her bed. She holds out her hand for me to take, laughing softly. Her fingers are cold and thin beneath mine.

"You don't. Not at all. And nobody *ever* looks their best after a long flight."

"I don't know how Alex flies so often. I was convinced we were going down the whole time."

"Are you staying a while?"

I look up at Alex. We haven't discussed it. I have no idea what my plans are. I only have three more days of underwear. I have no idea if he wants me to meet his sisters, if Fleur would even let me into their home without killing me.

"I hope so," is all he says, looking at me with so much emotion in his eyes. Yellow happiness and red passion and the fierce blue of his unwavering loyalty.

I love it when he isn't gray.

"He was lost without you."

"*Mom.*"

"You were!"

"I think we had to take some time apart to work through some stuff for ourselves," I say, enjoying the feel of my hand in hers. It eases my mother's absence and makes it so much worse all at once.

Alex steps outside to take an urgent work call, and I scoot my chair closer to the edge of the bed so I can show Elise some photos of the clothes I bought at the charity shops with Colette. It seems to take her mind off things, at least.

Elise is easy to talk to. She doesn't ask me any of the questions I'd worried about. She asks me how my time with Colette was, how swimming is going, whether I'd like a cup of tea.

"I knew you were good for him from the very start," she says, smiling down at my lock screen when I've finished showing her all the random pictures in my camera roll so that I don't have to think of a new conversation topic.

I stare at the photo, taken last December. A blurry selfie outside the Nightshade mansion, snow gathered on our eyelashes, windburn on our cheeks. "Sometimes I think he's really extraordinary, and I'm . . ."

"Don't you dare say you're ordinary."

"A mug of hot chocolate is my idea of a big treat. Walking to the corner store is a day out."

That makes her laugh. "You're extraordinary, Ophelia. Don't fall into the same trap I did, don't let them make you believe that it's wealth or fame that makes a person. It's what you do in the quiet moments."

I think back to my last quiet moment. I think I spent it balancing a tube of Pringles and my phone on my stomach. "I guess so."

"He started drawing in color again."

That has my head snapping up. "What?"

"After he met you. He started drawing in color again, not just black and white."

I think back to the sketches I saw when I first met Alex. Messy, chaotic, often repetitive. Always in black charcoal.

And then to the first time he drew me, in bright orange pastel. To the artworks from the life drawing class: colored portraits in muted pastels.

"I didn't know that."

Her hand squeezes mine, her heavy-lidded gaze soft and sleepy. "Makes you seem quite extraordinary to me."

"He's very talented."

She glances at the door, like she's checking Alex is still on the phone. "I won't last forever, Ophelia. These past few months, right as my mind is making a little progress, I can feel my body giving up on me."

My swallow is thick, nostrils burning. "I know."

"Josie is almost eight, Charlotte ten," she says, like it's something I might not know. "If I died tomorrow, Alex would . . ."

He'd be the only parent figure in their life. "I know."

"I know raising children is not what anyone would want in a relationship at twenty-one."

"It's okay. You don't need to worry about that," I reassure her. "The girls aren't a hinderance. They're a learning curve, maybe. An adjustment for me to make, coming from a tiny family. But I wouldn't be with Alex if I was planning to run the second things get difficult."

She gives me a watery smile, eyes conveying more gratitude than words ever could. But she has it wrong. It's Alex who's saving me, no matter how much it looks like the other way round from the outside. Every second that Alex keeps breathing is a promise of the happy ending I'd long given up on.

He's the salve to the four-year-old ache in my chest. He's the hope of a family. He's complete and utter acceptance of me, as I am. No changes necessary.

Elise falls asleep to the backdrop of rhythmic beeps from the machines beside the bed. I stroke her hair and tell her about anything I can think of, doing a crossword aloud until Alex's voice interrupts me.

"She loves you."

I glance up, cheeks turning red. I hadn't realized he was there. "I love her, too. Was your call okay?"

"Yeah, just boring."

"I miss my mom," I say, quietly. I don't know why her and my dad are so heavy on my mind today. My mom cheated on my dad. She cheated on him with the wrong man, a heinous man.

But I miss her all the same.

"Does it ever not hurt?" he whispers, quiet enough that his mom can't hear him.

I want Alex to have honesty from me, not the *it'll get easier* that everyone churns out on autopilot. "It always hurts. The shock of it, the unfairness. It's ridiculous . . . like a movie you've seen a hundred times and yet you still think this time it *might* end differently. Every day it's like . . . maybe my dad *will* be flipping pancakes at the stove when I go downstairs, and all of this will have been some bad dream."

His palm settles on my shoulder, gently rubbing the tense muscles there.

"It's cliché, but it doesn't get easier. You just get better at managing it. It doesn't hurt any less, but the pain doesn't scare me as much as it used to."

When I tip my head back to see him, his smile is soft, grateful. "I can handle that."

"I'll be right there with you."

He drops a kiss on my forehead. "Do you want to go back to my place? You can shower, eat a decent meal, sleep in my bed."

"Who is home?"

"The girls will be home in the evening. And the housekeeper, the nannies, the chef, and the security guys."

I do a terrible job of concealing the worry in my voice. "All six of them?"

His sigh tickles the top of my head. "Fleur will cool off."

"She shouldn't have to. Home is her safe space. I don't want to infiltrate that and make her feel she can't be there. Especially right now."

His hands move to my hair, scratching my scalp in the way that he loves. "I'll give her a call and ask her what she thinks of you staying over."

I'd like that, but I keep my hopes down.

Chapter 21

OPHELIA

The notification on my phone makes me grin as one of Alex's security guys weaves through the lunchtime traffic, a comfortable silence in the shiny black car.

From: Alex Corbeau-Green

Subject: Lonely (adjective) *sad because one has no company.*

Date: Wednesday 9th April 12:03 EST

To: Ophelia Winters

Are you there yet?

Ps. Mia hides the good snacks in the cupboard beside the dishwasher.

So the data plan he's put my phone on works, then. I continue to be impressed by this cracked, dented six-year-old little machine.

I imagine the look on Alex's face if I were to utter that sentence aloud. He already thinks I'm a cavewoman.

From: Ophelia Winters

Subject: Impatient (adjective) *annoyed because you have to wait.*

Date: Wednesday 9th April 12:04 EST

To: Alex Corbeau-Green

Not yet. This city is kind of trafficky, if you haven't noticed.

I shut the screen off to take in the madness of the city around me, but it pings straight away.

From: Alex Corbeau-Green

Subject: Trafficky (error) *not a word.*

Date: Wednesday 9th April 12:05 EST

To: Ophelia Winters

We making up words, now? Text me when you get there, baby.

The car pulls up a short while later, outside a huge, terraced brownstone on a tidy street. "Wow," I say, craning my neck to absorb all four floors.

The security guy opens the door for me. I've already forgotten his name. There's so many of them to memorize. "I'll park the car, miss. Take the steps up to the door."

I creep into the house like I'm a burglar, holding my breath and walking on my toes, for some reason. The foyer is huge, all polished wood floors and a white staircase with a beige runner. There are shoes spilling out of the closet beside me, and children's drawings in white frames decorate the wall behind the stairs. There's a warmth in the air, the smell of baking wafting from somewhere.

This is a home. The London house was a cold, polished shell. This is homey in a way that I've missed *so* badly. I turn to the closet, kicking off my boots and putting them on a shelf with Alex's sneakers.

A cheery *hi* splinters the thick silence, and I let out an unholy shriek, dropping my bag.

The woman in front of me laughs, holding her hands out in apology. She's short and round, brown hair streaked with gray. "Sorry to scare you. I'm Ingrid, the housekeeper."

"I'm . . ."

"Ophelia. Alex told me you'd be here any minute," she finishes for me, a warm smile on her face. Is *everyone* in Alex's life this excited that he has a girlfriend?

"I . . . this is a beautiful home."

"It is. I love my job. I'll show you around."

She takes my bag for me, leading me into a kitchen, bright and airy with pale wood floors and white stone countertops. Huge glass doors at the far end lead out to a small garden, full of plants and trees. A tray of cooling blueberry muffins sits on the island, and if I wasn't too embarrassed, I'd beg her for one. They smell ridiculous. "Are the girls home?"

"Emily will pick them up from school in a few hours, so you have some time to yourself before then."

"I definitely need a shower."

"Here, I'll show you Alex's bathroom. He already had me go out and grab you some things. I can give you a full tour later, if you like. I'm guessing you're exhausted."

Alex's room is at the end of the second-floor hallway. A giant cream rug covers most of the hardwood floor, a huge teak bedframe at the center of the back wall. Maybe I'm just tired, but the white cloud of soft bedding looks like it'll be the comfiest thing in the world.

As always with his rooms, the space is immaculate, but the desk is utter chaos. Piles of sketchbooks, books, letters for his mom, study notes, architecture journals. There are at least a dozen sketches of me scattered across it all.

In the giant en suite—I'll never understand why a bathroom needs two sinks—there's a wicker basket with shampoo, nice soap, a hairbrush, tampons, some soft sweatpants, pajamas, cookies, and a packet of Jelly Babies.

Ophelia

I'm spoiled. Thank you.

Alex

Did Ingrid meet you?

Ophelia

Yes, she's lovely.

Alex

I have nightmares in which that woman retires. She's worked here for fifteen years.

Ophelia

I might marry her instead of you.

Alex

Her husband works for us too, as a driver.

Ophelia

Damn it. Never mind, then. Gonna shower and take a nap.

Alex

Send pic

That stupid emoji pings through, with the big watery eyes. I laugh, snapping a pic where the towel only *just* covers me.

Alex

You're so hot, baby.

Ophelia

This shower is definitely big enough for two.

Alex

I'll be home first thing, as long as Mom
looks okay. Cannot wait.

The shower is everything I needed. It washes away the stress, the flight, the panic from the lecture hall. When I step out in the fluffy towel and spot that Ingrid has left a warm muffin and a cup of tea on the side table, I think I might just curl up here and never leave.

I sit on the edge of the bed, peeling back the brown paper and taking a bite.

Jesus Christ, it's the best thing I've ever eaten. I flop back onto the white duvet, moaning around the food in my mouth.

The painting is on the ceiling above Alex's bed. *My* painting. The mess of fingers and handprints I made while he fucked me in London.

Ophelia

Nice view from the bed

Alex

Something's got to make the lonely
nights less lonely

Now my brain is full of all sorts of visions of Alex in this bed, so I bury myself under the duvet and let my imagination run wild.

* * *

A KNOCK AT the door startles me. The curtains are good enough that I have no idea what time it is, but my phone tells me it's just past five. I croak out a hello, voice hoarse.

"Hey, girl!"

I've never met Mia, but I'd know her voice anywhere from the endless FaceTime calls I've spoken to her on.

"You're home! Come in," I say, combing my fingers through my hair.

The door opens, and a flurry of long limbs and dark hair launches toward me like a flying squirrel. She lands on the bed with a thud, grinning ear to ear. "Oh my god, it's so cool that you're here."

"I can't believe I survived the flight."

"I know, right? Usually a very unreliable form of transport," she says teasingly.

"Oh, so Alex's attitude runs in the family?"

She laughs, flopping back beside me. "He's the worst of us all."

"How was school?"

She wiggles her feet, clad in white sports socks. "Fine. I had track practice."

"Does Evie like sports, too?"

She smiles at the mention of her twin sister. "Not really. She likes dancing. Actually, she likes figure skating. She's excited to meet you, too."

"I'm kind of nervous." I'm more than nervous. Meeting a load of miserable businessmen and CEOs? I'd be fine. Meeting teenage girls? Terrifying.

"Don't be. We can just eat popcorn and watch a movie together. Did you see my mom? Did she seem . . . well, obviously she's not fine, but did she seem okay?"

Concern creases her eyes and my heart squeezes. "It's hard for me to say. I don't know what she's normally like. But we had a good chat. She seemed cheerful, considering."

Mia stares at her feet, chewing her bottom lip. While Evie, Josie, and Charlotte have the blond hair and fair complexion of their father, Mia is all green eyes and dark hair, her skin a little sun-kissed. Although, anyone looks sun-kissed next to me. "Our mom is the best."

"She is."

"It's not fair that she's sick and my father isn't."

I nod, fiddling with the purple friendship bracelet on my wrist. I don't know what to say. I don't know how Alex does this: answer questions from the six of them, all at different stages of childhood, all at different stages of understanding what death really means.

"It's not fair Alex is dealing with all of this, either."

"No, it isn't." I have a hundred questions. About Alex as a child, about life when their father was still at home, about how he's really been these past few months. None of them are fair to ask a sixteen-year-old trying to navigate one of the most difficult weeks of her life.

"Ugh. What are we doing?" Mia asks. "We've gone straight to miserable talk. We should get up and be positive. There are blueberry muffins downstairs. And it's risotto for dinner. *And* there's ice cream in the freezer. I made it."

I stand up, pulling on Alex's Sorrowsong Rugby hoodie. I'd kill to see him back there, playing beside Vincenzo. "You can make ice cream?"

"It's really good, if I do say so myself."

From the top of the stairs, I can already hear the buzz of life downstairs. Ingrid's voice, but someone else's, too. A man's. And lots of laughter, despite the situation.

It's a home. It's a home and a family and it's a sink full of dishes and walls that aren't cold the whole way through.

I will myself not to get emotional. But it *is* emotional. Whatever this is, here in this house, it's the opposite of loneliness. "Sounds busy," I say, nervously.

"You come from a small family, right?"

I stutter, like I always do whenever I talk about my family, stuck somewhere in that horrible space between *is* and *was*. "Yeah. Well, it's just me now. Just me at home . . . um . . . but there was three of us. But no, I've never had a big family."

She flushes, like she's cursing herself for asking me that. "Shit, Ophelia. That was careless of me."

"No, no. It's fine. Really, it is."

"If you're overstimulated, you can just have a moment in Alex's room."

"Sounds perfect."

I reach the bottom of the stairs, and a girl I recognize as Josie flies round the kitchen doorway like she's been watching the stairs, waiting for me.

"Pheelz!"

I laugh, accepting her impressively forceful hug. "Pheelz? Did Vincenzo put you up to that?"

"Yeah." She squeezes me again. "Alex told me not to scare you away."

I hug her back, nose in her blond waves. "He did? We can't keep letting him get away with these comments."

"Let's take him down!"

"Deal."

She drags me into the kitchen, where I see Evie—who looks exactly like her twin sister but with lighter hair—Éléanor, who is twelve and the shiest of them all, and Charlotte, who, at ten years old, gave me the most efficient, businesslike handshake I've ever received. Ingrid is here, too, and a gray-haired man I'm assuming is her husband. There's another man, too, in a white chef's jacket. It really is chaos. Several versions of my name are cheered, each of the sisters enveloping me in a warm hug. Evie holds on to me an extra second. "I feel like I know you already; we've heard so much about you."

"Oh no. I don't want to know."

She laughs, placing a drink in my hand. "All good things!"

Everyone is in good spirits, but they all look so tired. I don't know how they're all doing it.

But as the evening rolls on, I start to understand it a little more. They all lean on each other. Everyone is involved, everyone is included. When someone seems down, everyone rallies around them, even Ingrid, who seems to love Elise as if she were a sister.

And even though Alex isn't here to guide me through it, I feel totally okay. *Welcome.*

But one absence is nibbling away at my conscience. I nudge Mia as we start pulling pasta bowls and glasses out of cupboards for dinner. "Where's Fleur?"

"I'm not sure. Probably in her room."

"Is that because of me?"

"No. She never really hangs out with us anymore. She didn't eat with us last night. It's not you, I promise."

I hate that I'm off on such a bad foot with her. I wish everything had played out differently.

The chef leaves a huge casserole dish full of risotto on the center of the table in the dining room, as well as a mountain of grated parmesan and some salad. I pull out a chair and sit down for my first family meal in years.

Laura flashes in my mind, as guilt-inducing as it is jarring. The coldness, quietness in her Inverness house no different to my own.

This right here is all she really wanted.

God, Laura. I am so sorry. I feel like I used her as a stepping stone to get here.

What Alex thinks about me is true: I *am* disgusted by the wealth they all have. It's more than anyone needs. But if I happened to discover my dad was actually a millionaire and was just keeping me humble, hiring someone who can cook would be my first order of business.

I tried to make Alex a chicken salad last year and we both got a *stomach bug*, as he assures me it was.

It was food poisoning.

But this risotto? Nothing short of incredible.

I'm sad Alex isn't here, but it's right that his mom has company.

"Are you still here over the weekend, Ophelia?" Mia asks, taking a second helping of the food.

"Yes, if you guys don't mind?"

Josie's voice is loud and clear beside me, her hand landing on mine. "We don't mind!"

"We can bake a birthday cake for Alex!"

Shit. Alex's birthday. He's impossible to buy for. He has enough money to buy a small island, but the things he really wants are things money can't buy.

"Sounds great. Red velvet, maybe."

"Soooo . . ." says Charlotte, in a terrible effort to seem casual. "You guys are all made up?"

I snort into my lemonade. "Yes, we're all made up."

"Are you gonna break up again?"

"Josie!" Mia pinches the bridge of her nose, glaring at her sister.

"What? We were gonna ask her."

"We were going to interrogate her in a more subtle manner," says Mia, through her laughter.

"We've been waiting for Alex to get a serious girlfriend for ages," adds Evie, a solemn expression on her face. "We were worried it'd *never* happen. And then he left you, and like . . . obviously we love him, because he's our brother, but we wanted to strangle him. We never thought it was you who leaked the file. Well, none of us except . . ."

Another voice joins the fray, soft and lyrical just like Elise's, but the accent American, rather than French. "Wow, E. Thanks a lot."

The table quiets. I hope they don't notice the way my shoulders stiffen with tension. I know who it is before I turn. Should I stand? *No, she's not a fucking earl.* Go for a hug? She doesn't want to hug me. Handshake?

I turn to face Fleur. I've seen her in pictures, billboards, and magazines, but she's a lot more intimidating in the flesh. Her hair is dark like her brother's, long enough that it kisses the top of her belt. She's in an outfit that makes me realize that it's not low-waisted jeans that are the problem, it's me.

She has familiar piercing green eyes, and that sets me at ease. It's hard to feel any hostility to anyone who has Alex's eyes.

Still, anyone who can pull off low-waisted jeans makes my palms sweaty.

"Hey, Fleur," I say, quietly. "How are you?"

Dumb question. Despite the happy atmosphere in the house, it's pretty obvious all of these girls are struggling.

"Having kind of a shitty week, actually," she says, sinking into the vacant chair at the head of the table. She fills her plate with salad, the mood around the table a little grayer. Alex has given me a heads up about Fleur's feelings toward me, so I'm not really sure what to say. "How did my mom seem?"

"She seemed quite cheerful, I think."

She takes a mouthful, nude-colored nails tapping at her phone screen. Her skin is glowing, hair glossy, but the dark circles under her eyes are just as bad as Alex's. "Because Alex has finally found someone willing to put up with his shit."

Mia laughs. "I think we were worried you were a robot."

Evie nods in agreement. "He's always had a creative imagination."

"But he builds the *best* pillow forts."

I grin down at Josie. Based on the way he kitted out the rental car on Boxing Day, I can believe that.

I always knew how much he's done for his sisters, how hard he works to keep some semblance of normality in their lives, but seeing it here now, I have this sudden urge to reach beneath his skin and cradle his soft heart in both my hands.

But I can't do that, so I settle for a quick text.

Ophelia
I love you.

Ophelia
So much.

The rest of the dinner passes in quiet conversation. Fleur doesn't say another word, and she's first to leave the table. Still, I feel like our first meeting could've gone a lot worse, considering the fact that a month ago, she wanted to remove my head from my shoulders.

The rest of us are all eating Mia's homemade ice cream when my phone buzzes in my lap.

Alex
My love for you keeps my heart beating.

I feel my cheeks turning pink. I never know what to say back to these things, just like I don't know how I got so lucky. I send him a thumbs-up emoji, only because I know it'll make him laugh. He thinks I'm a bad texter.

I probably am a bad texter.

I SPEND THE first few hours of the night wide awake, staring at my terrible piece of artwork on the ceiling. A thick blanket of silence settles over the house, the hum of the outside world barely audible.

I pad down to the kitchen in my new—brown, of course—pajamas for a glass of water, whispering a quiet hello to the security guys in the foyer. I take a sip and turn to take in my surroundings.

The dishwasher churns quietly, full to the brim from a busy evening of home-cooked food. More children's drawings decorate the wall, and there's a folder filled to the brim of handwritten recipes.

In the still darkness of the kitchen, I spot a shadowed form outside, sat on the garden bench with his forehead resting in his hand.

I fill up a second glass of water and slide open one of the double doors. The stone path is cold on my bare feet, my pajamas a thin barrier against the chill. The wind whispers through the bushes, tousling my hair as I walk toward the defeated form on the bench.

Alex exhales a long stream of smoke, eyes on the starless sky above us. "I'm bad company tonight, Twist."

He's trying to get me to leave, but it isn't working. It won't work. We've done that once, and it was a mistake.

"Not for me. Never for me." I sit down on the bench beside him, watching the cigarette glow on his next inhale. "You came back early."

"The next nurse on shift was a bit stricter with visiting hours."

I run my hand over his back, feeling the heat of his skin even through his hoodie. His head drops again. I wish I could take some of the weight off his shoulders. "She's okay, though?"

"Mentally, she's surprisingly upbeat. Her heart and liver are just giving up."

I lean my head on his shoulder, which softly rises and falls with his slow breaths. It's peaceful out here. The chaos of the city is a muted hum. The air is crisp, but not cold. I can see why Elise likes to spend her days on this bench.

"I will quit," he says, putting a second cigarette between his lips. The lighter battles the breeze, illuminating the hand Alex cups around it. He looks so tired. "I will. Just not this week."

I take the box off him, because two is enough, and slip it into my pocket. He offers me the one between his fingers.

"No, thanks. I like normal-flavored air. Just plain, original, vanilla air."

He laughs. "Fuck me, then."

I grin back at him in the soft orange glow cast by the porch light. "Fuck you, then."

"Evie texted me to say that you're cool."

Now it's my turn to laugh. If I could pick one adjective that I'm not, it'd be *cool*. When I was twelve, my mom asked my grandma to say something nice about me and the best word she could come up with was *sturdy*. She slapped me on the thigh like a retired man slaps his old car and said, *She wouldn't blow away in a strong wind, that one.*

Nothing like a female family member to humble you at an early age.

I miss them all now, though.

"Your sisters are great. I like them all, Fleur included."

"They are. I don't know how they've not turned out terrible."

I swing my legs where I sit, the garden quiet save for the sporadic noise of my feet catching the tile beneath us.

"I might never get better, Ophelia."

This is unlike him. I've seen a lot from Alex, but never much insecurity. "Alex. I'm miserable. Cynical. Grumpy. Glass half empty. In the future you envision for us, am I a cheerful, happy-go-lucky optimist who skips her way down the stairs every morning?"

He almost shudders, which makes me laugh. I don't know why he is so charmed by my grumpiness. "Fuck no. You grumble all day."

He snuffs out the cigarette on the metal arm of the bench and drags me onto his lap, rinsing his mouth with water from the glass.

His hands run over my thighs, over the soft fabric that covers them. He leans into the curve of my neck and takes a slow inhale, like he needs me in his bloodstream more than the nicotine. "I'm frightened by my love for you."

"I'm frightened by the idea of not having a slice of toast in the next five minutes."

His laugh is warm and rumbly against my throat, and his fingers sink into my hips as though he can't bear to let go. "One more minute."

I drop a swift kiss to the top of his head. "If all you could ever offer me is quiet weekends and difficult mornings, that's more than enough."

"You're just grumpy, though. I'm depressed. It's a different beast. Depression is exhausting to be around. Grumpiness isn't."

"I know it's a different beast, but it's the same love."

Finally, he meets my eyes. His are full of worry, but I don't need a mirror to know that mine are full of certainty.

"The same love," he repeats, like it's an unfamiliar concept. Like he'd never considered the fact that I might love him just as unconditionally as he does me. Somewhere, two car horns beep. Someone shouts. Our eyes stay completely locked, like no one exists but us.

"DO YOU WANT anything for your birthday?" I ask, sitting on the stool at the kitchen island, watching Alex put four slices of bread in the toaster and push the button down.

"You. Backward. Forward. Sideways. In the shower. On my desk."

On his desk. *Fuck.* My knees press together. "*Alex.*"

"You're present enough for the next hundred birthdays, Ophelia."

"If you don't say something, I'll have to go rogue. I'll get you interpretive dancing lessons."

He's grinning, at last, as he pulls a jar of chocolate spread from the cupboard that very clearly says *Mia's – DO NOT TOUCH* on it and opens it. "I'll interpretive dance for you any day of the week, Twist. No need to pay for lessons."

He dips a knife into the jar, then, standing between my legs, he holds it up for me to lick.

I run my tongue along the cool metal, watching his pupils dilate.

I'm hyperaware of the square inches where our bodies touch. Hyperaware of the pulse that drums a thick, lazy rhythm in my neck. Hyperaware of the way the width of his body forces my thighs apart, of how rough his jeans feel against me. Time seems to slow, the distant *tick tick tick* of a clock in the hall sounding like it's been submerged in treacle.

When I reach the top of the blunt blade and wrap my lips around the very tip to gather the chocolate there, a hoarse curse escapes him.

My pulse slides from my throat to somewhere deep in my belly. One of his hands grips the knife so hard that veins bulge over his forearm, and the other slides up the side of my neck. My breaths come thicker and faster, each one inflating this balloon of tension between us.

"*Fuck*, Ophelia," he breathes out, as I swallow the chocolate on a quiet moan. The air is dense, like we're in the thicket of a rainforest. His exhale is animalistic. Mine is frantic.

This is what he does to me. I'm unraveled.

"I desperately need a good reason not to fuck you right here on this island."

My thighs squeeze, but with him between them, there's nowhere for them to go. "Don't threaten me with a good time."

He hooks a finger in the front of my pajama shirt and tugs it forward, eyes dropping to the opening he's just created.

The expression on his face is *anything* but gray.

I spread my legs wider so we're flush against each other, breaths heaving, control on the brink of snapping.

The toaster pops, making us both jump.

I drag in a desperate inhale like I've just run a marathon.

He steps back, raking two hands through his hair and opening a drawer to retrieve a clean knife. "God, Ophelia. I can't have any rational thoughts around you."

"I'd definitely be up for fucking on the kitchen island."

His back turns, muscular shoulders flexing as he spreads butter and chocolate onto all four slices and slides two over to me. "One night when it's just us here. No kids."

I put the knife in the sink while he pours me a cup of tea. If the atmosphere around us had a color, it'd be a soft lilac: those first wisps of sunrise on a quiet spring morning.

It spreads a yellow-orange sort of happiness to all the dark, dusty corners of my body. There's something so extraordinarily ordinary about us, feeling like my soul has been set alight while unloading the dishwasher beside him, feeling the cracks in my heart fuse shut while we wait the two minutes for our Cup Noodles to be ready.

Alex inhales his toast in four bites, practically hopping from foot to foot while I munch through mine, like a dog waiting for me to drop a crumb. The toast does a bad job of muffling my amusement.

"What?"

"You."

Another little shuffle from foot to foot. "What about me?"

"You want me to finish so we can go upstairs and fuck."

He stills, but he looks like he's been caught red-handed, the faintest blush kissing his cheeks. "Do you wanna?"

I fold the entire second slice of toast into my mouth like a piece of bread-based origami, hoping that's answer enough, and he lets out the most wonderful laugh, tossing me over his shoulder, carrying me out of the kitchen, and taking the stairs three at a time.

Chapter 22

ALEX

[DRAFT]

From: Alex Corbeau-Green

Subject: Dribble (noun) *You drool on your pillow, just to let you know. And you sleep talk.*

To: Ophelia Winters

If the rest of my birthdays begin like this one, then I'd like to live forever.

IT'S MY BIRTHDAY. Twenty-four.

I don't know why, but it feels significant.

Over the years, I've prayed not to reach twenty-four, and here I am. Alive and breathing and feeling and aging, just like everyone else.

Oddly enough, I'm someone who enjoys my birthday. I'm not one for presents or parties, but I'm one for time spent with family. I'm one for the look of pride and relief in my mom's eyes at the knowledge that I've made it another year. My depression *does* feel like an illness, and every birthday feels like an achievement as much as it feels like an exhausting feat of endurance.

This birthday in particular, I feel blessed. Ophelia's presence in New York has flipped my week on its head. When I'm not pulling my hair out from stress and trying to juggle four hundred things at once, I'll sit down and fully appreciate what she did for me by getting on that plane. It's too much for me to think about right now, a kindness too great for my brain to accept.

I vowed as soon as my eyelids swung open this morning that I wouldn't think about my father today. He doesn't deserve it. It's not like I have any real birthday memories beyond the age of ten that I associate him with, anyway. Green Aviation, his favorite child, took up too much of his time.

And after a mind-alteringly hot shower with my girl to start my twenty-fifth year, I spent the second half of my morning in a cramped hospital room with the eight women who put meaning behind my every action, purpose behind my every breath.

My mom's recovery is slow, but she's coming home. Ophelia seems in no rush to go back to Scotland. Fleur is speaking to me.

Today I feel surrounded by reasons to keep going.

Now I'm going through my emails in my office at home while Ophelia cooks me "the meal of a lifetime" for lunch, which may well be code for something that'll make me shit myself, if history is anything to go by.

I love Ophelia, and I think she's wonderful, but she's the worst cook on the planet.

In the future I'm building for us in my head, I cook. She sits at the kitchen island and moans about the state of the world and how everything is becoming a QR code nowadays.

Maybe it's my good mood, but I burn through my inbox in record time. The weekly update from the sales team doesn't feel as dry as it usually does. The marketing strategy I've been forwarded seems to make sense. The negotiations with the French airports are progressing. The overambitious LinkedIn warriors in my inbox don't make me want to put my head through the desk.

The folder of Deleted Items glares at me; one email in there teases me, taunts me all through my work days.

Carmichael wasn't lying when he wrote to me. Sorrowsong's architecture program *is* gaining more and more credibility.

Ophelia appears in the doorway, wearing a white apron over the green dress she bought in London.

I love that dress. I love the girl in it. I love what they do together.

She places an orange liquid in front of me with a small curtsy, dropping a cocktail umbrella in it. "Your drink, *mademoiselle.*"

I smother my laugh in my hand. She's really going all out. "Do you know what *mademoiselle* means?"

"No."

I take a sip, *trying* to keep both eyes open. One gently sneaks shut while my esophagus melts away. I'm not entirely convinced that isn't a glass of battery acid.

Her eyes are bright, excited. "Do you love it?"

"Love it."

"Then why are you wincing?" She snatches it from me, takes a sip, then immediately coughs it all over my desk. "That's fucking horrendous."

"It's lovely," I say, struggling to keep a hold on my laughter. She furiously brings up the recipe on her phone. Her face falls. "Ah. A tablespoon of lemon juice. Not a cup. I'll remake it."

"Pass that on to Rocco, though. He's always looking for new ways to melt padlocks from doors."

"Wanker," she breathes, on her way out the door.

Ten minutes pass, and then twenty. No drink reappears. On top of my work for once, I follow the vague smell of fire into the kitchen and find Ophelia's MacBook open on the island with *how to unburn steak* typed into the search bar.

I find her in the back kitchen, taking something out of the microwave. Her hair is in a messy bun, though more red tendrils have escaped than remain. She's looks like she's in the worst mood ever, which amuses me greatly.

"Fuck you for having a birthday. Fuck steak. Fuck lunch as a concept. Fuck frying pans. Fuck recipe websites. Why do I have to read about your uncle's fucking gallstones to read how long to cook a steak for? And fuck the stove, too. It's lying about being on medium. It's on high."

I lean against the doorway, a fond warmth spreading its way through my blood. This is what I want. This is what I want *forever*. "Going well, then."

She spoons green beans onto a plate with far more force than necessary. "A cow died for this, Alex!"

"I'm sure it's not that bad."

She leads me into the main kitchen, where two steaks masquerading as lumps of charcoal sit in the cast-iron skillet on the stove. When she drops one onto each plate, they clank like charcoal, too.

"It—"

"Shut up." She's pouting, hard, as she tosses a few potatoes on each plate and puts salt and pepper on them, like that'll save this car crash.

I sit down at the kitchen island, dragging the plate toward myself and biting the inside of my cheek.

"Happy fucking birthday," she mutters, sitting down beside me. I can see she's desperately trying not to laugh, too.

The potatoes aren't even bad. The green beans are definitely almost edible.

"You're not even going to try the steak?" she asks, looking down at the blackened mass on the plate, expression dejected.

"I'm all right, thanks. I'd quite like to finish the day with my molars intact."

That earns me a whack with a dishcloth. "Alex!"

I hook my finger under the strap of her green dress, dragging her closer to me. She swats my hand like it's a fly. "Is this how you usually treat the staff in restaurants?"

I give her my most charming smile. "Only the sexy, grumpy redheads."

"You better tip well."

"Oh, I have a tip you can have," I whisper, watching her bury her face in her hands.

She's blushing when she emerges, the very corners of her mouth turned up. "You're a terrible flirt."

I stick out my bottom lip, hands landing on her ass. The soft lines of her body have me in a tailspin, my head so far in the clouds that I've forgotten all my issues. "Flirt back. Don't leave me hanging—it's my birthday."

"Only if you leave me a good review on Tripadvisor."

I grin against her neck. "Five stars. *Chef was so hot that I can only assume that the steak must've burst into flames on contact.*"

She leans into my touch, my hands threading through the bright copper strands that have buried themselves so deep into my chest that they're holding my fragile heart together. "Seven letters," she whispers, "First letter *B. The chef might give you one, if you're lucky.*"

I shift on the stool. The thought of Ophelia on her knees, here, has my next sentence stuck in traffic. My brain has short-circuited.

But the patter of bare feet coming through the foyer reminds me why my errant thoughts must remain just thoughts. Josie skids around the doorway, face wrinkling. "Ew. Were you kissing?"

"We would *never*," I say, scandalized. I pick her up with one arm and swing her into my arms. She has a piece of paper clutched in her clammy little hand. "What you got there?"

"It's for Pheelz."

"Woah, on *my* birthday?" I set her down. "Better give it to her, then."

Josie drags Ophelia to the end of the kitchen island, sticking a homemade poster against the white marble. There's a stick figure that's obviously me, and another with an orange mass of hair.

Welcome to our family, Ophelia is scrawled across the top.

It may be a messy kid's drawing, but I know as soon as I read it that it'll feel like a swift punch of emotion straight to the gut for Ophelia. I place my palm on her lower back, just so she knows I'm here.

She stares at the poster, looking lost for words. "I . . . uhh . . ."

Josie's greasy little finger lands on the orange chaos that juts out from one stick figure's head. "That's you."

Ophelia's pale brown lashes blink rapidly, lips pressed together in a tight line. "It's . . ."

"You don't like it?"

I scrunch my hand through Josie's blond waves. "Give her a second, J. She's got to take it in."

"It's . . ." Ophelia starts and stops again, but I know. It's the reason she's hung on all these years. "I love it, Josie. Please may I keep it?"

"Yeah!" Josie exclaims, hugging Ophelia and charging out of the kitchen like she hasn't just thrown a stick of dynamite at the walls Ophelia has spent so many years building around her heart.

The silence is heavy. The mood is heavy. Her breath is heavy, laden with unshed tears. She clutches the poster so hard, like someone might snatch it from her at any moment. For a girl so full of snarky remarks, her next sentence comes out so quiet. So unsure. "Can I spend Christmas with you guys this year?"

I fold her into my arms, feeling the shudder of a sob ripple up her spine. "I'd be disappointed if you didn't, Twist."

"*This* year, though? Like . . . in eight months?" she reiterates into my chest, like she can't believe I've said yes, that she's made it through the loneliness and out the other side.

Something about the moment feels like daybreak. The first ray of sun after a long, dark night. The first shard of hope, illuminating two people who were on the edge of giving up.

"*Please?*" she adds, misinterpreting my silence for indecision. Something in my chest splinters. It makes me want to crawl beneath her skin and stitch all the little cracks up one by one.

I bury my face in her hair, inhaling that cinnamon coffee scent of hers. "This year and every year until midnight."

A hundred years from now.

MY MOM IS home, propped up on a giant pile of pillows and pushing the small portion of food on her plate around without taking a bite.

I've left Ophelia in the comfortable surroundings of the living room, playing online Scrabble with some terrible TV show on in the background. Not *MasterChef*. Cooking has become a sore subject since Steakgate.

I didn't know that Scrabble was the sort of game you could get all worked up over, but she manages. Every single night. If *WordBuster89* could hear what she's saying about them, they'd probably never look in the mirror again.

She's a funny one, my Ophelia.

Putting a tomato onto a fork, Mom smiles at the sound of Mia and Evie screeching about something in the garden. I wish she'd eat. I don't think she could get much thinner.

I'm about to coax her into eating a bite when she nods over to the framed sketch on her bedside table. I did it years ago, messily scribbled on the back of a napkin while we sat in a café in Paris. "You never talk about architecture anymore."

I shrug. It's been a long while since I've had time to think about my future. "It was a pipe dream."

"Says who?"

"Me. I've got to keep my head in Green. I don't know anything about architecture."

"That's the point, Alex. Your father made you forget it, but you're not supposed to know everything. You show up to university to learn. You pick a topic that inspires you, and *then* you study it."

Well, when she says it like that, it sounds obvious. A simple truth beaten out of me by my father. He didn't take it well, that first time I told him I didn't want Green.

From the minute you were born I knew you'd let me down.

"You always said you'd run an architecture firm. I know you haven't ticked building a public library off your bucket list, unless you're really good at keeping secrets."

I fiddle with the ring on my pinky, wishing she wouldn't inflate my hopes like this. "Maybe once the girls are in college."

"You'll leave Green soon. You could go back to university, finish the degree you started at Yale. You could even start a company while you're there."

She's described the dream I fought so hard to forget. But it's so complicated. With my mom how she is and the girls at home, adding something else into my schedule would likely finish me off.

But my mom has this hopeful expression on her face, and she's reached into the darkest pit of my chest and stoked a fire I thought long extinguished.

"I'll look into it."

Chapter 23

ALEX

The film of sun that glows through my curtains paints Ophelia in a sepia wash, flooding the room in a soft, warm light. After a couple of weeks of gray, rainy mornings in the city, this one feels like a luxury.

My phone reads just past 7 a.m., and I've already worked out, showered, and had an early call with Harwood. The difference between my good mornings and my bad ones is staggering.

I shut the bathroom door quietly, then slip into some shorts and beneath the covers, unlocking my phone. The tabs open on my search engine are an accurate representation of the inside of my brain. Brochures for houses in New York, Edinburgh, and London. Architecture course information for Yale. Doctors for my mom and schools for the girls in New York and the UK. A whole host of cooking schools for Mia. A desperate search for something, anything that'll change Fleur's mind about trading college for modeling with her shitty boyfriend's dad as an agent.

My mind has become spaghetti. No real direction or plan. Just chaos and a need for change. So many decisions, and yet I'm paralyzed by all of them.

Ophelia stirs beside me, grumbling something incoherent into the pillow.

A week of waking up like this, and I never want it to end. It's the elephant in the room: the fact that Sorrowsong's Easter break is coming to an end and the end-of-year exams are barreling toward her.

She'll have to leave soon.

I swipe my thumb over her cheek. I can't count her freckles, no matter how hard I try. There are so many, all piled up on top of one another over her nose and cheeks.

Her lashes flutter open, eyes puffy from sleep. "Hey."

I swipe the hair from her face. "Morning. Sleep well?"

She pouts, eyebrows creasing in a frown. "You know for a fact that I didn't sleep well."

"Funny. I seem to remember it was you begging for another round last night."

She rolls onto her side so her face is buried in my chest. "Yeah, well, you're old and misremembering things."

I trail my fingers down the dip of her spine, enjoying the feel of her against me. The dark cloud inside me is quiet. "I actually found a gray hair yesterday."

She makes an appreciative hum in the back of her throat. "You'll be so hot when you go gray . . . are you going to the gym?" she mumbles. Sunlight kisses her breasts, paints her thighs, burnishes her hair to a fiery shine. There's something so beautiful about her. It's not the most original word, but it's the one that flashes through my mind every time I look at her.

"Already been."

She pulls away, looking genuinely disgusted. "You people sicken me."

"I couldn't sleep, anyway."

She props herself up on her elbow, suddenly more awake. I shamelessly let myself drink in the view. "Bad mood day?"

"No, I'm feeling good. Just hard to sleep in late with you beside me."

She bats her lashes at me. "Because I'm too pretty?"

She may be being ironic, but it's *exactly* that. If I had my way, she'd never sleep. I spread a line of kisses over her chest, enjoying the way her hips rock when I swirl my tongue around her nipple. This is a dangerous game. I'm going to be late. "Nah, it's the snoring."

She pulls the duvet over her head in a rage. Leaving to go to work has never been so impossible. I don't know how anyone does it. "I'm never wearing lace again."

"No," I plead, pulling it off her, the sound of her laughter echoing around the room. "This is too harsh a punishment."

It's been three days since Ophelia bought herself a set of lingerie on a shopping trip with the girls that I wasn't invited to. I've bought her two more since, and added *Ophelia in red lace* to the list of things I have but will never deserve.

I press my mouth to hers, taking her face in my hands and swallowing her soft sigh. She sinks her fingers into my aching biceps, her tongue parting my lips. I swear thinking rational thoughts wasn't this hard ten minutes ago. She hooks her leg around mine, my thigh resting between hers.

The shameless grind of her hips against the hard muscle of my leg makes me smile. I think Ophelia must obsess over my thighs almost as much as I obsess over hers, my name a gasped breath from her lips. I graze my teeth along the shell of her ear, so desperate to sink myself into her that it hurts. "So wet, Ophelia."

"Only for you," she breathes, condemning me to an unproductive day of daydreams behind my desk.

In the future I cling onto, this is how all my days start.

"I have to go," I manage, in what might be the greatest display of self-sacrifice in history.

Any other meeting I'd toss aside in favor of a lazy morning in bed with Ophelia, but not this one.

The first appointment in my diary today is months in the making.

When I started weighing my options for my replacement, Mike was the only person I was considering. Today I'll ask Luis if he wants my job. I've caught an almost-costly mistake from Mike three times in as many weeks and seen him fly off the handle in meetings in a way that makes me wince, reminding me of terrible nights at home with my father.

"No," she whispers, like I've betrayed her.

I sink my teeth into her shoulder. Hard. "Later."

I'M TWENTY PAGES deep into reviewing a contract from our legal team for a new deal with a French airport—a deal that has taken me about three times as long to close as it should've—when Ophelia calls.

I glance at the time. *Fuck.* Seven p.m. has long gone. I text Jacqueline and apologize, telling her to head home.

Ophelia's voice is a welcome comfort, soft and husky through my AirPods. "Mr. Corbeau."

I can't even force a smile through the guilt that crushes my chest. "Miss Winters."

"How's work?"

"I completely lost track of time."

"That's okay. Are you feeling less stressed?"

"Yeah, I got a lot done today with the French deal and the press conference."

"Then that's all that matters."

But it isn't all that matters. In fact, it's exactly what shouldn't matter.

"How'd it go with Luis?"

"Good. Very good. His vision for Green matches mine."

"And Mike?"

I lean back in my chair and stretch my arms above my head. That's a conversation for tomorrow that I'm really not looking forward to. "Haven't told him he's not getting the job."

"How do you think he'll take it?"

"Terribly, I imagine."

"I'd cry while telling him."

"I might, at this rate."

"I need to head back, Alex."

I put my pen down, shutting my eyes. I knew she'd say this, eventually. It's been looming over us for more than a week. "You don't have to," I say, fighting that unreasonable part of me, the one my father nurtured, the one that wants to lock her in my basement and not let her leave.

"I know I don't."

I want to be so selfish. To tell her she doesn't need money anymore, or to go back to that house near Inverness. That I could get her into any university, anywhere. Pay off her tuition fees. Pay for a new house.

But it's against everything she stands for. She's trying to build her own identity.

She takes my silence as a question, explaining her decision. "I've thought about staying, Alex. I have. But I have prayed and prayed for friends, for a chance at a career, for a life that isn't fueled by revenge. A life that belongs to *me*. I have a friendship group, a scholarship, a place on the swim team."

"I know."

"I owe seventeen-year-old Ophelia better than giving that all up."

Like I have, twice.

My conversation with my mother weighs heavy on my mind.

For a horrible, unkind second, I almost think she's lucky to have so much freedom. Then I think about the hug Josie gave me as I walked out the door, the coffee my mom delivered to my bedside table, the way Mia always leans out the window to say good morning, the way it's those seven women who have given me purpose for the past twenty-four years, and I feel disgusted with myself.

I remember the way the cold in that house of hers had sunk its way into the foundations, the cardboard boxes of possessions that Ophelia had packed up alone. The untouched double bedroom at the top of the stairs. The word *lucky* sours on my tongue.

"I didn't mean that you *have* done that," Ophelia blurts out, when the silence stretches on.

"I know, baby. You're right for going home."

"Worst case, it's just over two years long distance. We can manage that. I could come here once I've graduated, maybe."

All those houses I've looked at in the UK float through my mind. But I don't know if the girls would agree. And my mom needs stability, not another huge life event. God, what I wouldn't do to live close to Ophelia.

Being five inches from her makes me grumpy, let alone three thousand miles. But she's right. With a lot of late-night phone calls and long showers, maybe I could survive it.

"You can take a jet home."

"I'm going to just try to fly on a normal plane."

"I'll help you book a flight later."

"Thank you. I love you," she says, voice wobbling. She's upset. I start packing my things straight away.

"I love you, too. Talk to me."

"I don't know what's wrong. I started my period. Charlotte made me an anklet." Her voice cracks, her next sentence revealing what's really the matter. "I killed Laura. I think of her every time I feel happy."

"Shall I get you a hot chocolate on the way back?"

I hear a muffled sniff. "Yeah. Maybe that'll fix me."

"If it doesn't, we'll find something else."

I keep Ophelia on the line until I have to get into the elevator, promising I'll see her soon.

Mike gets in one floor down, giving me a quick nod. He presses the button for the garage, even though I've already pressed it. "Congrats on the contract."

"Thought we were never going to land that one."

The elevator plunges into silence as it descends. Mike whistles a quiet tune, flashing me a quick glance. "How are things going with that girl of yours?"

It's an odd question. In fact, there's an odd atmosphere in the elevator. Mike's jaw is so tense that I'm surprised his molars haven't turned to dust. "It's going fine."

When Mike leans forward and hits the button for the sixth floor, which is only ever used for storage and by the janitors, I catch the faintest whiff of alcohol on his breath. As the red floor number on the small screen behind him ticks down, an alarm bell rings somewhere in the back of my mind. My skin prickles with awareness, that horrible, suffocating feeling of dread creeping up my throat.

Something isn't right here.

It all happens in a flash. I lunge for the red emergency override button, but Mike's fist crashes into mine and then comes flying at my face. I block his punch, but the force slams me into the mirror behind us, the explosive pain across my back so sharp that my vision turns white.

His next swing at me is sloppy, easy for me to dodge. His fist shatters the cracked mirror, sending shards of glass to the floor. I land a harsh blow to the left side of his face, slamming him against the other end of the elevator. He thrashes when my hands grip his neck, the ring on his finger cutting across my cheek. But I don't let up. Not when a life with Ophelia is at stake.

"Did my father put you up to this?" I grit out, as his punches lose strength. The elevator rattles to a stop on the maintenance floor, but I don't release him.

"You were never planning to make me CEO, were you?" he wheezes, the grip of my fingers stealing his oxygen away.

"I'm sure as fuck not going to now." He gasps for air, begs for his life. I tighten my hold on him. "Answer the question."

His eyes flick over my shoulder at the sound of the dented doors scraping open, and the fear in his expression melts into something like relief.

A rough hand clamps a cloth over my mouth; my next inhale feels like a ball of fire barreling down my airway and into my lungs, chemicals against delicate skin. It feels like the whole office building lurches sideways.

Somewhere in the haze that floods my brain with confusion, I hear my father's voice.

And that's when I realize this isn't some newfound anger about the CEO job. This is a far more elaborate plan.

I swing my head back, feeling it connect with flesh and bone behind me, but the hand over my mouth doesn't move.

"Missed me, *son*?"

Even though the world is swimming, the words my father hisses in my ear permeate the thick fog. A sharp pain amid a dull, pixelated ache.

Nausea churns my stomach. I feel just as helpless as I did when I was a child.

I'm no good to them dead.

It's the sentence I've whispered to the mirror on the worst of my days, in the lowest of my moods. It kept me alive then, and it'll keep me alive now.

Consciousness slips between my fingers, and all that I can think of as the world fades to black is that strange, wonderful girl I left at home.

Chapter 24

OPHELIA

"Is this a good idea?" I ask Russell, the Corbeau-Greens' driver, as he pulls up outside Alex's office building.

It's 9 p.m., Alex isn't home yet, and his phone location has him *still* at work.

So here Fleur and I are, coming to make sure he's okay, or to rescue him from a mountain of paperwork. Whatever is necessary.

I just hope he doesn't mind me interrupting him when he's clearly swamped.

"Better than him spending a night at his desk."

Fleur and I have managed not one but *two* conversations on the drive. She's telling me about fashion campaigns from brands I've never heard of, and I'm nodding and saying things like *true, barrel jeans are so dead* (I have two pairs), and *yeah, cellular beauty is* definitely *the way* (I have no idea what that is).

Even if I had to google every person and place that she mentioned in order to keep up, it's definitely something for the win column.

In the front, Russell undoes his seat belt. "I'll go in with you, miss."

I imagine Alex at his lowest, or fast asleep on his desk. He probably wouldn't want Fleur or the staff there. "No, no. You stay with Fleur. He might not want company. We'll be out in a few minutes."

I step out the car, inhaling a heavy breath of air thick with the scent of rain and something uniquely New York City. I'm nervous. Why I am nervous?

The silver Green Aviation logo above the doors likely doesn't help.

When the doorman lets me into the quiet lobby, I'm not sure I could look any more out of place if I tried. Everything is shiny: the floor is marble, and the reception desk has the largest bouquet of flowers I've ever seen perched on a *plinth*, for Christ's sake.

This place must go through an incredible amount of window and glass polish.

The reception desk is empty, which is strange. I would've thought they always have someone here. For the third time, my call to Alex goes to voicemail.

Could he be in a session with Harwood?

At the row of elevators, I hit the shiny button on the wall with a bad feeling sinking into my chest.

The elevator beside me is stuck on floor six, a little red triangle flashing beside the number. When a pair of doors slide open, I press the button for the penthouse floor, but the key card reader beside the number pad flashes red.

Great. I need an access card. Obviously I need an access card.

I glance around the hallway. Where is everyone? I thought everyone in this city was a workaholic.

I pace down the hallway of elevators, searching for . . . anything. An employee, a dropped access card, a janitor. I find a conference suite, whatever the fuck that means, and a coffee shop, both just as deserted as the rest of the building. It's only when I'm turning to go and ask the doorman on the street outside for help that I spot a folded piece of paper wedged in the windowless door at the end of the hall.

Oh God. This is like a real-life horror movie. I put my foot in the door to keep it unlocked and unfold the note between shaky fingers. It's going to be a ransom note, it's going to be a horrible photo, it's going to be—

It's blank.

It's a doorstop. That's as underwhelming as it is relieving.

I call Alex again with no answer, peering up the stairwell; it's not like the polished marble stairs with that ridiculous LED striplighting in the foyer. This looks like more of a maintenance stairwell, devoid of color save for the abandoned mop and bucket beside me.

I look back at the hallway of elevators, my eyes snagging on that *one* elevator, still stuck on floor six.

I feel tied to Alex in a way neither of us has ever been able to explain. All the time I've spent trying to snap the strings between us has only tied them tighter.

And I just *know* something's wrong.

My worry for Alex's mood turns into a different kind of worry entirely. I take the first few steps quietly, but I'm running by the time I reach the sixth floor, and, sure enough, the access door is propped open just enough for it not to lock.

It's not cold, but my teeth are chattering, fingers trembling as I dial 911 and press my phone to my ear.

Silence.

I don't have enough service on this floor to call for help.

I glance back toward the stairwell. I had service in the foyer, but I can't turn back. Not if Alex is up here and in danger.

Somewhere deep in my chest, I know exactly what—exactly *who*—is happening here.

This is the moment I've imagined a thousand times over. This was always between Cain and me.

I slip through the door and into the unlit hallway, feet silent against the white flooring as I pace past an empty break room, a room full of cables and wires and glowing lights, then a cleaning supplies closet.

It's deathly still.

I pull open a closet door, wincing at the creak of the hinges as I search the shelves for something, anything to use as a weapon.

A crowbar. I'll never call myself unlucky again, because there's a crowbar on the bottom shelf, sandwiched between two dustpans. It's cool to the touch when I clutch it to my chest, heavier than I imagined.

I dial 911 over and over, but the call keeps failing as I hurry down the hallway until I skid to a halt outside the elevator.

Smashed glass. Dented metal. Alex's phone, face down in a splatter of blood. And ironically, an odd sense of numbness washes over me. My fear for his safety melts everything else away, all the possible decisions and *what should I dos* converge into a single plan. I'm a woman possessed.

I follow the bloody trail, holding my crowbar in front of me like a baseball bat until I hear the sound of voices.

Holy shit, I'm really doing this.

A deep voice dripping with fury splinters the quiet: "Release the jet, Alex." I hear a nauseating thud, a choked grunt that I know must come from Alex.

I stop outside the door, back pressed to the wall.

"I'll give you one more chance, Alex, because I'd really rather not hurt you any more than I need to. Clear me a jet, get me out of the States, and you'll be home in time for breakfast tomorrow."

I hold my breath, leaning toward the small window in the door to some sort of control room and *fuck*. There are two of them. A smartly dressed man with a badly beaten face, and a hooded figure with his back to me that can only be Cain Green.

Cain steps to the left, and my stomach plummets six floors.

Alex is tied to a chair and he looks in a bad way.

His hair is a mess, tumbling over his forehead just enough to leave the cut above his eyebrow visible. Blood trickles over his temple and my heart pounding in my ears is the only thing I can hear.

I'm so consumed by rage, I almost smash my way through the door without a single thought. My hand is wrapped around the handle, the other clutching the crowbar, when Cain turns ever so slightly.

A gun glints in his left hand.

All confidence I had fizzles out. I'm out of my depth.

I flinch when his hand grips his son's jaw, forcing him to look up.

Oh, Alex. I'm so fucking sorry I didn't come earlier.

He looks so hurt. Blood trickles from his mouth, but it's the grief swimming in his gaze that knocks the air from my lungs.

Cain thrusts a phone into Alex's face, tightening his grip on the gun. Someone speaks on the other line, and I just watch, helpless, as the last of the fight leaves his body.

"Alex?"

"Dan, hi," he rasps. "I need a jet, off the record. One passenger. I've got a passport. Can you sort it for me tonight?"

"Thought Green was done with all that, Corbeau."

Alex's eyes drift shut. His father presses the barrel of the gun into his temple to wake him up. "Yeah, well . . . something came up."

"How are you gonna sweeten the deal?"

His head drops forward in defeat, blood dripping onto his lap. "Five hundred thousand."

"Eight."

"Fuck you," he rasps, voice hoarse. Cain clicks the safety off the gun. I clamp my hand over my mouth to muffle my sharp inhale, but Alex's head snaps up.

My eyes connect with his for the briefest of seconds, and even in the dark I see the fear in them, the horror that I'm here. *Go*, his say. *Never*, mine say back.

I pause for a moment, drag in the first steady breath I've taken since I got out the car. You can do this, Ophelia. *Think*.

I duck out of view, a plan forming. As a final hope, I text Russell. ***911.*** I glance to the end of the L-shaped hallway, say a prayer, and run round the corner. I wrap my clammy hands around the handle of the door to the room beside me and push it open.

Then I slam it shut, hard.

I press my back to the wall, chest heaving as I wait and hope.

I hear a door open at the end of the hall, hear the other guy tell Cain he'll investigate the noise, silence whatever janitor has made the mistake of coming up here after hours.

Thud, thud, thud.

Footsteps approach. My hands tighten around the crowbar. I wait and I wait and I wait for what feels like forever.

Now.

I lunge round the corner, slamming into something—someone. We both crash to the floor, and a white-hot flash of pain shoots up my thigh when my knee absorbs the impact.

The man in the suit kneels opposite me, red faced with fury. His eyes widen when they meet mine, and then he does exactly what I want him to. He shouts Cain's name.

I expect my usual indecision, a second of hesitation, but there is none. The crowbar slams against his skull with a surprisingly quiet crack, and then he's nothing but a wheezing, cursing pile of navy cashmere and polished leather on the floor.

My legs feel like jelly, but they carry me into a supply closet halfway down the hall, nonetheless.

I hide between racks of chemicals, watching the thin strip of frosted glass in the door as a shadow comes to a stop outside. I hold both hands over my mouth, don't dare blink, don't dare breathe. My stomach sinks, dread and relief in equal measure when the telltale whoosh of my message to Russell finally sounds.

For a sickening, awful second, I think Cain knows I'm in here. And then I hear a choked grunt from the guy down the hall, and Cain takes off running.

Alex. All I can think about is reaching him, helping him.

Heart thudding a rapid rhythm in my throat, I inch the door open, doing my best to ignore the pain in my leg, and listen. Cain's footsteps thud round the corner into the second hallway as he makes a break for his accomplice.

When I skid into the room, the despair in Alex's eyes almost brings me to my knees. He spits blood from his mouth, a desperate plea in his voice. "Go, Twist. Please go."

"I'm saving you," I whisper, though I doubt it comforts him. I squat behind his chair, frantically untying his hands.

"*Go*. He'll be back."

"I'm not leaving you here." I pull one rope loose, grappling for purchase with the other. Alex's head slumps forward, breathing labored. I shake my head, voice a whole lot surer than I feel. "Stay with me, Corbeau, I'm getting you out of here."

His voice is barely audible when it comes. "He built a model train with me on my eleventh birthday."

My hands blur, eyes sting, but I force away the tears. "I'm so sorry, Alex."

"He built a train with me and now *this*."

The second restraint drops to the blood-spattered floor. I round the chair to face him, hurriedly glancing over my shoulder. Bruises are forming above his right eye, and I'd do anything to take away his pain. I'd suffer for a lifetime if it meant he'd be happy. "Can you walk?"

"Get out of here, Ophelia."

I hook my arms beneath his and haul him to his feet, a hand on his waist as I drag him on shaky legs into the hallway. The elevators. I just need to get us into an elevator.

"Are you hurt?"

I can't help letting slip a disbelieving laugh as we near the silver doors. I leave him leaning against the wall and lurch to hit the elevator button, fumbling at his waist to get his ID badge from his belt. "Let's worry about you before we—"

A lazy drawl caresses my back, a voice so similar to his son's. "Ophelia Winters. What a delightful surprise."

I freeze where I stand, lashes drifting shut for just a moment. "Cain."

"You wouldn't be taking my son from me, would you?"

I turn to face him, square my shoulders, and keep my gaze level even as he raises his gun. Alex steps in front of me.

"Out of the way, Alex. I wasn't *really* planning to kill her, but since she's flown all this way . . ."

I try to move, try to push Alex toward the elevator but he's a wall of solid muscle, even injured and dazed.

Cain only smiles wider, and just the sight of him makes me sick. He has been the rotten core of my life for so long, the epicenter of all that is bad. "I warned you about distractions, son. Look what she's turned you into. Don't make me go through you."

"Alex, go," I plead. "This was always between your father and me. This has nothing to do with you."

"This has everything to do with me."

Cain has a glint in his eye: unhinged, crazed, a man with nothing left to lose.

He says he'd shoot Alex to get to me, and in that moment, I believe him.

I take a step to the right. Cain has a clear shot. Alex is none the wiser. The authorities must be close. If I can just keep Alex alive for a moment longer—

A gunshot cracks through the air, and I wait. Wait for the agony, wait for the blood, wait for the red-hot fire of a bullet in my skin.

And yet . . .

At the end of the hall, Cain slumps to the floor, a puddle of blood forming beneath his left leg.

With a high-pitched ringing in my ears, I look for a gun in Alex's empty hands, he looks for a gun in mine, and then we both look up in slow motion.

At the end of the clinical, white hallway, Fleur lowers her weapon.

Chapter 25

ALEX

You know, this is kind of fun," I say, putting one of the minuscule spokes on the train wheels with a set of tweezers.

My dad leans back in his chair, admiring our handiwork. "Of course it is. It's a waste of time. Everything that's fun is a waste of time."

Dad's been increasingly . . . not himself this past year. It started off with tense dinners, conversations on eggshells and too many refills of his wine glass. Now we're lucky to see him at dinner at all. The twins seem to be the only thing that stops him from flying off the rails lately. Their second birthday party last week was the first time I saw him smile in . . . months, actually.

"It's not often your only son turns eleven," he says. That infinitesimal hint of pride in his voice has me feeling ten feet tall.

"Unless the new baby is a boy."

His jaw tenses. I've said the wrong thing, somehow.

His palm lands on my shoulder, so hard that if he wasn't so volatile, I'd tell him it hurt. "I started joining my father in the office on weekends when I was your age."

"Oh, I . . ."

"You'll be fine. You'll make a fine CEO for Green one day."

"I . . . well . . ."

Another clap on the shoulder, hard enough this time that I realize he knows exactly what he's doing. "I know you wouldn't let me down, boy."

"ALEX."

I jolt awake, startled by sounds and smells that are so familiar now after the year my mother has had. My breaths are rapid, my dream about my father a memory I'd almost forgotten.

I open my eyes and *shit*, since when is operating an eyelid this painful?

"Hey." A gentle hand lands on my shoulder when I try to sit up. I trace my blurry gaze up one thin, tanned arm.

"Fleur?"

And just like that, it all comes back to me. The fight in the elevator, my father's fist, Ophelia's appearance, Fleur shooting dad.

Fleur shooting dad.

I think I'm going to be sick.

"Breathe, Alex, you're okay. Ingrid and the twins will be here soon. Mom's not really lucid enough to come."

"Ophelia," I manage, though my throat is raw.

"I think they sent her for some tests."

It's like all the fragmented pieces of myself suddenly pull together to form a single panicked thought. "She's hurt?"

No, no, no, no, no.

I push myself up in the bed, but Fleur pushes me back down. "It's just a knee X-ray. She'll cope on her own."

"You . . . oh my god, Fleur, you . . ."

"I couldn't watch what he does to you and Mom anymore, Alex. Seventeen years of it was enough."

"But you . . ."

"Russell and I were outside when Ophelia texted us for help. I knew Russell's been keeping a gun in the car since dad went missing, just in case. The rest is a blur."

"Is he . . ." Christ, I can't even form a sentence. Too rattled, too worried for Ophelia, too hurt.

"He's in a different hospital. He's definitely going to jail for the rest of his life. Mike's here, somewhere."

He's alive.

Relief courses through me, for Fleur, not for him. I don't want that weight looming over her.

I want him to rot behind bars.

"What did he want?"

I squint at the dark cityscape outside the window, like I'll find any answers there. "He was trying to get a flight to Greece."

He had a whole new life ready to go over there. The final, desperate hope of a coward who'd run out of options. He was having trouble bribing a contact at the airport, needed me to ensure his safe escape.

My vision swims, the pain in my head almost blinding. "Did Ophelia's knee . . . is she hurt? Is it bad?"

"Oh man, you're obsessed."

"Is she on her own?"

I can't lose her.

"She asked Brendan to send her the CCTV video of her whacking Mike round the head with a crowbar so she can keep it as a trophy. I think she's okay."

I huff out a laugh, but it spreads agony across my ribs. "Are you okay?"

She picks at her cuticles, stares down at her lap. "I think so."

"You think so, *but* . . ." I encourage, hearing the unspoken word dangling from the end of her sentence.

"I think I'm like him."

"Dad?"

She straightens up, squares her shoulders like this is a thought she's been trying to face for a long time. "There's something wrong with me."

I reach for her hand, desperate for her not to go down this line of thinking, like I have for too long. "Fleur, *no*."

"I thought about shooting him for so long. Watched him rant at the dinner table and listened to him shout at you downstairs and just thought how easy it would be to make him just . . . shut up."

"That doesn't—"

She interrupts me with a squeeze of my hand, and the wide-eyed panic in her expression guts me. "You think you're the rotten branch. You think you got his bad." Her bottom lip wobbles, and God, there isn't much worse than watching your little sister cry. "It's *me*. I have all the worst parts of him. The anger and the bad thoughts and the twisted excitement at the downfall of others. Pulling that trigger is the only thing that's made any of it . . . slow down."

"Fleur," I whisper, hardly feeling the pain in my ribs when I drag her into my arms. *When was the last time I hugged her?* "I used to think that, too. I still do, sometimes."

Her voice is muffled, arms around my neck. "Really?"

"Really. Shall we find you someone to talk to about this?"

"You're so boring and adult now," she groans, seemingly keen for a topic change. "Are *you* okay?"

Am I? It's been a long time since I've felt okay. But it almost feels within reach. "I will be."

Fleur stands and leans over to grab something from the table, holding up my phone. "You have over a hundred missed calls from Vincenzo."

Another one pops up just as she turns the phone to face me.

"Pick it up or he'll never stop."

She does, and there's Vincenzo's giant, stupid, anxiety-ridden face filling the screen. "Alex, *fuck*."

I frown, trying to get my eyes to focus. "Where are you?"

He glances over his shoulder, and I realize he's in a car. He pulls over, running two hands down his face. My chest constricts. "I was driving to the fucking airport because you weren't picking up and Ophelia said you were hurt and my dad couldn't find you in the hospital and . . ." He gives a rough growl. He looks distraught, shoulders sinking under a decade-long ability to blame himself if anyone he cares about gets hurt. "You look like shit, Alex. *Fuck*."

"Wow, thanks," I say, trying to lighten the mood enough to dislodge this crushing ball of emotion stuck in my throat.

"It's not funny."

I swallow. "I'm okay. I'll call you later?"

His whole body deflates with a huge breath of relief. "Yeah. Love you."

"Love you, too."

Fleur gives Vincenzo a little wave and hangs up. "You have about a thousand other—"

A flash of copper in the doorway catches my eye. Fleur trails off, slipping out the door to leave Ophelia and me alone.

And she looks so fucking beautiful and so . . . unharmed.

And then it all just hits me. Over a decade of gray gives way to everything I've been numb to. I think about Josie, crying out for a dad she knows no wrong about. About my earliest memories of my father, dancing my mom around the kitchen, cheering on the sideline of my first football games. Our first vacation before my dad spiraled into evil, before my mom took such a sharp downturn. Christmases that weren't spent on edge.

That life died a long time ago now, but this feels like the final draw of the curtains.

I expected anger. I imagined myself on the other side of my father's jail cell, laughing at him. I didn't think it'd be grief that has me feeling so broken.

The sob that works its way up my throat is silent, but I hear her soft intake of breath as she runs over to the bed and folds me in her arms. "Oh, *Alex*."

I drag her cinnamon scent into my lungs. "I'm so tired."

Her fingers thread through my hair behind my head. "I know."

"I don't think I could've shot him," I manage, like it's a confession to my worst sin. The air reeks of disinfectant and disgust. "Even after all he's done, I don't think I could've."

She clutches me tighter, face buried in my neck. I can feel her tears on my shoulder. "That's okay, he's your dad. That's okay. You've been through enough."

I don't know what I did to deserve her. This sweet girl who can overlook my father's sins for a future with me.

"None of it feels like a win." Dead or alive, imprisoned or on the run, sorry or not sorry. None of it makes anything feel better.

She runs her fingers through my hair, her other hand stroking my back as I drag in a shuddering breath. Exhaustion saps the life from my bones. "It isn't a win at all, Alex. Whoever gave you the impression that this was a situation to be won or lost, they were lying." She pulls away, gaze sincere like she *really* wants me to hear her. "There is more strength in mercy than there is in cruelty. You stood in front of the man who tried to make you a monster and you showed him that every effort he made was in vain."

"I know, but he . . ."

A tender hand swipes my hair from my eye, and I swear I feel a crack in my heart stitch itself together. "Forgive yourself."

I trail my gaze from her swollen bottom lip to the chest that rises in steady, sure breaths. "Is your knee okay?"

She can't squash her smile. "It's fine. Nothing's broken. And never mind my knee, you should see what I can do with a crowbar."

I could just ask her to marry me right here.

Not romantic, Alex.

Christ, I love her. I love them all. I love them all so much it aches. I'm desperate to have all eight of them in my arms.

I'm going to get them away from all of this. I'm not going to let any of them know fear like this ever again.

Chapter 26

OPHELIA

The ache in my knee wakes me up, like it has each morning for the past seven days.

And just like every other day this week, a snoring Josie is wedged between Alex and me in bed.

I fly home late tonight.

I'm trying not to think about it.

I fly *home*. I keep saying that, but I don't even know where home is, anymore. When I say the word in my head, no picture or place accompanies it. Really, I'm just flying back to Scotland before I get expelled.

I miss Colette, Magda, and Divya, too. I'm craving a movie night with them, so we can unpack the events of the last few weeks with popcorn and beers. They spam my phone all day, constantly checking on me in the group chat.

Alex is asleep beside me—someone so in love with me that he bought the car we spent our first night together in.

It feels like I have six little sisters now. Elise is like a third parent in my life, dishing out the best advice. Cain Green is in hospital, likely his last stop before heading to a maximum-security prison to live out the rest of his days. He'll never shred another family apart again.

It's surreal. It's *ridiculous.*

Peace is all Alex and I have ever longed for, and I'm beginning to feel it. It's here in this room. It's in the way the line between his brows is relaxed as he sleeps. It's in the way that Cain is finally out of their lives. It's in first couple of cardboard boxes Alex has packed up, preparing to move anywhere that isn't here.

He shifts slightly, opening an eye. The bruise on his eyebrow is fading, and though it's only been a week, the events that transpired in his office are fading, too.

Cain Green has been shackled to me for years. I've been dragging him around like a heavy weight, turning even the most level of days into an uphill climb. But when Fleur shot him, I finally let go.

Cain may die soon, or in thirty years. But seeing him on the floor, begging for whatever scraps of his life remained, I realized that watching his family move on, losing his children, losing his wife—it's punishment enough for me.

"What's on that mind of yours?"

"Guess."

He smiles. "Knowing you, it's either the pointlessness of life and the decay of modern society, or croissants."

I laugh softly. "I feel quite . . . positive."

He frowns, looking so genuinely alarmed as he checks the

temperature of my forehead that my laughter gets loud enough to wake Josie.

Alex prods his sister and cocks his head toward me. "Ophelia's in a good mood, Jo."

She frowns, spinning to face me. "Weird." Two small arms wrap around me, clad in bright blue Spider-Man pajamas. "I don't want you to go."

"I know. I'm so sorry. But Alex has been very kind and paid for a clever doctor to help me talk about my fear of flying."

"So you can visit?"

"Exactly."

She squishes her face into me. *Don't cry, don't cry, don't cry.*

I *love* having a big family.

Alex stands, tugging a T-shirt over his head. He points at Josie. "Jelly and butter?"

She whoops with joy at the knowledge that our toast-in-bed party is making its appearance for the fourth consecutive morning.

I watch Alex head out into the hallway, my eyes lingering on the way his muscular shoulders taper down to a narrow waist, on the way his thighs fit into those gray sweatpants.

I do love Josie as my own personal hot-water bottle in bed, but I need to catch him alone today. Maybe in the shower.

The door creeps open, and then Charlotte is beside us. "Are you *really* leaving today?"

"I have to go. But I'll be back."

"Pinky swear?"

"Pinky swear."

"Double pinky swear?" comes a voice from the hallway. Elise leans against the doorframe, a fragile smile on her face. "I'm going to miss you sorely, Ophelia."

"I'll miss you more," I reply, struck by just how true that is. I've been here for *weeks*. I haven't stayed anywhere other than Sorrowsong or the house near Inverness for this long in my life.

The mornings are hectic here, the evenings packed full of dance recitals, tennis games, movie nights, arguments, tears, family dinners, and exasperating bedtime routines. In a month, Sorrowsong will close for the summer, and I'll head back to my parents' house. And though I've enjoyed my time here, I just know it's going to make the silence bite harder.

But I'll tread water, just like I tell Alex to do, because this distance is temporary. We'll get our time, and it'll be even sweeter when it comes.

I pat the space on the other side of Josie and Charlotte, inviting Elise to sit. Her whole face brightens, and my hand steadies her as she lowers herself onto the mattress. Other than one particularly bad day earlier this week, her moods have been more stable. The highs aren't so high, the lows aren't so low. But years of eating disorders, drug use, surgeries, stress, and health trials are catching up with her.

She looks so fragile.

Her hand slips into mine. "If you're in that house alone, call us every night. We'll put the phone at the dinner table if we have to."

"I'll try to visit you guys before the end of the year."

She winks at me like she knows something I don't. "We'll see."

Charlotte sits up, her hair sticking up at every possible angle. "Maybe we can visit Ophelia, too!"

Elise drops a kiss to her forehead. "Maybe we can, *mon chou*."

"Is Dad coming back?" Josie asks, for the four hundredth time this week.

"No, my love."

"But—"

"Your dad wasn't very kind to Alex, Fleur, and me. And he *especially* wasn't very kind to Ophelia. That's why he can't come back."

"We didn't even finish playing *Animal Crossing* at Christmas."

I don't know how Elise does it. No frustration, no impatience, no anger, no sadness. Just a kind warmth in her eyes as she promises them that she'll learn to play it with them.

Alex comes in, balancing three plates of toast. I know one was supposed to be for him, because it has peanut butter on it, but he smiles at Charlotte and gives it to her instead, handing the buttered one to me and the strawberry jam to Josie. The ravens inked into his skin flutter as he stretches those thick arms above his head, exposing a thin strip of muscle at his waist.

If I don't get an hour alone with him today, I'll just cancel my flight.

Oh god. *The flight.* I drag my palms down my cheeks. Alex is at my side in a second, shaking his head. "We're not worrying about the trip home until ten p.m., remember?"

"Okay," I rasp, wiping my sweaty palms on my thighs.

A tiny voice in my head tells me to stay. To worry about my education later, to catch up with my friends on the phone.

But the girls go back to school tomorrow and Alex back to work. This cocoon we've been in, the calm after the storm, will burst.

I owe it to my younger self to fly home.

* * *

I COULDN'T BRING myself to get on the first flight.

But a serious pep talk from Alex and a threatening text from Belladonna about missing the swim meet next week had me on the next flight an hour later, promising to pay Alex back for both tickets—or all four, if you count the ones he bought to accompany me to the plane steps.

The flight back felt a lot shorter than the one to New York, so short that when I watch the wheels touch down with my nose pressed against the acrylic window, I can still feel the dried tears on my cheeks and the ghost of Alex's lips on mine.

"I might lose a finger in a minute," the seventy-something-year-old lady beside me says, as people stand to grab their bags before they're even allowed to. I glance down, and, sure enough, no blood is flowing to her hand. I release it quickly, cheeks turning red.

Mabel is my new best friend. She held my hand the whole way, let me trade my weird salad pot for her bread roll. When I convinced myself that the wing looked a bit worse for wear, she reminded me I have no fucking idea what I'm talking about. I told her about my fear of flying, and then we talked shit about her ex-husband for six hours.

"Safe travels up to the Highlands," she says with a warm smile.

"Thank you," I say, chewing my lip as I look at the train prices. It's not the fourteen-hour journey time that bothers me—I've managed my fair share of horrendous travel days since I lost my parents—but the price.

There is *no* reason for a train to cost that much.

Mabel scowls at my phone, too. "Robbing bastards, aren't they?"

I hang my duffel over my shoulder, following her off this horrific flying tin can. "Couldn't have put it better myself."

My feet hit the tarmac, and I have half a mind to kiss it. I feel like the star of one of those videos you see of astronauts returning to Earth from space. I will never take solid ground for granted ever again.

"I did it!" I exclaim, suddenly overcome with emotion. Then Mabel and I are bouncing around like two footballers who've just scored the winning penalty.

"I can't jump anymore, I'll piss myself," she says, stopping abruptly. "*Never* have kids."

I pick up her bag, too, and head inside the terminal at a busy London Heathrow. She scowls as we join the short queue at passport control. "I hate these new machines. Whatever was wrong with the people in the booths?"

I watch a woman put her passport in upside down. "Same."

"And *everything* is becoming an app now."

"Oh my god, *thank you*!" I say, hands dragging down my cheeks. "No one else understands. Why do I need an app to claim a free croissant? Why can't they just give me one anyway?"

"World's gone to shit," she grumbles, as a short man in uniform directs her to a passport machine. I scan mine, turning to see where Mabel is. She makes eye contact with me, mimicking shooting herself in the head as the man asks her to step back from the machine and head to a booth instead.

I don't want to leave her without saying goodbye, so I pull my phone from my pocket and switch it from airplane mode. Heart rate not yet below one fifty, I type out a text to Alex while I sit and wait for Mabel to stop flirting with the older gentleman checking her passport.

Ophelia

Made it!! And I only cried twice.

It takes a minute to send, but when it does, a reply comes straight away. It's past five in the morning there.

Alex

I miss you. Proud to be yours.

The picture attached is the little highland cow I got him for his birthday, resting on the pillow beside him, right where I should be.

Mabel appears, giving me a warm smile.

Why am I emotional? Is it sad that I'm so much better at befriending older people?

"Funny how you get attached to people after a only few hours," she says, echoing my thoughts aloud.

I wrap her in a hug, squeezing tight as the whir of people goes on around us.

"Things have been ever so lonely since my daughter passed," she says, voice wobbling. "Maybe we could be phone friends."

"I was too scared to ask you," I say, on a laugh.

"In case I thought you were trying to get into my will?"

"*Mabel!* No!"

She laughs, pulling away and handing me her phone, open on her contacts. I smile at the name she's already put in. *Ophelia Scared of Flying*.

I put her in mine, too. *Mabel Not Scared of Flying.*

"You'll have to come for tea next time you're in Yorkshire."

"I promise I will."

She takes my hand in hers, the skin tanned and mottled with age, giving me a sincere look. "If he's the right fella for you, you'll get through the long distance."

I squeeze her one last time, setting her off in the direction of the luggage claim. I head to Arrivals, trying to talk myself into spending the last of my emergency savings on a series of train tickets, even though it was supposed to be for driving lessons.

I wander aimlessly through to the airport foyer. It's people-watching heaven. Men in sharp suits and earpieces hold iPads with people's names in unhelpfully small text. That surely cannot be the most effective way to do it. Mabel would agree with me.

A girl with a giant backpack runs past me, leaping into the waiting arms of her parents. A couple kiss under the harsh airport lights, his hand lifting the tote bag off his husband's shoulder. A woman and three toddlers whoop with excitement as a man jogs over, a big grin on his face.

A year ago, a *month* ago, it probably would've made me cry. A year ago, I found grief in the joy of others, self-doubt in the beauty of my friends.

I wait for the misery and the envy to hit me, but it doesn't. All it does is warm my heart, restore my faith in the world a little more.

Or maybe I'm so happy to not be forty thousand feet in the air that I've gone delirious.

A flash of orange catches my eye, a ridiculous bundle of gold, orange, and yellow balloons, and another foil balloon shaped like a star. Each balloon has a letter on it.

YOU SURVIED.

I'm so distracted by the message, I almost miss the hands beneath them, waving frantically. Hardly notice Colette, Magda, and Divya bouncing around to get my attention, holding a flattened cardboard box that says *Welcome Back Ophelia* in big pink letters.

I gape at them like a goldfish, feet seeming to grow roots into the vinyl flooring of the airport.

I . . . *what*?

And then I'm just like that girl with the big hiking backpack, rushing past people to get to them. We collide in a group hug so enthusiastic that it momentarily knocks the air from my lungs, makes me realize how right I was to come home. Colette's Chanel perfume invades my lungs. "You did it!"

"I did it!"

"Do you like the balloons?" They rearrange them again.

"I *survied.*"

Colette sticks out her glossy bottom lip. "They only had one *V* balloon in stock at the party store we went to on the way down."

Divya sighs, thrusting a take-away cup of tea into my hand. "Apparently some bitch Vivian is having a birthday party."

"Slag," mumbles Magda, in her trademark black lipstick.

Colette claps her hands, leading us to the exit. Her satin mini-dress has some sort of neck scarf built in, the cream fabric the same shade as her heels. *How does she not get cold?* "Let's go!"

Eike is stood outside a bigger car than usual in the pickup area, on what looks to be a bit of a tense phone call.

"How's Eike?" I ask Colette, as we head toward him.

"I'm surprised he's climbed out of my stepfather's ass long enough to drive us home, let's just put it that way."

"Are you going to ask for a new driver?"

"They're all shit, Ophelia. The next one will be, too. They're not really drivers. They're just spies who report back on my every move."

I glance over at Eike, who is pacing the drop-off zone with his phone pressed to his ear. I can't help but feel some sympathy for him—I'm sure Colette's tweed-wearing, old-money stepdad is a nightmare client.

"I'm sorry. We can catch up at Sorrowsong."

"I would *love* that. Apparently, Hemlock is opening up a cozy café in their common room to the other houses."

"You know it's been a slow month at Sorrowsong when this is what we're excited about," says Divya, as Eike comes over and takes my bag off my shoulder. Magda takes the front seat, sliding her purple headphones over her braids, and I think she's asleep before we've even paid the charge at the airport barrier.

Colette presses a button to put a screen up between us and Eike and then turns to face me like she's been holding a piece of information in for days. "I caught Belladonna making out with a groundskeeper."

"*What?*"

Divya nods, looking like she might burst with excitement at the fact we're all back together. "And I caught my lecturer making out with Carmichael's new PA!" She waves her hand like she's trying to dismiss her own conversation topic. "What am I even talking about? You first! Tell us *everything*."

I lean back in the plush leather seat, taking a sip of my tea. Alex's mom, the fight with his father, the fact that things between Alex and me couldn't be any better, the flights, Mabel, Fleur. *Christ.* Suddenly I'm glad the drive is two days long. "We have so much to talk about."

Chapter 27

ALEX

To say the media storm following the break-in last week has been intense would be putting it mildly. My family and I have become some sort of public fascination, a spectacle for all to see.

I'm tired of it.

My laptop is hooked up to the TV above the fireplace, and I'm sweating so much I look like a glazed donut. I must've delivered thirty presentations this year—to politicians, to CEOs, to scarily mean schoolchildren, to shareholders—yet I've never been as nervous as I am for this one.

Josie puts down her toy robot to take a fistful of popcorn from Mia's bowl. "What about school?"

"Well, that's a really great question, Jo." I lean against the bookshelves. "You'd have to go to a new school, with new people."

"What about Fleur and college?" asks Evie, ever the advocate for her sisters.

"I'm not going to college," interjects Fleur, without taking her eyes off her phone.

Mia, Élé, and Charlotte have been up for moving to the United Kingdom since long before I went to Sorrowsong. Josie and Evie, I'm not so sure on. It was Fleur I was most worried about convincing, but she's completely uninterested, scrolling mindlessly on her phone.

"Fleur, please join us," Mom says softly.

She scowls back at her. "I'm here, aren't I?"

"That's not what I mean."

"Yes, fine, Alex. It all looks fine." She shrugs. "I'll be eighteen in less than a year, and then I can move wherever I like. This doesn't really affect me."

I deflate against the shelves. I want to mend the jagged edges of my relationship with Fleur. I want her genuine opinion. All six of these girls are children. All six of them *have* to come before Ophelia. They deserve that much. If any one of them desperately wants to stay, we'll stay.

"Of course it affects you, Fleur."

"You literally didn't care about a single one of my opinions for all of last year, Alex."

I shut my eyes for a second, letting out a long exhale. "Well, I'm trying to put things right."

"Go back to the yard!" says Éle, and I flick back to the brochure of the eight-bedroom country house a few miles out of Edinburgh.

This feels ridiculous, but my mother encouraged me to at least try.

Charlotte nods approvingly at the large yard and paddock. "We could get chickens."

Mom leans over to wipe some ice cream off her bottom lip. "Scotland wouldn't be forever. It'd just be for a few years. *Then* we'd settle down forever. Somewhere else."

"I hate this house," Mia says, waving her hand around our New York living room. There are a few grumbles of agreement. When I see the foyer, I see my mother curled in a ball at the bottom of the stairs, convinced the staff are out to get her. The office makes me taste the metallic tang of blood, the harsh bite of my father's fist when he couldn't punch the economy, so I was the next best thing.

A small smile sneaks across Evie's face, that tiny little sliver of impulsiveness beneath the reserved personality that couldn't be more different to her twin's. "I'm all for it."

My next exhale comes out as a small laugh of disbelief. "Really?"

"Why not? It sounds fun. Everyone at school looks at Mia and me like we're a charity case, so . . . it's not like I'd miss it. And Scotland sounds cool. And in two years, we'd go to college anyway . . . so . . . yeah. I'm in."

My mother voices her agreement, and then three more follow.

Fleur just shrugs. Josie looks the most hesitant of all. "So . . . what about if we want to go to France on vacation?"

"We can still go. It's even closer from there."

"And . . . pizza?"

"Plenty of pizza over there, too. Maybe not as good as New York pizza, but still good. How about we let the others get to bed and discuss it over some cereal?"

She slides off the sofa, slipping her hand into mine. Mia gives me a wink, a huge smile on her face.

My mom is folding hand towels in the pantry when I go in for a fresh box of cereal, Josie is sitting at the island in the kitchen. "I love that house, Alex."

"Me too."

"I'll talk to Fleur."

I pick up the cereal box from the pantry and start heading back to the other room, but some invisible hand stops me in the doorway. A question burns a hole in my mind, has been for weeks. I've been waiting for my mom's mood to steady out a little, and here we are. "Mom, can I ask you something?"

"Of course. Always."

"Carmichael told me that it was you who asked him to convince the board not to let me take Green over."

Her hands freeze as they fold a dishcloth. "Did he also tell you that I asked him never to tell you that?"

"Yes."

"I can never decide if I like that man."

"It's not true, right?"

"It is true."

"Do you realize what that could've cost us?"

"I calculated the risks very thoroughly. I did what's best for you."

"And Dad continuing to go unchallenged is best for me?"

"Being the CEO of Green is everything I never wanted you to have. You told me on your sixth, seventh, eighth birthday, your sixteenth birthday, your *twenty-third* birthday, that taking over your father's company was your idea of hell."

"Until it became a survival decision. One I would make again and again, a hundred times over."

"I did what I thought best for my son."

"But you could've consulted me."

She turns back to the towels, away from me. Away from the discussion. Guilt rolls in, blanketing my anger.

"*Maman.*"

"*Laisse-moi tranquille.*"

A small voice filters in from the kitchen. "I'm bloody starving."

Our laughter shatters the tension. "Where does she pick up these things?"

"Ophelia might be responsible for that one."

I wrap my mom in a hug, inhaling the scent of the perfume she's worn for as long as I can remember. "I'm sorry."

"I just want what's best for you, Alex. And I didn't think that was Green."

I grab the cereal box and pour two bowls, pulling out a stool to sit beside my littlest sister, who is getting alarmingly un-little. "Cereal *after* bedtime. Don't you ever say I'm not good to you."

"This should be every day."

"So, you're not too sure about Scotland, huh?"

"Well . . . I have a thousand million billion questions."

"Oh my god. We're gonna need more cereal."

She giggles, leaning her head against my arm, asking me questions until past midnight.

ALL THREE GUARDS are stony faced as the middle one wheels my father into the visitation room at a high-security correctional facility upstate. I quash the myriad emotions that bubble up my throat, fighting hard to meet him eye to eye.

I can't believe he's alive. That he lived yet my mother's time is running out.

"Cain," I say, as the guard kicks the brake on the chair and steps back.

He looks pale. Tired. His frosty blue eyes are dull, hair fading to silver.

"Alex. I didn't think you'd visit." He looks almost hopeful, like I might've forgiven him. Better extinguish those hopes quickly.

"I'm here to say goodbye, to tell you that we will not be visiting you. If the girls want to come when they're eighteen, they can. But I wouldn't keep your hopes up."

That snatches his next sentence away. His mouth opens and closes, opens again, closes again. He looks devastated, but I can't find it in myself to care.

I pop my knuckles, frustrated by his silence but well aware he'd only piss me off if he spoke. "I'm done with you."

"Did she survive? The girl?"

"Ophelia is fine."

"I want to talk to Fleur."

"Fleur is going through enough."

"I want to make things right between her and I," he says, but his eyes are glittering with ill intentions. I've seen his version of making things right. The whispered threats, the harsh bite of his words that sting so much more than his fists ever could, and the drunken, saccharine apologies that had my too-kind mother forgiving him each night.

I won't have him feed his poison to Fleur.

My laugh is bitter, acidic on my tongue. "We're long past that. What you did to Mom is irreparable." I shake my head, simultaneously desperate to leave and longing to understand just how he ended up so terrible. "I remember you loving her."

"Of course I love her, I—"

"Just loved Green more." I try to let it go, but I just can't. "They told you she had a medical condition, and you told them she was just high-maintenance. I was twenty-one, driving her to hospital visits so you could fuck your secretaries."

"I'm sorry, Alex," he snaps, but the telltale flexing of his fingers tell me the only thing he's truly sorry about is the guards and the cuffs that prevent him from touching me. "What more do you want me to say?"

I don't even know. Sorry is all he can say, but it doesn't feel enough. It's *so* unsatisfying. I hardly recognize him sitting opposite me, hardly understand how anyone could think I look like him.

I rise to stand, unsure what anyone could say to make any of this less terrible. "*Well.* Have a good rest of your life."

"It's not too late to turn yourself around. Lose the girl, cut the distractions. You could be worth something, Alex."

Ophelia crosses my mind. The way those brown eyes brighten when they meet mine. The pink tinge that kisses her nose when I compliment her. My voice is soft and sure when it comes. "I am worth something, dad."

It's the gentlest reply I could've given, and yet he flinches like he's truly, finally understanding that all his efforts to turn me into him have been in vain. And for the shortest of seconds, it's like the past ten years of emotions pass through his expression at once. It's gone in an instant, but the strong line of his shoulders droops a little lower than it did when he came in.

It's the punishment he deserves, and no guilt hits me.

I'm halfway out the door when his voice stops me. I expect a final, cutting blow. A remark that'll haunt my lowest of days. But it's just a quiet, dejected, "Look after the girls."

"I've been doing that for a very long time."

And then I walk out, leaving the crushing weight he piled onto my shoulders for so long behind.

I unlock my phone as I pace out of the foyer and into the sunny parking lot beyond, dragging in a desperate lungful of fresh air. *Finally.* I slip a cigarette between my lips, thumbs hammering out a text.

Alex

It's done. I don't think I'll ever see him again.

Robert Harwood

A day we've talked about for years. How do you feel?

Alex

I don't really feel anything at all

Robert Harwood

I think you've been grieving his loss for a long time before today.

He's probably right.

There's one thing left on my list of things to do this Sunday, something I seem to carry over from day to day.

I scroll through my contacts, but a call from Ophelia pops up before I reach the name I'm looking for.

Her voice is always so welcome, a metronome for my heartbeat, a salve for my wounds. "How did it go?"

"I don't know, really. I don't really know how well it went or how I'm feeling."

"That's okay. If you were jumping for joy, I'd understand. If you were weeping in the car, I'd get it, too."

I don't know how I ended up with her in my life. She's not just a reason to tread water, she's a whole life raft. "Fuck, I miss you."

"Does your heart ache?" she asks, tone teasing.

"And my dick."

Her laughter is soft and happy, followed by a yawn. It must be late for her. "Sucks for you."

"I was actually about to make a call."

"Oh?"

"Yeah . . . it's . . . I don't want to tempt fate."

"Tell me when you're ready. I love you."

The call drops, and my grin in the reflection of my car is ridiculous, a glint in my eye I've never really noticed before.

I don't look like him at all.

I don't *feel* like him anymore.

I extinguish my cigarette and press my phone to my ear, letting it ring.

"I thought I'd never hear from you again."

I take a deep breath, swallow my pride. "Is it too late to take you up on your offer?"

Chapter 28

OPHELIA

Sorrowsong took the phrase *April showers* seriously, but May is turning out to be even worse.

The month is drawing to a close, and there's hardly been a day it hasn't rained. The tarn is full to bursting, the river choppy and rough.

It's been a month since my friends picked me up at the airport. A month of long distance with Alex. A month of Cain locked behind bars. A month of my grades and my swim performance being my main concern.

A month of leaving wildflowers on the riverbank where I scattered Laura's ashes.

I leave the exam hall with a good feeling—a renewed desire to have a career, a life, a future.

My boots sink into the mud of the path to the mansion, everything softened by the rain. Thick slate clouds hang low over the castle, the highest turret lost in the mist. Summer is most definitely *not* in the air.

But for once, I see why Colette loves it here. The castle, the dark hallways, the low light in the library, the constant rumble of thunder that she says helps her sleep. She thinks Sorrowsong is something straight out of a fairy tale.

Can't say I agree on that one, but I'm glad for her.

I almost slip three times on my way down the muddy bank, but it's worth it. The tarn is never busy. It feels like my own private space here, more so than my room. The memories that haunted me here—a hand holding me underwater, water in my lungs—are fading, replaced by lazy afternoon swims, floating on my back and watching the birds flit between the trees.

At the water's edge, I tug off my skirt, tights, and jumper to reveal my swimsuit beneath. I slip my phone into my boot, but not before I click on a notification from one of the stupid financial news sites I subscribed to.

Green Aviation has rallied after the dip it took last week following the arrest of COO Mike Wilson and the surprise decision of CEO Alex Corbeau-Green to step down after just five months in charge, something he states was always part of the plan. Shareholders find confidence in new CEO Luis Bennett's five-year strategy to reshape and rebuild the company. Corbeau-Green retains control of Synx, the cybersecurity firm he acquired in January, and remains on the board of Green Aviation.

I send it to Alex. His decision to keep Synx was a surprise even to me, but I think he secretly enjoys running a company. Just not *that* company.

Ophelia

It's doing just fine without you.

Alex
Who'd have thought appointing a CEO who isn't twenty-three and completely passionless would help?

I smile at the screen as I type, blanketed in my tranquil surroundings.

Ophelia
Going for a swim.

Alex
Be safe, baby.

I wade into the freezing water, letting it snatch my breath away, letting it sting my toes, letting it turn my skin white.

No pool could ever compare.

I swim until my arms burn, and then I float onto my back and stare at the rumbling sky. The wind licks across the surface of the water, chilling my face.

"Hey, Mom and Dad," I whisper, for the first time in a while. "I . . . uhh . . . I did it."

They probably don't even know what I mean. *I* don't even know what I mean. My list of accomplishments is getting longer than I ever imagined.

I took down Cain Green. When you type his name into Google, none of the results are good.

I killed Bancroft. Erased his miserable existence from this earth.

I went to university, like they always wanted me to.

I fell in love.

My tears are lost to the inky mass of water as I tell them about it all, wishing so badly that I was doing this at our kitchen table with their smiling faces looking back at me.

"I made a seventy-six-year-old friend called Mabel. We play Scrabble online once a week. We met for dinner in York last week."

I think I talk to them for longer than I ever have. So long that I feel my final shred of resentment against them, my frustration that they got in that helicopter to save a short amount of time on the journey home, sink to the bottom of the lake.

I don't have the energy to hate my mother for what she did.

I don't have the energy to hate myself for telling them to rush home that day, either.

I think that one day, maybe, I could accept that it is Cain Green who is ultimately responsible for Laura's death.

By the time my legs carry me up the bank of the tarn, it feels like the cold has sunk all the way into my bones.

My phone is ringing when I reach it.

"Hey."

Alex's voice is like warm honey against the chill. "Hey. I have news."

I hold my breath, don't ask, *can't* ask.

"My offer on a house has been accepted. It's all going to happen pretty quick."

London. I daren't hope, but my traitorous heart quickens anyway, fluttering like a bird taking flight in my chest. "The house that you looked at upstate?"

I hear his smile, hear the weightlessness of it. "Nah."

"Don't tell me you're coming to London," I say, so quiet I'm surprised he even hears it. I'm standing at the edge of the water, shivering, clutching my phone in both hands. "Don't get my hopes up like this."

"Scotland."

"I—"

What?

"You still there, Twist?"

"I . . . you . . . all of you . . . you're moving?"

"Just for two years."

My mind is a montage of family Christmases and busy dinners. Weekends visiting him, a group of people watching my swim meets.

It's like the loneliness that burrowed itself into the marrow of my bones almost five years ago is starting to trickle into the soil at my feet.

"Alex, I . . ." My next breath is a shudder, a failed attempt at not crying. "I don't believe you."

"This isn't sudden, baby. It's been in the works a while, I just didn't want to get your hopes up."

"But your mom, she . . ."

"There's a great team in Edinburgh who'll look after her. And Jack's parents visit Sorrowsong every two months to see him. They're going to see my mom each time."

I'm not sure if I'm laughing or crying. "And the girls, they . . . Fleur. Fleur cannot be happy about this."

"Shitbag Boyfriend is moving to London for better modeling opportunities, so Fleur is keen. Ingrid and Russell are coming, too. Mom has been their best friend for twenty years. I think we're all ready to leave our memories here behind."

I tip my head back against the light spatter of rain and laugh at the ridiculousness of it all.

I hear a short inhale, his tone hesitant. "I can finish the last two years of the architecture degree I started."

"At Edinburgh? You spoke to them?"

His voice is rough with emotion. "Well . . . yeah, but . . ."

He trails off, but I leap in to fill the silence. "Alex! You didn't tell me!"

"I didn't trust myself to follow through with it. After we've graduated, we'll move, Ophelia. Wherever is best for the girls. It might be London, might be Paris, but it could be back to the States."

"That's okay," I whisper, holding my phone so tight it might shatter. "I'll be right there with you."

"Well, I better go. I have a hundred bits of paperwork to do."

"I can't believe this is real."

"Me neither. I love you. I'll see you soon."

"I love you," I squeak, bouncing up and down in the mud like a fool.

I dress slowly, fingers shaking too much to lace my boots.

A ray of sun splits the cloud, spilling a bright blue stain across the white sky and flooding the darkest corners of the path with light.

I trudge up the hill with a little less force that I usually do, and I have half a mind to turn around and sprint back into the water to tell my dad the news, to tell him that I'm starting to forget what complete isolation feels like, to tell him to stop worrying about me.

But sometimes I think he probably knew in those thirteen seconds that he spiraled down toward the earth that I'd be okay. His belief in me never wavered before that day; I don't know why that would've changed then.

Still, when I float in that lake, it feels like I'm talking into a paper cup tied to a string, and I'd kill for him to be holding the other end just one more time.

When I reach the Nightshade mansion gardens, Belladonna is there, hovering between the two cracked gargoyle statues that stand at the end of the path. She frowns when she sees me, looking at me like I've grown a second head. "What has you looking so happy?"

"I'm . . . just in a good mood."

She leans in just an inch, cerulean gaze bouncing between both of my eyes. "Have you taken something?"

A small laugh slips out of me, which only makes things worse. "No, of course not. Can't I just be in a good mood?"

"You give me the creeps, Winters," she mutters, leaning back again. The faintest little glimmer of amusement sparks in her eyes as she turns to leave, and I wonder if she knows exactly what has me in such a good mood.

My phone buzzes in my hand, an endless string of excited texts from Alex's sisters rolling through.

A small wave of guilt washes over me, like a whole family is being uprooted and moved because of me and my fear of flying. But like she's living inside my messy brain, Elise sends a rare text.

Elise

This is good for all of us. Not just you, and not just Alex. If you saw the way the girls are throwing their clothes into suitcases you'd believe me. It's a two-year vacation.

Ophelia
It just feels like it wouldn't have happened
if Alex hadn't have met me.

Elise
A lot of great things wouldn't have
happened if Alex hadn't met you.
I love you. I'll see you soon.

I slip my phone into my swim bag, craning my neck to take in all the Elizabethan grandeur of the Nightshade mansion. Save for the bullet holes in one of the doors, it's kind of . . . beautiful.

It feels like a lifetime ago I was stood here for the first time, watching Vincenzo and Alex with a heart full of a hate and a life devoid of anything warm.

I was wrong—wrong about them, wrong about so many things. Sorrowsong isn't my downfall at all. It's my chance at a new beginning.

Chapter 29

ALEX

I reverse into Carmichael's spare parking spot just as the rain begins, filling the mild September air with the rich scent of damp earth.

It takes a little over three hours to drive from our house to Sorrowsong Castle, and I've experienced all four seasons in that time.

I can't believe it's a year since I parked my car in this space for the first time, a bedraggled, miserable redhead in my passenger seat.

My life is unrecognizable from where it was then. Gray has split itself up into all the other colors. Ophelia has stitched a silver lining into the black cloud that lives in my head.

The first six weeks in Scotland have been as chaotic as I expected. The girls are adjusting, some better than others. Fleur and Evie have gotten into hiking. Mia forages for cooking ingredients in the expansive gardens of our home. Charlotte and Élé are nervous about school. My mom is more at peace than I've ever seen her, free of the shadow that my father cast her in, free of the memories that plagued the house in Manhattan.

She's not cured by any stretch of the imagination. *I'm* not cured by any stretch of the imagination. But it feels like we're in the shallows, no treading water necessary.

I leave my bags in the car, finding Belladonna waiting for me at the drawbridge, *almost* smiling.

She's a chronic overachiever, top of her class—top of the university—so for her to have to stay here an extra semester because she skipped an assignment to travel back to New York when my mom collapsed is not something I take lightly.

The Morellos represent everything I'm trying to cut out of my life, yet I'd rather die than lose them.

She drops a set of keys into my hand, followed by and an access card to the Nightshade mansion. "Might've shuffled rooms around a little. Have you told her yet?"

"No. But I'm really hoping she's pleased."

"She'll be pleased. All she's done this week is mope."

Sounds like my girl.

I never hated Sorrowsong, not the same way Ophelia does. But I suppose that makes sense—it was built for people like me, people rich enough not to fear the law.

The forests beside me are fading into a hundred shades of copper and gold, busy with red deer and foxes. The castle is a masterpiece in gothic architecture: ceilings held aloft by ribbed vaults and windows that arch into the sharpest of points. Shadows cling to every statue, the light of the day starting to fade.

The Victorian glasshouse is glossy with rain when it appears between the pines, the iron hinges creaking when I pull open the door. It's even darker inside, but I spot her immediately. She's flying through the water, lost in her own world like she always is when she's swimming.

I don't know how long I watch her glide across the surface. I've never really been able to keep track of time around her. When my love-drunk mind eventually convinces my legs to move forward, she's stopped to check her time on her watch.

She startles, alarm melting into shock when she sees it's me.

"I . . . uhh . . . *what*?"

"Hey," I say, not even trying to bite down my grin. "I'm Alex."

"No shit, Sherlock. Why are you here?"

My darling girlfriend. Always so pleased to see me.

She must read my thoughts, because she tosses her goggles onto the edge of the pool and says, "I mean, *hi*, obviously. But also . . . what?"

I lean down and hold out my hand for her to shake, like we're strangers. Like she isn't the air in my lungs and the reason they still function. "I'm new here."

She's laughing now, like I've lost my mind. I think I have. British roads will do that to a man. Her hand slips inside mine. "You . . . you *what*?"

"I just started my second year. Figured I'd come and ask the hottest girl here on a date."

"At Edinburgh, Alex. You're about two hundred miles out."

"At Sorrowsong."

Her face turns pale, I see what I see every time anything good presents itself in her life: the glimmer of soaring hopes, and the way she extinguishes them, just in case. "I don't understand."

"I ate my pride a while back. Called Carmichael and begged him to let me finish the degree I started at Yale here."

If the pool wasn't shallow enough for her to stand in, I'd worry she'd go into shock and drown. Her words are stuttered and confused when they come. "But your mom. Your sisters. The drive is over three hours."

Her hand is still in mine, her whole body frozen. "I'll go home every weekend, every holiday. I'll go home when my mom needs extra support. But she's doing great at the moment, the girls are starting school this week. They're the ones who encouraged me to do this. And it beats a seven-hour flight to New York, any day. It's two years. I'll survive two years of scenic five a.m. drives if it means I get to wake up and fall asleep next to you."

She opens her mouth. Closes it. Opens it again. Closes it. Laughs. Holds up her free hand in a *what the fuck?* motion.

She yanks me into the pool before I can stop her, and my whole body sinks beneath the surface. It's supposed to be heated, but the cold reaches beneath my clothing and snatches my breath away. When I emerge, she's breathless and giggling, freckles rapidly disappearing in the rosy flush creeping over her cheeks.

My hands gravitate to her waist, dragging her to me. Heat from her skin sinks into mine, thaws my heart, warms my blood. Her forehead presses to mine, and our lips are painfully close to touching.

"If this is a prank, it's a cruel one," she says, her voice barely audible over the water that laps around us.

"And if it's reality?"

"Then it's far more than I deserve."

I grin, holding her face in both my hands with my mother's words echoing around my mind. "We deserve each other."

Water trickles over her bottom lip, sticks her brown eyelashes together. "You're staying in the Nightshade mansion?"

My hands slide down her back, picking her up so her legs wrap around my hips. "Got us a *really* good room. But we'll keep your current one, too, in case you need time alone."

"This *cannot* be real."

I see it in her eyes, the disbelief that she deserves a happy ending, the need to deny herself good things, to erect walls around her heart.

But that's okay, because I am patient. I'll disassemble those walls brick by brick if I need to. Let her add bricks, if it makes her feel safe. If it takes me two years, 730 midnights, to convince her she deserves joy, then it'll be 730 midnights well spent.

"I love you," I murmur, the words sitting on the tip of my tongue so frequently these days that they must've tattooed themselves there.

She peppers me with kisses, like she can't get enough of me. Each one is like a hand reaching back in time, mending that child in me who wanted nothing more than to be accepted by his father.

Her hands roam over the wet white fabric of my shirt. "*Fuck.* I love you more."

Her mouth turns hungrier, teeth sinking into my bottom lip. I swallow her moan, letting it sink lower and lower until it's a hot ball of need at the bottom of my abdomen.

She pulls away, eyes swirling with desire. "Is it socially acceptable to fuck in a communal swimming pool?"

"How should I know?"

"You're the one with . . . experience."

"I forgot everything that came before you when you wore that backless dress on your date for Shawn."

"*Ah*. How could I forget. The Great Cryptocurrency Lecture of First Year."

"Say, Ophelia," I say, doing my best Shawn impression, "I know you're just trying to survive the day, but have you tried diversifying away from traditional financial assets?"

"Oh, I don't know, Shawn," she replies, batting her eyelashes at me. It's sarcastic, but it still makes me hard. "Have you tried folding yourself in half and inserting yourself into the paper shredder?"

My laughter echoes around the huge glass structure, the quiet tinkling of rain starting somewhere above us.

"I think Belladonna would put *me* in the shredder if she knew we fucked in here," I say to Ophelia's great disappointment. "Changing rooms?"

"Tetanus sounds like a great way to start the year." She drops her eyes to my wet shirt, her chest rising and falling with each heavy breath. Her fingers skate over the fabric that covers my shoulder, and her forehead crumples into a frown at the unfamiliar shadow beneath. "What is this?"

"Take a look," I whisper, watching her delicate fingers undo a few more buttons until she can peel the shirt from my skin. Her eyes widen at what she sees, but I can't drag mine from her.

Her touch traces the robin on my left shoulder, wings spread wide as it takes flight with the other birds that sweep across my body. It's the only one with any color: a streak of orange down its chest. "When?"

"A few weeks ago."

"*Alex*."

"You've painted the world in color, Ophelia. It's the least I could do."

"And you taught me to fly," she mutters, under her breath. Her eyes return to mine, full of life. "You've got it *bad*, Corbeau."

Hopelessly, calamitously bad. "And you, Winters."

Her mouth is hot and wet when it finds mine again. "Ah, fuck it," she mutters, sliding the straps of her swimsuit off her shoulders.

She's everything. She's the words, the clues, the black spaces that hold the whole puzzle together. She's every color in my paint set, and the brush that turns them into something beautiful.

She's the one thing I was once too scared to dream she'd be:

Mine.

Epilogue

ALEX

FOUR YEARS LATER

One of my favorite things about Ophelia is how red she goes when I sing her "Happy Birthday" each year.

This year is no exception, her face buried in her hands as I sing the final line, lighting shitty gas station candles haphazardly stuck into shortbread cookies and Jelly Babies. "Twenty-five. How does it feel?"

Her cheeks turn even pinker when she leans forward to blow them both out. Her floral dress—a birthday present from me—clings to her in a way that makes me wish so badly that we didn't have evening plans. "It feels . . ." She lies back against the grass, staring up at the copper leaves of the tree above us with a contented sigh. "It feels so peaceful."

Our weekend away to celebrate her twenty-fifth birthday always had to be to Scotland. We've missed it since we left after our graduation two years ago.

The first threads of autumn are beginning to stitch their way across the landscape. The sun paints her hair in shades of red and gold, the leaves fading from yellow to orange.

Orange is my favorite color.

It's Ophelia. It's my mood on so many days, lately. It's the shade of the small diamond that looks so pretty on her ring finger. It's the sunset where I married her last year, the flowers tucked into Vincenzo's pocket as he walked her down the aisle. It's the fire that crackles in the hearth of our crumbly, badly insulated, money trap of a cottage in the English countryside. It's the stupid beans on toast that Josie, Charlotte, and Élé eat before school.

It's the robin that sat on my mother's windowsill during her final weeks.

I survived my mother's death. Somehow, we *all* survived it.

I thought I wouldn't, but here I am. Alive and grateful.

If I thought I knew grief after my dad went to jail, I was *so* wrong. This grief felt inescapable, unsurvivable, completely and utterly overwhelming. It drowned the delicate tissue of my lungs in tar, filled my skull with lead, shackled my limbs to the bed.

I couldn't breathe most nights, couldn't work, couldn't talk as I desperately tried to make sense of a world where my mother would die and my father would live.

It was Ophelia who forced us to eat, Ophelia who explained it to Josie over and over with the patience of a saint, Ophelia who stood at my side at her wake and finished the speech that I could not. It was Ophelia who told me the world would *never* make sense, and the sooner I accept it, the better. When the girls went to bed each night and I fell apart, it was Ophelia who pieced me back together again like I was a puzzle she knew so well that she could do it upside down and blindfolded.

On those days where we miss her so painfully that it feels insurmountable, it's *still* Ophelia who leads us through.

All her patients at the clinic where she works as a childhood grief counselor couldn't be in better hands.

Somewhere, at some point, I must've done something right.

"Fucking candles. Absolute waste of time," she grumbles, as she passes me a shortbread splattered in orange candle wax.

"World's gone to shit," I mutter, echoing the favorite phrase of Mabel, who lives in the tiny cabin at the end of our garden. Only Ophelia would befriend an elderly woman on a plane and get so attached that she adopted her as a grandmother for all of us.

She wraps her lips around the shortbread, torturing me without meaning to. I've really fucked up by making plans for us tonight. I'd rather recreate last night. "It really has."

I lie back beside her, the early September sun a warm, soft blanket on my skin. This feels surreal. Every day feels surreal with her.

I trace my finger over her clear phone case, over the torn-out crossword page that lives inside. I run it over all the letters that sit in the shaded gray boxes, hastily written on one of the best days of my life. Except Ophelia got a clue wrong, so the shaded letters spell *MARAY ME*.

Had the same effect, though.

"Cheers," she says, knocking her shortbread against mine as if it were a flute of champagne.

"To you turning twenty-five."

"And to Raven Architecture landing its first big project!"

That feels surreal, too. A university building in London felt like a ridiculous project to pitch for in our third year of business, but I poached some of the best architects out there, took the time to build the company up carefully, and after a slow first year and then two more years of trying to prove myself, it's starting to pay off.

If my father's surname had to be attached to the company that rotted his brain, rotted our family life, rotted my own childhood, then it had to be my mother's name on the company that represents the final domino falling in my father's vision for his firstborn child.

I haven't gone back to visit him. Not once. I accept his call at Christmas each year, listen to his apologies. I wish him merry Christmas and hang up, and just like the day I walked out of the visitation room the last time I saw him, I feel nothing.

"And to Robert marrying Jacqueline!" Ophelia chimes, bringing me back into the here and now. *Fucking Robert.* Poached my assistant and then married her.

"And to Mia getting her first restaurant job."

I cried for so long when Mia moved out two months ago that Ophelia thought someone had died.

"And Evie getting in a show on the fucking West End," she says, like she can't believe we haven't covered that one yet.

We've had a lot of wins this year. I wish my mom was here to see them.

"I've booked the whole front row for us." I let my most exasperated sigh drift up into the cloudless sky. "And cheers to Fleur, I guess."

She presses her lips together to suppress a laugh. Fleur is engaged. The whole ordeal knocked ten years off my life. I'm going to go gray by thirty, at this rate. I do *not* approve, but Ophelia does, and I suppose that's vaguely comforting.

She props herself up on an elbow, gazing down at me in the meadow. Her hair is longer, nails longer, freckles darker from time outside. A tiny fine-line tattoo decorates her collarbone, identical to the one on my ring finger. A small circle with a line extending from the center to the top. A clock pointing to midnight.

She's still that pessimistic, grumpy girl I almost ran over outside Sorrowsong's twisted gates. Sunshine makes her hot and annoyed, paper straws turn her murderous. Musicals and festive cheer make her never want to leave the house again.

But there's a confidence about her now, a healthy glow beneath the pale skin that used to be tinged with a bluish hue. The shadows beneath her eyes are put there by our love of late-night showers together, and not by the nightmares that used to plague her dreams.

Raising the girls is so much easier with such a perfect role model for them at home.

She sweeps my messy hair from my forehead, her mouth twisting into a small smile. "What's on your mind?"

I lean up to place a soft kiss on her lips. "That I'd like you to live to one hundred and twenty-five."

"I'd be as wrinkly as a prune."

"I'd love that."

She snorts, her head landing in the space between my biceps and my chest. "No, you would not."

I can hardly squash my smile long enough to kiss her. "Mmhmm. I'd take that prune home. Kiss it. Get it a blanket. Butter it some toast."

Her laughter makes the sun look dull as she playfully shoves me away. "You're full of shit, Corbeau."

But I'm not. I watched my mother die without a wrinkle, and Ophelia's parents died before their hair had gone gray, so the ability to watch time carve lines in her lovely face is my every birthday wish.

She sits up, muttering something about how gingers aren't built for the sun. It gives me the perfect opportunity to check my phone. I have a whole load of unread messages in the group chat for her surprise party tonight.

Party might be a stretch. But we're all going to sit down with music at a reasonable volume around large bowls of chips in varying flavors, just the way she likes it.

Still at Sorrowsong completing her medicine degree, Divya hasn't traveled far, but for the others—for Colette, Fleur, the twins, Vin, Belladonna, Magda, Mabel, Jack, all of her friends from work—coming to Scotland is a long day of travel. I hope it'll help Ophelia realize just how important she is to so many people. That families don't have to be tied by blood. That she has put her little thread of copper through the hearts of so many people, a web that extends around the globe.

Colette sends a picture of the living room of the house we're renting for the weekend, decorated with pillows and balloons and raspberry cupcakes that look so good that they could only be the work of Mia.

Alex

Don't let Vincenzo eat them all.

Vincenzo

Well, that's rude.

Fleur

He's literally got one in his mouth while he's typing.

Divya

Alex, come back. Everyone is driving me crazy.

Evie

We're hungry.

Mia

Mabel is four sherrys deep. She wants to know if there is a karaoke machine.

Alex

If there was a karaoke machine, Ophelia would flee her own party.

Vincenzo

Because I'm such a great singer?

Jack

If Vinnie was on the mic, I'd be fleeing right beside her.

Belladonna
If Vinnie was on the mic, we'd all bleed
out of our ears and die.

I bite down my smile, shutting my phone off on the onslaught of messages in the group chat. "Do you want to head off?"

She turns to face me where she sits, the hair at her nape glowing, lit from behind by the sun. The most unruly strands are set alight, a warm glow catching her dress. I wish I had my paints with me, but I settle for a quick photo of her on my phone instead.

She slips her hand into mine when we stand, brushing the leaves from the skirt of her dress. "We'd better. I'm hungry."

THE CLOCK IN the kitchen seems to tick so loud in the silent house, the hands some way past two in the morning.

Everyone is asleep but us, haphazardly crammed into the guest rooms and on the sofas in the sitting rooms. This house is so full of love and laughter that I'm surprised the walls aren't sagging, bending under the sheer weight of it all.

I do miss the little ones, though.

She sighs wistfully. "Is it sad that I miss Jo, Élé, and Charlotte?"

I laugh, setting a cup of tea in front of her. "I was thinking the same."

Ophelia gives me a sleepy, tipsy smile from where she's sitting at the kitchen table. Her mascara is smudged, and there's pizza sauce on the strap of her dress, somehow.

Falling in love isn't the right description. I've been plummeting since I met her, haven't stopped since. Each day when I think I might find the bottom, that my feelings for her couldn't intensify any more, she does something else that sends the ground flying away from me again.

"That was one of the best evenings of my life," she says, voice so soft that it hardly breaks the silence.

"And mine."

"Thank you."

"Thank *you*."

Her eyes crinkle at the edges, filling with warmth. "We deserve each other."

I'm not sure I'll ever deserve her, but I agree anyway. "That we do."

I lean against the oak countertop, eyes bouncing around the kitchen. The sink is overflowing with plates, bowls, cutlery, wine bottles, glasses, tumblers. The mess spills onto the draining board and onto the counter. A pile of wrapping paper and opened envelopes surrounds the overflowing trash can. There are so many shoes and coats at the front door that I couldn't open it even if I wanted to.

I'm always wary of complaining about mess these days, of wishing it away or rushing to clear it up.

I'll never forget Ophelia's parents' house that first Christmas. The lack of mess, the lack of *things*, the lack of bowls in the sink. I know from the way she's staring, eyes glassy, at the dishes on the counter that she's thinking the same.

I promised her once that she'd never know that awful, bone-eating, soul-crushing silence again, and it's a promise I'll never break.

I wander over to the table, stand behind her, and snake my arms around her waist. My chin rests on the top of her head. "You were beautiful, tonight."

"If I was, it's your doing."

KEEP READING FOR AN EXCLUSIVE BONUS CHAPTER

THREE MONTHS LATER

Breathe, breathe, breathe.

I roll forward in the too-cold pool, and it's perfectly timed. For once. My legs drive me away from the tile, and I'm swimming again.

Even by my standards—much higher these past few months—I know this is going to be a good time. And each time my left ear breaks the surface, I can hear the echoed shouting and cheering around Sorrowsong's greenhouse.

My arms are burning, my lungs are on fire, I'm not *entirely* convinced my legs are still attached, and yet I think I might be . . . enjoying myself? It's a new concept, recently discovered: Swimming for pleasure. Not for medals, not to pass the time, and not to stave away the grief and despair.

When my hand hits the tile for the final time and I pull off my goggles and drag in a desperate lungful of air, Belladonna is nodding at me where she stands at the edge of the pool. *PR*, she mouths at me, and sure enough, it's my best time ever

It's not enough to win the race—some girl from Bath University is literally going to the Olympics—but it's second place.

When I tug off my cap, one word rises above the unfocused

buzz in the greenhouse, chanted louder and clearer than the rest of the chatter. *Ophelia, Ophelia, Ophelia.* I turn to face them, that small crowd gathered to my left who are here *just* for me. You'd think I had set a new world record, judging by the way Alex and Vincenzo are celebrating.

Mia, Evie, and Fleur are here, waving printed out pictures of my face stuck to wooden skewers. Elise, too, wrapped in a big jacket and a scarf that covers most of her face. They're *all* waving, and it's so ridiculous, given that most of the other seats are empty. I might be the only university student in the country whose family has shown up for a sports event, but I don't care. I missed out on this for the last few years of high school. I will not take it for granted now.

There's an empty seat beside Elise, and I just know that somehow, in some way, my dad is in it, shouting and hollering in the way I always told him was embarrassing.

Alex mouths something at me. *I fucking love you, I think. I love fucking you,* I mouth back, and he laughs.

I climb out the pool, slipping my feet into flip-flops and smiling at the outdated floor tile like a complete idiot. A towel slips around my shoulders, a whispered caress against the top of my head.

"I love fucking you, too."

"Later?"

Alex turns me to face him. "I don't think we're going to escape Vincenzo's poker night. He's literally put it in my calendar so I can't forget."

I glance over my shoulder toward Vinnie, where he's letting Mia and Evie beat him up with paper versions of my face. "A poker night sounds great, actually. What time do you finish rugby?"

His thumb swipes a droplet of water from my jaw, gaze dipping to my lips for the briefest of seconds. "Seven." His expression turns hopeful. "But I don't *have* to go?"

"Yes, you do, you insatiable fool." I shove his chest, but he doesn't distance himself from me. He never did. He never does. "Go to rugby. We'll play poker after."

His bottom lip makes an appearance, but those green irises are glittering, and *my god*, he is tempting. But there's something about Alex, twenty-four, living like a twenty-four-year-old should; two months of rugby practice, poker nights, drinks with friends, hangovers and takeout boxes and lazy mornings. That storm cloud over his shoulders seems to lessen every time I watch him, Jack, and Vinnie jog their way up the path to the mansion.

"Not really the time or the place for"—Belladonna appears beside us, waving her fingers in our general direction—"whatever this is. You two are insufferable. See you in the locker room, Winters."

Alex grins down at me. "Better not upset the boss."

"I'm going to miss her." Belladonna is in her last few weeks at Sorrowsong, and I'm alarmingly sad about that. "I'll see you guys later?"

"Later."

I stare down at my hand, a full house, with an expression that I'm hoping says *oh no, I'm so sad about my hand.*

"Ophelia has a full house," says Belladonna, breaking the silence.

"What?" I clutch my cards to my chest. "I do *not*."

"You're terrible at faking being sad."

"Well, maybe I have a royal flush," I snap, over Alex's laughter.

"If you had a royal flush you'd be too excited to look sad."

"Alex!" I cry. "Defend me!"

Alex stops laughing long enough to lean over and peek at my cards. It spoils the game, but we've been going for hours and Belladonna has run out of things to win at this point. Vincenzo and Colette are drunk. Divya is furious at the whole situation, insisting it *must* be rigged. Alex has been too busy running his fingers along the hem of my skirt to truly focus on the game, and I've been losing without excuse.

My ears, chest, nose, and cheeks seem to flush red at every good hand, and Belladonna remains stony and impassive, face shrouded in shadow where we're all splayed out across the chesterfield sofas in the Nightshade library.

"Wow, that's a bad hand," Alex mutters, trying to rescue me.

Belladonna scowls. "You used to have a backbone, Corbeau."

Alex's fingers dip beneath my skirt, dancing along the tights that cover my thighs. If he goes up any farther, he'll discover that they're stockings. "Did I? I don't remember."

Belladonna rolls her eyes at us, but she's not *quite* succeeding at squashing that tiny glimmer of fondness in them. Colette shows her hand to Vincenzo, asking him for the thirtieth time if an ace is good or bad.

Alex's thumb swipes an inch higher, and I lose focus on the game. Belladonna probably wins. I don't know. I don't really care.

Jack shuffles the cards while Vinnie tops off the glasses. They're all laughing at something, but I'm stuck on the way my pulse has moved from my chest to my upper thighs, the hot touch of his fingers scorching a path along my skin.

"Can't we play Scrabble?" asks Divya.

I perk up at that, the promise of letter tiles and wordplay enough to distract me from my ridiculously attractive boyfriend, apparently. "*Yes*!"

"Scrabble is for cowards," Belladonna mutters, and Vincenzo tips his glass toward her in agreement.

"That makes zero sense."

"We can play, but if anyone puts *zoo* on a triple word, I'm leaving Sorrowsong early."

One inch higher, and he's found his way to smooth, bare skin. I hear Alex's sip of whiskey catch in his throat. His fingers grip the fabric that covers my legs, like he can hardly believe his luck. He's up and standing behind the sofa with his hands on my shoulders before I take my next breath. "Ophelia and I have to get to bed."

"What? No you don't," grumbles Vincenzo.

"I have to drive to see Mom and the girls in the morning."

Vincenzo scowls at him, narrowing his eyes in a way that says *I can't argue with that excuse, but I know it's bullshit*. Alex goes to bed late and wakes up at the crack of dawn most days.

He slips his hand around mine and tugs me to my feet, planting the softest kiss beneath my ear. "Are you happy to go, Twist?" he asks, quiet enough for only me to hear.

My swallow is thick, my voice hoarse. I hope the library is dark enough for the others not to notice the way my face flames. "Yeah."

I bid the others goodnight, distracted by Alex and his hands and his thighs and his eyes and his hair. He steers us between dusty shelves of forgotten books, two wide hands encircling my waist. He pauses behind me somewhere between outdated medicine textbooks and Latin texts, then sinks his teeth into my shoulder with a rough growl. "I could just fuck you right here."

God above. "Would you?"

The noise that escapes him is tortured. "Is that a request?"

"Yeah."

He kisses the spot where his teeth just were, arms tightening around me. "Another time. I've been thinking about taking you to bed all day."

He has me in his arms before I can reply, carrying me effortlessly up the winding staircase to the third floor, and it's the lightness in his footsteps today, the ease with which he laughs, that fill me with so much hope for the future. He's keeping his promise to me; fixing me like I'm fixing him.

ACKNOWLEDGMENTS

TO MR. WOODS (the original yearning blueprint), who, as I am typing this, is making me a hot chocolate at 1 a.m. to fuel me over my deadline. I love you so much, I'm so fortunate to be doing life with you.

My wonderful parents and twin brother, who, despite my most valiant dissuading efforts, will unfortunately read this book. Love you.

To my agent, Daisy, for the incredible amount of carbohydrates you have fed me over the past year, and for your suspicious amount of faith in me.

Rosie, Becky, and the rest of my amazing team of agents at PFD, who make all my books and translations possible—thank you so much! I have never witnessed such incredible and ruthless organization (please come and help me sort out my life).

To Kinza, Clare, Meg, Chloe, and the whole Pan Macmillan team who have made so many of my publishing dreams come true. I am so grateful for your belief in, and enthusiasm for, Sorrowsong!

Nicole and the fantastic Zando Slowburn team, for all the invaluable support and help in making Alex and Ophelia's story happen.

To all my translators and teams overseas, I am so excited that Alex and Ophelia will meet so many readers in so many languages, all thanks to your hard work.

Ada and Julia—I would be so lost, and so bored, without you two. I am so lucky to have you around!

To my wonderful friend Erin, whom I couldn't possibly be any more thankful to know.

Somme, Kath, Ali, Ellie, Jess, Ki, Carol-Anne, EJ, Stef, Zarin, Meg, Georgia, Rebecca, Soraya—the best support system I could ever wish for!

To Emily, for yet another beautiful cover.

To you, the readers! If you follow me on Instagram, you'll see me delivering a poorly edited, rambling "thank you" message far too often. But I mean every word—I am truly so unbelievably thankful to be sharing this story with you. None of this would be possible without you, and meeting/talking to you guys is the best part about all of this.

Oh, and to my little dog, Juno, of course!

ABOUT THE AUTHOR

AUTUMN WOODS is an aerospace engineer by day, romance author by evening and weekend. She currently lives in the South West of the UK with Mr. Woods and their dog.

She loves to write strong FMCs, and dark and twisty MMCs, wrapping them in cottagecore and dark academia worlds.

When not writing or reading, she's usually painting, baking, or spending time outdoors.

Instagram: @autumnwoods.author

TikTok: @autumn.woods.author